Dear Reader,

I'm delighted to welcome you to a very special
Bestselling Author Collection for 2024! In
celebration of Harlequin's 75 years in publishing,
this collection features fan-favorite stories from
some of our readers' most cherished authors. Each
book also includes a free full-length story by an
exciting writer from one of our current programs.

Our company has grown and changed since its
inception 75 years ago. Today, Harlequin publishes
more than 100 titles a month in 30 countries
and 15 languages, with stories for a diverse
readership across a range of genres and formats,
including hardcover, trade paperback, mass-market
paperback, ebook and audiobook.

But our commitment to you, our romance reader,
remains the same: in every Harlequin romance, a
guaranteed happily-ever-after!

Thank you for coming on this journey with us. And
happy reading as we embark on the next 75 years of
bringing joy to readers around the world!

Dianne Moggy

Vice-President, Editorial

Harlequin

A prolific author of more than one hundred books, **Diana Palmer** got her start as a newspaper reporter. A *New York Times* bestselling author and voted one of the top ten romance writers in America, she has a gift for telling the most sensual tales with charm and humor. Diana lives with her family in Cornelia, Georgia. Visit her website at dianapalmer.com.

Delores Fossen, a *USA TODAY* bestselling author, has written over a hundred and fifty novels, with millions of copies of her books in print worldwide. She's received a Booksellers' Best Award and an RT Reviewers' Choice Best Book Award. She was also a finalist for a prestigious RITA® Award. You can contact the author through her website at deloresfossen.com.

TRUE BLUE

NEW YORK TIMES **BESTSELLING AUTHOR**
DIANA PALMER

H Harlequin

BESTSELLING AUTHOR COLLECTION

 **Harlequin®**
BESTSELLING
AUTHOR
COLLECTION

Recycling programs
for this product may
not exist in your area.

ISBN-13: 978-1-335-14675-5

True Blue

First published in 2011. This edition published in 2024
with revised text.
Copyright © 2011 by Diana Palmer
Copyright © 2024 by Diana Palmer, revised text edition.

Sheriff in the Saddle
First published in 2022. This edition published in 2024.
Copyright © 2022 by Delores Fossen

All rights reserved. No part of this book may be used or reproduced in any
manner whatsoever without written permission.

Without limiting the author's and publisher's exclusive rights, any
unauthorized use of this publication to train generative artificial intelligence
(AI) technologies is expressly prohibited.

This is a work of fiction. Names, characters, places and incidents are
either the product of the author's imagination or are used fictitiously. Any
resemblance to actual persons, living or dead, businesses, companies,
events or locales is entirely coincidental.

For questions and comments about the quality of this book, please
contact us at CustomerService@Harlequin.com.

TM and ® are trademarks of Harlequin Enterprises ULC.

 Harlequin Enterprises ULC
22 Adelaide St. West, 41st Floor
Toronto, Ontario M5H 4E3, Canada
www.Harlequin.com

Printed in U.S.A.

CONTENTS

Also by Diana Palmer

Long, Tall Texans

The Wyoming Men

Visit her Author Profile page at Harlequin.com,
or dianapalmer.com, for more titles!

TRUE BLUE

Diana Palmer

Chapter 1

"We could lose the case," San Antonio Detective Sergeant Rick Marquez muttered as he glared at one of the newest detectives on his squad.

"I'm really sorry," Gwendolyn Cassaway said, wincing. "I tripped. It was an accident."

He stared at her through narrowed dark eyes, his sensual lips compressed. "You tripped because you're nearsighted and you won't wear glasses." Personally, he didn't think the lack of them did anything for her, if vanity was the issue. She had a pleasant face, and an exquisite complexion, but she was no raving beauty. Her finest feature was her wealth of thick platinum-blond hair that she wore in a high bun on top of her head. She never wore it down.

"Glasses get in my way and I can't ever get them clean enough," she muttered. "That coating just causes

smears unless you use the proper cleaning materials.
And I can't ever find them," she said defensively.

He drew in a long, exasperated breath and perched
on the edge of the desk in his office. In the posture,
his .45 Colt ACP in its distinctive leather holster was
displayed next to his badge on his belt. So were his
powerful legs, and to their best advantage. He was tall
and muscular, without it being obvious. He had a light
olive complexion and thick long black hair that he wore
in a ponytail. He was very attractive, but he couldn't
ever seem to wind up with a serious girlfriend. Women
found him useful as a sympathetic shoulder to cry on
over their true loves. One woman refused to date him
when she realized that he wore his pistol even off duty.
He'd tried to explain that it was a necessary thing, but
it hadn't given him any points with her. He went to the
opera, which he loved, all alone. He went everywhere
alone. He was almost thirty-one, and lonelier than ever.
It made him irritable.

And here was Gwen making it all worse, messing
up his crime scene, threatening the delicate chain of
evidence that could lead to a conviction in a complex
murder.

A college freshman, pretty and blonde, had been
brutally assaulted and killed. They had no suspects and
trace evidence was very sketchy already. Gwen had almost contaminated the scene by stepping too close to
a blood smear.

He was not in a good mood. He was hungry. He was
going to be late for lunch, because he had to chew her
out. If he didn't, the lieutenant surely would, and Cal
Hollister was even meaner than Marquez.

"You could also lose your job," Marquez pointed out. "You're new in the department."

She grimaced. "I know." She shrugged. "I guess I could go back to the Atlanta P.D. if I had to," she said with grim resignation. She looked at him with pale green eyes that were almost translucent. He'd never seen eyes that color.

"You just have to be more careful, Cassaway," he cautioned.

"Yes, sir. I'll do my best."

He tried not to look at the T-shirt she was wearing under a lightweight denim jacket with her jeans. It was unseasonably warm for November but a jacket felt good against the morning chill.

On her T-shirt was a picture of a little green alien, the sort sold in novelty shops, with a legend that read, Have You Seen My Spaceship? He averted his eyes and tried not to grin.

She tugged her jacket closer. "Sorry. But they don't have any regulations against T-shirts here, do they?"

"If the lieutenant sees that one, you'll find out," he said.

She sighed. "I'll try to conform. It's just that I come from a very weird family. My mother worked for the FBI. My father was, uh, in the military. My brother is…" She hesitated and swallowed. "My brother *was* in military intelligence."

He frowned. "Deceased?"

She nodded. She still couldn't talk about it. The pain was too fresh.

"Sorry," he said stiffly.

She shifted. "Larry died very bravely during a covert

ops mission in the Middle East. But he was my only sibling. It's hard to talk about."

"I can understand that." He stood up, glancing at the military watch he wore on his left wrist. "Time for lunch."

"Oh, I have other plans..." she began quickly.

He glared at her. "It was a remark, not an invitation. I don't date colleagues," he said very curtly.

She blushed all the way down to her throat. She swallowed and stood taller. "Sorry. I was... I meant...that is..."

He waved the excuses away. "We'll talk about this some more later. Meanwhile, please do something about your vision. You can't investigate a crime scene you can't see!"

She nodded. "Yes, sir. Absolutely."

He opened the door and let her go out first, noticing absently that her head only came up to his shoulder and that she smelled like spring roses, the pink ones that grew in his mother's garden down in Jacobsville. It was an elusive, very faint fragrance. He approved. Some women who worked in the office seemed to bathe in perfume and always had headaches and allergies and never seemed to think about the connection. Once, a fellow detective had had an almost-fatal asthma attack after a clerical worker stood near him wearing what smelled like an entire bottle of perfume.

Gwendolyn stopped suddenly and he plowed into her, his hands sweeping out to grasp her shoulders and steady her before she fell from his momentum.

"Oh, sorry!" she exclaimed, and felt a thrill of pleasure at the warm strength of the big hands holding her so gently.

He removed them at once. "What is it?"

She had to force her mind to work. Detective Sergeant Marquez was very sexy and she'd been drawn to him since her first sight of him several weeks before. "I meant to ask if you wanted me to check with Alice Fowler over at the crime lab about the digital camera we found in the murdered woman's apartment. By now, she might have something on the trace evidence."

"Good idea. You do that."

"I'll swing past there on my way back to the office after lunch," she promised, and beamed, because it was a big case and he was letting her contribute to solving it. "Thanks."

He nodded, his mind already on the wonderful beef Stroganoff he was going to order at the nearby café where he usually had lunch. He'd been looking forward to it all week. It was Friday and he could splurge.

Tomorrow was his day off. He was going to spend it helping his mother, Barbara, process and can a bushel of hothouse tomatoes she'd been given by an organic gardener with a greenhouse. She owned Barbara's Café in Jacobsville, and she liked to use her organic vegetables and herbs in the meals she prepared for her clients. They would add to the store of canned summer tomatoes that she'd already processed earlier in the year.

He owed her a lot. He'd been orphaned in junior high school and Barbara Ferguson, who'd just lost her husband in an accident, and suffered a miscarriage, had taken him in. His mother had once worked for Barbara at the café just briefly. Then his parents—well, his mother and stepfather—had died in a wreck, leaving a single, lonely child all on his own. Rick had been a terrible teen, always in trouble, bad-tempered and

moody. He'd been afraid when he lost his mother. He
had no other living relatives of whom he was aware, and
no place to go. Barbara had stepped in and given him
a home. He loved her no less than he'd loved his real
mother, and he was quite protective of her. He never
spoke of his stepfather. He tried not to remember him
at all.

Barbara wanted him to marry and settle down and
have a family. She harped on it all the time. She even
introduced him to single women. Nothing helped. He
seemed to be an eternally on-sale item in the matri-
monial market that everybody bypassed for the fan-
cier merchandise. He laughed shortly to himself at the
thought.

Gwen watched him leave and wondered why he'd
laughed. She was embarrassed that she'd thought he was
asking her to lunch. He didn't seem to have a girlfriend
and everybody joked about his nonexistent love life. But
he wasn't attracted to Gwen in that way. It didn't matter. No man had ever liked her, really. She was everybody's confidante, the good girl who could give advice
about how to please other women with small gifts and
entertainments. But she was never asked out for herself.

She knew she wasn't pretty. She was always passed
over for the flashy women, the assertive women, the
powerful women. The women who didn't think sex before marriage was a sin. She'd had a man double over
laughing when she'd told him that, after he expected a
night in bed in return for a nice meal and the theater.
Then he'd become angry, having spent so much money
on her with nothing to show for it. The experience had
soured her.

"Don Quixote," she murmured to herself. "I'm Don Quixote."

"Wrong sex," Detective Sergeant Gail Rogers said as she paused beside the newcomer. Rogers was the mother of some very wealthy ranchers in Comanche Wells, but she kept her job and her own income. She was an amazing peace officer. Gwen admired her tremendously. "And what's that all about?" she asked.

Gwen sighed, glancing around to make sure they weren't being overheard. "I won't give out on dates," she whispered. "So men think I'm insane." She shrugged. "I'm Don Quixote, trying to restore morality and idealism to a decadent world."

Rogers didn't laugh. She smiled, very kindly. "He was noble, in his way. An idealist with a dream."

"He was nutty as a fruitcake." Gwen sighed.

"Yes, but he made everyone around him feel of worth, like the prostitute whom he idealized as a great lady for whom he quested," came the surprising reply. "He gave dreams to people who had given them up for harsh reality. He was adored by them."

Gwen laughed. "Yes, I suppose he wasn't so bad at that."

"People should have ideals, even if they get laughed at," Rogers added. "You stick to your guns. Every society has its outcasts." She leaned down. "Nobody who conformed to the rigid culture of any society ever made history."

Gwen brightened. "That's true." Then she added, "You've lived through a lot. You got shot," Gwen recalled hearing.

"I did. It was worthwhile, though. We broke a cold case wide-open and caught the murderer."

"I heard. That was some story."

Rogers smiled. "Indeed it was. Rick Marquez got blindsided and left for dead by the same scoundrels who shot me. But we both survived." She frowned. "What's wrong? Marquez giving you a hard time?"

"It's my own fault," Gwen confided. "I can't wear contacts and I hate glasses. I tripped in a crime scene and came close to contaminating some evidence." She grimaced. "It's a murder case, too, that college freshman they found dead in her apartment last night. The defense will have a field day with that when the perp is caught and brought to trial. And it will be my fault. I just got chewed out for it. I should have, too," she said quickly, because she didn't want Rogers to think Marquez was being unfair.

Rogers's dark eyes searched hers. "You like your sergeant, don't you?"

"I respect him," Gwen said, and then flushed helplessly.

Rogers studied her warmly. "He's a nice man," she said. "He does have a temper and he does take too many chances. But you'll get used to his moods."

"I'm working on that." Gwen chuckled.

"How did you like Atlanta?" Rogers asked conversationally as they headed for the exit.

"Excuse me?" Gwen said absently.

"Atlanta P.D. Where you were working."

"Oh. Oh!" Gwen had to think quickly. "It was nice. I liked the department. But I wanted a change, and I've always wanted to see Texas."

"I see."

No, she didn't, Gwen thought, and thank goodness for that. Gwen was keeping secrets that she didn't dare divulge. She changed the subject as they walked together to the parking lot to their respective vehicles.

Lunch was a salad with dressing on the side, and half a grilled cheese sandwich. Dessert, and her drink, was a cappuccino. She loved the expensive coffee and could only afford it one day a week, on Fridays. She ate an inexpensive lunch so that she could have her coffee.

She sipped it with her eyes closed, smiling. It had an aroma that evoked Italy, a little sidewalk café in Rome with the ruins visible in the distance...

She opened her eyes at once and looked around, as if someone could see the thoughts in her head. She must be very careful not to mention that memory, or other similar ones, in regular conversation. She was a budding junior detective. She had to remember that. It wouldn't do to let anything slip at this crucial moment.

That thought led to thoughts of Detective Marquez and what would be a traumatic revelation for him when the time came for disclosure. Meanwhile, her orders were to observe him, keep her head down and try to discover how much he, or his adoptive mother, knew about his true background. She couldn't say anything. Not yet.

She finished her coffee, paid for her meal and walked out onto the chilly streets. So funny, she thought, the way the weather ran in cycles. It had been unseasonably cold throughout the South during the spring then came summer and blazing, unrelenting heat with drought and wildfires and cattle dying in droves. Now it was November and still unseasonably warm, but some weather experts said snow might come soon.

The weather was nuts. There had been epic drought throughout the whole southern tier of America, from

Arizona to Florida, and there had been horrible wildfires in the southwestern states. Triple-digit tempera-
tures had gone all summer in south Texas. There had
been horrible flooding on the Mississippi River due to
the large snowmelt, from last winter's unusually deep
snows up north.

Now it was November and Gwen was actually sweat-
ing long before she reached her car, although it had
been chilly this morning. She took off her jacket. At
least the car had air-conditioning, and she was turning
it on, even if it was technically almost winter. Idly, she
wondered how people had lived in this heat before air-
conditioning was invented. It couldn't have been an easy
life, especially since most Texans of the early twentieth century had worked on the land. Imagine, having
to herd and brand cattle in this sort of heat, much less
plow and plant!

Gwen got into her car and drove by the crime lab
to see if Alice had found anything on that digital camera. In fact, she had. There were a lot of photos of people who were probably friends—Gwen could use face
recognition software to identify them, hopefully—and
there was one odd-looking man standing a little distance behind a couple who was smiling into the camera against the background of the apartment complex
where the victim had lived. That was interesting and
suspicious. She'd have to check that man out. He didn't
look as if he belonged in such a setting. It was a mid-
range apartment complex, and the man was dingy and
ill kempt and staring a little too intently. She drove back
to her precinct.

Her mind was still on Marquez, on what she knew,

and he didn't. She hoped he wasn't going to have too hard a time with his true history, when the truth came out.

Barbara glared at her son. "Can't you just peel the tomato, sweetie, without taking out most of it except the core?"

He grimaced. "Sorry," he said, wielding the paring knife with more care as he went to work on what looked like a bushel of tomatoes, a gift from an organic gardener with a hothouse, that his mother was canning in her kitchen at home. Canning jars simmered in a huge tub of water, getting ready to be filled with fragrant tomato slices and then processed in the big pressure cooker. He glared at it.

"I hate those things," he muttered. "Even the safest ones are dangerous."

"Baloney," she said inelegantly. "Give me those."

She took the bowl of tomatoes and dunked them into a pot of boiling water. She left them there for a couple of minutes and fished them out in a colander. She put them in the sink in front of Rick. "There. Now they'll skin. I keep telling you this is a more efficient way than trying to cut the skins off. But you don't listen, my dear."

"I like skinning them," he said with a dark-eyed smile in her direction. "It's an outlet for my frustrations."

"Oh?" She didn't look at him, deliberately. "What sort of frustrations?"

"There's this new woman at work," he said grimly.

"Gwen." She nodded.

He dropped the knife, picked it back up and stared at her.

"You talk about her all the time."

"I do?" It was news to him. He didn't realize that.

She nodded as she skinned tomatoes. "She trips over things that she doesn't see, she messes up crime scenes, she spills coffee, she can't find her cell phone…" She glanced at him. He was still standing there, with the knife poised over a tomato. "Get busy, there, those tomatoes won't peel themselves."

He groaned.

"Just think how nice they'll taste in one of my beef stew recipes," she coaxed. "Go on, peel."

"Why can't we just get one of those things that sucks the air out of bags and freeze them instead?"

"What if we have a major power outage that lasts for days and days?" she returned.

He thought for a minute. "I'll go buy twenty bags of ice and several of those foam coolers."

She laughed. "Yes, but we can't tell how the power grid is going to cope if we have one of those massive CMEs like the Carrington Event in 1859."

He blinked. "Excuse me?"

"There was a massive coronal mass ejection in 1859 called the Carrington Event," she explained. "When it hit earth, all the electrics on the planet went crazy. Telegraph lines burned up and telegraph units caught fire." She glanced at him. "There wasn't much electricity back in those days—it was in its infancy. But imagine if such a thing happened today, with our dependence on electricity. Everything is connected to the grid these days, banks, communications corporations, pharmacies, government, military and the list goes on and on. Even our water and power are controlled by computers. Just imagine if we had no way to access our computers."

He whistled. "I was in the grocery store one day when the computers went offline. They couldn't process credit cards. Most people had to leave. I had enough cash for bread and milk. Then another time the computers in the pharmacy went down, when you had to have those antibiotics for the sinus infection last winter. I had to come home and get the checkbook and go back. People without credit cards had real problems."

"See?" She went back to her tomatoes.

"I suppose it would be a pretty bad thing. Is it going to happen, you think?"

"Someday, certainly. The sun has eleven year cycles, you know, with a solar minimum and a solar maximum. The next solar maximum, some scientists say, is in 2012. If we're going to get hit, that would have my vote for the timeline."

"Twenty-twelve," he groaned, rolling his eyes. "We had this guy come in the office and tell us we needed to put out a flyer."

"What about?"

"The fact that the world is ending in 2012 and we have to have tin-foil hats to protect us from electromagnetic pulses."

"Ah. EMPs," she said knowledgeably. "Actually, I think you'd have to be in a modified and greatly enlarged version of a Leiden jar to be fully protected. So would any computer equipment you wanted to save." She glanced at him. "They're developing weapons like that, you know," she added. "All it would take is one nicely placed EMP and our military computers would go down like tenpins."

He put down the knife. "Where do you learn all this stuff?" he asked, exasperated.

"On the internet." She pulled an iPod out of her pocket and showed it to him. "I have Wi-Fi in the house, you know. I just connect to all the appropriate websites." She checked her bookmarks. "I have one for space weather, three radars for terrestrial weather and about ten covert sites that tell you all the stuff the government won't tell you…"

"My mother, the conspiracy theorist," he moaned.

"You won't hear this stuff on the national news," she said smartly. "The mainstream media is controlled by three major corporations. They decide what you'll get to hear. And mostly it's what entertainer got drunk, what television show is getting the ratings and what politician is patting himself on the back or running for reelection. In my day—" she warmed to her theme "—we had real news on television. It was local and we had real reporters out gathering it. Like the Jacobsville paper still does," she added.

"I know about the Jacobsville paper," he said with a sigh. "We hear that Cash Grier spends most of his time trying to protect the owner from getting assassinated. She knows all the drug distribution points and the drug lords by name, and she's printing them." He shook his head. "She's going to be another statistic one day. They've killed plenty of newspaper publishers and reporters over the border for less. She's rocking the boat."

"Somebody needs to rock it," Barbara muttered as she peeled another tomato skin off and tossed it into a green bag to be used for mulch in her garden. She never wasted any organic refuse. "People are dying so that another generation can become addicted to drugs."

"I can't argue that point," he said. "The problem is that nothing law enforcement is doing is making much of a dent in drug trafficking. If there's a market, there's going to be a supply. That's just the way things are."

"They say Hayes Carson actually talked to Minette Raynor about it."

That was real news. Minette owned the *Jacobsville Times*. She had two stepsiblings, Shane, who was twelve, and Julie, who was six. She'd loved her step-mother very much. Her stepmother and her father had died within weeks of each other, leaving a grieving Minette with two little children to raise, a newspaper to run and a ranch to manage. She had a manager to handle the ranch, and her great-aunt Sarah lived with her and took care of the kids after school so that Minette could keep working. Minette was twenty-five now and unmarried. She and Hayes Carson didn't get along. Hayes blamed her, God knew why, for his younger brother's drug-related death, even after Rachel Conley left a confession stating that she'd given Bobby Carson, Hayes's brother, the drugs that killed him.

Rick chuckled. "If there's ever a border war, Minette will stand in the street pointing a finger at Hayes so the invaders can get him first."

"I wonder," Barbara mused. "Sometimes I think where there's antagonism, there's also something deeper. I've seen people who hate each other end up married."

"Cash Grier and his Tippy," Rick mused.

"Yes, and Stuart York and Ivy Conley."

"Not to mention half a dozen others. Jacobsville is growing by leaps and bounds."

"So is Comanche Wells. We've got new people there, too." She was peeling faster. "Did you notice that Grange bought a ranch in Comanche Wells, next to the property that his boss owns?"

Rick pursed his sensual lips. "Which boss?"

She blinked at him. "What do you mean, which boss?"

"He works as ranch manager for Jason Pendleton. But he also works on the side for Eb Scott," he said. "You didn't hear this from me, but he was involved in the Pendleton kidnapping," he added. "He went to get Gracie Pendleton back when she was kidnapped by that exiled South American dictator, Emilio Machado."

"Machado."

"Yes." He peeled the tomato slowly. "He's a conundrum."

"What do you mean?"

"He started out, we learned, as a farm laborer down in Mexico, from the time he was about ten years old. He was involved in protests against foreign interests even as a teenager. But he got tired of scratching dirt for a living. He could play the guitar and sing, so he worked bars for a while and then through a contact, he got a job as an entertainer on a cruise ship. That got boring. He signed on with a bunch of mercs and became known internationally as a crusader against oppression. Afterward, he went to South America and hired on with another paramilitary group that was fighting to preserve the way of life of the native people in Barrera, a little nation in the Amazon bordering Peru. He helped the paramilitary unit free a tribe of natives from a foreign corporation that was trying to kill them to get the oil-rich land on which they were living. He developed a taste for defending the underdog, moved up in the ranks of the military until he became a general." He smiled. "It seems that he was a natural leader, because when the small country's president died four years ago, Machado was elected by acclamation." He glanced at her. "Do you realize how rare that is, even for a small nation?"

"If people loved him so much, how is it that he's in Mexico kidnapping people to get money to retake his country?"

"He wasn't ousted by the people, but by a vicious and bloodthirsty military subordinate who knew when and how to strike, while Machado was on a trip to a neighboring country to sign a trade agreement and offer an alliance against foreign corporate takeovers."

"I didn't know that."

"It's sort of privileged info, so you can't share it," he told her. "Anyway, the subordinate killed Machado's entire staff, and sent his secret police to shut down newspapers and television and radio stations. Overnight, influential people ended up in prison. Educators, politicians, writers—anyone who might threaten the new regime. There have been hundreds of murders, and now the subordinate, Pedro Mendez by name, is allying himself with drug lords in a neighboring country. It seems that cocaine grows quite nicely in Barrera and poor farmers are being 'encouraged' to grow it instead of food crops on their land. Mendez is also nationalizing every single business so that he has absolute control."

"No wonder the general is trying to retake his country," she said curtly. "I hope he makes it."

"So do I," Rick replied. "But I can't say that in public," he added. "He's wanted in this country for kidnapping. It's a capital offense. If he's caught and convicted he could wind up with a death penalty."

She winced. "I don't condone how he's getting the

money," she replied. "But he's going to use it for a noble reason."

"Noble." He chuckled.

"That's not funny," she said shortly.

"I'm not laughing at the word. It's Gwen. She goes around mumbling that she's Don Quixote."

She laughed out loud. "What?"

He shook his head. "Rogers told me. It seems that our newest detective won't give out on dates and she groups herself with Don Quixote, who tried to restore honor and morality to a decadent world."

"My, my!" She pursed her lips and smiled secretively.

"I don't want to marry Gwen Cassaway," he said at once. "I just thought I'd mention that, because I can read minds, and I don't like what you're thinking."

"She's a nice girl."

"She's a woman."

"She's a nice girl. She has a very idealistic and romantic attitude for someone who lives in the city. And I ought to know. I have women from cities coming through here all the time, talking about unspeakable things right in public with the whole world listening." Her lips made a thin line. "Do you know, Grange was having lunch next to a table of them where they were discussing men's, well, intimate men parts," she amended, clearing her throat, "and Grange got up from his chair, told them what he thought of them for discussing a bedroom topic in public in front of decent people and he walked out."

"What did they do?"

"One of them laughed. One of the others cried. Another said he needed to start living in the real world instead of small town 'stupidville.'" She grinned. "Of course, she said it after he'd already left. While he was talking, they didn't say a word. But they left soon after. I was glad. I can't choose my clientele and I've only ever ordered one person to leave my restaurant since I've owned it," she added.

She dragged herself back to the present. "But the topic of conversation was getting to me, too. People need to talk about intimate things in private, not in a public place with their voices raised. We don't all think alike."

"Only in some ways," he pointed out, and hugged her impulsively. "You're a nice mother. I'm so lucky to have you for an adoptive parent."

She hugged him back. "You've enriched my life, my sweet." She sighed, closing her eyes in his warm embrace. "When I lost Bart, I wanted to die, too. And then your mother and stepfather died, and there you were, as alone as I was. We needed each other."

"We did." He moved away and smiled affectionately. "You took on a big burden with me. I was a bad boy."

She groaned and rolled her eyes. "Were you ever! Always in fights, in school and out. I spent half my life in the principal's office and once at a school board meeting where they were going to vote to throw you right out of school altogether and put you in alternative school." Her face hardened. "In their dreams!"

"Yes, you took a lawyer to the meeting and buffaloed them. First time it ever happened, I heard later."

"I was very mad."

"I felt really bad about that," he said. "But I put my nose to the grindstone after, and tried hard to make it up to you."

"Joined the police force, went to night school and got

your associate degree, went to the San Antonio Police Department and worked your way up in the ranks to sergeant," she agreed, smiling. "Made me *so* proud!"

He hugged her again. "I owe it all to you."

"No. You owe it to your hard work. I may have helped, but you pulled yourself up."

He kissed her forehead. "Thank you. For everything."

"You're my son. I love you very much."

He cleared his throat. Emotions were difficult for him, especially considering his job. "Yeah. Me, too."

She grinned. The smile faded as she searched his large, dark eyes. "Do you ever wonder about your mother's past?"

His eyebrows shot up. "What a question!" He frowned. "What do you mean?"

"Do you know anything about her friends? About any male friends she had before she married your step-father?"

He shrugged. "Not really. She didn't talk about her relationships. Well, I wasn't old enough for her to con-fide in me, either, you know. She never was one to talk about intimate things," he said quietly. "Not even about my real father. She said that he died, but she never talked about him. She was very young when I was born. She did say she'd done things she wanted forgiveness for, and she went to confession a lot." He studied her closely. "You must have had some reason for asking me that."

She put her lips tightly together. "Something I over-heard. I wasn't supposed to be listening."

"Come on, tell me," he said when she hesitated.

"Cash Grier was having lunch with some fed. They

were discussing Machado. The fed mentioned a woman named Dolores Ortíz who had some connection to General Machado when he lived in Mexico."

Chapter 2

"Dolores Ortíz?" he asked, the paring knife poised in midair. "That was my mother's maiden name."

"I know."

Rick frowned. "You mean my mother might have been romantically involved with Emilio Machado?"

"I got that impression," Barbara said, nodding. "But I wasn't close enough to hear the entire conversation. I just got bits and pieces of it."

He pursed his lips. "Well, my father died around the time I was born, so it's not impossible that she did meet Machado in Mexico. Although, it's a big country."

"You lived in the state of Sonora," she pointed out. "That's where Machado had his truck farm, they said."

He finished skinning the tomato and reached for another one. "Wouldn't that be a coincidence, if my mother actually knew him?"

"Yes, it would."

"Well, it was a long time ago," he said easily. "And she's dead, and I never knew him. So what good would it do for them to dig up an old romance now?"

"I have no idea. It bothered me, a little. I mean, you're my son."

"Yes, I am." He glanced at her. "I love it when people get all flustered and start babbling when you introduce me. You're blonde and fair and I'm dark and obviously Hispanic."

"You're gorgeous, my baby," she teased. "I just wish women would stop crying on your shoulder about other men and start trying to marry you."

He sighed. "Chance would be a fine thing. I carry a gun!" he said with mock horror.

She glowered at him. "All off-duty policemen carry guns."

"Yes, but I might shoot somebody accidentally, and it would get in the way if I tried to hug somebody."

"I gather that somebody female mentioned that?"

He sighed and nodded. "A public defender," he said. "She thought I was cute, but she doesn't date men who carry. It's a principle, she said. She hates guns."

"I hate guns, too, but I keep a shotgun in the closet in case I ever need to defend myself," Barbara pointed out.

"I'll defend you."

"You work in San Antonio," she said. "If you're not here, I have to defend myself. By the time Hayes Carson could get to my place, I'd be...well, not in any good condition if somebody tried to harm me."

That had happened once, Rick recalled with anger. A man he'd arrested, after he'd been released, had gone after Rick's adoptive mother for revenge. It was just chance that Hayes Carson had stopped by when he was off duty, in his unmarked truck, to ask her about catering an event. The ex-convict had piled out of his car and come right up on the porch with a drawn gun—in violation of parole—and banged on the door demanding that Barbara come outside. Hayes had come outside, disarmed him, cuffed him and taken him right to jail. The man was now serving another term in prison, for assault on a police officer, trespassing, attempted assault, possessing a firearm in violation of parole and resisting arrest. Barbara had testified at his trial. So had Hayes.

Rick shook his head. "I hate having you in danger because of my job."

"It was only the one time," she said, comforting him. "It could have been somebody who carried a grudge because their apple pie wasn't served with ice cream or something."

He smiled. "Dream on. You even make the ice cream you serve with it. Your pies are out of this world."

"Don't you have an in-house seminar coming up at work?" she asked.

He nodded.

"Why don't you take a couple of pies back with you?"

"That would be nice. Thank you."

"My pleasure." She pursed her lips. "Does Gwen like apple pie?"

He turned and stared at her. "Gwen is a colleague. I never, never date colleagues."

She sighed. "Okay."

He went back to work on the tomatoes. This could turn into a problem. His mother, well-meaning and loving, nevertheless was determined to get him married. That was one area in which he wanted to do his own

prospecting. And never in this lifetime did he want
to end up with someone like Gwen, who had two left
feet and the dress sense of a Neanderthal woman. He
laughed at the idea of her in bearskins carrying a spear.
But he didn't share the joke with his mother.

When he went to work the next day, it was qualifying time on the firing range. Rick was a good shot,
and he kept excellent care of his service weapon. But
the testing was one of the things he really hated about
police work.

His lieutenant, Cal Hollister, could outshoot any man
in the precinct. He scored a hundred percent regularly.
Rick could usually manage in the nineties but never a
perfect score. He always seemed to do the qualifying
when the lieutenant was doing his, and his ego suffered.

Today, Gwen Cassaway also showed up. Rick tried
not to groan out loud. Gwen would drop her pistol, accidentally kill the lieutenant and Rick would be prosecuted for manslaughter...

"Why are you groaning like that?" Hollister asked
curtly as he checked the clip for his .45 in preparation
for target shooting.

"Just a stray thought, sir, nothing important." His
eyes went involuntarily to Gwen, who was also load-
ing her own pistol.

On the firing range, shooters wore eye protection and
ear protection. They customarily loaded only six bullets into the clip of the automatic, and this was done at
the time they got into position to fire. The pistol would
be held at low or medium ready position, after being
carefully drawn from its snapped holster for firing, with
the safety on. The pistol, even unloaded, would never

be pointed in any direction except that of the target and the trigger finger would never rest on the trigger. When in firing position, the safety would be released, and the shooter would fire at the target using either the Weaver, modified Weaver, or Isosceles shooting stance.

One of the most difficult parts of shooting, and one of the most important to master, was trigger pull. The pressure exerted on the trigger had to be perfect in order to place a shot correctly. There were graphs on the firing range that helped participants check the efficiency of their trigger pull and help to improve it. Rick's was improving. But his lieutenant consistently showed him up on the gun range, and it made him uncomfortable. He tried not to practice or qualify when the other man was around. Unfortunately, he always seemed to be on the range when Rick was.

Hollister followed Rick's gaze to Gwen. He knew, as Rick did, that she had some difficulty with coordination. He pursed his lips. His black eyes danced as he glanced covertly at Gwen. "It's okay, Marquez. We're insured," he said under his breath.

Rick cleared his throat and tried not to laugh.

Hollister moved onto the firing line. His thick blond hair gleamed like pale honey in the sunlight. He glanced at Gwen. "Ready, Detective?" he drawled, pulling the heavy ear protectors on over his hair.

Gwen gave him a nice smile. "Ready when you are, sir."

The Range Master moved into position, indicated that everything was ready and gave the signal to fire.

Hollister, confident and relaxed, chuckled, aimed at the target and proceeded to blow the living hell out of it.

Rick, watching Gwen worriedly, saw something incredible happen next. Gwen snapped into a modified Weaver position, barely even aimed and threw six shots into the center of the target with pinpoint accuracy.

His mouth flew open.

She took the clip out of her automatic, checked the cylinder and waited for the Range Master to check her score.

"Cassaway," he said eventually, and hesitated. "One hundred percent."

Rick and the lieutenant stared at each other.

"Lieutenant Hollister," the officer continued, and was obviously trying not to smile, "ninety-nine percent."

"What the hell…!" Hollister burst out. "I hit dead center!"

"Missed one, sir, by a hair," the officer replied with a twinkle in his eyes. "Sorry."

Hollister let out a furious bad word. Gwen marched right up to him and glared at him from pale green eyes.

"Sir, I find that word offensive and I'd appreciate it if you would refrain from using it in my presence," she said curtly.

Hollister's high cheekbones actually flushed. Rick tensed, waiting for the explosion.

But Hollister didn't erupt. His black eyes smiled down at the rookie detective. "Point taken, Detective," he said, and his deep voice was even pleasant. "I apologize."

Gwen swallowed. She was almost shaking. "Thank you, sir."

She turned and walked off.

"Not bad shooting, by the way," he commented as he removed the clip from his own pistol.

She grinned. "Thanks." She glanced at Rick, who

was still gaping, and almost made a smart remark. But she thought better of it in time.

Rick let out the breath he'd been holding. "She trips over her own feet," he remarked. "But that was some damned fine shooting."

"It was," the lieutenant agreed. He shook his head. "You can never figure people, can you, Marquez?"

"True, sir. Very true."

Later that day, Rick noted two dignified men in suits walking past his office. They glanced at him, spoke to one another and hesitated. One gestured down the hall quickly, and they kept walking.

He wondered what in the world was going on.

Rogers came into his office a few minutes later, frowning. "Odd thing."

"What?" he asked, his eyes on his computer screen where he was running a case through VICAP.

"Did you see those two suits?"

"Yes, they hesitated outside my office. Who are they, feds?"

"Yes. State Department."

He burst out laughing as he looked at her with large, dancing brown eyes. "They think I'm illegal and they're here to bust me?"

"Stop that," she muttered.

"Sorry. Couldn't resist it." He turned to her. "We have high level immigration cases all the time where the State Department gets involved."

"Yes, but mostly we deal with the enforcement branch of the Department of Immigration and Naturalization, with ICE. Or we deal with the DEA in drug cases, I know that. But these guys aren't from Austin. They're from D.C."

"The capitol?"

"That's right. They've been talking to the lieutenant all morning. They're taking him to lunch, too."

"What's going on? Any idea?"

She shook her head. "Only that gossip says they're on the Machado case."

"Yes. He's wanted for kidnapping." He didn't add what Barbara had told him, that his own birth mother might have once known Machado in the past.

"He's not in the country."

"And how would you know that?" Rick asked her with pursed lips. "Another psychic insight?" he added, because she had a really unusual sixth sense about cases.

"No. I ran into Cash Grier over at the courthouse. He was up here on a case."

"Our police chief from Jacobsville," he acknowledged.

"The very same. He mentioned that Jason Pendleton's foreman is on temporary leave because of Machado."

"Grange," Rick recalled, naming the foreman. "He went into Mexico to retrieve Gracie Pendleton when she was kidnapped by Machado's men for ransom."

"Yes. It seems the general took a liking to him, had him investigated and offered him a job."

Rick blinked. "Excuse me?"

"That's what I said when Grier told me." She laughed. "The general really does have style. He said somebody had to organize his mercs when he goes in to retake his country. Grange, being a former major in the army, seemed the logical choice."

"His country is Barrera," Rick mused. "Nice name, since it sits on the Amazon River bordering Colombia, Peru and Bolivia. Barrera is Spanish for barrier."

"I didn't know that, only having completed two years of college Spanish," she replied blithely.

He made a face at her.

"Anyway, it seems Grange likes the idea of being a crusader for democracy and freedom and human rights, so he took the job. He's in Mexico at the moment helping the general come up with a plan of attack."

"With Eb Scott offering candidates, I don't doubt," Rick added. "He's got the cream of the crop at his counterterrorism training center in Jacobsville, as far as mercs go."

"The general is gathering them from everywhere. He has a couple of former SAS from Great Britain, a one-eyed terror from South Africa named Rourke whose nickname is Deadeye…"

"I know him," Rick said.

"Me, too," Rogers replied. "He's a pill, isn't he? Rumored to be the natural son of K. C. Kantor, who was one of the more successful ex-mercs."

"Yes, Kantor became a billionaire after he gave up the lifestyle. He has a daughter who married Dr. Micah Steele in Jacobsville, and a godchild who married into the ranching Callister family up in Montana." His eyes narrowed. "Where is the general getting the money to finance his revolution?"

"Remember that he gave Gracie back without any payment. But then he nabbed Jason Pendleton for ransom, and Gracie paid it with the money from her trust fund?"

"Forgot about that," Rick said.

"It ran to six figures. So he's bankrolled. We hear he also charged what's left of the Fuentes cartel for protection while he was sharing space with them over the border."

"Charging drug lords rent in their own turf?" Rick asked.

"And getting it. The general has a pretty fearsome reputation," she added. She laughed. "He's also a incredibly handsome," she mused. "I've seen a photograph of him. They say he has a charming personality, reveres women and plays the guitar and sings like an angel."

"A man of many talents."

"Not the least of which is inspiring troops." Rogers sighed. "But it has to be unsettling for the State Department, especially since the Mexican government is up in arms about having Machado recruit mercs to invade a sovereign nation in South America while living in their country."

"Why are they protesting to us? We aren't helping him," Rick pointed out.

"He's on our border."

"If they want us to do something about Machado, they could do something about the militant drug cartels running over our borders with automatic weapons to protect their drug runners."

"Chance would be a fine thing."

"I guess so. None of that explains why the State Department is gumming up our office," he added. "This is San Antonio. The border is that way." He pointed out the window. "A long, long drive that way."

"I know. That's what puzzled me. So I pumped Grier for information."

"What did he tell you?"

"He didn't. Tell me anything," she added grimly. "So I had my oldest son pump his best friend, Sheriff Hayes Carson, for information."

"Did you get anything from him?"

She bit her lower lip. "Bits and pieces." She gave him a worried look. She couldn't tell him what she found out. She'd been sworn to secrecy. "But nothing really concrete, I'm sorry to say."

"I suppose they'll tell us eventually."

"I suppose so."

"When is this huge invasion of Barrera going to take place? Any timeline on that?"

"None that presented itself." She sighed. "But it's going to be a gala occasion, from what we hear. The State Department would have good reason to be concerned. They can't back a revolution…"

"One of the letter agencies could help with that, of course, without public acknowledgment."

Letter agencies referred to government bureaus like the CIA, which Rick assumed would have been in the forefront of any assistance they could legally give to help install a democratic government friendly to the United States in South America.

"Kilraven used to belong to the CIA," Rick murmured. "Maybe I could ask him if he knows anything."

"I'd keep my nose out of it for the time being," Rogers cautioned, foreseeing trouble ahead if Rick tried to interfere at this stage of the game. "We'll know soon enough."

"I guess so." He glanced at her and asked, "Hear about what happened on the firing range this morning?"

Her eyes brightened. "Did I ever! The whole department's talking about it. Our rookie detective outshot the lieutenant."

"By a whole point." Rick grinned. "Imagine that. She falls into potted plants and trips over crime evidence, but she can shoot like an Old West gunslinger." He shook his head. "I thought I'd pass out when she started firing that automatic. It was beautiful. She never even seemed to aim. Just snapped off the shots and hit in the center every single time."

"The lieutenant's a good loser, though," Rogers commented. "He bought a single pink rose and laid it on her desk after lunch."

Rick's eyes narrowed and his expression grew cold. "Did he, now?"

The lieutenant was a widower. Nobody knew how he lost his wife, he never spoke of her. He didn't even date, as far as anyone knew. And here he was giving flowers to Gwen, who was young and innocent and impressionable...

"I said, do you think that could be construed as sexual harassment?" Rogers repeated.

"He gave her a flower!"

"Well, yes, but he wouldn't have given a man a flower, would he?"

"I'd have given Kilraven a flower after he nabbed the perp who blindsided me in the alley and left me for dead," he said, tongue-in-cheek.

She sighed. She felt in her pocket for the unopened

pack of cigarettes she kept there, pulled it out and looked at it with sad eyes. "I miss smoking. The kids made me quit."

"You're still carrying around cigarettes?" he exclaimed.

"Well, it's comforting. Having them in my pocket, I mean. I wouldn't actually smoke one, of course. Unless we have a nuclear attack, or something. Then it would be okay."

He burst out laughing. "You're incorrigible, Rogers."

"Only on Mondays," she said after a minute. She glanced at her watch. "I have to get back to work."

"Let me know if you find out anything else, okay?"

"Of course I will." She smiled.

She felt a twinge of guilt as she walked out of his office. She wished she could tell him the truth, or at least prepare him for what she knew was coming. He had a surprise in store. Probably not a very nice one.

"But I made corned beef and cabbage," Barbara groaned when Rick phoned her Friday afternoon to say he wasn't coming home that night.

"I know, it's my favorite, and I'm sorry," he said. "But we've got a stakeout. I have to go. It's my squad." He sighed. "Gwen's on it, and she'll probably knock over a trash can and we'll get burned."

"You have to think positively." She hesitated. "You could bring her home with you tomorrow. The corned beef will still be good and I'll cook more cabbage."

"She's a colleague," he repeated. "I don't date colleagues."

"Does your lieutenant date colleagues?" she asked

with glee. "Because I heard he left her a single rose on her desk. What a lovely, romantic man!"

He gnashed his teeth and hoped the sound didn't carry. He was tired of hearing that story. It had gone the rounds at work all week.

"You could put a rose on her desk..."

"If I did, it would be attached to a pink slip!" he snapped.

She gasped, hesitated and turned off the phone. It was the first time he'd ever snapped at her.

Rick groaned and dialed her number back. It rang and rang. "Come on. Please?" he spoke into the busy signal. "I'm sorry. Come on, let me apologize..."

"Yes?" Barbara answered stiffly.

"I'm sorry. I didn't mean to snap at you. I really didn't. I'll come home for lunch tomorrow and eat corned beef and cabbage. I'll even eat crow. Raw." There was silence on the end of the line. "I'll bring a rose?"

She laughed. "Okay, you're forgiven."

"I'm really sorry. Things have been hectic at work. But that's no excuse for being rude to you."

"No, it's not. But I'm not mad."

"You're a nice mother."

She laughed. "You're a nice son. I love you. I'll see you at lunch tomorrow."

"Have a good night."

"You have a careful one," she said solemnly. "Even rude sons are hard to come by these days," she added.

"I'll change my ways. Honest. See you."

"See you."

He hung up and sighed heavily. He couldn't imagine why he'd been so short with his own mother. Perhaps he needed a vacation. He only took time off when he was threatened. He loved his job. Being sergeant of an eight-detective squad in the Homicide Unit, in the Murder/Attempted Murder detail, was heady and satisfying. He assigned lead detectives to cases, reviewed cases to make sure everything necessary was done and kept up with what seemed like tons of paperwork, as well as reporting to the lieutenant on caseloads. But maybe a little time off would improve his temper. He'd talk to the lieutenant about it next week, he resolved. For now, he had work to do.

Gwen had been assigned as lead detective on the college student's murder case downtown. It was an odd sort of case. The woman had been stabbed by person or persons unknown, in her own apartment, with all the doors locked and the windows shut. There were no signs of a struggle. She was a pretty young woman with no current boyfriend, no apparent enemies, who led a quiet life and didn't party.

Gwen wanted very much to solve the case. She'd told Rick that Alice Fowler had found prints on a digital camera that featured an out-of-place man in the background. Gwen was checking that out. She was really working hard on the mystery.

But in the meantime, she'd been pressed into service to help Rick with a stakeout of a man wanted for shooting a police officer in a traffic stop. The officer lived, but he'd be in rehab for months. They had intel that the shooter was hiding out in a low class apartment building downtown with some help from an associate. But they couldn't find him there. So Rick decided to stake out the place and try to catch him. The fact that it was a Friday night meant that the younger, single detectives were trying to find ways not to get involved. Even the night detectives had excuses, pending cases that they simply couldn't spare time away from. So Rick ended up with Gwen and one young and eager patrol officer, Ted Sims, from the Patrol South Division who'd volunteered, hoping to find favor with Rick and maybe get a chance at climbing the ladder, and working as a detective one day.

They were set up in a ratty apartment downtown, observing a suspect across the alley in another run-down apartment building. They had all the lights off, a telescope, a video camera, listening devices, warrants to allow the listening devices, and as much black coffee as three detectives could drink in an evening. Which was quite a lot.

"I wish we had a pizza." Officer Sims sighed.

Rick sighed, too. "So do I, but the smell would carry and the perp would know we were watching him."

"Maybe we could put the pizza outside his door and he'd go nuts smelling it and rush out to grab it and we could grab him," Sims mused.

"What do you have in that bottle besides water?" Gwen asked, with twinkling green eyes.

Sims made a face. "Just water, sadly. I could really use a cold beer."

"Shut up," Marquez groaned. "I'm dying for one."

"We could ask Detective Cassaway to investigate the beer rack at the local convenience store and confiscate a six-pack for the crime scene investigation unit," Sims joked. "Nobody would have to know. We could threaten the owner with health violations or something."

Gwen gave him a cold look. "We don't steal."

Marquez gave him an even more vicious look. "Ever."

He flushed. "Hey," he said, holding up both hands, "I was just kidding!"

"I'm not laughing," she returned, unblinking.

"Neither am I," Marquez seconded. His face was hard with suppressed anger. "I don't want to hear talk like that from a sworn police officer."

"Sorry," he said, swallowing hard. "Really. Bad joke. I didn't mean I'd actually do it."

Gwen shrugged. Sims was very young. "I'm missing that new science fiction show I got hooked on," she groaned. "It's making me twitchy."

"I watch that one, too," Rick replied. "It's not bad."

"You could record it," Sims suggested. "Don't you have a DVR?"

She shook her head. "I'm poor. I can't afford one."

Rick glared at her. "We work for one of the best-paying departments in the southwest," he rattled off. "We have a benefits package, expense accounts, access to excellent vehicles…"

"I have a monthly rent bill, a monthly insurance bill, a car payment, utilities payments and I have to buy bullets for my gun," she muttered. "Who can afford luxuries?" She glared at him. "I haven't had a new suit in six months. This one looks like moths have nested in it already."

Rick's eyebrows arched up. "Surely, you've got more than one suit, Cassaway."

"Two suits, twelve blouses, six pair of shoes and assorted…other things," she said. "Mix and match and I'm sick of all of it. I want haute couture!"

"Good luck with that," Rick remarked.

"Luck won't do it."

"Hey, is this the guy we're looking for?" Sims asked suddenly, looking through the telescope.

Chapter 3

Rick and Gwen joined him at the window. Rick snapped a photo of the man across the street, using the telephoto feature, plugged it into his small computer and, using a new face recognition software component, compared it to the man he'd photographed.

"Positive ID. That's him," Rick said. "Let's go get him."

They ran down the steps, deploying quickly to the designations planned earlier by Rick.

The man, yawning and oblivious, stepped out onto the sidewalk next to a bus stop sign.

"Now," Rick yelled.

Three people came running toward the stunned man, who started to run, but it was far too late. Rick tackled him and took him down. He cuffed his hands behind his back and chuckled as the man started cursing.

"I ain't done nothin'!" he wailed.

"Then you don't have a thing to worry about."

The man only groaned.

"That was a nice takedown," Gwen said as they cleared their equipment out of the rented apartment, after the man had been taken away by the patrol officer.

"Thanks. I try to keep in shape."

She didn't dare look at him. She was having a hard enough time not noticing how very attractive he was.

"You know," he mused, "that was some fine shooting down at HQ."

She beamed. "Thanks." She glanced up. "At least I do have one saving grace."

"Probably more than one, Cassaway."

She shouldered her purse. "Are we done for the night?"

"Yes. I'll input the report and you can sign it tomorrow. I snapped at my mother. I have to go home and try to make it up to her."

"She's very nice."

He turned, frowning. "How do you know?"

"I came through Jacobsville when I had to interview a witness in that last murder trial," she reminded him. "I had lunch at the café. It's the only one in town, except for the Chinese restaurant, and I like her apple pie." She added that last bit to make sure he knew she wasn't frequenting his mother's café just because she was his mother.

"Oh."

"Has she owned the restaurant a long time?"

He nodded. "She opened it a couple of years before I was orphaned. My mother worked for her as a cook just briefly."

Gwen nodded, trying to be low-key. "Is your mother still alive? Your biological mother?" she asked while looking through her purse for her car keys.

"She and my stepfather died in a wreck when I was almost in my teens. Barbara had just lost her husband and had a miscarriage the month before it happened. She was grieving and so was I. Since I had no other family, and she knew me, she adopted me."

She flushed. "Oh. Sorry, I didn't mean to pry. I was just curious."

He shrugged. "Most everybody knows," he said easily. "I was born in Mexico, in Sonora, but my mother and stepfather came to this country when I was a toddler and lived in Jacobsville. My stepfather worked at one of the local ranches."

"What did he do?"

"Broke horses." The way he said it was cold and short, as if he didn't like being reminded of the man.

"I had an uncle who worked ranches in Wyoming," she confided. "He's dead now."

He studied her through narrowed eyes. "Wyoming. But you're from Atlanta?"

"Not originally."

He waited.

She cleared her throat. "My people are from Montana, originally."

"You're a long way from home."

"Yes, well, my parents moved to Maryland when I was small."

"I guess you miss the ocean."

She nodded. "A lot. It wasn't a long drive from our house. But I go where they send me. I've worked a lot of places—" She stopped dead, and could have bitten her tongue.

His eyebrows were arching already. "The Atlanta P.D. moves you around the country?"

"I mean, I've worked a lot of places around Atlanta."

"Mmm-hmm."

"I didn't always work for Atlanta P.D.," she muttered, trying to backpedal. "I worked for a risk organization for a year or two, in the insurance business, and they sent me around the country on jobs."

"A risk organization? What sort of work did you do?"

"I was a sort of security consultant." It wasn't quite the truth, but it wasn't quite a lie, either. She glanced at her watch as a diversion. "Oh, goodness, I'll miss my television show!"

"God forbid," he said dryly. "Okay. We're done here."

"It didn't take as long as I expected," she commented on the way out. "Usually stakeouts last for hours if not days."

"Tell me about it," he said drolly. "Is your car close by?"

She turned at the foot of the steps. "It's across the street, thanks," she said, because she knew he was offering to walk her to it. He was a gentleman, in the nicest sort of way.

He nodded. "I'll see you Monday, then."

She smiled. "Yes, sir."

She turned and walked away. Her heart was pounding and she was cursing herself mentally. She'd almost blown the whole thing sky-high!

Barbara was her usual, smiling self, but her eyes were sad when Rick showed up at the door the night before he was due home.

"You said tomorrow?" she murmured.

He stepped into the house and hugged her, hard, rocking her in his arms. He heard a muffled sob. "I felt bad," he said at her ear. "I upset you."

"Hey," she murmured, drawing away to dab at her eyes, "that's what kids are supposed to do."

He smiled. "No, it's not."

"Want some coffee?"

"Yes!" he said at once, pulling off his suit coat and loosening his tie as he followed her to the kitchen. He swung the coat around one of the high-back kitchen chairs at the table and sat down. "I've been on stake-out, with convenience-store coffee." He made a face. "I think they keep it in the pot all day to make sure it doesn't pass for hot brown water."

She laughed as she made a fresh pot. "There's that profit margin to consider," she mused.

"I guess."

"Did you catch a crook?"

"We did, actually. That new face recognition software we use is awesome. Pegged the guy almost immediately."

"New technology." She shook her head. "Cameras everywhere, face recognition software, pat downs at the airport…" She turned and looked at him. "Isn't all that supposed to make us feel safer?"

"No, it's supposed to actually make you safer," he corrected. "It makes it harder for the bad guys to hide from the law."

"I guess so." She got out cups and saucers. "I made apple pie."

"You don't even need to ask. I had a hamburger earlier."

"You live on fast food."

"I work at a fast job," he replied. "No time for proper meals, now that I'm in a position of responsibility."

She turned and smiled at him. "I was so proud of you for that promotion. You studied hard."

"I might have studied less if I'd realized how much paperwork would be involved," he quipped. "I have eight detectives under me, and I'm responsible for all the major decisions that involve them. Plus I have to co-ordinate them with other services, work around court dates and emergency assignments... Life was a lot easier when I was just a plain detective."

"You love your job, though. That's a bonus."

"It is," he had to agree.

She cut the pie, topped it with a scoop of homemade ice cream and served it to him with his black coffee. She sat down across from him and watched him eat it with real enjoyment, her hands propping up her chin, elbows on the tablecloth.

"You love to cook," he responded.

She nodded. "It isn't an independent woman thing, I know," she said. "I should be designing buildings or running a corporation and yelling at subordinates."

"You should be doing what you want to do," he replied.

"In that case, I am."

"Good cooks are thin on the ground." He finished the pie and leaned back with his coffee cup in his hand, smiling. "Wonderful food!"

"Thanks."

He sipped coffee. "And the best coffee anywhere."

"Flattery will get you another slice of pie."

He chuckled. "No more tonight. I'm fine."

"Are you ever going to take a vacation?" she asked.

"Sure," he replied. "I've already arranged to have Christmas Eve off."

She glared at him. "A vacation is longer than one night long."

He frowned. "It is? Are you sure?"

"There's more to life than just work."

"I'll think about that, when I have time."

"Have you watched the news today?" she asked.

"No. Why?"

"They had a special report about violence on the border. It seems that the remaining Fuentes brother sent an armed party over the border to escort a drug shipment and there was a shootout with some border agents."

He grimaced. "An ongoing problem. Nobody knows how to solve it. Bottom line, if people want drugs, somebody's going to supply them. You stop the demand, you stop the supply."

"Good luck with that." She laughed hollowly. "Never going to happen."

"I totally agree."

"Anyway, they mentioned in passing that one of the captured drug runners said that General Emilio Machado was recruiting men for an armed invasion of his former country."

"The Mexican Government, we hear, is not pleased with that development and they're angry at our government because they think we aren't doing enough to stop it."

"Really?" she exclaimed. "What else do you know?"

"Not much, but you can't repeat anything I tell you," he added.

She grinned. "You know I'm as silent as a clam. Come on. Talk."

"Apparently, the State Department sent people into our office," he replied. "We know they talked to our lieutenant, but we don't know what about."

"State Department!"

"They do have their fingers on the pulse of foreign governments," Rick reminded her. "If anybody knows what's really going on, they do."

"I would have thought one of those other government agencies would have been more involved, especially if the general's trying to recruit Americans for a foreign military action," she pondered.

His eyebrows arched.

"Well, it seems logical, doesn't it?" she asked.

"Actually, it does," he agreed. "I know the FBI and the CIA have counterterrorism units that infiltrate groups like that."

"Yes, and some of them die doing it," Barbara recalled. She grimaced. "They say undercover officers in any organization face the highest risks."

"The military also has counterterrorism units," he replied. He sipped his cooling coffee. "That must be an interesting sort of job."

"Dangerous."

He smiled. "Of course. But patriotic in the extreme, especially when it comes to foreign operatives trying to undermine democratic interests."

"Doesn't the general's former country have great deposits of oil and natural gas?" she wondered aloud.

"So we hear. It's also in a very strategic location, and the general leans toward capitalism rather than socialism or communism. He's friendly toward the United States."

"A point in his favor. Gracie Pendleton says he sings like an angel," she added with a smile.

"I heard."

"Yes, we had that discussion earlier." She was also remembering another discussion over the phone and her face saddened.

He reached across the table and caught her hand in his. "I really am sorry, Mom," he said gently. "I don't know what came over me. I'm not usually like that."

"No, you're not." She hesitated. She wanted to remark that it wasn't until she asked about the lieutenant giving Gwen a rose that he'd gone ballistic. But in the interests of diplomacy, it was probably wiser to say nothing. She smiled. "How about I warm up that coffee?" she asked instead.

Gwen answered the phone absently, her mind still on the previews of next week's episode of her favorite science fiction show.

"Yes?" she murmured, the hated glasses perched on her nose so that she could actually see the screen of her television.

"Cassaway, anything to report?"

She sat up straighter. "Sir!"

"No need to get uptight. I'm just checking in. The wife and I are on our way to a party, but I wanted to make sure things are progressing well."

"They're going very slowly, sir," she said, curling up in her bare feet and jeans and long-sleeved T-shirt on her sofa. "I'm sorry, I haven't found a diplomatic way to get him talking about the subject and find out what he knows. He doesn't like me…."

"I find that hard to believe, Cassaway. You're a good kid."

She winced at the description.

He cleared his throat. "Sorry. Good woman. I try to be PC, you know, but I come from a different generation. Hard for us old-timers to work well in the new world."

She laughed. "You do fine, sir."

"I know this is a tough assignment," he replied. "But I still think you're the best person for the job. You have a way with people."

"Maybe another type of woman would have been a better choice," she began delicately, "maybe someone more open to flirting, and other things…"

"With Marquez? Are you kidding? The guy wrote the book on staunch outlooks! He'd be turned off immediately."

She relaxed a little. "He does seem to be like that."

"Tough, patriotic, a stickler for doing the right thing even when the brass disapproves, and he's got more guts than most men in his position ever develop. Even went right up in the face of a visiting politician to tell him he was putting his foot in his mouth by interfering with a homicide investigation and would regret it when the news media got hold of the story."

She laughed. "I read about that."

"Takes a moral man to be that fearless," her boss continued. "So yes, you're the right choice. You just have to win his confidence. But you're going to have to move a little faster. Things are heating up down in Mexico. We can't be caught lagging when the general makes his move, you know? We have to have intel, we have to be in position to take advantage of any opportunities that present themselves. The general likes us. We want him to continue liking us."

"But we can't help."

He sighed. "No. We can't help. Not obviously. We're in a precarious position these days, and we can't be seen to interfere. But behind the scenes, we can hope to influence people who are in a position to interfere. Marquez is the obvious person to liaison with Machado."

"It's going to be traumatic for him," Gwen said worriedly. "From the little intel I've been able to acquire, he has no idea about his connection to Machado. None at all."

"Pity," he replied. "That's going to make it harder." He put his hand over the receiver and spoke to someone. "Sorry, my wife's ready to leave. I have to go. Keep me in the loop, and watch your back," he added firmly. "We're trying to get the inside track. There are other people, other operatives, around who would love nothing better than to see us fall on our faces. Other countries would do anything to get a foothold in Barrera. I don't need to tell you who they are, or from what motives they work."

"No, sir, you don't," she agreed. "I'll do the best I can."

"You always do," he said, and there was faint affection in his tone. "Have a good evening. I'll be in touch."

"Yes, sir."

She hung up the cell phone and sat staring at it in her hand. She felt a chill. So much was riding on her ability to be diplomatic and quick and discreet. It wasn't her first difficult assignment; she was not a novice.

But until now, she'd had no personal involvement. Her growing feelings for Rick Marquez were complicating things. She shouldn't care so much about how it would hurt him, but she did. If only there was a way, any way, that she could give him a heads-up before the fire hit the fan. Perhaps, she thought, she might be able to work something out if she spoke to Cash Grier. They shared a similar background in covert ops and he knew Marquez. It was worth a try.

So Friday morning, her day off, Gwen got in her small, used foreign car and drove down to Jacobsville, Texas.

Cash Grier met her at the door of his office, smiling, and led her inside, motioning to a chair as he closed the door behind him, locked it and pulled down the shade.

She pursed her lips with a grin. "Unusual precautions," she mused.

He smiled. "I'd put a pillow over the telephone if I thought there might be a wire near it. An ambassador's family habitually did that in Nazi Germany in the 1930s. Even did it in front of the head of the Gestapo once."

Her eyebrows arched as she sat down. "I missed that one."

"New book, about the rise of Hitler, and firsthand American views on the radical changes in society there in the 1930s," he said as he sat down and propped his big booted feet on his desk. "I love World War II history. I could paper my walls with books on the European Theatre and biographies of Patton and Rommel and Montgomery," he added, alluding to three famous World War II generals. "I like to read battle strategies."

"Isn't that a rather strange interest for a guy who

worked alone for years, except with an occasional spotter?" she asked, tongue-in-cheek. It was pretty much an open secret that Grier had been a sniper in his younger days.

He chuckled. "Probably."

"I like history, too," she replied. "But I lean more toward political history."

"Which brings us to the question of why you're here," he replied and smiled.

She drew in a long breath and leaned forward. "I have a very unpleasant assignment. It involves Rick Marquez."

He nodded and his face sobered. "I know. I still have high-level contacts in your agency."

"He has no idea what's about to go down," she said. "I've argued with my boss until I'm blue in the face, but they won't let me give Marquez even a hint."

"I think his mother knows," he said. "She asked me about it. She overheard some visitors from D.C. talking about connections."

"Do you think she's told him anything?"

"She might know that his mother was romantically involved with Machado at some point. But she wouldn't know the rest. His mother was very close about her private life. Only one or two people even knew what happened." He grimaced. "The problem is that one of the people involved had a cousin who married a high-level agent in D.C., and he spilled his guts. That started this whole chain of events."

"Hard to keep a secret like that, especially one that would have been so obvious." She frowned. "Rick's stepfather must have known. From what little information I've been able to gather about his past, he and his stepfather didn't get along at all."

"The man beat him," Grier said harshly. "A real jewel of a human being. It's one reason Rick had so many problems as a kid. He was in trouble constantly right up until the wreck that killed his mother and stepfather. It was a tragedy that produced golden results. Barbara took him in, straightened him out and put him on a path that turned him into an exemplary citizen. Without her influence…" He spread his hands expressively.

Gwen stared at her scuffed black loafers. Idly, she noticed that they needed some polish. She dressed casually, but she liked to be as neat as possible. One day her real identity would come out, and she didn't want to give the agency a black eye by being slack in her grooming habits.

"You want me to tell him, don't you?" Grier asked.

She looked up. "You know him a lot better than I do. He's my boss, figuratively speaking. He doesn't like me very much, either."

"He might like you more if you'd wear your damned glasses and stop tripping over evidence in crime scenes," he said, pursing his lips. "Alice Mayfield Jones Fowler, who works in the Crime Scene Unit in San Antonio, was eloquent about the close call."

Gwen flushed. "Yes, I know." She pushed the hated glasses up on her nose, where they'd slipped. "I'm wearing my glasses now."

"I didn't mean to be critical," he said, noting her discomfort. "You're a long way from the homicide detective you started out to be," he added. "I know it's a pain, trying to relearn procedure on the fly."

"It really is," she said. "My credentials did stand up

to a background check, thank goodness, but I feel like I'm walking on eggshells. I let slip that my job involved a lot of traveling and Marquez wondered why, since I was apparently working for Atlanta Homicide."

"Ouch," he said.

"I have to remember that I've never been out of the country. It's pretty hard, living two lives."

"I haven't forgotten that aspect of government work," he agreed. "It's why I never had much of a personal life, until Tippy came along."

Everybody local knew that Tippy had been a famous model, and then actress. She and Cash had a rocky trip to the altar, but they had a little girl almost two years old and it was rumored that they wanted another child.

"You got lucky," she said.

He shrugged. "I guess I did. I never could see myself settling down in a small town and becoming a family man. But now, it's second nature. Tris is growing by leaps and bounds. She has red hair, and green eyes, like her mama's."

Gwen noted the color photo on his desk, with himself and Tippy, with Tris and a boy who looked to be in his early teens. "Is that Tippy's brother?" she asked, indicating the photo.

"Rory," he agreed. "He's fourteen." He shook his head. "Time flies."

"It seems to." She leaned back again. "I miss my dad. He's been overseas for a long time, although he's coming back soon for a talk with some very high-level people in D.C. and rumors are flying. Rick Marquez has no idea what sort of background I come from."

"Another shock in store for him," he added. "You should tell him."

"I can't. That would lead to other questions." She sighed. "I'd love to meet my dad at the airport when he flies in. We've had a rough six months since my brother, Larry, died overseas. Dad still mourns my mother, and she's been gone for years. I miss her, too."

"I heard about your brother from a friend in the agency. I'm truly sorry." His dark eyes narrowed. "No other siblings?"

She shook her head.

"My mother's gone, too. But my dad's still alive, and I have three brothers," he replied with a smile. "My older brother, Garon, is SAC at the San Antonio FBI office."

"I've met him. He's very nice." She studied his face. He was a striking man, even with hair that was going silver at the temples. His dark eyes were piercing and steady. He looked intimidating sitting behind a desk. She could only imagine how intimidating he'd look on the job.

"What are you thinking so hard about?" he queried.

"That I never want to break the law in your town." She chuckled.

He grinned. "Thanks. I try to perfect a suitably intimidating demeanor on the job."

"It's quite good."

He sighed. "I'll talk to Marquez's mother and plant clues. I'll do it discreetly. Nobody will ever know that you mentioned it to me, I promise."

"Least of all my boss, who'd have me on security details for the rest of my professional life," she said with a laugh. "I don't doubt he'd have me transferred as liaison to a police department for real, where he'd make sure I was assigned to duty at school crossings."

"Hey, now, that's a nice job," he protested. "My patrolmen fight over that one." He said it tongue-in-cheek. "In fact, the last one enjoyed it so much that he transferred to the fire department. It seems that a first-grader kicked him in the leg, repeatedly."

Her fine eyebrows arched. "Why?"

"He told the kid to stay in the crosswalk. Seems the kid had a real attitude problem. The teachers couldn't deal with him, so they finally called us, after the kicking incident. I took the kid home, in the patrol car, and had a long talk with his mother."

"Oh, dear."

His face was grim. "She's a single parent, living alone, no family anywhere, and this kid is one step away from juvy," he added, referencing the juvenile justice system. "He's six years old," he said heavily, "and he already has a record for disobedience and detention at his school."

"They put little kids in detention in grammar school?" she exclaimed.

"Figure of speech. They call it time-out and he sits in the library. Last time he had to go there, he stood on one of the library tables and recited the Bill of Rights to the head librarian."

Her eyes widened in amusement. "Not only a troublemaker, but brilliant to boot."

He nodded. "Everybody's hoping his poor mother will marry a really tough hombre who can control him before he does something unforgivable and gets an arrest record."

She laughed. "The things I miss because I never married," she mused, shaking her head. "It's not an incentive to become a parent."

"On the other end of the spectrum, there's Tippy and me," he replied with a smile. "I love being a dad."

"It suits you," she said.

She got to her feet. "Well, I have to get back to San Antonio. If Sergeant Marquez asks, I had to talk to you about a case, okay?"

"In fact, we really do have a case that might connect," he said surprisingly. "Sit back down and I'll tell you about it."

Chapter 4

Sergeant Marquez came into the office two days later, looking grim. He motioned to Gwen, indicated a chair and closed the door.

She remembered her trip to Cash Grier's office, and wondered if Grier had had time to talk to her superior officer's mother and the information had trickled down.

"The cold case squad has a job for us," he said as he sat down, too.

"What sort of job?"

"They dug up an old murder. It was committed back in 2002 and a man went to prison on evidence largely given by one person. Now it seems the person who gave evidence has been arrested and convicted for a similar crime. They want to know if we can find a connection."

"Well, by chance, that was the case I just spoke to Chief Grier about down in Jacobsville," she told him, happy that she could make a legitimate connection to her impromptu trip out of town. "He has an officer who knew the prisoner's family and could place the man at a party during the murder."

"Did he give evidence?" he asked.

She shook her head. "He was never called to testify," she said. "Nobody knows why."

"Isn't that interesting."

"Very. So the cold case squad wants us to wear out some shoe leather on their behalf?"

He grimaced. "They have plenty of manpower, but they've got two people out sick, one just transferred to the white collar crime unit and their sergeant said they don't want to let this case get buried. Especially not when a similar crime was just committed here. Your case. The college woman who was murdered. It needs investigation, and they don't have enough people." He smiled. "Besides, there's the issue of not stepping on the toes of another unit's investigation."

"I can understand that."

"So, we'll see if we can make a connection, based on available evidence. I'm assigning you as lead detective on this case, as well as on the college freshman murder. Find a connection. Catch the perp. Make me proud."

She grinned at him. "Actually, that might be possible. I just got some new information from running a check on the photo of that odd man in the murder victim's camera. The one I mentioned to you?"

"Yes, I recall that."

She pulled up a file on her phone. "This is him. I used face recognition software to pick him out." She showed him the mug shot on her phone. "The perp. His name is Mickey Dunagan. He has a rap sheet. It's a long one. He's been prosecuted in two aggravated assault cases, never convicted. Here's the clincher. He has a thing for young college girls. He was arrested for attempted assault a few months ago, on a girl who went to the same college as our victim. I have a detective from our unit en route to question her today, and we're interviewing people at the apartment complex about the man in the photograph. If his DNA is on file, and I'm betting it is since he's served time during his trials, and there's enough DNA from the crime scene to type and match…"

"Good work!" he said fervently.

She grinned. "Thanks, sir."

"I wish we could get ironclad evidence that he killed the victim." He grimaced. "Not that ironclad evidence ever got a conviction when some silver-tongued gung-ho public defender got the bit between his teeth."

"Impressive mixing of metaphors, sir," she murmured dryly.

He actually made a face at her. "Correct my grammar, get stakeout duty for the next two months."

"I would never do that!" she protested with wicked, twinkling eyes.

He smiled back. She was very pretty when she smiled. Her mouth was full and lush and sensuous…

He sat back in his chair and forced himself not to notice that. "Get busy."

"I'll get on it right now."

"Just out of curiosity, who was the officer who could place the convicted murderer at a party when the other murder was committed?"

"Officer Dan Travis," she said. "He's at the Jacobsville Police Department. I'm going to drive down and talk to him tomorrow." She checked the notes on her phone.

"Dunagan was arrested for assault by a patrolman in South Division named Dave Harris. I'm going to talk to him afterward. He might remember something that would be helpful."

"Good. Keep me in the loop."

"I will." She got up and started for the door.

"Cassaway."

She turned at the door. "Sir?"

His dark eyes narrowed. He seemed deep in thought. He was. He had a strange sense that she knew something important that she was hiding from him. He read body language very well after his long years in law enforcement. He'd once tripped a bank robber up when he noticed the man's behavior and deliberately engaged him in conversation. During the conversation, he'd gotten close enough to see the gun the man was holding under his long coat. Rick had quickly subdued him, cuffed him, and taken him in for questioning. The impromptu encounter had solved a whole string of unsolved bank robberies for the cold case unit, and their sergeant, Dave Murphy, had taken Rick out to lunch in appreciation for the help.

"Sir?" Gwen prompted when he didn't reply.

He sat up straight. His eyes narrowed further as he stared at her. She was almost twitching. "What do you know," he said softly, "that you aren't telling me?"

Her face flushed. "No...nothing. I mean, there's... nothing," she faltered, and could have bitten her tongue for making things worse.

"You need to think about your priorities," he said curtly.

She drew in a long breath. "Believe me, I am."

He grimaced and waved his hand in her direction. "Get to work."

"Yes, sir."

She almost ran out of the office. She was flushed and unsettled. Lieutenant Hollister met her in the hall, and frowned.

"What's up?" he asked gently.

She bit her lip. "Nothing, sir," she said. She drew in a long breath. She wanted, so badly, to tell somebody what was going on.

Hollister's black eyes narrowed. "Come into my office for a minute."

He led her back the way she'd come, past a startled Marquez, who watched the couple go into the lieutenant's office with an expression that was hard to classify.

"Sit down," Hollister said. He went behind his desk and swung up his long, powerful legs, propping immaculate black boots on the desk. He crossed his arms and leaned back precariously in his chair. "Talk."

She shifted restlessly. "I know something about Sergeant Marquez that I'm not supposed to discuss with anybody."

He lifted a thick blond eyebrow. He even smiled. "I know what it is."

Her green eyes widened.

"The suits who came to see me earlier in the week were feds," he said. "I know who you really are, and what's going on." He sighed. "I want to tell Marquez, too, but my hands are tied."

"I went to see Cash Grier," she said. "He's out of the loop. He can't do anything directly, but he might be able to let something slip at Barbara's Café in Jacobsville.

That would at least prepare Sergeant Marquez for what's about to go down."

"Nothing can prepare a man for that sort of revelation, believe me." His eyes narrowed even more. "They want Marquez as a liaison, don't they?"

She nodded. "He'd be the best man for the job. But he's going to be very upset at first and he may refuse to do anything."

"That's a risk they're willing to take. They don't dare interfere directly, not in the current political climate," he added. "Frankly, I'd just go tell him."

"Would you?" she asked, and smiled.

He laughed deeply and then he shook his head. "Actually, no, I wouldn't. I'm too handsome to spend time in prison. There would be riots. I'd be so much in demand as somebody's significant other."

She laughed, too. She hadn't realized he had a sense of humor. Her face flushed. She looked very pretty.

He cocked his head. "You could just ask Marquez to the ballet and tell him yourself."

"My boss would have me hung in Hogan's Alley up at the FBI Academy with a placard around my neck as a warning to other loose-lipped agents," she told him.

He grinned. "I'd come cut you down, Cassaway. I get along well with the feds. But I'm not prejudiced. I also get along with mercenaries."

"There's a rumor that you used to be one," she fished.

His face closed up, although he was still smiling. "How about that?"

She didn't comment.

He swung his long legs off the desk and stood up. "Let me know how it goes," he said. He walked her to the door. "It's not a bad idea, about asking him to the ballet. He loves ballet. He usually goes alone. He can't get girlfriends."

"Why not?" she asked. She cleared her throat. "I mean, he's rather attractive."

"He wears a gun."

"So do you," she pointed out, indicating the holster. "In fact, we all wear them."

"True, but he likes women who don't," he replied. "And they don't like men who wear guns. He doesn't date colleagues, he says. But you might be able to change his mind."

"Fat chance." She sighed. "He doesn't like me."

"Go solve that murder for the cold case unit, and they'll lobby him for you," he teased.

"How do you know about that?" she asked, surprised.

"I'm the lieutenant," he pointed out. "I know everything," he added smugly.

She laughed. She was still laughing when she walked down the corridor.

Rick heard her from inside his office. He threw a scratch pad across the room and knocked the trash can across the floor with it. Then he grimaced, in case anybody heard and asked what was going on. He couldn't have told them. He didn't know himself why he was behaving so out of character.

The man Gwen was tracking in her semiofficial disguise was an unpleasant, slinky individual who had a rap sheet that read like a short story. She'd gone down to Jacobsville and interviewed Officer Dan Travis. He seemed a decent sort of person, and he could swear that the man who was arrested for the murder was at a holiday party with him, and had never even stepped outside.

He had told the assistant DA, but the attorney refused to entertain evidence he considered hearsay. Travis gave her the names of two other people she could contact, who would verify the information. She took notes and arranged for a deposition to be taken from him.

Her next stop was Patrol South Division, in San Antonio, to talk to the arresting officer who'd taken Dunagan in for the attempted assault on a college woman a few months ago, Dave Harris. He was working that day, but was working a wreck when she phoned him. So she arranged to meet him for lunch at a nearby fast food joint.

They sat together over hamburgers and fries and soft drinks, attracting attention with his uniform and her pistol and badge, conspicuously displayed.

"We're being watched," she said in a dramatic tone, indicating two young women at a nearby booth.

"Oh, that's just Joan and Shirley," he said. He looked toward the women, waved and grinned. One of them flushed and almost knocked over her drink. He was blond and blue-eyed, nicely built, and quite handsome. He was also single. "Joan's sweet on me," he added in a whisper. "They know I always eat here, so they come by for lunch. They work at the print shop downtown. Joan's a graphic artist. Very talented."

"Nice," she murmured, biting into the burger.

"Why are you doing a cold case?" he asked as he finished his salad and sipped black coffee.

"It ties in with a current one we're working on," she said, and related what Cash Grier had told her.

His dark eyebrows arched. "They never called a prime witness in the case?"

"Strange, isn't it?" she agreed. "That would be grounds

for a mistrial, I'd think, but I'll need to talk to the city attorney's office first. The man who was convicted has been in prison for almost a year."

"Shame, if he's innocent," the patrolman replied.

"I know. Fortunately, such things don't happen often."

"What about the suspect in your current case?"

"A nasty bit of work," she replied. "I can place him at the scene of the crime, and if there's enough trace evidence to do a DNA profile, I think I can connect him with it. Her neighbors reported seeing him around her apartment the morning before the murder. If he's guilty, I don't want him to slip through the cracks on my watch, especially since Sergeant Marquez assigned me to the case as chief investigator."

"Really? How many other people are helping you with the case?"

"Let's see, right now, there's me and one other detective that I borrowed to help question witnesses."

He sighed. "Budget issues again?"

"Afraid so. I can manage. If I need help, the cold case unit will lend me somebody."

"Nice group, that cold case unit."

She smiled. "I think so, too."

"Now about the perp," he added, leaning forward. "This is how it went down."

He described the scene of the assault where he'd arrested Dunagan, the persons involved, the witnesses and his own part in the arrest. Gwen made notes on her phone and saved the file.

"That's a big help," she told him. "Thanks."

He smiled. "You're very welcome." He checked his watch. "I have to get back on patrol. Was there any other information you needed?"

"Nothing I can't find in the file. I appreciate the summary of the case, and your thoughts on it. That really helps."

"You're welcome. Anytime."

"Shame about the latest victim," she added as they got up and headed to the trash bin with their trays. "She was very pretty. Her neighbors said she went out of her way to help people in need." She glanced at him. "We had one of your fellow officers on stakeout with us the other night. Sims."

He paused as he dumped the paper waste and placed the tray in its stack on the refuse container top. "He's not our usual sort of patrol officer."

"What do you mean?" she asked, frowning.

"I really can't say anything. It's just that he has an interesting background. There are people in high positions with influence," he added. He smiled. "But he's not my problem. I think you'll do well in the homicide unit. You've got a knack for sorting things out, and you're thorough. Good luck on the case."

"Thanks. Thanks a lot."

He smiled. "You're welcome."

She drove back to the office with her brain spinning. What she'd learned was very helpful. She might crack the case, which would certainly give her points with Rick Marquez. But there was still the problem of what she knew and couldn't tell him. She only hoped that Cash Grier would be able to break some ground with her sergeant.

Cash Grier had a thick ham sandwich with homemade fries and black coffee and then asked for a slice of Barbara's famous apple pie and homemade ice cream.

She served it with a grin. "Don't eat too much of this," she cautioned. "It's very fattening." She was teasing, because he was still as trim as men ten years his junior, and nicely muscled.

He pursed his lips and his black eyes twinkled. "As you can see, I'm running to fat."

She laughed. "That'll be the day."

He studied her quietly. "Can you sit down for a minute?"

She looked around. The lunchtime rush was over and there were only a couple of cowboys and an elderly couple in the café. "Sure." She sat down across from him. "What can I do for you?"

He sipped coffee. "I've been enlisted to get some information to your son without telling him anything."

She blinked. "That's a conundrum."

"Isn't it?" He put down the coffee cup and smiled. "You're a very intelligent woman. You must have some suspicions about his family history."

"Thanks for the compliment. And yes, I have a lot." She studied his hard face. "I overheard some feds who ate here talking about Dolores Ortíz and her connection to General Machado. Dolores worked for me just briefly. She was Rick's birth mother."

"Rick's stepfather was a piece of work," he said coldly. "I've heard plenty about him. He mistreated livestock and was fired for it on the Ballenger feedlot. Gossip is that he did the same to his stepson."

Her face tautened. "When I first adopted him, I lifted my hand to smooth back his hair—you know, that thing mothers do when they feel affectionate. He stiffened and cringed." Her eyes were sad. "That's when I first knew that there was a reason for his bad behavior. I've never hit him. But someone did."

"His stepfather," Grier asserted. "With assorted objects, including, once, a leather whip."

"So that's where he got those scars on his back," she faltered. "I asked, but he would never talk about it."

"It's a blow to a man's pride to have something like that done to him," he said coldly. "Jackson should have been sent to prison on a charge of child abuse."

"I do agree." She hesitated. "Rick's last name is Marquez. But Dolores said that was a name she had legally drawn up when Rick was seven. I never understood."

"She didn't dare put his real father's name on a birth certificate," he replied. "Even at the time, his dad was in trouble with the law in Mexico. She didn't want him to know about Rick. And, later, she had good reason to keep the secret. She married Craig Jackson to give Rick a settled home. She didn't know what sort of man he was until it was too late," he added coldly. "He knew who Rick's real father was and threatened to make it public if Dolores left him. So she stayed and Rick paid for her silence."

Barbara was feeling uncomfortable. "Would his real father happen to be an exiled South American dictator, by any chance?"

Grier nodded.

"Oh, boy."

"And nobody can tell him, because a certain federal agency is hoping to talk him into being a go-between for them, to help coax Machado into a comfortable trade agreement with our country when he gets back into power. Which he certainly will," he added quietly. "The thug who took over his government has human rights advocates bristling all over the world. He's tortured people, murdered dissenters, closed down public media outlets… In general, he's done everything possible to outrage anyone who believes in democracy. At the same time, he's pocketing money from sources of revenue and buying himself every rich man's perk that he can dream up. He's got several Rolls-Royce cars, assorted beautiful women, houses in most affluent European cities and his own private jet to take him to them. He doesn't govern so much as he flaunts his position. Workers are starving and farmers are being forced to grow drug crops to support his extravagant lifestyle." He shook his head. "I've seen dictators come and go, but that man needs a little lead in his diet."

She knew what he was alluding to. "Any plans going to take care of that?" she mused.

"Don't look at me," he warned. "I'm retired. I have a family to think about."

"Eb Scott might have a few people who would be interested in the work."

"Yes, he might, but the general isn't lacking for good help." He glanced up as one of Barbara's workers came, smiling, to refill his coffee cup. "Thanks."

She grinned. "You're welcome. Boss lady, you want some?"

Barbara shook her head. "Thanks, Bess, I'm already flying on a caffeine high."

"Okay."

"So who has to do the dirty work and tell Rick the truth?" Barbara asked.

Grier didn't speak. He just smiled at her.

"Oh, darn it, I won't do it!"

"There's nobody else. The feds have forbidden their

agents to tip him off. His lieutenant knows, but he's been gagged, too."

"Then how in the world do they expect him to find out? Why won't they just tell him?"

"Because he might get mad at them for being the source of the revelation and refuse to cooperate. And there isn't anybody else they can find to do the job of contacting Machado."

"They could ask Grange," Barbara said stubbornly. "He's already working for the general, isn't he?"

"Grange doesn't know."

"Why me?" she groaned. "He'll be furious!"

"Yes, but you're his mother and he loves you," he replied. "If you tell him, he'll get over it. He might even be receptive to helping the feds. If they tell him, he'll hold a grudge and they'll never find anyone halfway suitable to do the job."

She was silent. She stared at the festive tablecloth worriedly.

"It will be all right," he assured her gently.

She looked up. "We've already had a disagreement recently."

"You have? Why?" he asked, surprised, because Rick's devotion to his adopted mother was quite well-known locally.

She grimaced. "His lieutenant gave the new detective, Gwen Cassaway, a rose, and I mentioned it in a teasing way. He went ballistic and I hung up on him. He won't admit it, but I think he's got a case on Gwen."

"Well!" he mused.

That was a new and interesting proposition. "Couldn't she tell him?" she asked hopefully.

"She's been cautioned not to."

She sighed. "Darn. Does everybody know?"

"Rick doesn't."

"I noticed."

"So you have to tell him. And soon."

"Or what?"

He leaned forward. "Or six government agencies will send operatives down here to disparage your apple pie and accuse you of subverting government policy by using organic products in your kitchen."

She burst out laughing. "Yes, I did hear that a SWAT team of federal agents raided a farm that was selling unpasteurized milk. Can you believe that? In our country, in this day and time, with all the real problems going on, we have to send armed operatives against people living in a natural harmony with the earth?"

"You're kidding!" he exclaimed.

"I wish I was," she replied. "I guess we're all going to be force-fed Genetically Modified Organisms from now on."

He burst out laughing. "You need to stop hanging out on those covert websites."

"I can't. I'd never know what was really going on in the world, like us having bases on the moon."

He rolled his eyes. "I have to get back to work." He stood up. "You'll tell him, then."

She stood up, too. "Do I have a choice?"

"You could move to Greenland and change your name."

She made a face at him. "That's no choice. Although I would love to visit Greenland. They have snow."

"So do we, occasionally."

"They have lots of snow. Enough to make many snowmen. South Texas isn't famous for that."

"The pie was great, by the way."

She smiled. "Thanks. I do my best."

"I'd have to leave town if you ever closed up," he told her. "I can't live in a town that doesn't have the best food in Texas."

"That will get you extra ice cream on your next slice of apple pie!" she promised him with a grin.

But she wasn't grinning when she went home. It disturbed her that she was going to have to tell her son something that would devastate him. He wasn't going to be pleased. Other than that, she didn't know what the outcome would be. But Grier was right about one thing; it was better that the information came from his mother rather than from some bureaucrat or federal agent who had no personal involvement with Rick and didn't care how the news affected him. It did make her feel good that so far, they hadn't blurted it out. By hesitating, they did show some compassion.

Rick went to his mother's home tired. It had been a long day of meetings and more meetings, with a workshop on gun safety occasioned by the accidental discharge of a pistol by one of the patrol officers. The bullet went into the asphalt but fortunately didn't ricochet and hit anything, or anyone. The officer was disciplined but the chain of command saw an opportunity to emphasize gun safety and they took it. The moral of the story was that even experienced officers could mishandle a gun.

Privately, Marquez wondered how Officer Sims ever got through the police academy, because he was the officer involved. The same guy who'd gone on stakeout with him and Cassaway. He didn't think a lot of the young man's ethics and he'd heard that Sims had an uncle high up in the chain of command who made sure he kept his job. It was disturbing.

"You look worn-out," Barbara said gently. "Come sit down and I'll put supper on the table."

"It's late," he commented, noting his watch.

"We can have supper at midnight," she teased. "Nobody's watching. I'll even pull down the shades if it makes you happy."

He laughed and hugged her. "You're a treasure, Mom. I'll never marry unless I can find a girl like you."

"That's sweet. Thanks."

She started heating up roast beef and buttered rolls, topping off his plate with homemade potato salad. She put the plate in front of him. "Thank goodness for microwave ovens." She laughed. "The cook's best friend."

"This is delicious." He closed his eyes, savoring every bite. "I had a sandwich for lunch and I only had time to eat half of it between meetings."

"I didn't even eat lunch," she said, dipping into her own roast beef.

"Why not?"

"I had a talk with Cash Grier and afterward I lost my appetite."

He stopped eating and stared at her with narrowed eyes. "What did he tell you?"

"Something everybody knows and nobody has the guts to tell you, my darling," she said, stiffening herself mentally. "I have some very unpleasant news."

He put down his fork. "You've got cancer." His face paled. "That's it, isn't it? You should have told me…!"

He got up and hugged her. "We'll get through it together. I'll never leave your side…"

She pulled back, flattered. "I'm fine," she said. "I don't have anything fatal. That isn't what I meant. It's about you. And your real father."

He blinked. "My real father died not long after I was born…"

She took a deep breath. "Rick, your real father is across the border in Mexico amassing a private army in preparation for invading a South American country."

He sat down, hard. His light olive complexion was suddenly very pale. All the gossip and secrecy suddenly made sense. The feds were all over his office, not because they were working on shared cases, but because of Rick.

"My father is General Emilio Machado," he said with sudden realization.

Chapter 5

"My father is a South American dictator," Rick repeated, almost in shock.

"I'm afraid so." Barbara pulled up a chair facing him and held his hand that was resting on the table. "They made me tell you. Nobody else wanted to. I'm so sorry."

"But my mother said my father was dead," he repeated blankly.

"She only wanted to protect you. Machado was in trouble with the Mexican authorities when he lived in the country because he was opposed to foreign interests trying to take over key industries where he lived. He organized protests even when he was in his teens. He was a natural leader. Later, Dolores didn't dare tell you because Machado was the head of a fairly well-known international paramilitary group and that would have made you a target for any extremist with a grudge. He was in the news a lot when you were a child."

"Does he know?" Rick persisted. "Does he know about me?"

Barbara bit her lower lip. "No. She never told him." She sighed. "After Cash told me who your father was, I remembered something that Dolores told me. She said your father was only fourteen when he fathered you. She was older, seventeen, and there was no chance that her family would have let her marry him. She wanted you very much. So she had you, and never even told her parents who the father was. She kept her secret. At least, until she married your stepfather. Cash said that your stepfather got the truth out of her and used it to keep her with him. She didn't dare protest or he'd have made your real identity known. A true charmer," she added sarcastically.

"My stepfather was a sadist," he said quietly. "I've never spoken of him to you. But he made my life hell, and my mother's as well. I got in trouble with the law on purpose. I thought maybe somebody would check out my home life and see the truth and help us. But nobody ever did. Not until you came along and offered my mother work."

"I tried to help," she agreed. "Dolores liked cooking for me, but your stepfather didn't like her having friends or any interest outside of him. He was insanely jealous."

"He also couldn't keep a job. Money was tight. You used to sneak me food," he recalled with a warm smile. "You even came to visit me in the detention center. My mother appreciated that. My stepfather wouldn't let her come."

"I knew that. I did what I could. I tried to get our police chief at the time to investigate, but he was the sort of man who didn't want to rock the boat." She laughed.

"Can you imagine Cash Grier turning a blind eye to something like that?"

"He'd have had my stepfather pilloried in the square." Rick smiled, then sobered. "My father is a dictator," he repeated again. It was hard to believe. He'd spent his whole life certain that his biological father was long dead.

"A deposed dictator," Barbara corrected. "His country is going to the dogs under its new administration. People are dying. He wants to accomplish a military coup, but he needs all the help he can get. Which brings us to our present situation," she added. "A paramilitary group is going down to Barrera with him, including some of Eb Scott's guys, some Europeans, one African merc and with ex-army Major Winslow Grange, Jason Pendleton's foreman on his Comanche Wells ranch, to lead them."

"All that firepower and the government hasn't noticed?"

"It wouldn't do them a lot of good. Machado's in Mexico, just over the border," Barbara said. "They can't mount an invasion to stop him. But they can try to find a way to be friendly without overt aid."

"Ah. I see. I'm the goat."

She blinked. "Excuse me?"

"They're going to tether me out to attract the puma."

"Puma." She laughed. "Funny, but one of my customers said that's what the local population calls 'El General.' They say he's cunning and dangerous like a cat, but that he can purr when he wants to." Her face softened. "For a dictator, he's held in high esteem by most democracies. He's intelligent, kind, he reveres women and he isn't afraid to fight for justice."

"Does he wear a red cape?" Rick murmured.

She shook her head. "Sorry."

"Who's in on this?" he asked narrowly. "Does my lieutenant know?"

"Yes," she said. "And there's a covert operative somewhere in your organization," she added. "I got that tidbit from a patrol officer who has a friend on the force in San Antonio. A guy named Sims."

"Sims." His face closed up. "He's got connections. And he's a total ethical wipeout. I hate having a guy like that on the force. He got careless with a pistol and almost shot himself in the foot. He's the reason we just had a gun safety workshop."

"Learning gun safety is not a bad thing."

He sighed. "I know." He was trying to adjust to the shock of his parentage. "Why didn't my mother tell me?" he burst out.

"She was trying to protect you. I'm certain that she would have told you eventually," she added. "She just didn't have time before she died."

He grimaced. "What am I supposed to do now, walk over the border, find the general and say, hey, guess what, I'm your kid?"

"I don't really think that would be wise," she replied. "I'm not sure he'd believe it in the first place. Would you?"

"Now there's a question." He leaned back in the chair, his dark eyes focused on the tablecloth. "I suppose I could have a DNA profile done. There's a private company that can at least rule out paternity by blood type. If mine is compatible with the general's, it might help convince him... Wait a minute," he added coldly. "Why the hell should I care?"

"Because he's your father, Rick," she said gently. "Even though he doesn't know."

"And the government's only purpose in telling me is to help reunite us," he returned angrily.

"Well, no, they want someone to convince the general to make a trade agreement with us once he's back in power. They're certain that he will be, which is why they want you to make friends with him."

"I'm sure he'll be overjoyed to know he has a grown son who's a cop," he said coldly. "Especially since he's wanted by our government for kidnapping."

She leaned forward with her chin resting in her hands, propped by her elbows. "You could arrest him," she pointed out. "And then befriend him in jail. Like the mouse that took the thorn out of the lion's paw and became its friend."

He made a face at her. "I can't walk across the border and arrest anyone. I might have been born in Mexico, but I'm an American citizen. And I did it the hard way," he added firmly. "Legally."

She grimaced.

"Sorry," he said after a minute. "I know you sympathize with all the people hiding out here who couldn't afford to wait for permission. In some of their countries, they could be killed just for paying too much attention to the wrong people."

"It's very bad in some Central American states," she pointed out.

"It's very bad anywhere on our border."

"And getting worse."

He got up and poured himself another cup of coffee. His big hand rested on the coffeemaker as he switched it off. "Who's the mole in my office?"

"I honestly don't know," she replied. "I only know that Sims told his friend, Cash Grier's patrolman, about it. He said it was someone from a federal agency, working undercover."

"I wonder how Sims knew."

"Maybe he's the mole," she teased.

"Unlikely. Most feds have too much respect for the law to abuse it. Sims actually suggested that we confiscate a six-pack of beer from a convenience store as evidence in some pretended case and threaten the clerk with jail if he told on us."

"Good grief! And he works for the police?" she exclaimed, horrified.

"Apparently," he replied. "I didn't like what he said, and I told him so. He seemed repentant, but I'm not sure he really was. Cocky kid. Real attitude problem."

"Doesn't that sound familiar?" she asked the room at large.

"I never suggested breaking the law after I went through the academy and swore under oath to uphold it," he replied.

"Are you sure you didn't overreact, my darling?" she asked gently.

"If I did, so did Cassaway. She was hotter under the collar than I was." He laughed shortly. "And then she beat the lieutenant on the firing range and he let out a bad word. She marched right up to him and said she was offended and he shouldn't talk that way around her." He glanced at her ruefully. "Hence, the rose."

"Oh. An apology." She looked disappointed. "Your lieutenant is very attractive," she mused. "And eligible. I thought he might find Miss Cassaway interesting. Or something."

"Maybe he does," he said vaguely. "God knows why. She's good with a gun, I'll give her that, but she's a walking disaster in other ways. How she ever got a job with the police, I'll never know." He didn't like talking about Cassaway and the lieutenant. It got under his skin, for reasons he couldn't understand.

"She sounds very nice to me."

"Everybody sounds nice to you," he replied. He smiled at her. "You could find one good thing to say about the devil, Mom. You look for the best in people."

"You look for the worst," she pointed out.

He shrugged. "That's my job."

He was thoughtful, and morose. She felt even more guilty when she saw how disturbed he really was.

"I wish there had been some other way to handle this," she muttered angrily. "I hate being made the fall guy."

"Hey, I'm not mad at you," he said, and bent to kiss her hair. "I just…don't know what to do." He sighed.

"'When in doubt, don't,'" she quoted. She frowned. "Who said that?"

"Beats me, but it's probably good advice." He put down his cooling coffee and stretched, yawning. "I'm beat. Too many late nights finishing paperwork and going on stakeouts. I'm going to bed. I'll decide what to do in the morning. Maybe it will come to me in a dream or something," he added.

"Maybe it will. I'm just sorry I had to be the one to tell you."

"I'll get used to the idea," he assured her. "I just need a little time."

She nodded.

* * *

But time was in short supply. Two days later, a tall, elegant man with dark hair and eyes, wearing a visitor's tag but no indication of his identity, walked into Rick's office and closed the door.

"I need to talk to you," he said.

Rick stared at him. "Do I know you?" he asked after a minute, because the man seemed vaguely familiar.

"You should," he replied with a grin. "But it's been a while since we caught Fuentes and his boys in the drug sting in Jacobsville. I'm Rodrigo Ramirez. DEA."

"I knew you looked familiar!" Rick got up and shook the other man's hand. "Yes, it has been a while. You and your wife bought a house here last year."

He nodded. "I work out of San Antonio DEA now instead of Houston, and she works for the local prosecutor, Blake Kemp, in Jacobsville. With her high blood pressure, I'd rather she stayed at home, but she said she'd do it when I did it." He shrugged. "Neither of us was willing to try to change professions at this late date. So we deal with the occasional problem."

"Are you mixed up in the Barrera thing as well?" Rick asked curiously.

"In a way. I'm related, distantly, to a high official in Mexico," he said. "It gives me access to some privileged information." He hesitated. "I don't know how much they've told you."

Rick motioned Ramirez into a chair and sat down behind his desk. "I know that El General has a son who's a sergeant with San Antonio P.D.," he said sarcastically.

"So you know."

"My mother told me. They wanted me to know, but nobody had the guts to just say it," he bit off.

"Yes, well, that could have been a big problem. Depending on how you were told, and by whom. They were afraid of alienating you."

"I don't see what help I'm going to be," Rick said irritably. "I didn't know my biological father was still alive, much less who he was. The general, I'm told, has no clue that I even exist. I doubt he'd take my word for it."

"So do I. Sometimes government agencies are a little thin on common sense," he added. He crossed his elegant long legs. "I've been elected, you might say, to do the introductions, by my cousin."

"Your cousin...?"

"He's the president of Mexico."

"Well, damn!"

Ramirez smiled. "That's what I said when he told me to do it."

"Sorry."

"No problem. It seems we're both stuck with doing something that goes against the grain. I think the general is going to react very badly. I wish there was someone who could talk to him for us."

"Like my mother talked to me for the feds?" he mused.

"Exactly."

Rick frowned. "You know, Gracie Pendleton got along quite well with him. She refused to even think of pressing charges. She was asked, in case we could talk about extradition of Machado with the Mexican government. She said no."

"I heard. She's my sister-in-law, although she's not related to my wife. Don't even ask," he added, waving his hand. "It's far too complicated to explain."

"I won't. But I remember Glory very well," he reminded Ramirez. "Cash Grier and I taught her how to shoot a pistol without destroying cars in the parking lot," he added with a grin.

Ramirez laughed. "So you did." He sobered. "Gracie might be willing to speak to the general, if we could get word to him," Ramirez said.

"We had a guy in jail here who was one of the higher-ups in the Fuentes organization. He's going on probation tomorrow."

"An opportunity." Ramirez chuckled.

"Apparently, a timely one. I'll ask him if he'd have the general call Gracie. Now, how do you get Gracie to do that dirty work for you?"

"I'll have my wife bribe her with flowers and chocolate and Christmas decorations."

"Excuse me?" Rick asked.

"Gracie loves to decorate for Christmas. My wife has access to a catalog of rare antique decorations. Gracie can be bribed, if you know how," he added.

Rick smiled. "An assistant district attorney working a bribe. What if somebody tells her boss?"

"He'll laugh," Ramirez assured him. "It's for a just cause, after all."

Rick started down to the jail in time to waylay the departing felon. He spoke to the probation officer on the way and arranged the conversation.

The man was willing to take a message to the general, for a price. That put them on the hot seat, because neither man could be seen offering illegal payment to a felon.

Then Rick had a brainstorm. "Wait a second." He'd spotted the janitor emptying trash baskets nearby. He took the man to one side, handed him two fifties and told him what to do.

The janitor, confused but willing to help, walked over to the prisoner and handed him the money. It was from him, he added, since the prisoner had been pleasant to him during his occupation in the jail. He wanted to help him get started again on the outside.

The prisoner, smiling, understood immediately what was going on. He took the money graciously, with a bow, and proceeded to sing the janitor's praises for his act of generosity. So the message was sent.

Gwen Cassaway was sitting at Rick's desk when he went back to his office, in the chair reserved for visitors. He hated the way his heart jumped at the sight of her. He fought down that unwanted feeling.

"Do they have to issue us these chairs?" she complained when he came in, closing the door behind him. "Honestly, only hospital waiting rooms have chairs that are more uncomfortable."

"The idea is to make you want to leave," he assured her. "What's up?" he added absently as he removed his holstered pistol from his belt and slid it into a desk drawer, then locked the drawer before he sat down. "Something about the case I assigned you to?"

She hesitated. This was going to be difficult. "Something else. Something personal."

He stared at her coolly. "I don't discuss personal issues with colleagues. We have a staff psychologist if you need counseling."

She let out an exasperated sigh. "Honestly, do you have a steel rod glued to your spine?" she burst out.

Then she realized what she'd said, clapped her hand over her mouth and looked horrified at the slip.

He didn't react. He just stared.

"I'm sorry!" she said, flustered. "I'm so sorry! I didn't mean to say that…!"

"Cassaway," he began.

"It's about the general," she blurted out.

His dark eyes narrowed. "Lately, everything is. Don't tell me. You're having an affair with him and you have to confess for the sake of your job."

She drew in a long breath. "Actually, the general *is* my job." She got up, opened her wallet and handed it to Rick.

He did an almost comical double take. He looked at her as if she'd grown leaves. "You're a fed?"

She nodded and grimaced. She took back the wallet after he'd looked at it again, just to make sure it didn't come from the toy department in some big store.

She put it back in her fanny pack. "Sorry I couldn't say something before, but they wouldn't let me," she said heavily as she sat down again, with her hands folded on her jeans.

"What the hell are you doing pretending to be a detective?" he asked with some exasperation.

"It was my boss's idea. I did start out with Atlanta P.D., but I've worked in counterterrorism for the agency for about four years now," she confessed. "I'm sorry," she repeated. "This wasn't my idea. They wanted me to find out how much you knew about your family history before they accidentally said or did something that would upset you."

He raised an eyebrow. "I've just been presented with a father who's an exiled South American dictator, whose existence I was unaware of. They didn't think that would upset me?"

"I asked Cash Grier to talk to your mother," she said. "You can't tell anybody. I was ordered not to talk to you about it. But they didn't say I couldn't ask somebody else to do it."

He was touched by her concern. Not that he liked her any better. "I wondered about your shooting skills," he said after a minute. "Not exactly something I expect in a run-of-the-mill detective."

She smiled. "I spend a lot of time on the gun range," she replied. "I've been champion of my unit for two years running."

"Our lieutenant was certainly surprised when he found himself outdone," he remarked.

"He's very nice."

He glared at her.

She wondered what he had against his superior officer, but she didn't comment. "I was told that a DEA officer is going to try to get someone to speak to General Machado about you."

"Yes. Gracie Pendleton will talk with him. Machado likes her."

"He kidnapped her!" she exclaimed. "And the man she's now married to!"

He nodded. "I know. He also saved her from being assaulted by one of Fuentes's men," he added.

"Oh. I didn't know that."

"She's fond of him, too," he replied. "Apparently, he makes friends even of his enemies. A couple of feds I know think he's one of the better insurgents," he added dryly.

"He did install democratic government in Barrera," she pointed out. "He instituted reforms that did away with unlawful detention and surveillance, he invited the foreign media in to oversee elections and he ousted half a dozen petty politicians who were robbing the poor and making themselves into feudal lords. From what we understand, one of those petty politicians helped Machado's second-in-command plan the coup that ousted him."

"While he was out of the country negotiating trade agreements," Rick agreed. "Stabbed in the back."

"Exactly. We'd love to have him back in power, but we can't actually do anything about it," she said quietly. "That's where you come in."

"The general doesn't even know me, let alone that I'm his biological son," he repeated. "Even if he did, I don't think he's going to jump up and invite me to baseball games."

"Soccer," she corrected. "He hates baseball."

His eyebrows lifted. "How do you know that?"

"I have a file on him," she said. "He likes strawberry ice cream, his favorite musical star is Marco Antonio Solís, he wears size 12 shoes and he plays classical guitar. Oh, he was an entertainer on a cruise ship in his youth."

"I did know about that. Not his shoe size," he added with twinkling dark eyes.

"He's never been romantically linked with any particular woman," she continued. "Although he was good friends with an American anthropologist who went to live in his country. She'd found an ancient site that was revolutionary and she was involved in a dig there. Apparently, there are some interesting ruins in Barrera."

"What happened to her?"

"Nobody knows. We couldn't even ascertain her name. What I was able to ferret out was only gossip."

He folded his hands on his desk. "So, you're a fed, I'm one detective short and you're supposed to be heading a murder investigation for me," he said curtly. "What do I do about that?"

"I've been working on it," she protested. "I'm making progress, too. As soon as we get the DNA profile back, I may be able to make an arrest in the college freshman's murder, and solve a cold case involving another dead coed. I have lots of information to go on, now, including eyewitness testimony that can place the suspect at the murdered woman's apartment just before she was killed."

He sat up. "Nice!"

"Thank you. I have an appointment to talk to her best friend, also, the one who took the photo that the suspect showed up in. She gave a statement to the crime scene detective that the victim had complained about visits from a man who made her uneasy."

"They'll let you continue to work on my case, even though you're a fed?"

"Until something happens in the general's case," she said. "I'm keeping up appearances."

"You slipped through the cracks," he translated.

She laughed. "Thanksgiving is just over the horizon and my boss gets a lot of business done in D.C. going from one party to another with his wife."

"I see."

"When is Mrs. Pendleton going to talk to the general, did the DEA agent say?"

He shook his head. "It's only a work in progress right now." He leaned back in his chair. "I thought my father was dead. My mother told me he was killed when I was just a baby. I didn't realize I had a father who never even knew I was on the way."

"He loves children," she pointed out.

"Yes, but I'm not a child."

"I noticed."

He glared at her.

She flushed and averted her eyes.

He felt guilty. "Sorry. I'm not dealing with this well."

"I can understand that," she replied. "I know it must be hard for you."

She had a nice voice, he thought. Soft and medium in pitch, and she colored it in pastels with emotion. He liked her voice. Her choice of T-shirts, however, left a lot to be desired. She had on one today that read Save a Turkey, Eat a Horse for Thanksgiving. He burst out laughing.

"Do you have an open line to a T-shirt manufacturer?" he asked.

"What? Oh!" She glanced down at her shirt. "Well, sort of. There's this online place that lets you make your own T-shirts. I do a lot of business with them, designing my own."

Now he understood her quirky wardrobe.

"Drives my boss nuts," she added with a grin. "He thinks I'm not dignified enough on the job."

"I'm sure you have casual days, even in D.C."

"I don't work in D.C.," she said. "I get sent wherever I'm needed. I live out of a suitcase mostly." She smiled wanly. "It's not much of a life. I loved it when I was younger, but I'd really love to have someplace permanent."

"You could get a job in a local office."

"I guess." She shrugged. "Meanwhile, I've got one right here. I'm sorry I didn't tell you who I was at first," she added. "I would have liked to be honest."

He sensed that. He grimaced. "It's hard for me, too, trying to understand the past. My mother, my adopted mother," he said, just to clarify the point, "said that the general was only fourteen when he fathered me. I'll be thirty-one this year, in late December. That would make him—" he stopped and thought "—forty-five." His eyebrows arched. "That's not a great age for a dictator."

She laughed. "He was forty-one when he became president of Barrera," she said. "In those four years, he did a world of good for his country. His adopted country."

"Yes, well, he's wanted in this country for kidnapping," he reminded her.

"Good luck trying to get him extradited," she cautioned. "First the Mexican authorities would have to actually apprehend him, and he's got a huge complex in northern Sonora. One report is that he even has a howitzer."

"True story," he said, leaning back in his chair. "Pancho Villa, who fought in the Mexican Revolution, was a folk hero in Mexico at the turn of the twentieth century. John Reed, a Harvard graduate and journalist, actually lived with him for several months."

"And wrote articles about his adventures there. They made them into a book," she said, shocking him. "I had to buy it from a rare book shop. It's one of my treasures."

Chapter 6

"I've read that book," Rick said with a slow smile. "*Insurgent Mexico*. I couldn't afford to buy it, unfortunately, so I got it on loan from the library. It was published in 1914. A rare book, indeed."

She shifted uncomfortably. She hadn't meant to let that bit slip. She was still keeping secrets from him. She shouldn't have been able to afford the book on her government salary. Her father had given it to her last Christmas. That was another secret she was keeping, too; her father's identity.

"And would you know Pancho Villa's real name?" he asked suddenly.

She grinned. "He was born Doroteo Arango," she said. The smile faded a little. "He changed his name to Pancho Villa, according to one source, because he was hunted by the authorities for killing a man who raped his younger sister. It put him on a path of lawlessness, but he fought all his life for a Mexico that was free of foreign oppression and a government that worked for the poor."

He smiled with pure delight. "You read Mexican history," he mused, still surprised.

"Well, yes, but the best of it is in Spanish, so I studied very hard to learn to read it," she confessed. She flushed. "I like the colonial histories, written by priests in the sixteenth century who sailed with the *conquistadores*."

"Spanish colonial history," he said.

She smiled. "I also like to read about Juan Belmonte and Manolete."

His eyebrows arched. "Bullfighters?" he exclaimed.

"Well, yes," she said. "Not the modern ones. I don't know anything about those. I found this book on Juan Belmonte, his biography. I was so fascinated by it that I started reading about Joselito and the others who fought bulls in Spain at the beginning of the twentieth century. They were so brave. Nothing but a cape and courage, facing a bull that was twice their size, all muscle and with horns so sharp…" She cleared her throat. "It's not PC to talk about it, I know."

"Yes, we mustn't mention blood sports," he joked. "The old bullfighters were like soldiers who fought in the world wars—tough and courageous. I like World War II history, particularly the North African theater of war."

Her eyes opened wide behind the lenses of her glasses. "Rommel. Patton. Montgomery. Alexander…"

His lips fell open. "Yes."

She laughed with some embarrassment. "I'm a history major," she said. "I took my degree in it." She didn't add that she came by her interest in military history quite naturally, nor that her grandfather had known General George S. Patton, Jr., personally.

"Well!"

"You have an associate's degree in criminal justice and you're going to night school working on your B.A.," she blurted out.

He laughed. "What's my shoe size?"

"Eleven." She cleared her throat. "Sorry. I have a file on you, too."

He leaned forward, his large dark eyes narrow. "I'll have to compile one on you. Just to be fair."

She didn't want him to do that, but she just nodded. Maybe he couldn't dig up too much, even if he tried. She kept her private life very private.

She stood up. "I need to get back to work. I just wanted to be honest with you, about my job," she said. "I didn't want you to think I was being deliberately deceitful."

He stood up, too. "I never thought that."

He walked with her to the door. "Uh, is the lieutenant still bringing you roses?" he asked, and could have slapped himself for even asking the question.

"Oh, certainly not," she said primly. "That was just an apology, for using bad language in front of me."

"He's a widower," he said as they reached the door.

She paused and looked up at him. He was very close all of a sudden and she felt the heat from his body as her nostrils caught the faint, exotic scent of the cologne he used. He smelled very masculine and her heart went wild at the proximity. Her head barely topped his shoulder. He was tall and powerfully built, and she had an almost overwhelming hunger to lay her head on that shoulder and press close and bury her lips in that smooth, tanned throat.

She caught her breath and stepped back quickly. She looked up into his searching eyes and stood very still, like a cat in the sights of a hunter. She couldn't even think of anything to say.

Rick was feeling something similar. She smelled of wildflowers today. Her skin was almost translucent and he noticed that she wore little makeup. Her hair was caught up in a high ponytail, but he was certain that if she let it down, it would make a thick platinum curtain all the way to her waist. He wanted, badly, to loosen it and bury his mouth in it.

He stepped back, too. The feelings were uncomfortable. "Better get back to work," he said curtly. He was breathing heavily. His voice didn't sound natural.

"Yes. Uh, m-me, too," she stammered, and flushed, making her skin look even prettier.

He started to open the door for her. But he paused. "Someone told me that you like *The Firebird*."

She laughed nervously. "Yes. Very much."

"The orchestra is doing a tribute to Stravinsky Friday night." He moved one shoulder. He shouldn't do this. But he couldn't help himself. "I have two tickets. I was going to take Mom, but she's going to have to cater some cattlemen's meeting in Jacobsville and she can't go." He took a breath. "So I was wondering…"

"Yes." She cleared her throat. "I mean, if you were going to ask me…?" she blurted, embarrassed.

Her nervousness lessened his. He smiled at her in a way he never had, his chiseled mouth sensuous, his eyes very dark and soft. "Yes. I was going to ask you."

"Oh." She laughed, self-consciously.

He tipped her chin up with his bent forefinger and looked into her soft, pale green eyes. "Six o'clock? We'll have dinner first."

Her breath caught. Her heartbeat shook her T-shirt. "Yes," she whispered breathlessly.

His dark eyes were on her pretty bow of a mouth. It was slightly parted, showing her white teeth. He actually started bending toward it when his phone suddenly rang.

He jerked back, laughing deeply at his own helpless response to her. "Go to work," he said, but he grinned.

"Yes, sir." She started out the door. She looked back at him. "I live in the Oak Street apartments," she said. "Number 92."

He smiled back. "I'll remember."

She left, with obvious reluctance.

It took him a minute to realize that his phone was still ringing. He was going to date a colleague and the whole department would know. Well, what the hell, he muttered to himself. He was really tired of going to concerts and the ballet alone. She was a fed and she wouldn't be here long. Why shouldn't he have companionship?

Gwen got back to her own office and leaned back against the door with a long sigh. She was trembling from the encounter with Rick and so shocked at his invitation that she could barely get her breath back. He was going to date her. He wanted to take her out. She could barely believe it!

While she was savoring the invitation, her cell phone rang. She noted the number and opened it.

"Hi, Dad," she said, smiling. "How's it going?"

"Rough, or don't you watch the news, pudding?" he asked with a laugh in his deep voice as he used his nickname for her.

"I do," she said. "I'm really sorry. Politicians should let the military handle military matters."

"Come up to D.C. and tell the POTUS that," he murmured.

"Why can't you just say President of the United States?" she teased.

"I'm in the military. We use abbreviations."

"I noticed."

"How's it going with you?"

"I'm working on a sensitive matter."

"I've been talking to your boss about it," he replied. "And I told him that I don't like having you put on the firing line like this."

She winced. She could imagine that encounter. Her boss, while very nice, was also as bullheaded as her father. It would have been interesting to see how it ended.

"And he told you…?"

He sighed. "That I could mind my own damned business, basically," he explained. "We're a lot alike."

"I noticed."

"Anyway, I hope you're packing, and that the detective you're working with is, also."

"We both are, but the general isn't a bad man."

"He's wanted for kidnapping!"

"Yes, well, he's desperate for money, but he didn't really hurt anybody."

"A man was killed in his camp," he returned curtly.

"Yes, the general shot him for trying to assault Gracie Pendleton," she replied. "He caught him in the act.

Gracie was bruised and shaken, but he got to her just in time. The guy was one of the Fuentes organization."

There was a long silence. "I didn't hear that part."

"Not many people have."

He sighed. "Well, maybe he's not as bad a man as I thought he was."

"We want him on our side. He has a son that he didn't know about. We're trying to get an entrée into his camp, to make a contact with him. It isn't easy."

"I know about that, too." He paused. "How's your love life?" he teased.

She cleared her throat. "Actually, Sergeant Marquez just invited me to a symphony concert."

There was a longer pause. "He likes classical music?"

"Yes, and the ballet." Her eyes narrowed. "And no smart remarks, if you please."

"I like classical music."

"But you hate ballet," she pointed out. "And you think anybody who does is nuts."

"So I have a few interesting flaws," he conceded.

"He's also a military history buff," she added quickly. "World War II and North Africa."

"How ironic," he chuckled.

She smiled to herself. "Yes, isn't it?"

He drew in a long sigh. "You coming home for Christmas?"

"Of course," she agreed. She smiled sadly. "Especially this year."

"I'm glad." He bit off the words. "It hasn't been easy. Larry's wife calls me every other night, crying."

"Lindy will adjust," she said softly. "It's just going to take time. She and Larry were married for ten years and they didn't have children. That will make it harder for her. But she's strong. She'll manage."

"I hope so." There was a scraping sound, as if he was getting up out of a chair. "His commanding officer got drunk and wrecked a bar up in Maryland, while he was on R&R," he said.

"Larry's death wasn't his fault," she replied tersely. "Any officer who goes into a covert situation knows the risks and has to be willing to take them."

"I told him that," her father replied. "Damn it, he cried…!" He cleared his throat, choking back the emotion. "I called up Brigadier Langston and told him to get that man some help before he becomes a statistic. He promised he would."

"General Langston was fond of Larry, too," she said quietly. "I remember him at the funeral…"

There was a pause. "Let's talk about something else."

"Okay. How do you feel about giving chickens the vote?"

He burst out laughing.

"Or we could decide where we're going to eat on Christmas Eve, because I'm not spending my days off in the kitchen," she said.

"Good thing. We'd starve or die of carbon monoxide poisoning," he replied.

"I can cook! I just don't like to."

"If you'd use timers, we'd have food that didn't turn black before we got to eat it," he said. "I can cook anything," he added smugly.

"I remember." She sighed. "Rick's mom is a great cook," she replied. "She owns a restaurant."

"She does? You should marry him. You'd never have to worry about cooking again." He chuckled.

She blushed. "It's just a date, Dad."

"Your first one in how many years…?"

"Stop that," she muttered. "I date."

"You went to the Laundromat with a guy who lived in your apartment building," he burst out. "That's not a date!"

"It was fun. We ate potato chips and discussed movies while our clothes got done," she replied.

He shook his head. "Pudding, you're hopeless."

"Thanks!"

"I give up. I have to go. I've got a meeting with the Joint Chiefs in ten minutes."

"More war talk?"

"More withdrawal talk," he said. "There's a rumor that the POTUS is going to offer me Hart's job."

"You're kidding!"

"That's what they're saying."

"Will you take it?" she asked, excited.

"Watch the news and we'll find out."

"That would be great!"

"I might be in a position to do something more useful," he said. "But, we'll see. I guess I'd do it, if they ask me."

"Good for you!"

"Say, do you ever see Grange?"

"Grange? You mean, the Pendletons' foreman?" she asked, disconcerted.

"Yes. Winslow Grange. He was in my last overseas command." He smiled. "Had a real pig of an officer, who sent him into harm's way understrength and with a battle plan that some kindergarten kid could have come up with. Grange tied him up, put him in the trunk of his own car and led the assault himself. He was invited to leave the army with an honorable discharge or be court-martialed. He left. But he came back to testify against his commanding officer, who was dishonorably discharged after a nasty trial."

"Good enough for him," she said curtly.

"I do agree. Anyway, Winslow is a friend of mine. I'd love to see him sometime. You might pass that along. We could always use someone like him in D.C. if he gets tired of horse poop."

She wondered if she should tell her father what his buddy Grange was rumored to be doing right now, but that was probably a secret she should keep. "If I see him, I'll tell him," she promised.

"Take care of yourself, okay? You're the only family I've got left." His deep voice was thick with emotion.

"Same here," she replied. "Love you, Dad."

"Mmm-hmm." He wasn't going to say it out loud. He never did. But he loved her, so she didn't make a smart remark.

"I'll call you in a few days, just to check in. Okay?"

"That's a deal." His hand went over the receiver. "Yes, I'm on my way," he told someone else. "Gotta go. See you, kid."

"Bye, Dad."

He hung up. She put the phone back in her pocket. It seemed to be a day for revelations.

She had a beautiful little couture black dress, with expensive black slingbacks and a frilly black shawl that she'd gotten in Madrid. She wore those for her date with Rick, and she let her hair down, brushing it until it was shiny, like a pale satin curtain down her back. She left her glasses off for once. If she wasn't driving, she didn't need them, and a symphony concert didn't really require perfect vision.

Rick wore a dinner jacket and a black tie. His own hair was still in its elegant ponytail, but tied with a neat black ribbon. He looked very sharp.

He stared at her with disconcerting interest when she opened the door, taking in the nice fit of her dress with its modest rounded neckline and lacy hem that hit just at mid-calf. Her pretty little feet were in strappy high heels that left just a hint of the space between her toes visible. It was oddly sexy.

"You look…very nice," he said, his eyes taking in her flushed, lovely complexion and her perfect mouth, just dabbed with pale lipstick.

"Thanks! So do you," she replied, laughing nervously.

He produced a box from behind his back and handed it to her. It was a beautiful cymbidium orchid, much like the ones she had back at her father's home that the housekeeper faithfully misted each day.

"It's lovely!" she exclaimed.

He raised one shoulder and smiled self-consciously. "They wanted to give me one you wore around the wrist, but I explained that we weren't going to a dance and I wanted one that pinned."

"I like this kind best." She took it out of the box and pinned it to the dress, smiling at the way it complemented the dark background. "Thanks."

"My pleasure. Shall we go?"

"Yes!"

She grabbed her evening bag, closed the door and locked it and let him help her into his pickup truck.

"I should have something more elegant to drive than this," he muttered as he climbed in beside her.

"But I love trucks!" she exclaimed. "My dad has one that he drives around our place when he's home."

He grinned. "Well, maybe I'll get a nice car one day."

"It doesn't matter what you go in, as long as it gets you to your destination," she pointed out. "I even like Humvees."

His eyebrows arched. "And where do you get to ride in those?"

She bit her tongue. "Uh…"

"I forgot. Your brother was in the military, you said," he interrupted. "Sorry. I didn't mean to bring back sad memories for you."

She drew in a long breath. "He died doing what he felt was important for his country," she replied. "He was very patriotic and spec ops was his life."

His eyebrows arched.

"He died in a classified operation," she added. "His commanding officer just went on a huge bender. He feels responsible. He ordered the incursion."

His eyes softened. "That's the sort of man I wouldn't mind serving under," he said quietly. "A man with a conscience, who cares about his men."

She smiled. "My dad's like that, too. I mean, he's a man with a conscience," she said quickly.

He didn't notice the slip. He reached out and touched her soft cheek. "I'm sorry for your loss," he said. "I don't have siblings. But I wish I did."

She managed a smile. "Larry was a wonderful brother and a terrific husband. His wife is taking it hard. They didn't have any kids."

"Tough."

She nodded. "It's going to be hard to get through Christmas," she said. "Larry was a nut about it. He came home to Lindy every year and he brought all sorts of foreign decorations with him. We've got plenty that he sent us…"

He moved closer. His big hands framed her face and lifted it. Her pale green eyes were swimming in tears. He bent, helpless, and softly kissed away the tears.

"Life is often painful," he whispered. "But there are compensations."

While he spoke, his chiseled lips were moving against her eyelids, her nose, her cheeks. Finally, as she held her breath in wild anticipation, his lips hovered just over her perfect bow of a mouth. She could feel his breath, taste its minty freshness, see the hard curve of his lips that filled her vision to the exclusion of anything else.

She hung there, at his mouth, her eyes half-closed, her skin tingling from the warm strength of his hands framing her face, waiting, waiting, waiting…!

He drew in an unsteady breath and bent closer, logic flying out the window as the wildflower scent of her made him weak. Her mouth was perfect. He wanted to feel its softness under his lips, taste her. He was sure that she was going to be delicious…

The sudden sound of a horn blowing raucously on the street behind them shocked them apart. He blinked, as if he was under the influence of alcohol. She didn't seem much calmer. She fumbled with her purse.

"I guess we should go," he said with a forced laugh. "We want to have enough time to eat before the concert."

"Y…yes," she agreed.

"Seat belt," he added, nodding toward it.

"Oh. Yes! I usually put it on at once," she added as she fumbled it into place.

He laughed, securing his own.

Her shy smile made him feel taller. Involuntarily, his fingers linked with hers as he started the truck and pulled out into traffic. He wouldn't even let himself think about how he'd gone in headfirst with a colleague, against all his best instincts. He was too happy.

They ate at a nice restaurant in San Antonio, one with a flamenco theme and a live guitarist with a Spanish dancer in a beautiful red dress with puffy sleeves and the ruffled, long-trained dress that was familiar to followers of the dance style. The performance was short, but the applause went on for a long time. The duet was impressive.

"What a treat," she said enthusiastically. "They're so good!"

"Yes, they are." He grinned. "I love flamenco."

"So do I. I bought this old movie, *Around the World in 80 Days,* and it had a guy named Jose Greco and his flamenco dance troupe in it. That's when I fell in love with flamenco. He was so talented," she said.

"I've seen tapes of Jose Greco dancing," he replied. "He truly was phenomenal."

"My mother used to love Latin dances," she said dreamily, smiling. "She could do them all."

"Is she still alive?" he asked carefully.

She hesitated. She shook her head. "We lost her when I was in my final year of high school. Dad was overseas and couldn't even come back for the funeral, so Larry and I had to do everything. Dad never got over it. He was just starting to, when Larry died."

"Why couldn't your father come home?" he asked, curious.

She swallowed. "He was involved in a classified mission," she said. She held up a hand when he started to follow up with another question, smiling to lessen the sting. "Sorry, but he couldn't even tell me what he was doing. National security stuff."

His eyebrows arched. "Your dad's in the military?"

She hesitated. But it wouldn't hurt to agree. He was. But Rick would be thinking of a regular soldier, and her dad was far from regular. "Yes," she replied.

"I see."

"You don't, but I can't say any more," she told him.

"I guess not. Wouldn't want to tick off the brass by saying something out of turn, right?" he teased.

"Right." She had to fight a laugh. Her father was the brass; one of the highest ranking officers in the U.S. Army, in fact.

The waiter who took their order was back quickly with cups of hot coffee and the appetizers, buffalo wings and French fries with cheese and chili dip.

Rick tasted the wings and laughed as he put it quickly back down. "Hot!" he exclaimed.

"I'm glad I'm wearing black," she sighed. "If I had on a white dress, it would be red-and-white polka dotted when I finished eating. I wear most of my food."

His dark eyebrows arched and he grinned. "Me, too."

She laughed. "I'm glad it's not just me."

He tried again with the French fries. "These are really good. Here. Taste."

She let him place it at her lips. She bit off the end and sighed. "Delicious!"

"They have wonderful food, including a really special barbecue sauce for the wings. Want to know where they got it?" he asked mischievously.

"From your mother?" she guessed.

He shook his head. "It seems that FBI senior agent Jon Blackhawk came here to eat with his brother, Kilraven, one night. Jon tasted their barbecue sauce, made a face, got up, walked into the kitchen and proceeded to have words with the chef."

"You're kidding!"

"I'm not. It didn't come to blows, but only because Jon put on an apron and showed the chef how to make a proper barbecue sauce. When the chef tasted it, so the story goes, he asked which cordon bleu academy in Paris Mr. Blackhawk had attended. He got the shock of his life when Jon named it." He grinned. "You see, he actually went to Paris and took courses. His new wife is one lucky woman. She'll never have to go in the kitchen unless she really wants to."

"I heard about them," she replied. "That's one interesting family."

He munched a French fry thoughtfully. "I'd love to have kids," he said solemnly. "A big family to make up for what I never had." His expression was bitter. "Barbara is the best mother on the planet, but I wish I'd had brothers and sisters."

"You do at least still have a father living," she pointed out.

"A father who's going to get the shock of his life when he's introduced to his grown-up son," he said. "And I wonder if Ramirez has had any luck getting his sister-in-law to approach the general."

As if in answer to the question, his cell phone began vibrating. He checked the number, gave her a stunned glance and got to his feet. "I'll be right back. I have to take this."

She nodded. She liked his consideration for the other diners. He took the call outside on the street, so that he wouldn't disturb other people with his conversation.

He was back in less than five minutes. He sat back down. "Imagine that," he said on a hollow laugh. "Gracie talked to the general. He wants us to come to the border Monday morning for a little chat, as he put it."

Her eyebrows arched. "Progress," she said, approving.

He sighed. "Yes. Progress." He didn't add that he had misgivings and he was nervous as hell. He just finished eating.

Chapter 7

Rick was preoccupied through the rest of the meal. Gwen didn't talk much, either. She knew he had to be unsettled about the trip to the border, for a lot of reasons.

He held her hand on the way to the car, his strong fingers tangling in hers.

"It will be all right," she blurted out.

They reached the passenger door and he paused, looking down at her. "Will it?"

"You're a good man," she said. "He'll be very proud of you."

He was uncertain. "You think?"

She loved the smell of his body, the warm strength of it near her. She loved everything about him. "Yes."

He smiled tenderly. She made him feel tall, powerful, important. Women had made him feel undervalued for years, mostly by thinking of him as nothing more than a friend. Gwen was different. She was a working girl, from his own middle-class strata. She was pretty, in her way, and smart. And she knew her way around a handgun, he thought amusedly. But she also stirred his senses in a new and exciting way.

"You're nice," he said suddenly.

She grimaced. "Rub it in."

"No. Nice, in a very positive way," he replied. His expression was somber. "I don't like sophisticated women. I like brains in a woman, and even athletic outlooks. But I do mind women who think of themselves as party favors. You get me?"

She smiled. "I feel the same way about men like that."

He smiled. "You and I, we don't belong in a modern setting."

"We'd look very nice in a Victorian village," she agreed. "Like Edward in the *Twilight* vampire series of books and movies. I love those. I guess I've seen the movies ten times each and read the books on my iPod every night."

"I don't watch vampire movies. I like werewolves."

"Oh, but there are werewolves in them, too. Nice werewolves."

"You're kidding."

She hesitated. "I've got all the DVDs. I was wondering…"

He moved a step closer, so that she was backed into the car door. "You were wondering?"

"Uh, yes, if you'd like to maybe watch the movies with me?" she asked him. "I could make a pizza. Or we could…order…one…?"

She was whispering now, and her voice was breaking because his mouth had moved closer with every whispered word until it was right against her soft lips.

"Gwen?"

"Hmm?"

"Shut up," he whispered against her lips, and his crushed down on them with warm, sensual, insistent hunger.

A muffled sob broke from her throat as she lifted her arms and pressed her body as close as she could get it to his tall, powerful form. He groaned, too, as the insane delight pulsed through him like fire.

He moved, shifting her, so that one long leg was between her skirt, and his mouth was suddenly invasive, starving.

"Detective!"

He heard a voice. It sounded close. And shocked. And angry. He lifted his head, still reeling from Gwen's soft mouth.

"Hmm?" he murmured, turning his head.

"Detective Sergeant Marquez," a deep, angry voice repeated.

"Sir!" He jumped back, almost saluted, and tried to look normal. He hoped his jacket was covering a blatant reminder of his body's interest in Gwen's.

"What the hell are you doing?" Lieutenant Hollister asked gruffly.

"It's okay, sir," Gwen faltered. "He was, uh, helping me get my earring unstuck from my dress."

He blinked and scowled. "What?"

"My earring, sir." She dangled it in her hand. "It caught on my dress. Detective Marquez was helping me get it loose. I guess it did look odd, the position we were in." She laughed with remarkable acting ability.

"Oh. I see." Hollister cleared his throat. He shoved his hands in his pockets. "I'm very sorry. It looked, well, I mean…" He cleared his throat again. He scowled. "I thought you didn't date colleagues," he shot at Marquez, who had by reciting multiplication tables made a remarkably quick recovery.

"I don't, sir," Marquez agreed. "We both like flamenco, and there's a dancer here…"

Hollister held up his hand and declared, "Say no more. That's why I came. Alone, sadly," he added with a speculative and rather sad look at Gwen.

"She's a great dancer," Gwen said. "And that guitarist!"

He nodded. "Her husband."

"Really!" Gwen exclaimed.

"Oh, yes. They've appeared all over Europe. I understand they're being considered for a bit part in a movie that's filming near here next year."

"That would be so lovely for them," Gwen enthused.

Rick checked his watch. "We'd better go. I've got an appointment early Monday morning. I thought I'd brush up on my Spanish over the weekend," he added dryly.

"Yes, I heard about that," Hollister said quietly. "It will go all right," he told Rick. "You'll see."

Rick was touched. "Thanks."

Hollister shrugged. "You're a credit to my department. Don't let him talk you into going to South America, okay?"

Rick smiled. "I'm not much good with rocket launchers."

"Me, neither," the lieutenant agreed. He glanced at

Gwen and smiled. "Well, sorry about the mistake. Have a good evening."

"You, too, sir," Gwen said, and Rick nodded assent.

Hollister nodded back and walked, distracted, toward the restaurant.

Rick helped Gwen into the truck and burst out laughing. So did she.

"Did I ever tell you that I minored in theater in college?" she asked. "They said I had promise."

"You could make movies," he said flatly. He shook his head as he started the truck. "Quick thinking."

"Thanks." She flushed a little.

Neither of them mentioned that they'd been so far gone that anything could have happened, right there in the parking lot, if the lieutenant hadn't shown up. But it was true. Also true was the look the lieutenant had been giving them. He seemed to have more than the usual interest in Gwen. He wasn't really the sort of man to put a rose on a woman's desk unless he meant it. Rick was thinking that he had some major competition there, if he didn't watch his step. Hollister's tone hadn't been one of outraged decorum so much as jealous anger.

Rick left Gwen at her door. He was more cautious this time, but he did pull her close and kiss her goodnight with barely restrained passion.

She held him, kissing him back, loving the warm, soft press of his mouth on hers.

"I'm out of practice," he murmured as he stepped back.

"Me, too," she said breathlessly, her eyes full of stars as they met his in the light from the security lamps.

"I guess we could practice with each other," he murmured dryly.

She flushed and laughed nervously. "I'd like that."

"Yes. So would I." He bent again, brushing his mouth lightly over hers and forcing himself not to go in headfirst. "Are you coming along, in the morning?"

She nodded. "I have to."

He smiled. "Good. I could use the moral support."

She smiled back. "Thanks."

"Well. I'll see you at the office Monday."

"Yes."

He turned and took a step. He stopped. He turned. She was still standing there, her expression confused, waiting, still...

He walked back to her. "Unlock the door," he said quietly.

She fumbled the key into the lock and opened it. He closed it behind him, his arms enveloping her in the dark hallway, illuminated by a single small lamp in the living room. His mouth searched for hers, found it, claimed it, possessed it hungrily.

His arms were insistent, locking her against the length of his powerful body. She moaned, a sound almost like a sob of pleasure.

He was feeling something very similar.

"What the hell," he whispered into her lips as he bent and lifted her, still kissing her, and carried her to the long, soft sofa.

They slid down onto it together, his body covering hers, one long leg insinuating itself between her skirt, between her soft thighs. His lean hands went to the back of the dress, finding the hook and the zipper.

She didn't even have the presence of mind to protest.

She was drowning in pleasure. She'd never felt anything remotely similar to the sensations that were washing over her like ripples of unbelievable delight.

He slid the dress off her arms, along with the tiny straps of the black slip she wore under it, exposing a small, black-lace bra that revealed more than it covered. She had pretty little breasts, firm and very soft.

His hand slid under the bra, savoring the warm softness of the flesh, exciting the hard little tip, making her shiver with new sensations.

She hadn't done this before. He knew it without being told. He smiled against her mouth. It was exciting, and new, to be the first man. He never had been. Not that there had even been that many women that he'd been almost intimate with. And, in recent years, nobody. Like Gwen, he'd never indulged in casual sex. He was as innocent, in his way, as she was. Well, he knew a little more than she did. When he touched his mouth to her breast, she lifted toward his lips with a shocked little gasp. He smiled as his mouth opened, taking the hard tip inside and pulling at it gently with his tongue.

Her nails bit into the muscles of his arms as he removed his jacket and tie and shirt, wanting so badly to be closer, closer…

She felt air on her skin and then the hard, warm press of hair and muscle as they locked together, both bare from the waist up.

His mouth was insistent now, hungry, demanding. She felt his hand sliding up her bare thigh and she knew that very soon they would reach a point from which there was no return.

"N…no," she whispered, pushing at his chest. "Rick? Rick!"

He heard her voice through a bloodred haze of desire that locked his muscles so tightly that he could barely move for the tension. She was saying something. What? It sounded like...no?

He lifted his head. He looked into wide, uneasy green eyes. He felt her body tensed, shivering.

"I'm sorry..." she began.

He blinked once, twice. He drew in a breath that sounded as ragged as he felt. "Good Lord," he exhaled.

She swallowed. They were very intimate. Neither of them had anything on above the waist. His hand was still on her thigh. He removed it quickly and lifted up just a little, his high cheekbones flushing when he got a sudden, stark, uninterrupted view of her pretty pink breasts with tight little dusky pink tips very urgently stating the desire of the owner for much more than looking.

Embarrassed, she drew her hands up over them as he levered himself away and sat up.

"I'm sorry," he said, averting his eyes while she fumbled her dress back on. "I didn't mean to..."

"Of c-course not," she stammered. "Neither did I. It's all right."

He laughed. His body felt as if it had been hit with a bat several times in strategic places and he ached from head to toe. "Sure it is."

"Oh, I'm sorry!" she groaned. She wasn't experienced, but she had friends who were, and she knew what was wrong with him. "Here, just a sec."

She went to the kitchen and came back with a cold beer from the fridge. "Detective Rogers comes over from time to time and she likes this brand of light beer," she explained. "I don't drink, but I think people need to sometimes. You need to, a little…?"

He gave her an exasperated sigh. "Gwen, I'm a police detective sergeant!"

"Yes, I know…"

"I can't take a drink and drive!"

She stared at him, looked at the beer. "Oh."

He burst out laughing. It broke the ice and slowly he began to feel normal again.

She looked around them. His jacket and shirt and tie, and her shoes and his holster and pistol were lying in a heap beside the sofa.

His gaze followed hers. He laughed again. "Well."

"Yes. Uh. Well." She looked at the can of beer, laughed, and set it down. Her glasses were where she'd tossed them on the end table but she didn't put them on. She didn't want to see his expression. She was already embarrassed.

He put his shirt and tie back on and slipped into his jacket before he replaced the holstered pistol on his belt. "At least you don't object to the gun," he mused.

She shrugged. "I usually have a concealed carry in my purse," she confessed.

His eyebrows arched. "No ankle holster?" he asked.

She made a face. "Weighs down my leg too much."

He nodded. He looked at her in a different way now. Possessively. Hungrily. He moved forward, but he only took her oval face in his hands and searched her eyes, very close up. He was somber.

"From now on," he said gently, "we say good-night at the door. Right?"

He was hinting at a relationship. "From now on?" she said hesitantly.

He nodded. He searched her eyes. "There aren't that many women running around loose who belong to the Victorian era, don't mind firearms and like to watch flamenco dancing."

She smiled with pure delight. "I was going to say the same about you—well, you're not a woman, of course."

"Of course."

He bent and kissed her very softly. He lifted his head and his large brown eyes narrowed. "If Hollister puts another rose on your desk, I'm going to deck him, and I don't care if he fires me."

Her face became radiant. "Really?"

"Really." His jaw tautened. "You're mine."

She flushed. She lowered her eyes to his strong neck, where a pulse beat very strongly. She nodded.

He hugged her close, rocked her in his arms. He drew in a long breath, finally, and let her go. He smiled ruefully. "After we get through talking with the general, Monday, I'm going to take you to meet my mother."

"You are?"

"You'll love her. She'll love you, too," he promised. He glanced at his watch and grimaced. "I have to get going. I'll pick you up here at 6:00 a.m. sharp, okay?"

"I could drive to the office…"

"I'll pick you up here."

She smiled. Her eyes were bright with pleasure. "Okay."

He chuckled. "Lock the door after me."

"I will. I really enjoyed the flamenco."

"So did I. I know another Latin dance club over on the west side of town. We'll go there next time. Do you like Mexican food?"

"Love it."

He smiled. "Theirs is pretty hot."

"No worries, I don't have any taste buds left. I eat jalapenos raw," she added with a grin.

"Whew! My kind of girl."

She grinned. "I noticed."

He laughed, kissed her hair and walked out the door. After he climbed back into the pickup truck, he paused and waited until she was safely in her apartment before he drove off.

She didn't sleep that night. Not a wink. She was too excited, exhilarated and hungrily, passionately really in love for the first time in her life.

Rick was somber and nervous Monday morning when he picked Gwen up for the drive to the border. It had turned cold again and she was wearing a sweater and thick jeans with a jacket and boots.

"Summer yesterday, winter today," she remarked, readjusting her seat belt.

"That's Texas," he said fondly.

"Is Ramirez going to meet us at the border station?"

"Yes," he said. "He and Gracie."

Her eyebrows arched. "Mrs. Pendleton is coming, too? Isn't that dangerous?"

"We're not going over the border," he reminded her. "Just up to it."

"Oh. Okay."

He glanced at her, warm memories of the night before still in his dark eyes. She was lovely, he thought. Pretty and smart and good with a gun.

She felt his eyes but she didn't meet them. She was nervous, too. She worried about how he might feel when he learned the truth about her own background. She was still keeping secrets. She hoped he wouldn't feel differently when he learned them.

But right now, the biggest secret of all was about to be revealed to a man who had no apparent family and seemed to be content with his situation. Gwen wondered how the general would feel when he was introduced to a son he didn't even know existed.

They pulled up to the small border station, which wasn't much more than an adobe building beside the road, next to a cross arm that was denoted as the Mexican-American border, with appropriate warning signs.

A tall, sandy-haired man came out to meet them. He introduced himself as the border patrol agent in charge, Don Billings, and indicated a Lincoln Town Car sitting just a little distance way. He motioned.

The car pulled up, stopped and Rodrigo Ramirez got out, going around to open the door for his sister-in-law, Gracie Pendleton. They came forward and introductions were made.

Gracie was blonde and pretty and very pregnant. She laughed. "The general is going to be surprised when he sees me," she said with a grin. "I didn't mention my interesting condition. Jason and I are just over the moon!"

"Is it a boy or a girl?" Gwen wanted to know.

"We didn't let them tell us," she said. "We want it to be a surprise, so I bought everything yellow instead of pink or blue."

Gwen laughed. "I'd like it to be a surprise, too, if I ever had a baby." Her eyes were dreamy. "I'd love to have a big family."

Rick was watching her and his heart was pounding. He'd like a big family, too. Her family. He cleared his throat. Memories of last night were causing him some difficulty in intimate places. He thought of sports until he calmed down a little.

"He should be here very soon," Ramirez said.

Even as he spoke, a pickup truck came along the dusty road from across the border, stopped and was waved through by the border agent.

The truck stopped. Two doors opened. Winslow Grange, wearing one of the very new high-tech camouflage patterned suits with an automatic pistol strapped to his hip, came forward. Right beside him was a tall, elegant-looking Hispanic man with thick, wavy black hair and large black eyes in a square face with chiseled lips and a big grin for Gracie.

"A baby?" he enthused. "How wonderful!"

She laughed, taking his outstretched hands. "Jason and I think so, too. How have you been?"

"Very busy," he said, indicating Grange. "We're planning a surprise party." He wiggled his eyebrows at the border agent. "I'm sorry that I can't say more."

"So am I." The border patrolman chuckled.

Gwen came forward, her eyes curious and welcoming at the same time. "You and I haven't met, but I think you've heard of me," she said gently. She held out her hand. "I'm Gwendolyn Cassaway. CIA."

He shook her hand warmly, and then raised it to his lips. He glanced at the man with her, a tall young man with long black hair in a ponytail and an oddly familiar face. "Your boyfriend?" he asked, lifting an eyebrow at the reaction the young man gave when he kissed Gwen's hand.

"Uh, well, uh, I mean..." She cleared her throat. "This is Detective Sergeant Ricardo Marquez, San Antonio Police Department."

General Emilio Machado looked at the younger man with narrowed, intent eyes. "Marquez."

"Yes."

Machado was curious. "You look familiar, somehow. Do I know you?"

He studied the general quietly. "No. But my birth mother was Dolores Ortíz. She was from Sonora. I look like her."

Machado stared at him intently. "She lived in Sonora, in a little village called Dolito. I knew her once," he said. "She married a man named Jackson," he added coldly.

"My stepfather," Rick said curtly.

"I have heard about your late stepfather. He was a brutal man."

Rick liked Machado already. "Yes. I have the scars to prove it," he added quietly.

Machado drew in a long breath. He looked around him. "This is a very unusual place to meet with federal agents, and I feel that I am being set up."

"Not at all," Gwen replied. "But we do have something to tell you. Something that might be upsetting."

Nobody spoke. There were somber, grim faces all around.

"You brought a firing squad?" Machado mused, looking from one to the other. "Or you lured me here to arrest me for kidnapping Gracie?"

"None of the above," Gwen said quietly. She took a deep breath. This was a very unpleasant chore she'd been given. "We were doing a routine background check on you for our files and we came across your relationship with Dolores Ortíz. She gave birth to a child out of wedlock down in Sonora. Thirty-one years ago."

Machado was doing quick math in his head. He looked at Rick pointedly, with slowly growing comprehension. The man had looked familiar. Was it possible…? He moved a step closer and cocked his head as he studied the somber-faced young man.

Then he laughed coldly. "Ah. Now I see. You know that I have spies in my country who are even now planting the seeds of revolution. You know that I have an army and that I am almost certain to retake the government of Barrera. So you are searching for ways to ingratiate yourself with me…excuse me, with my oil and natural gas reserves as well as my very strategic location in South America." He gave Rick a hard glance. "You produce a candidate for my son, and think that I will accept your word that he is who he says he is."

"I haven't said a damned thing," Rick snapped back icily.

Machado's eyebrows shot up. "You deny their conclusion?"

Rick glared at him. "You think I'm thrilled to be lined up as the illegitimate son of some exiled South American dictator?"

Machado just stared at him for a minute. Then he burst out laughing.

"Rick," Gwen groaned from beside him.

"I was perfectly content to think my real father was in a grave somewhere in Mexico," Rick continued. "And then she showed up with this story…" He pointed at Gwen.

She raised her hand. "Cash Grier told your mother," she reminded him quickly. "I had nothing to do with telling you."

"All right, my mother told me," he continued.

"Your mother is dead," Machado said, frowning.

"Barbara Ferguson, in Jacobsville, adopted me when my mother and stepfather were killed in an auto accident," Rick continued. "She runs the café there."

Machado didn't speak. He'd never considered the possibility that Dolores would become pregnant. They'd been very close until her parents discovered them one night in an outbuilding and her father threatened to kill Machado if he ever saw him again. He'd gone to work for a big landowner soon afterward and moved to another village. He hadn't seen Dolores again.

Could she have been pregnant? They'd done nothing to prevent a child. But he'd only been fourteen. He couldn't have fathered a son at that age, surely? In fact, he'd never fathered another child in the years since, and he had been coaxed into trying, at least once. The attempt had ended in total failure. It had hurt his pride, hurt his ego, made him uncertain about his manhood. He had thought, since then, that he must be sterile.

But here was, if he could believe the statement, proof of his virility. Could this really be his son?

He moved forward a step. Yes, the man had his eyes. He had Dolores's perfect teeth, as well. He was tall and powerfully built, as Machado was. His hair was long and black and straight, without the natural waves that were in Machado's. But, then, Dolores had long black hair that was smooth as silk and thick and straight.

"You think I would take your word for something this important, even with Gracie's help?" he asked Rick.

"Hey, I didn't come here to convince you of anything," Rick said defensively. "She—" he indicated Gwen "—got him—" he nodded at Ramirez "—to call her—" he pointed toward Gracie "—to have you meet us here. I got pulled into it because some feds think you'll listen to me even if you won't listen to them." He shrugged. "Of course, they haven't decided what to have me tell you just yet. I presume that's in the works and they'll let me know when they can agree on what day it is."

Machado listened to him, pursed his lips and laughed. "Sounds exactly like government policy to me. And I should know. I was head of a government once." His eyes narrowed and glittered. "And I will be, once again."

"I believe you," Gwen agreed.

"But for now," Machado continued, studying Rick. "What evidence exists that you really are my son? And it had better be good."

Chapter 8

"Don't look at me," Rick said quietly. "I didn't come here to prove anything."

Gwen moved forward, removing a paper from her purse. "We were sure that you wouldn't accept anyone's word, General," she said gently. "So we took the liberty of having a DNA profile made from Sergeant Marquez's last physical when blood was drawn." She gave Rick an apologetic glance. "Sorry."

Rick sighed. "Accepted."

The general read the papers, frowned, read some more and finally handed them back. "That's pretty convincing."

Gwen nodded.

He glanced at Rick, who was standing apart from the others, hard-faced, with his hands deep in the pockets of his slacks.

The general studied him from under thick black eye-
lashes, with some consternation. His whole life had just
been turned upside-down. He had a son. The man was
a law enforcement officer. He was not bad-looking,
seemed intelligent, too. Of course, there was that se-
vere attitude problem…

"I don't like baseball," Rick said curtly when he noticed how the general was eyeing him.

Machado's thick eyebrows levered up. "You don't
like baseball…?"

"In case you were thinking of father-son activities,"
Rick remarked drolly. "I don't like baseball. I like soccer."

Machado's dark eyes twinkled. "So do I."

"See?" Gwen said, grasping at straws, because this
was becoming awkward. "Already, something in common…"

"Get down!"

While she was trying to understand the quick command from the general, Rick responded by tackling
her. Rodrigo had Gracie in the limo, which had bulletproof glass, and Machado hit the ground with his pistol drawn at the same time Grange opened up with an
army-issue repeating rifle.

"What the hell…!" Rick exclaimed as he leveled his
own automatic, along with Gwen, at an unseen adver-
sary, tracking his direction from the bullets hitting the
dust a few yards away.

"Carver, IED, now!" Grange called into a walkie-
talkie.

Seconds later, there was a huge explosion, a muffled
cry, and a minute later, the sound of an engine starting

and roaring, a dust cloud becoming visible as a person or persons unknown took off in the distance.

Grange grinned. "I always have a backup plan," he remarked.

"Good thing," Gwen exclaimed. "I didn't even consider an ambush!"

"Your father would have," Grange began.

She held up her hand and gave a curt shake of her head.

"You know her father?" Rick asked curiously.

"We were poker buddies, a few years back," Grange said. "Good man."

"Thanks," Gwen said, and she wasn't referring totally to the compliment. Grange would keep her secret; she saw it in his eyes.

Rick was brushing thick dust off his jacket and slacks. "Damn. They just came back from the dry cleaner."

"You should wear cotton. It cleans better," Machado suggested, indicating his own jeans and cotton shirt.

"Who was that, do you think?" Gwen asked somberly.

"Fuentes." Machado spat. "He and I have parted company. He amuses himself by sniping at me and my men."

"The drug lord? I thought his family was dead!" Gwen exclaimed.

"Most of it is. This is the last one of the Fuentes brothers, the stupid one, and he's clinging to power by his fingernails," the general told her. "He spies on me for a federal agency. Not yours," he told Gwen with a smile.

Ramirez left Gracie in the car and came back. "I don't think she should risk coming out here in the open," he said.

"I agree. She is all right?" Machado asked with some concern.

"Yes. Gracie really has guts," he replied. He frowned. "Which agency is Fuentes spying for?"

"Yours, I think, my friend," Machado told the DEA agent.

Ramirez let out a sigh. "We know there's a mole in our agency, someone very high level. We've never found out who it is."

"You should set Kilraven on him," Gwen mused dryly.

"I probably should," Ramirez agreed. "But we have our hands full right now with Mexican military coming over the border to protect drug shipments." He glanced toward the border patrol agent, who was talking to Gracie through a cracked window. "Our men on the border are in peril, always. We almost lost one some months ago, an agent named Kirk. He was very nearly killed. He left the agency and went back to his brothers on their Wyoming ranch. A great loss. He was good at his job, and he had contacts that we now lack."

"I can get you all the contacts you need," Machado promised. He glanced toward the distant hill where the sniper had been emplaced. "First I must deal with Fuentes."

"I didn't hear you say that," Gwen said firmly.

"Nor I," Ramirez echoed.

"Well, I did," Rick replied coldly. "And you're still wanted on kidnapping charges in my country, even though Mrs. Pendleton refuses to press them."

Machado's large eyes widened. "You would turn your own father in to the authorities?"

Rick's eyes narrowed. "The law is the law."

"You keep a book of statutes on your person?" the general asked.

Rick glared at him. "I've been a cop for a long time."

"Amazing. I have spent my life breaking most of the laws that exist, and here I find a son, a stranger, who goes by the book." His eyes narrowed. "I think perhaps they rigged the DNA evidence." He gave the detective a disparaging look. "I would never wear a suit like that, or grow my hair long. You look like a—what is the expression?—a hippie!"

Rick glared at him.

The general glared back.

"Uh, the sniper?" Ramirez reminded them. "He may have gone for reinforcements."

"True." Machado turned to Grange. "Perhaps you should order a sweep on the surrounding hills."

Grange smiled. "I already have."

"Good man. We will soon have a proper government in my country and you will be the commander of the forces in my country."

Ramirez choked. Gwen colored. Rick looked at them, trying to figure out why the hell they were so disturbed.

"We should go," Ramirez said, indicating the car. "I promised her husband that I would have her home very quickly. He might send a search party for us. Not a man to make an enemy of."

"Absolutely," Grange agreed.

"Thank you for making this meeting possible," Machado said, extending his hand to Ramirez.

Ramirez shook it, and then grinned. "It wasn't my idea. I'm related to the president of Mexico. He thought it would be a good idea."

Machado was impressed. "When I retake my country, perhaps you can speak to him for me about a trade agreement."

Ramirez admired the confidence in the other man's voice. "Yes, perhaps I can. Keep well."

"And you."

Gwen and Marquez waved them off before turning back to Machado.

"We should be going, too," Marquez said stiffly. "I have to get back to work."

Machado nodded. He studied his son with curious, strange eyes. "Perhaps, later, we can meet again."

"Perhaps," Rick replied.

"In a place where we do not have to fear an attack from my enemies," Machado said, shaking his head.

"I don't think we can get to Mars yet," Rick quipped.

Machado laughed. "Grange, we should go."

"Yes, sir."

Machado took Gwen's hand and kissed the back of it tenderly. "It has been a pleasure to meet you, *señorita,*" he said with pure velvet in his deep voice.

Rick stepped in, took Gwen's hand and pulled her back. He glared at Machado, which made Gwen almost giddy with delight.

Machado's dark eyes twinkled. "So it is like that, huh?"

"Like what?" Rick asked innocently. He dropped Gwen's hand and looked uncomfortable.

"Never mind. I will be in touch."

"Thank you for coming," Gwen told the general.

"It was truly a pleasure." He winked at her, gave Rick a droll look and climbed back into the truck with Grange. They disappeared over the border. Rick stood staring after the truck with mixed feelings. Then he turned, said goodbye to the border agent and walked back to his truck with Gwen.

Rick kept to himself for the next couple of days. Gwen didn't intrude. She knew that he was dealing with some emotional issues that he had to resolve in his own mind.

Meanwhile, she went on interviews with neighbors of the murdered college freshman, the case she'd been assigned to as lead detective.

"Did she have any close friends that you know of?" she asked the third neighbor, an elderly woman who seemed to have a whole roomful of cats. They were clean, brushed, well fed and there was no odor, so she must be taking excellent care of them.

"Oh, you've noticed the cats?" the woman asked her with a grin that made her seem years younger. "I'm babysitting."

Gwen blinked. "Excuse me?"

"Babysitting. I have four neighbors with cats, and we've had a problem with animals disappearing around here. So they leave their cats with me while they're at work, and I feed them. It's a nice little windfall for me, since I'm disabled, and the owners have emotional security since they don't have to worry about their furry 'families' going missing."

Gwen laughed. "Impressive."

"Thanks. I love animals. I wish I could afford to keep a cat, but I can't. This is the next best thing."

Gwen noted several pill bottles on the end table by the elderly lady's recliner.

"By the time I pay for all those out of my social security check," she told Gwen, "there's not much left over for bills and food."

Gwen winced. "That's not right."

The woman sighed. "The economy is terrible. I expect something awful will have to happen to finally set things right." She looked at Gwen over her glasses. "I don't expect to still be around then. But if aliens exist, and they want somebody to experiment on..." She raised her hand. "I'm ready to go. To some nice, green planet with lots of meadows and trees and no greedy humans destroying it all for a quick profit."

"You and I would get along," Gwen said with a smile.

The woman nodded. "Now, back to my neighbor. I do keep a watch on the apartment complex, mostly to try to protect myself. I can't fight off an intruder and I don't own a gun. So I make sure I know who belongs here and who doesn't." Her eyes narrowed. "There was a grimy young man with greasy hair who kept coming to see the college girl. She was trying to be nice, you could tell from her expression, but she never let him inside. Once, the last time he came, the police went to her apartment and stayed for several minutes."

Gwen's heart jumped. If there had been police presence, there would be a report, with details of the conversation. She jotted that down on her phone app, making virtual notes.

"That thing is neat," the elderly lady said. "One of my cat-owning friends has one. He can surf the net on it, buy groceries, books, all sorts of things. I never realized we had such things in the modern world. I suppose I live in the past."

Gwen made a mental note to make sure this nice lady

got a phone and several phone cards for Christmas, from an anonymous source. It would revolutionize her life.

"Yes, they are quite nice," Gwen said. She smiled. "Thanks for talking to me. You've been a very big help."

"It was my pleasure. I know you young folks don't have much free time, but if you're ever at a loose end, you can come and see me and I'll tell you about the FBI in the seventies."

Gwen stared at her.

"I was a federal agent," the woman told her. "One of the first women in the bureau."

"I would love to hear some stories about those days," Gwen told her. "And I'll make time."

The wrinkled face lit up. "Thank you!"

"No, thank you. I'm fond of pioneers," she replied.

She told Rick about the elderly woman.

"Yes, Evelyn Dorsey." He nodded, smiling. "She's something of a legend over at the FBI field office. Garon Grier goes to see her from time to time." He was the SAC, the special agent in charge, at the San Antonio Field Office now. "She shot it out with a gang of would-be kidnappers right over on the 410 Loop. Hit two of them before they shot her, almost fatally, and escaped. But she had a description of the car, right down to the license plate number, and she managed to get it out on the radio before she passed out. They nabbed the perps ten miles away. Back in those days, the radio was in the car, not on a belt. It was harder to be in law enforcement."

"I expect so. Ms. Dorsey was very helpful on our college freshman case, by the way. We did have a patrol unit respond to the freshman's call. I'm tracking down the officer who filed the report now."

"I hope we can catch the guy," he replied.

"The cold case unit wants him very badly. They think he's connected to the old case they're working on," she said. "One of those detectives was related to the victim in it."

"Sad."

"Yes." She moved closer to the desk. "You doing okay?"

He grimaced. "No," he said, with a faint smile.

"Why don't you come over and watch the *Twilight* movies with me tonight? We can order a pizza."

He cocked his head and the smile grew. "You know, that sounds like a very good idea."

She grinned. "Glad you think so. I like mushrooms and cheese and pepperoni."

His eyebrows lifted. "Have you been checking out my profile?"

"No. Why?"

"That's my favorite."

She beamed. "Another thing in common."

"We'll find more, I think."

"Yes."

Rick wasn't comfortable with so-called chick flicks, but he was drawn into the movie almost at once. He barely noticed when the pizza delivery girl showed up, and only lifted his hand for the plate and coffee cup without taking his eyes off the screen.

Gwen was delighted. It was her favorite film. She kicked off her shoes and curled up beside him on the sofa to watch it again, sipping coffee and munching pizza in a contented silence. It was amazing, she thought, how comfortable they were with each other, even at this early stage of their relationship.

He glanced at her while the vampire was showing off his skills to the heroine on the screen. "You're right. This is very good."

"So are the books. I love all of them."

"I guess I'll have to buy them. It isn't often you find so many likable people in a story chain."

She sipped coffee. "You know, I hadn't thought of it that way, but you're right. Even the vampires are likable."

"Odd, isn't it? Likable monsters."

"But they aren't really monsters. They're just misunderstood living-challenged people."

He burst out laughing.

"More pizza?" she asked.

"I think I could hold one more slice."

"Me, too." She jumped up and went to get it.

After they finished eating, she curled up against him through the heroine's introduction to her boyfriend's family, the baseball game in the rain, the arrival of the more dangerous vampires, the heroine's brush with death and, finally, her appearance at the prom in a cast with her boyfriend.

"That was a roller coaster ride," he remarked. "Are there more?"

"Two more. Want to watch the next one?"

He turned toward her, his dark eyes on her radiant face. He pursed his lips. "Yes, I would. But not right now." He pulled her across his lap. "I'm suffering from affection deprivation. Do you think you could assist me?"

"Could I!" she whispered as his mouth came down on hers.

Each kiss became harder, more urgent. As they grew

accustomed to the feel and taste of each other, the pleasure grew and it became more difficult to pull back.

He actually groaned when he found himself lying over her with half their clothes out of the way, just like before. He buried his face in her warm, frantically pulsing throat.

"I'm dying," he ground out.

"Me, too," she whispered back, shivering.

He lifted his head. His eyes were tormented. "How do you feel about marriage?"

She blinked.

He realized that he, the most non-impulsive man on earth, was doing something totally out of character. But he was already crazy about Gwen and the lieutenant was lurking. Even Machado had been giving her long looks. He didn't want her to end up with some other man while he was waiting for the right moment to do something. And besides, he was traditional, so was she, and there was this incredible, almost unbelievable physical compatibility.

He sighed. "Look, we get along very well. We're incredibly suited physically. We have similar jobs, outlooks on life, philosophies, and we're on the same social level. Why don't we drive over the border and get married? Right now. Afterward," he added with a speaking glance, "we can do what we're both dying to do without lingering feelings of guilt."

Her lips parted. She should have challenged that social level comparison immediately, but her body was on fire and all she could think of was relief. She loved him. He was at least fond of her. They both wanted kids. It would work. She would make it work.

"Yes," she blurted out.

He forced himself to get up and he pulled out his cell phone, scrolled down a list of names and punched in a button. "Yes. Ramirez? Sorry to call so late. Can you get me a direct line to the general? I need his help on a—" he glanced at Gwen "—personal matter."

Ramirez sighed. "All right. But you owe me one."

"Yes, I do."

There was a pause, another pause. Rick motioned Gwen for a pencil and paper. He wrote down a number. "Thanks!" he told Ramirez, and hung up. He dialed the number.

"Yes, it's your—" he hesitated "—your son. How do you feel about giving away the bride at a Mexican wedding? Oh, in about thirty minutes."

There was a burst of Spanish from the other end of the line. Rick replied in the same language, protesting that he wasn't up to anything immoral, he was trying to make sure everything was done properly and that meant a proper wedding. The general seemed to calm down. Another hesitation. Rick grinned.

"Thanks," he said, and hung up. He turned to Gwen and pursed his lips. "Do you have a white dress?"

"Do I have a white dress!" she exclaimed, and ran into the next room to put it on.

She left her hair long. The dress was close-fitting, with puffy sleeves and a draped beaded shawl. She looked young and very innocent. And most incredibly sexy.

Rick's body reacted to her visibly. He cleared his throat. "Don't notice that," he said curtly.

"Oh. Okay." She giggled as she joined him and looked up into his dark eyes. "Are you sure?" she asked hesitantly.

He framed her face in his hands and kissed her with breathless tenderness. "I don't know why, but I've never been so sure of anything. No cold feet?"

She shook her head. Her eyes were full of dreams. "Oh, no. Not at all."

He smiled. "Same here. We can share ammunition, too, so it will be cost effective to get married."

She burst out laughing. "I'll be sure to tell my father that when I explain why I didn't invite him to the ceremony."

He grimaced. "I'll have to do the same for my mother. But we don't have time to get them all together. We're eloping."

"Your father will have to be the audience," she said.

"My father." He smiled. "Let's go."

The general was waiting for them at the border. They followed him down a long dusty road to a small village and stopped in front of a mission church with a shiny new bell.

"I donated the bell," the general informed them proudly. "They are good people here, and the priest is a nice young man, from the United States." He hesitated, glancing from one to the other. "I did not think to ask which religious denomination…?"

"Catholic." They both spoke at once, stared at each other, and then burst out laughing.

"We hadn't discussed it before," Rick said.

"Well, it will be good," the general said with a big smile. "Come, the priest is waiting. You two, you're sure about this?"

Gwen looked at Rick with her heart in her eyes. "Very."

"Very, very," Rick added, his dark eyes shining.

"Then we shall proceed."

The general took Gwen down the aisle of the church on his arm. The whole village came to watch, including a number of small children who seemed to find the blonde lady's hair fascinating.

The priest smiled benevolently, read the marriage service. Then they came to the part about a ring.

Rick turned white. "Oh, no."

The general punched him. "Here. I remember everything." He handed him a small circle of gold that looked just right for Gwen's hand. "Something old. It belonged to my *abuela*," he added, "my grandmother." He smiled. "She would want it to stay in the family."

"It's beautiful," Gwen whispered. "Thank you."

The general nodded. Rick took the small circle of gold and slid it gently onto Gwen's finger, where it was a perfect fit. The priest pronounced them man and wife, and Rick bent to kiss her. And they were married.

Neither of them remembered much about the rest of the evening. Back at Gwen's apartment, there was a feverish removal of cotton and lace, followed by an incredibly long session in bed that left them both covered in sweat, boneless with pleasure and totally exhausted.

Not that exhaustion stopped them. As soon as they were breathing normally again, they reached for each other, and started all over.

"You know, it never occurred to me that marriage would be so much fun," Rick commented when they were finally sleepy.

Gwen, curled up against him, warm and satisfied, laughed softly. "Me, either. I always thought of it as something a little more dignified. You know, for children and…" She stopped.

He turned and looked down at her guilty face. "Hey. You want kids. I want kids. What's the problem?"

She relaxed. "You make it seem so simple."

"It is simple. Two people fall in love, get married and have a family." His eyes were on fire with his feelings. "We'll grow old together. But not right away. Maybe not at all," he added worriedly, "when my mother realizes that I got married without even telling her."

"My dad is going to go ballistic, too," she replied. "But he couldn't have come even if I'd had time to ask him. He's tied up with military stuff right now."

"Is he on active duty?"

"Oh, yes," she said, and there was another worry. She still had to tell Rick who her dad was, and all about the family he'd married into. That might be a source of discord. So she wasn't about to face it tonight.

She curled up close and wound her arms around him. "For a guy who never indulged, you're very good."

He laughed. "Compliment returned." He hugged her close. "They said it comes naturally. I guess it does. Of course, there were all these books I read. For educational purposes only."

She grinned. "I read a few of those, too."

He bent and brushed his mouth gently over hers. "I'm glad we waited," he said seriously, searching her eyes. "I know we're out of step with the world. But I don't care. This was right for us."

"Yes, it was. Thank you for having enough restraint," she added. "We couldn't have counted on me for it. I was on fire!"

"So was I. But I was thinking about later, generations

later, when we tell our grandchildren and great-grand-children about how it was when we fell in love and got married." He closed his eyes. "It's a golden memory. Not a legalization of something that had gone on before."

She pressed her mouth into his warm, muscular shoulder with a smile. "And the nicest thing is that you're already my best friend."

"You're mine, too." He kissed her hair. "Go to sleep. We'll get up tomorrow and face the music."

"What?"

"I was just thinking," he mused, "that the lieutenant is going to foam at the mouth when we tell him."

"What?" she exclaimed.

"Just a hunch." He thought the lieutenant had a case on Gwen. Maybe, maybe not. But he was expecting fireworks the next day.

Chapter 9

"Fireworks" was, if anything, an understatement.

"You're married?" Lieutenant Hollister exclaimed.

Gwen moved a little closer to Rick. "Yes. Sorry, we would have invited you, but we didn't want the expense of a big wedding, so we eloped," she told him, stretching the truth.

"Eloped." Hollister leaned back in his chair with a grumpy sigh. He glared at Marquez. "Well, it was certainly quick."

"We knew how we felt at once," Rick replied with a smile at his wife. "No sense having a long engagement."

She smiled back. "Absolutely."

"Well, congratulations," Hollister said after a minute. He got up, smiled and shook hands with both of them. "How did your mother take it?" he asked Rick.

Rick grimaced. "Haven't told her."

"Why don't you two take the day off and call it a honeymoon," Hollister suggested. "Gail Rogers can sub for you," he told Rick. "I don't want Barbara coming after me with a bazooka because she heard the news from somebody else."

"Good idea," Rick said. "Thanks!"

"My pleasure. A wedding present. A short one," he added. "You have to be back on the job tomorrow. And when are we losing you?" he asked Gwen.

She wasn't sure what he meant, and then she realized that she belonged to a federal agency. "I'm not sure. I'll have to talk to my boss and he'll have to discuss it with the captain here."

Hollister nodded. "You've done very well. I'll be sorry to lose you."

She smiled. "I'll be sorry to go. I may have to make some minor adjustments in my career path, as well," she added with a worried glance at Rick. "I don't really want to keep a job that sends me around the world every other week. Not now."

Hollister pursed his lips. "We can always use another detective," he pointed out. "You'd pick it back up in no time, and we have all sorts of workshops and training courses."

She beamed. "You mean it?"

"Of course," he assured her.

"Wait a minute, you'd give up working for the feds, for me?" Rick asked, as if he couldn't quite believe it.

"I would," she said solemnly. "I'm tired of living out of a suitcase. And I really like San Antonio." She didn't add that she was also very tired of the D.C. social scene and being required to hostess parties for her dad. It was never enjoyable. She didn't like crowds or parties. To give him his due, neither did her father. But he was certainly going to be in the center of the Washington social whirl very soon. She dreaded having to tell Rick about it.

"Well," Rick said, and couldn't resist a charming smile.

She laughed. "And now for the really hard part. We have to break the news to your mother."

"She'll kill me," he groaned.

"No. We'll take her a pot of flowers," Gwen said firmly. "She's a gardener. I know she wouldn't mind a bribe that she could plant."

They all laughed.

And actually, Barbara wasn't mad. She burst into tears, hugged them both and rambled on for several minutes about how depressed she'd been that women never seemed to see Rick as a potential mate as much as a shoulder to cry on.

"I'm just so happy!"

"I'm so glad," Gwen enthused. "But we still brought you a bribe."

"A bribe?" Barbara asked, wiping away tears.

Gwen went onto the porch and came back inside carrying a huge potted plant.

"It's an umbrella plant!" Barbara exclaimed. "I've wanted one for years, but I could never find one the right size. It's perfect!"

"I thought you could plant it," Gwen said.

"Oh, no, I'll let it live inside. I'll put grow lights around it and fertilize it and..." She hesitated. "You two didn't have to get married?"

They howled.

"She's as Victorian as we are," Rick told his mother with a warm smile.

"That's wonderful! Welcome to the stone age, my dear!" she told Gwen and hugged her, hard.

"Where are you going to live? In San Antonio?" Barbara asked, resigned.

Gwen and Rick had discussed this. "The old Andrews place is up for sale, right in downtown Jacobsville," Rick said, "next door to the Griers. In fact, I put in an offer for it this morning."

"Oh!" Barbara started crying again. "I thought you'd want to live where your jobs are."

Explanation about Gwen's job could come later, Rick decided. "We want to live near you," Rick replied.

"Because when the kids come along," Gwen added with a grin, "you'll want to be able to see them."

Barbara felt her forehead. "Maybe I'm feverish. You want to have kids?"

"Oh, yes," Gwen replied, smiling.

"Lots of kids," Rick added.

"I can buy a toy store," Barbara murmured to herself. "But first I need to stock up on organic seeds, so that I can make healthy stuff for the baby."

"We just got married yesterday," Rick pointed out.

"That's right, and this is November." She went looking for a calendar. "And nine months from now is harvest season!" she called back.

Rick and Gwen shook their heads.

They stayed for supper, a delicious affair, and then settled down to watch the news. Gwen, sitting contentedly beside her husband, had no warning of what was about to happen.

A newscaster smiled as a picture of a four-star general, very well-known to the public, was splashed across the screen. "And this just in. Amid rumors that he was retiring or resigning from the service, we have just learned that General David Cassaway, former U.S. Commander in Iraq, has been named director of the Central Intelligence Agency. General Cassaway, a former covert ops commander, has commanded American troops in Iraq for the past two years. He was rumored to be retiring from the military, but it seems that he was only considering a new job."

Barbara glanced at Gwen. "Why, what a coincidence. That's your last name."

The newscaster was adding, "General Cassaway's only son, Larry, died in a classified operation in the Middle East just a few months ago. We wish General Cassaway the best of luck in his new position. Now for other news…"

Rick was staring at Gwen as if she'd grown horns. "Your brother's name was Larry, wasn't it?" he asked. "The one who was killed in action?"

Barbara was staring. So was Rick.

Gwen took a deep breath. "He's my father," she confessed.

Rick wasn't handling this well. "Your father is the new head of the CIA?"

"Well, sort of," she said, nodding worriedly.

Rick knew about Washington society from people in his department who had to deal with the socialites in D.C. He was certain that there were no poor generals in the military, and the head of the CIA would certainly not be in line for food stamps.

"What sort of place do you live in, when you go home?" Rick asked very quietly.

Gwen sighed. "We have a big house in Maryland, on several acres of land. My dad likes horses. He raises, well, thoroughbreds." She was almost cringing by now.

"And drives a…?"

She swallowed. "Jaguar."

Rick got up and turned away with an exasperated sigh. "Why didn't you tell me?"

"Because I was afraid you'd do just what you're doing now," Gwen moaned. "Judging me by the company I keep. I hate parties. I hate receptions. I hate hostessing! I'm perfectly happy working a federal job, or a police job, any sort of job that doesn't require me to put on an evening gown and look rich!"

"Rich." Rick ran his fingers through his hair.

"I'm not rich," she pointed out.

"But your father is."

She grimaced. "He was born into one of the founding families. He went to Harvard, and then to West Point," she said. "But he's just a regular person. He doesn't put on airs."

"Sure."

"Rick—" she got up and went to him "—I'm not my family. I don't have money. I work for my living. For heaven's sake, this suit is a year old!"

He turned around. His face was hard. "My suit is three years old," he said stiffly. "I drive a pickup truck. I can barely afford tickets to the theater."

She gave him a strained look. "You'll get used to this," she promised him. "It will just take a little time. You've had one too many upsets in the past few weeks."

He sighed heavily. "We should have waited to get married," he ground out.

"No," she returned. "If we'd waited and you'd found out, you'd never have married me at all."

Before Rick could open his mouth and destroy his future, Barbara got up and stood between them. "She's right," she told her son. "You need to stop before you say something you'll regret. Let Gwen go home for to-night, and you sleep on it. Things will look better in the morning." She went to get her cell phone and dialed a number. She waited until the call was answered. "Cash? Gwen Cassaway's going back to San Antonio for the night and I don't want her driving up there alone, do you have someone who can take her?"

"No…!" Gwen protested.

Barbara held up a hand. She grinned. "I thought you might. Thanks! I owe you a nice apple pie." She hung up. "One of Cash's men lives in San Antonio and he's on his way home. He'll swing by and give you a lift. He won't mind, and he's very nice. His name is Carlton Ames. He'll take good care of you."

Rick was cursing himself for not letting Gwen drive her car down instead of insisting that she come with him. He didn't like the idea of her riding with another man. They were married. At least, temporarily.

"Go home and don't worry," Barbara said, hugging her. "It will be all right."

Gwen managed a smile. She looked at Rick, but he wouldn't meet her eyes. She drew in a long breath and put on her coat and picked up her purse. She walked out to the front porch with Barbara, who closed the door behind them.

"He's still upset about meeting his father," Barbara said gently. "He'll get over this. You just get a good night's sleep and don't worry. It will work out. I'm so happy he married you!" She hugged the younger woman again. "You're going to be very happy together once he gets over the shock."

"I hope you're right. I should have told him. I was afraid to."

"Have you talked to your father?"

She shook her head. "I have to do that tonight." She grimaced. "He's not going to be happy, either."

"Does he have prejudices…?" Barbara worried at once.

Gwen laughed. "Heavens, no! Dad doesn't see color or race or religion. He's very liberal. No, he'll be hurt that I didn't tell him first."

"That's all right then. You'll make it up with him. And with Rick. Oh, there's Carlton!"

She waved as an off-duty police car pulled up at the porch. A nice young man got out and smiled. "I'm going to have company for the ride, I hear?" he asked.

"Yes, this is my new daughter-in-law, Gwen." Barbara introduced them. "That's Carlton," she added with a grin. "She didn't drive her own car and she has to get back to San Antonio to pick it up. Thanks for giving her a ride."

"Should I follow you back down here, then?" he offered.

Gwen shook her head. "I have things to get together in my apartment. But thanks."

"No problem. Shall we go?"

Gwen looked toward the porch, but the door was still closed. She saw Barbara wince. She managed a smile. "I'll see you later, then," she said. "Have a good night."

"You, too, dear," Barbara said. She forced a smile. "Good night."

She watched them leave. Then she went back in the house and closed the door. "Rick?"

He was on the phone. She wondered who he could be calling at this hour of the night. Perhaps it was work.

He hung up and came into the living room, looking more unapproachable than she'd ever seen him. "I'm going for a drive. I won't be long."

"She was very upset," she said gently. "She can't help who her father is, any more than you can."

He looked torn. "I know that. But she should have told me."

"I think she was afraid to. She's very much in love, you know."

He flushed and looked away. "I won't be long."

She watched him go, feeling a new and bitter distance between them, something she'd never felt before. She hoped they could work things out. She liked Gwen a lot.

Rick pulled up to the country bar, locked the truck and walked inside. It was late and there were only a couple of cowboys sitting in booths. A man in the back motioned to Rick, who walked down the aisle to sit across from him.

The older man gave him an amused smile. "Should I be flattered that you called me when you needed sympathy? Why not talk to your mother?"

Rick sighed. "It's not really something a woman would understand," he muttered.

General Machado pursed his lips. "No? Perhaps not." He motioned to the waiter, who came over at once, grinning. "Coffee for my young friend, please."

"At once!"

Rick's eyebrows arched at the man's quick manner.

"He wants to go and help liberate my country," Machado told Rick with a grin. "I have the ability to inspire revolutions."

"I noticed," Rick said dryly.

General Emilio Machado leaned back against the booth, studying the young man who looked so much like himself. "You know, we do favor each other."

"A bit."

The waiter came back with the coffee, placing a mug in front of Rick, along with small containers of cream and sugar, and a spoon. "Anything else for you, sir?" he asked the general with respect.

"No, that will do for now, thank you."

"A pleasure! If you need anything, just call."

"I will."

The waiter scampered away. Machado watched Rick sip hot coffee. "Just married, and already you quarrel?"

"She lied to me. Well, she lied by omission," he corrected coolly.

"About what?"

"It turns out that her father is the new head of the CIA."

"Ah, yes, General Cassaway. He and Grange are friends."

Rick recalled an odd conversation that Gwen and Grange had shared at the first meeting with Machado at the border. It had puzzled him at the time. Now he knew that she had been cautioning Grange not to give away her identity. It made him even sadder.

"He's rich," Rick said curtly.

"And you are not." Machado understood the problem. "Does it matter so much, if you care for the woman?

What if it was your mother who was wealthy, and her father who was poor?"

He shifted restlessly. "I don't know."

"But of course you do. You would not care."

Rick sipped more coffee. He was losing the argument.

Machado toyed with his own cup. "I was a millionaire, in my country," he confided. "I had everything a man could possibly want, right down to a Rolls-Royce and a private helicopter. Perhaps I had too much, and God resented the fact that I spent more money on me than I did on the poor villagers who were being displaced and murdered by my underling's minions as he worked to bring in foreign oil corporations. The oil and natural gas are quite valuable, and the villagers considered them a nuisance that interfered with the fishing." He smiled. "They have no interest in great wealth. They live from day to day, quietly, with no clocks, no supermarkets, no strip malls. Perhaps they have the right idea, and the rest of the world has gone insane from this disease called civilization."

Rick smiled back. "It would be a less hectic life."

"Yes, indeed." His dark eyes were thoughtful. "I was careless. I will never be careless again. And the man who usurped my place and made my people suffer will pay a very high price for his arrogance and greed, I promise you." The look on his face gave Rick cold chills.

"We've heard what he did to private citizens," Rick agreed.

"That is my fault. I should have listened. A…friend of mine, an archaeologist, tried to warn me about what his people were doing to the native tribes. I thought she was overstating, trying to get me to clamp down on foreign interests in the name of preserving archaeological treasures."

"A female archaeologist?"

He chuckled. "There are many these days. Yes, she taught at a small college in the United States. She was visiting my country when she stumbled onto a find so amazing that she hesitated to even announce it before she had time to substantiate her claim with evidence." His face hardened. "There was gossip that they put her in prison. I shudder to think what might have been done to her. That will be on my soul forever, if she was harmed."

"Maybe she escaped," Rick said, trying to find something comforting to say. "Rumors and gossip are usually pretty far off the mark."

"You think so?" Machado's dark eyes were sad but hopeful.

"Anything is possible."

Machado sighed. "I suppose."

The waiter came scurrying up looking worried. "El General, there is a police car coming this way," he said excitedly.

Machado looked at Rick.

"I'm not involved in any attempts to kidnap or arrest you," he said dryly.

"Is the car local?" Machado asked.

"Yes. It is a Jacobsville police car."

Machado weighed his options. While he was trying to decide whether to make a break out the back door, a tall, imposing man in a police uniform with large dark eyes and his long hair in a ponytail came in the door, looked around and spotted Rick with the general.

Rick relaxed. "It's all right," he said. "That's Cash Grier."

"You know him?"

"Yes. He's our police chief. He's a good man. Used to be a government assassin, or that's the rumor," Rick mused.

Machado laughed under his breath.

Cash walked over to their table. He wasn't smiling. "I'm afraid I have some bad news."

"You're here to arrest me?" Machado asked dryly.

Cash glanced at him. "Have you broken the law?" he asked curiously. It was obvious that he didn't recognize the bar's famous patron.

"Not lately," Machado lied.

Cash looked back at Rick, who was going tense.

"Gwen," he burst out.

Cash grimaced. "I'm afraid so. There's been a wreck…"

Rick was out of the booth in a flash. "How badly is she hurt?" he asked at once, white-faced. "Is she all right?"

"They've transported her and Ames to Jacobsville General," he said quietly. "Ames is pretty bad. Ms. Cassaway has at the very least a broken rib…!" Rick was already out of the bar, running for his truck.

"Wait! I'm coming with you!" Machado called after him, and stopped just long enough to pay the waiter, who bowed respectfully.

Cash, confused by the two men, got back in his patrol car and followed the pickup truck down the long road to the hospital. To his credit, he didn't pull out his ticket book when he pulled in behind Rick at the emergency entrance.

"My wife, Gwen Cassaway," Rick told the clerk at the desk. "They just brought her in."

The clerk studied him. "Oh, that's you, Detective Marquez," she said, smiling. "Yes, and she's your wife? Congratulations! Yes, she's in X-ray right now. Dr. Coltrain is treating her…"

"Copper or Lou?" Rick asked, because the married Coltrains were both doctors.

"Lou," came the reply.

"Thanks."

"You can have a seat right over there," the clerk said gently, "and I'll have someone ask Dr. Coltrain to come see you, okay?"

Rick wanted to rush behind the counter, but he knew better. He ground his teeth together. "Okay."

"Be just a sec." The clerk picked up the phone.

"She will be all right," Machado told his son with a warm smile. "She has great courage for one so young."

Rick felt rocked to the soles of his feet. He never should have reacted as he had. He'd upset her. But… she hadn't been driving, and Ames was one of Cash's better drivers…

He turned to the police chief. "Ames wrecked the car? How?"

"That's what I'd like to know," Cash said curtly. "There was another set of tracks in the dirt nearby, as if a car had sideswiped them. I've got men tracking right now."

"If you need help, I can provide a tracker who might even excel your own," Machado offered quietly.

Cash had been sizing the other man up. He pursed his lips. "You look familiar."

"There are very few photographs of me," Machado replied.

"Yes, but we've met. I can't remember where. Maybe it will come back to me."

Machado raised an eyebrow. "It would be just as well if your memory lapses for the next few hours. My son can use the company."

"Your son?" Cash's dark eyes narrowed on the older man. "Machado."

The older man nodded and smiled.

"Gwen had a photo of you. I had to break the news to Rick's mother, about your connection to him."

"Ah, yes, that was how he was told. Ingenious." The general's expression sombered. "I hope she and the officer will be all right."

"So do I," Cash said. "I can't help being concerned about that other car."

Machado came a step closer. "The Fuentes bunch have much reason to interfere with my plans. They are being paid by my successor to spy on me. There is also a very high level mole in the DEA. I do not know who it is," he added. "But even I am aware of him."

"Damn," Cash muttered.

"Yes, things are quite complicated. I did not mean to involve the children in my war," he added, with a rueful glance at Rick, who was pacing the floor.

"No parent would. Sometimes fate intervenes. Her father should be told."

"Yes," Machado replied. "He should." He excused himself and spoke to Rick.

"Her father." Rick groaned. "How am I going to find him?"

Machado grinned. "I think I can solve that problem." He pulled out his disposable cell phone, one of many, and dialed a number. "Grange? Yes. Gwen has been injured in an automobile accident. I need you to call her father and tell him. We don't know details yet. She has at least a broken rib. The rest we don't know… but he should come."

There was a pause. "Yes. Thank you. She is at the Jacobsville hospital. Yes. All right." He hung up. "Grange and her father are friends. He will make the call."

Rick averted his eyes. "Hell of a way to meet in-laws," he muttered.

"I do agree," Machado said. He put an affectionate arm around his son's neck. "But you will get through it. Come. Sit down and stop pacing, before you wear a hole in the floor."

Rick allowed himself to be led to a chair. It was kind of nice, having a father.

Dr. Louise Coltrain came into the room in her white lab coat, smiling. She was introduced to Gwen's husband and father-in-law with some surprise, because no one locally knew about the wedding.

"Congratulations," she told Rick. "She'll be all right," she added quickly. "She does have a broken rib, but the other injuries are mostly bruises. Patrolman Ames has a head injury," she told Cash. "His prognosis is going to be trickier. I'm having him airlifted to San Antonio, to the Marshall Center. He's holding his own so far, though. Do you have a way to notify his family?"

Cash shook his head. "He doesn't have any family that I'm aware of. Just me," he added with a grim smile. "So I'm the one to notify."

She nodded. "I'll keep you in the loop. Detective

Marquez, you can see your wife now. I'll take you back..."

"Where the hell is my daughter?"

Rick felt a shiver go down his spine. That voice, deep and cold with authority, froze everyone in the waiting room. Rick turned to find the face that went with it, and understood at once how this man had risen to become a four-star general. He was in full uniform, every button polished, his hat at the perfect angle, his hard face almost bristling with antagonism, his black eyes glittering with it.

"And who's responsible for putting her in the hospital?" he added in a tone that was only a little less intimidating.

While Rick was working on an answer, Barbara came in the door, worried and unsettled by his call. She paused beside the military man who was raising Cain in the waiting room.

"My goodness, someone had his razor blade soup this morning, I see!" she exclaimed with pure hostility. "Now you calm down and stop shouting at people. This is a hospital, not a military installation!"

Chapter 10

General Cassaway turned and looked down at the willowy blonde woman who was glaring up at him.

"Who the hell are you?" he demanded.

"The woman who's going to have you arrested if you don't calm down," she replied. "Rick, how is she?" she asked, holding out her arms.

Rick came and held her close. "Broken rib," he said. "And some bruising. She'll be all right."

"Who are you?" General Cassaway demanded.

Rick turned. "I'm Gwen's husband. Detective Sergeant Rick Marquez," he said coldly, not backing down an inch.

"Her husband?"

"Yes. And he's my son," Barbara added.

"And also my son," General Machado said, joining them. He smiled at Barbara, who smiled back.

"You two are married?" Cassaway asked.

Barbara laughed. "No. He's much too young for me," she said.

Machado gave her an amused look. "I do like older women," he admitted.

She just shook her head.

"I want to see my daughter," Cassaway told Lou Coltrain.

"Of course. Come this way. You, too, Rick."

Cassaway was surprised at the first name basis.

"We all know each other here," Lou told him. "I'm a newcomer, so to speak, but my husband is from here. He's known Rick since Barbara adopted him."

"I see."

Gwen was heavily sedated, but her eyes opened and she brightened when she saw her husband and her father walk into the recovery room.

"Dad! Rick!"

Rick went on one side to take a hand, her father on the other.

"I'm so sorry," she began.

"Don't be absurd." Rick kissed her forehead. "I was an idiot. I'm sorry! I never should have let you go with Ames."

"Ames! How is he?" she asked. "The other car came out of nowhere! We didn't even see it until it hit us. There were three men in it…"

"Did you recognize any of them?"

"No," she replied. "But it could have been Fuentes. The last of the living brothers, the drug lords."

"By God, I'll have them hunted down like rats," Cassaway said icily.

"My father will beat you to it," Rick replied coolly.

"Just who is your father?" Cassaway asked suddenly. "He looks very familiar."

"General Emilio Machado," Rick said, and with a hint of pride that reflected in the tilt of his chin.

Cassaway pursed his lips. "Grange's boss. Yes, we know about that upcoming operation. We can't be involved, of course."

"Of course," Rick replied with twinkling eyes.

"But we are rooting for the good guys," came the amused comment.

Rick chuckled.

"So you're married," Cassaway said. He shook his head. "Your mother would have loved seeing you married." He winced. "I would have, too."

"I'm so sorry," she said. "But I hadn't told Rick who you were." She bit her lip.

"What did that have to do with anything?" the older man asked, puzzled.

"I'm a city detective," Rick said sardonically. "I wear three-year-old suits and I drive a pickup truck."

"Hell, I drive a pickup truck, too," the general said, shrugging. "So what?"

Rick liked the man already. He grinned.

"See?" Gwen asked her husband. "I told you he wasn't what you thought."

"Snob," the general said, glaring at Rick. "I don't pick my friends for their bank accounts."

"Sorry," Rick said. "I didn't know you."

"You'll get there, son."

"Congratulations on the appointment," Rick said.

The general shrugged. "I don't know how long I'll last. I don't kiss butt, if you know what I mean, and I say what I think. Not very popular to speak your mind sometimes."

"I think honesty never goes out of style, and has value," Rick replied.

The general's eyes twinkled. "You did good," he told his daughter.

She just smiled.

Out in the waiting room, Cash Grier was talking on the phone to someone in San Antonio while the general thumbed through a magazine. Barbara paced, worried. Gwen's father was a hard case. She hoped he and Rick would learn to get along.

Cash closed his flip phone grimly. "They found a car, abandoned, a few miles outside of Comanche Wells," he said. "We can't say for sure that it's the one that hit Ames, but it has black paint on the fender, and Ames's car is black. We ran wants and warrants on it—it was stolen."

"Fuentes," Machado said quietly. His dark eyes narrowed. "I have had just about enough of him. I think he will have to meet with a similar accident soon."

"I didn't hear you say that," Cash told him.

"Did I say something?" Machado asked. "Why, I was simply voicing a prediction."

"Terroristic threats and acts," he said, waving a finger at Machado. "And I'm conveniently forgetting your connection with the Pendleton kidnapping for the next hour or so. After that," he added with pursed lips, "things could get interesting here."

Machado grinned. "I will be long gone by then. My son needed me."

Cash smiled. "I have a daughter," he said. "She's

going on three years old. Red hair and green eyes and a temper worse than mine."

"I would like to have known my son when he was small," Machado said sadly. "I did not know about him. Dolores kept her secret all the way to the grave. A pity."

"It was nice for me, that you didn't know," Barbara said gently. "When I adopted him, he gave me a reason to live." She stood up. "Do you think things happen for a reason?" she asked philosophically.

"Yes, I do," Machado replied with a smile. "Perhaps fate had a hand in all this."

"Well, I suppose…" she began.

"I have to get back home," General Cassaway was saying as he walked out with Rick. "But it's been a pleasure meeting you, son." He shook hands with Rick.

"Same here," Rick told him. "I'll take better care of your daughter from now on. And I won't be so inflexible next time she springs a surprise on me," he added with a laugh.

"See that you aren't. Remember what I do for a living now," he told the younger man with a grin. "I can find you anywhere, anytime."

"Yes, sir," Rick replied.

The general turned to Machado. "And you'd better hightail it out of Mexico pretty soon," he said in a confidential tone. "Things are going to heat up in Sonora. A storm's coming. You don't want to be in its way."

Machado nodded. "Thank you."

"Oh, I have ulterior motives," Cassaway assured him. "I want that rat out of Barrera before he turns your country into the world's largest cocaine distribution center."

"So do I," Machado replied quietly. "I promise you, his days of power will soon come to an end."

"Wish I could help," Cassaway told him. "But I think you have enough intel and mercs to do the job."

"Including a friend of yours," Machado replied, smiling.

"A very good one. He'll get the job done." He shook hands with Machado. Then he turned to Barbara. "You've got a smart mouth on you."

She glared at him. "And you've got a sharp tongue on you."

He smiled. "I like pepper."

She shifted. "Me, too."

"She's a great cook," Rick said, sliding his arm around her shoulders. "She owns the local café here, and does most of the cooking for it."

"Really! I'm something of a chef myself," Cassaway replied. "I grow my own vegetables and I get a local grandmother to come over and help me can every summer."

Barbara moved closer. "I can, too. I like to dry herbs as well."

"Now I've got a herb garden of my own," the general said. "But it isn't doing as well as I'd like."

"Do you have a composter?" Barbara asked.

His eyebrows lifted. "A what?"

"A composter, for organic waste from the kitchen." She went on to explain to him how it worked and what you did with it.

"A fellow gardener," Cassaway said with a beaming smile. "What a surprise! So few women garden these days."

"Oh, we have plenty around Jacobsville who plant

gardens," Barbara said. "You'll have to come and visit us next summer. I can show you how to grow corn ten feet high, even in a drought," she added.

Cassaway moved a step closer. He was huge, Barbara thought, tall and good-looking and built like a tank. He had thick black hair and black eyes and a tan complexion. Nice mouth.

Cassaway was thinking the same thing about Barbara. She was tall and willowy and very pretty.

"I might visit sooner than that," he said in a low, deep tone. "Is there a hotel?"

"Yes, but I have a big Victorian house. Rick and Gwen can stay there, too. We'll have a family reunion." She flushed a little, and laughed, and then looked at Machado. "That invitation includes you, also," she added. "If you're through with your revolution by then," she said ruefully.

"I think that is a good possibility, and I will accept the invitation," Machado said. He kissed her hand and bowed. "Thank you for taking such good care of my son."

She smiled. "He's been the joy of my life. I had nobody until Rick needed a home."

"I only have a daughter," General Cassaway said sadly. "I lost my son earlier this year to an IED, and my wife died some years ago."

"I'm so sorry," Barbara said with genuine sympathy. "I miscarried the only child I ever had. It must be terrible to lose one who's grown."

"Worse than death," Cassaway agreed. He cleared his throat and looked away. He drew in a long breath. "Well, my adjutant is doing the ants' dance, so I guess we'd better go," he said, nodding toward a young officer standing in the doorway.

"The ants' dance?" Barbara asked.

"He moves around like that when he's in a hurry to do something, like he's got ants climbing his legs. Good man, but a little testy." He shrugged. "Like me. He suits me." He shook hands with Rick. "I've heard good things about you from Grange. Your police chief over there—" he nodded toward Cash, who was talking on the phone again "—speaks highly of you."

Rick smiled. "Nice to know. I love my job. I like to think I'm good at it."

"Take care of my little girl."

"You know I will."

He paused at Barbara and looked down at her with quiet admiration. "And I'll see you later."

She grinned. "Okay!"

He nodded at the others, and walked toward the young man, who was now motioning frantically.

Cash joined them a minute later. "Sorry, I wasn't trying to be rude. I've got a man working on the hit-and-run, and I've been checking in. There was an incident at the border crossing over near Del Rio," he added. "Three men jumped a border agent, knocked him out and took off over the crossing into Mexico. We think it was the same men who ran Ames off the road."

"Great," Rick muttered. "Just great. Now we work on trying to get them extradited back to the States. That will be good for a year, even if we can get a positive identification of who they are."

Machado pursed his lips. "I would not worry about that. Such men are easy to find, for a good tracker, and equally easy to deal with."

"I didn't hear that," Cash said.

Machado chuckled. "Of course not. I was, again, making a prediction."

"Thanks for coming with me," Rick told Machado. "And for the shoulder earlier."

Machado embraced his son in a bear hug. "I will always be around, whenever you need me." He searched the younger man's face. "I am very proud to have such a man for my son."

Rick swallowed hard. "I'm proud to have such a man for my father."

Machado's eyes were suspiciously bright. He laughed suddenly. "We will both be wailing in another minute. I must go. Grange is waiting for me in the parking lot."

"I can't say anything officially," Cash told the general. "But privately, I wish you good luck."

Machado shook his hand. "Thank you, my friend. I hope your patrolman will be all right."

"So do I," Cash said.

Rick walked Machado to the door. Outside, Winslow Grange was sitting behind the wheel of Machado's pickup truck, waiting.

Machado turned to his son. "When the time comes, I will be happy to let you become my liaison with the American authorities. And it will come," he added solemnly. "My country has many resources that will appeal to outside interests. I would prefer to deal with republics or democracies rather than totalitarian states."

"A wise decision," Rick said. "And when the time comes, I'll be here."

Machado smiled. *"Que vayas con Dios, mi hijo,"* he said, using the familiar tense that was only applied to family and close friends.

It made Rick feel warm inside, that his father already felt affection for him. He waved as the two men in the truck departed. He hoped his father wouldn't get killed in the attempt to retake Barrera. But, then, Machado was a general, and he'd won the title fairly, in many battles. He would be all right. Rick was certain of it.

Gwen came home two days later. She wore a rib belt and winced every time she moved. The lieutenant had granted her sick leave, but she was impatient to get back on the job. Rick had to make threats to keep her in bed at all, at Barbara's house.

"And I'm a burden on your poor mother," Gwen protested. "She has a business to run, and here she is bringing me food on trays…!"

"She doesn't mind," Rick assured her.

"Of course she doesn't mind," Barbara said as she brought in soup and crackers. "She's working on planning a fantastic Thanksgiving dinner in a couple of weeks. I'm going to invite your father," she told Gwen and then flushed a little. "I guess that would be all right. I don't know," she hesitated, looking around her. "He's head of the CIA and used to crystal and fine china…"

"He doesn't use the good place settings at home," Gwen said dryly. "He likes plain white ceramic plates and thick Starbucks coffee mugs and just plain fare to eat. He isn't a fancy mannered person, although he can blend into high society when he has to. He'll think of it as a welcome relief from the D.C. whirl. Which I'm happy to be out of," she added heavily. "I never liked having to hostess parties. I like working in law enforcement."

"Me, too," Rick said, smiling warmly at his wife. "I'm just sorry about what happened to you and Ames."

"Yes. Have we heard anything about Ames?"

"Cash Grier said that he regained consciousness this morning," Barbara said with a smile. "It's all coming back to him. He remembered what the men looked like. He got a better view of them than you did," she told the younger woman. "He recognized Fuentes."

"Fuentes himself?" Gwen was shocked. "Why would he do his own dirty work?"

"Fuentes knows that you're married to me, and that I'm General Machado's son," Rick said somberly. "I think he was trying to get back at the general, in a roundabout way. He may have thought it was me driving. He wouldn't have known that you were with Ames."

"Yes," Barbara said worriedly. "And he may try again. You can't go anywhere alone from now on, at least until Fuentes is arrested."

"He won't be," Rick said coldly. "Dozens of policemen have tried to pin him down, nobody has succeeded. He has a hideout in the mountains and guards at every checkpoint. An undercover agent died trying to infiltrate his camp a few weeks ago. I'd love to see him behind bars. It's trying to get him there that's the problem."

"Well, your father's not too happy with him right now," Barbara remarked.

"And the general has ways and means that we don't have access to," Gwen agreed.

"True," Rick said.

"I think we may hear some good news soon about Fuentes and his bunch," Barbara said. "But for now, my main focus is getting your wife back on her feet," she told her son. "Good food and a little spoiling always does the trick."

"You're a nice mother," Rick said.

"A very nice mother and I'm so happy that you're going to be mine, too," Gwen told her with a warm smile. She shifted in the bed and groaned.

"Time for meds," Barbara said, and went out to get them.

Rick bent and kissed Gwen gently between her eyes. "You get better," he whispered. "I have erotic plans for you at some future time very soon."

She laughed, wincing, and lifted her mouth to touch his. "You aren't the only one with plans. Darn this rib!"

"Bad timing, and Fuentes's fault," Rick murmured as he brushed her mouth tenderly with his. "But we have forever."

"Yes," she whispered, beaming. "Forever."

Thanksgiving came suddenly and with, of all things, snow! Rick and Gwen walked out into the yard at Barbara's house and laughed as it piled down on the bare limbs of the trees around the fence line.

"Snow!" she exclaimed. "I didn't know it snowed in Texas!"

"Hey, it snowed in South Africa twice in August," he pointed out. "The weather is loopy."

She smiled and hugged him, still wincing a little, because her rib was tender. She was healing quickly, though. Soon, she would be whole again and ready for more amorous adventures with her new husband.

"Is your father coming down?" he asked Gwen.

"Oh, yes. He said he wouldn't miss a homemade Thanksgiving dinner for the world. He can cook, but he hates doing it on holidays, and he mostly eats out. He's very excited. And not only about the meal," she added with an impish grin. "I think he likes your mother."

"Wouldn't that be a match?" he mused.

"Yes, it would. They're both alone and about the same age. Dad's quite a guy."

"But he's head of a federal agency. He lives in D.C. and she owns a restaurant here," Rick pointed out.

"If they really want to, they'll find a way."

"I guess so." He turned to her, in the white flaky curtain, and drew her gently to his chest. "The best thing I ever did in life was marry you," he said somberly. "I may not say it a lot but I love you very much."

She caught her breath at the tenderness in his deep voice. "I love you, too," she whispered back.

He bent and drew her mouth under his, teasing the upper lip with his tongue, parting her lips so that his could cover them hungrily. He forgot everything in the flashpoint heat of desire. His arms closed around her, enveloping her so tightly that she moaned.

He heard that, and drew back at once. "Sorry," he said quickly. "I forgot!"

She laughed breathily. "It's okay. I forgot, too. Just another week or two, and I'll be in fine shape."

He lifted an eyebrow and looked down at her trim, curvy body in jeans and a tight sweater. "I'll say you're in fine shape," he murmured dryly.

"Oh, you!" She punched him lightly in the chest.

"Shapely, sexy and sweet. I'm a lucky man."

She reached up and kissed him back. "We're both lucky."

He sighed. "I suppose we should go back inside and offer to peel potatoes."

"I suppose so."

He kissed her again, smiling. "In a minute."

She sighed. "Yes. In a minute...or two...or three..."

Ten minutes later, they went back inside. Barbara gave them an amused look and handed Rick a huge pan full of potatoes and a paring knife. He sighed and got to work.

The general came with an entourage, but they were housed in the local hotel in Jacobsville. General Cassaway did allow his adjutant and a clerk to move into Barbara's house with him, with her permission of course, and he had a case full of electronic equipment that had to find living space as well.

"I have to keep in touch with everyone in my department, monitor the web, answer queries, inform the proper people at Homeland Security about my activities," the general said, rattling off his duties. "It's a great job, but it takes most of my time. That's why I've been remiss in the email department," he added with a smile at Gwen.

"I think you do very well, considering how little free time you have, Dad," she told him.

"Thanks." He dug into the dressing, closing his eyes as he savored it and the giblet gravy. "This is wonderful, Barbara."

"Thank you," she replied, with a big smile. "I love to cook."

"Me, too," Gwen added. "Barbara's teaching me how to do things properly."

"She's a quick study, too," Barbara replied, smiling at her daughter-in-law. "Her corn bread is wonderful, and I didn't teach her that...it's her own recipe. She's very talented."

"Thanks."

"What about this Fuentes character who sideswiped that car you were in?" he asked Gwen suddenly.

"Strange thing," she replied, tongue-in-cheek. "Fuentes seems to have gone missing. Nobody's seen him since the wreck."

"How very odd," the general remarked.

"Isn't it?"

"How about the young man who was driving you?" he added as he dipped his fork into potato salad.

"He's out of the hospital and back at work," Gwen said warmly. "He's going to be fine, thank goodness."

"I'm glad about that." He glanced across the table at Rick. "I understand that your father has left Mexico."

Rick smiled. "Yes, I did hear about that."

"So things are going to heat up in Barrera very soon, I would expect," the general added.

Rick nodded. "Very soon."

"No more talk of revolution," Barbara said firmly. She got to her feet with a big grin. "I have a surprise."

She went into the kitchen and came back in with a huge coconut cream pie. She put it on the table.

"Is that…?"

"Coconut cream." Barbara nodded. "I heard that it's someone's favorite."

"Mine!" General Cassaway said. "Thanks!"

"My pleasure." She cut it into slices and put one on a saucer for him. "If you still have room after all that turkey and dressing…"

"I'll make room," he said with such fervor that everyone laughed.

The general stayed for two days. Rick and Gwen and Barbara drove him around Jacobsville and introduced him to people. He fit in as if he'd been born there. He was coming back for Christmas, he assured them. He had to do a vanishing act to get out of all those holiday parties in Washington, D.C.

Rick heard from his father, too. The mercenaries had landed in a country friendly to Machado, near the border of Barrera, and they were massing for an attack. Machado told Rick not to worry, he was certain of victory. But just in case, he wanted Rick to know that the high point of his life so far had been meeting his own son. Rick had been overwhelmed with that statement. He told Gwen later that it had meant more to him than anything. Well, anything except marrying her, of course.

They moved back into her apartment, because it was closer to their jobs, leaving Rick's vacant for the moment.

She went home early one Friday night and when Rick walked in the door, he found her standing by the sofa wearing a negligee set that sent his heart racing like a bass drum.

"Here I was trying on my new outfit and there you are, home early. What perfect timing!" she purred, and moved toward him with her hair long and soft around her shoulders, her arms lifting to envelope him hungrily.

He barely got the door closed in time, before they wound up in a feverish tangle on the carpet...

Chapter 11

"Your ribs," Rick gasped.

"Are fine," Gwen whispered, lifting to the slow, hard rhythm. Her eyes rolled back in her head at the overwhelming wave of pleasure that accompanied the movements. "Oh, my gosh!" she groaned, shivering.

"It just gets better...and better," he bit off.

"Yes...!" A high-pitched little cry escaped her tight throat. She opened her eyes wide as he began to shudder and she watched him. His body rippled in the throes of ecstasy. He closed his eyes and groaned helplessly as he arched up and gave himself to the pleasure.

Watching him set her own body on fire. She moved involuntarily, lifting, lifting, tightening as she felt the pleasure grow and grow and grow, like a volcano throwing out rocks and flame before it suddenly exploded and sent fiery rain into the sky. She was like the volcano, echoing its explosions, feeling her body burn and flame and consume itself in the endless fires of passion.

She couldn't stop moving, even when the pinnacle was reached and she was falling from the hot peak, down into the warm ashes.

"No," she choked. "No…it's too soon…!"

"Shhhhh," he whispered at her ear. "I won't stop until you ask me to." He brushed her mouth with his and moved back into a slow, deep rhythm that very quickly brought her from one peak to an even higher one.

He lifted his head and looked down at her pretty pink breasts, hard-tipped and thrusting as she lifted to him, her flat belly reaching up to tempt his to lie on it, press it into the soft carpet as the rhythm grew suddenly quick and hard and urgent.

"Now, now, now," she moaned helplessly, shivering as the pleasure began to grow beyond anything she'd experienced before in his arms. "Oh, please, now!"

He pushed down, hard, and felt her ripple around him, a flutter of motion that sent him careening off the edge into space. He cried out, his body contracting as he tried to get even closer.

They shuddered and shuddered together, until the pleasure finally began to seep into manageable levels. He collapsed on her, his body heavy and hard and hot, and she held him while they started to breathe normally again.

"That was incredible," she whispered into his throat.

"I thought we'd already found the limit," he whispered back. "But apparently, we hadn't." He laughed weakly. He lifted his head. "Your rib," he said suddenly.

"It's fine," she assured him. "I wouldn't have felt it

if it wasn't fine," she added with a becoming flush. She searched his dark eyes. "You're just awesome."

He grinned. "So are you." He lifted an eyebrow. "I hope you plan to make a habit of meeting me at the door in a see-through pink negligee. Because I have to tell you, I really like it."

She laughed softly. "It was impromptu. I was trying it on and I heard your key in the door. The rest is history."

He kissed her softly. "History indeed."

He started to lift away and she grimaced.

"Sorry," he said, and moved more gently. "We went at it a little too hard."

"No, we didn't," she denied, smiling even through the discomfort.

He led her into the bedroom and tucked them both into bed, leaving the clothes where they'd been strewn.

"We haven't had supper," she protested.

"We had dessert. Supper can wait." He pulled her into his arms and turned out the light. And they slept until morning.

Christmas Day brought a huge meal, the whole family except for General Machado, and holiday music around the Christmas tree in the living room of Barbara's house. Rick and Gwen had bid on the nearby house and the family selling it accepted. They were signing the papers the following month. It was an exciting time.

Barbara and General Gene Cassaway were getting along from time to time, but with minor and unexpected explosions every few hours. The general was very opinionated, it seemed, and he had very definite ideas on certain methods of cooking. Considering that he'd only started being a chef five years before, and Barbara had been doing it for years, they were bound to clash. And they did. The more they discussed recipes, the louder the arguments became.

Gwen had resigned her federal job, with her father's blessing, and was now working full-time as a detective on Rick's squad at San Antonio P.D.

Her fledgling efforts had resulted in murder charges against Mickey Dunagan, the man arrested but not convicted on assault charges concerning a college coed. He was also the subject of another investigation on a similar cold case, in which charges were pending. He'd been seen at the most recent victim's apartment before her death in San Antonio.

Faced with ironclad evidence of his guilt, a partial fingerprint and conclusive DNA matching fluids found on the victim's body, he'd confessed. A public defender had tried to argue that the Miranda rights hadn't been read, but the prisoner himself had assured his legal counsel that he'd been read them, and that he stood on his confession. He'd started crying. He hadn't meant to hurt any of them, but they were so pretty and he could never even get a girl to go out with him. He'd killed that other girl, too, because she'd made fun of him and laughed.

This girl he'd just killed, she'd been kind. He didn't care if he went to prison, he told Gwen. He didn't want to hurt anybody else.

She'd handed him over to the prosecutor's office with a sad smile. A murderer with a conscience. How unusual. But it didn't bring the dead women back. On the other hand, the cold case squad was feeling a sense of satisfaction. They owed Gwen a nice dinner, they told her, and would deliver anytime she asked. She also spoke with the parents of the dead women, and gave them some consolation, in the fact that the killer would be brought to justice and, most likely, without a long and painful trial that would only bring back horrible memories of the tragedies.

The San Antonio patrolman, Sims, who'd gone on stakeout with Rick and Gwen, had been resigned from the force suddenly, with no reason given. Nobody in the department knew what had happened.

Patrolman Ames in Jacobsville was happily back on the job and with no apparent ill effects.

Down in Barrera, there were rumors of an invasion. It was all over the news. General Cassaway, when asked about the truth of those rumors, just smiled.

Gwen handed Rick a wrapped gift and waited patiently for him to open it.

He looked inside and then back at her with wonder. "How did you know...?"

She grinned and nodded toward Barbara, who laughed.

"Thanks!" he said, pulling out a DVD of an important United States vs. Mexico soccer match that he'd had to miss because of work. "I'll really enjoy it."

"I know you saw the results, but it was a great game," Gwen said.

"Here. Open yours," he said, and handed her a small present.

She pulled it open. It was a jeweler's box. She pulled the lid up and there was a small, beautiful diamond ring.

He pulled it out and slid it onto her finger. "I thought you should have one. It isn't the biggest around, but it's given with my whole heart."

He kissed it. She burst into tears and hugged him close. "I wouldn't care if it was a cigar band," she said.

"I know. That's why I wanted you to have it."

"Sweet man," she murmured.

He sighed. "Happy man," he added, kissing her hair.

She looked up at him with eyes full of love. "You know," she said, glancing toward her mother and General Cassaway, who were looking at recipe books they'd given each other, "I think this is the best Christmas of my life."

"I know it's the best of mine," he replied. "And only the first of many."

"Yes," she said, smiling from ear to ear as she touched his cheek with her fingertips. "The first of many. Merry Christmas."

He kissed her. "Merry Christmas."

The sudden buzz of his cell phone interrupted them. He reached into his pocket with a grimace. It was probably a case and he'd have to go to San Antonio on Christmas Day....

He looked at the number. It was an odd sort of number....

"Hello?" he said.

"Feliz Navidad," a deep voice sang, "Feliz Navidad, Feliz Navidad, something-somethingy felicidad!"

"You forgot the words?" Rick laughed, delighted. "Shame! It's '*Feliz Navidad, próspero año y felicidad,*'" he added smugly.

"Yes, shame, but I am very busy and my mind is on other things. Happy Christmas, my son."

"Happy Christmas to you, Dad," he said, glowing because his father had taken time out of a revolution to wish him well.

"Things are going fine here. Perhaps soon you and your lovely wife will come to visit me, and I will send a plane for you."

"That would be nice," Rick said. He mouthed "Dad" to Gwen, who grinned.

"Meanwhile, be a good boy and Santa Claus will send you something very nice in the near future."

"I didn't get you anything," Rick said with sadness.

There was a deep chuckle. "You did. The hope of grandchildren. That is a gift beyond measure."

"I'll do my best," Rick replied, tongue in cheek.

There was an interruption. "Yes, I will be right there. Sorry. I have to go. Wish me luck."

"You know I do."

"And Happy Christmas, my son."

"Happy Christmas."

He hung up.

"That was a very nice surprise," Rick said.

She smiled. "Yes."

"It's not a simple recipe," the general was growling. "Nobody can make that right! It's a stupid recipe, it curdles every time!"

"It's not stupid, and yes, you can," Barbara growled back.

"I'm telling you, it's impossible! I know, I've tried!"

"Oh, for heaven's sake! Come on in here and I'll show you. It's not hard!"

"That's what you think!"

"Stop growling. It's Christmas."

The general made a face. "All right, damn it."

"Gene!"

He sighed. "Darn it."

"Much better," she said with a grin.

"I won't be reformed by a cook," he informed her. "And just in case you didn't notice, I'm head of the CIA!"

"In this house, you're an apprentice chef. Now stop muttering and come on. This is one of the easiest sauces in the world, and you won't curdle it if you'll just pay attention."

The general was still muttering as he followed Barbara into the kitchen. There was a loud rattle of pots and pans and the opening of the fridge. Voices murmured.

Rick pulled Gwen into his arms and kissed her hungrily. "I love you."

"I love you, too."

"See? I told you! That's curdling!"

"It's not curdling, it's reducing!"

"Damn it, you put the butter in too soon!" the general was raging.

"I did not!"

Rick rolled his eyes. "Do you think you could do something about your father?"

"If you'll do something about your mother," she returned with a grin.

"I'm not raising the heat. That book is wrong!" the general snapped.

Rick looked at Gwen. Gwen looked at Rick. In the kitchen, the voices were growing louder. Without a word, they went to the front door, opened it and ran for their car.

Rick was laughing. "They won't even miss us," he said as he started the vehicle. "And maybe if they're left alone, they'll make peace."

"You think?" she teased.

He drove off to the house they were buying, cut off the engine and stared at it.

"We're going to be very happy here," Gwen said, sighing. "I'll make a garden and your mother can teach me how to can."

"Yes." He pulled her close. "If she and your father don't kill each other," he added.

"They'll have to learn to get along."

"Ha!"

The phone rang. Rick opened it. "Hello?"

"Could you come home for a minute?" Barbara asked.

"Sure. If it's safe," he teased. "What do you need?"

"Well, we could use a little help in the kitchen."

"Making the sauce?"

"Getting hollandaise sauce out of hair. And curtains. And cabinets. And on walls..."

"Mom!" he exclaimed. "What happened?"

"He thought I was making it wrong and I thought he was making it wrong, and, well, we sort of, uh, tossed the pan up."

"Are you okay?"

"Actually, you know, I think he was right. It tastes pretty good with less salt."

"I see."

"He's looking for another frying pan, so could you hurry?" she whispered, and then hung up.

"What's going on?" Gwen asked.

He grinned as he started the car. "War of the Worlds Part I. We get to help clean up the carnage in the kitchen."

"Excuse me?"

"They trashed the hollandaise sauce all over the kitchen."

"At least they're speaking," she pointed out.

He just shook his head. The general and his mother might eventually agree to a truce, but Rick had a feeling that it was going to be a long winter.

He pulled Gwen close and kissed the top of her head. He could manage anything, he thought, as long as he had her.

She sighed and closed her eyes. "Too many cooks spoil the broth?" she wondered aloud.

"I was thinking the same thing," he agreed. "Let's go referee."

"Done!"

They drove home through the colorful streets, with strings of red and blue and yellow and green lights and garlands of holly and fir. In the middle of the town square was a huge Christmas tree full of decorations, under which were wooden painted presents.

"One day," Rick said, "we'll bring our kids here when they light the tree."

She beamed. "Yes," she said, and it was a promise. "One day."

The tree grew smaller and smaller in the rearview mirror as they turned down the long road that led to Barbara's house. It was, Rick thought, truly the best Christmas of his life. He looked down at Gwen, and he saw in her eyes that she was thinking the very same thing.

Two lonely people, who found in each other the answer to a dream.

* * * * *

Visit her Author Profile page at Harlequin.com,
or deloresfossen.com, for more titles!

SHERIFF IN THE SADDLE

Delores Fossen

Chapter 1

There's been a murder at the Triple R Ranch.

Sheriff Leigh Mercer figured those were words no cop wanted to hear, but the dispatcher had been dead certain that was what the 911 caller had said.

Since the Triple R Ranch was in the jurisdiction of the Dark River Police Department, it was Leigh's job to check it out. But she hoped like the devil that the caller had been wrong. There hadn't been a murder in her hometown of Dark River, Texas, in nearly a decade, and for reasons other than just the obvious, Leigh wanted to keep it that way.

"You think we should call in Jeb on this?" Deputy Rocky Callaway asked her.

There was an edge to his voice, and leaning forward in the passenger's seat of the cruiser, Rocky was drumming his fingers on his holstered sidearm. The deputy was showing some nerves, and that was the only reason Leigh didn't scald him with a glance for asking that question.

Still, the question set her teeth on edge.

Jeb Mercer was her father, and before Leigh had pinned on the sheriff's badge eighteen months ago, Jeb had held that particular title for over four decades. He'd trained her. Trained Rocky, too. And even though Leigh had been duly elected after her dad's retirement, there were plenty, including Rocky, who'd always think of Jeb as the "real" sheriff.

"No, we're not bringing in Jeb," she insisted.

It was two in the morning, and she didn't need him to hold her hand at a possible crime scene. She'd already gotten Rocky out of bed since he was the deputy on call, and right now he was the only backup she intended to have.

She stepped from the cruiser, the winter wind howling and swiping at her. Mercy, it was cold, a bone-deep kind of wet cold that poked like icy fingers through her buckskin coat and boots. Leigh suspected in less than an hour, the predicted sleet would start to come down in buckets and turn the roads into skating rinks.

The wind gusts flicked away any of the usual scents that she might have picked up from the ranch, but then again, *usual* didn't apply to the Triple R. It was sprawling with its hundreds of acres of prime pastures to accommodate the hundreds of Angus cattle and prize quarter horses raised there.

The sleek white limestone house qualified as sprawling, too. Three floors that stretched out so far that it'd take a serious wide-angle lens to get it all in one photo. Lights speared out from at least a dozen of the windows.

Leigh flipped up the collar of her coat and glanced around. She hadn't been to the Triple R in fourteen years, not since she'd come to a party here when she'd been a senior in high school. She had plenty of memories of that particular event.

Memories that she hoped wouldn't get in the way if something bad had truly gone on here tonight.

Giving his own thick coat an adjustment, Rocky clamped his hand on his gun as they walked up the steps, and Leigh rang the doorbell. She automatically checked around for any signs that something was off. Nothing. And only a couple of seconds ticked by before the large double doors opened. Leigh instantly recognized the silver-haired woman who answered.

Rosa Tyree.

That was one of the advantages of living in a small town. Leigh knew most folks, and in this case, she knew that Rosa was a housekeeper at the ranch. A longtime one, having worked there for longer than Leigh had been alive. She was also well aware that Rosa didn't usually look this frazzled.

"He won't let me in the room," Rosa volunteered right away. "He said I should wait down here for you." Shivering from the cold, she frantically motioned for them to come in, and when they did, she shut the doors.

"He?" Leigh questioned though she was pretty sure she already knew what Rosa's answer would be.

"Mr. Brodie," Rosa provided, and then she added, "Mr. *Cullen* Brodie."

Yep, Leigh had been right. Cullen Brodie was the owner of the Triple R, but his brother, Nick, and their father, Bowen, visited often. Leigh had been hoping for

Nick or Bowen since Cullen was a huge part of those memories that she hoped wouldn't get in the way.

"You made the 911 call?" Leigh asked the woman while she had a look around the foyer and the adjoining rooms.

Rosa nodded, followed her gaze. "The cleaning crew won't be in until morning to clear up from the party."

There was indeed some various glassware scattered on the tables in what Leigh supposed was called a great room. A room that lived up to the sprawling and plush standards of the rest of the ranch. There were also gleaming silver trays with remains of what had no doubt been tasty food. What was missing were guests, but maybe those who'd been invited to the engagement party had headed out so they could get home before the bad weather moved in.

"The, uh, body's at the back of the house," Rosa explained, fluttering her trembling fingers in that direction. "It's the big room at the end of the hall. Mr. Brodie's in there, too."

Leigh did a quick trip down memory lane and silently groaned. That was Cullen Brodie's bedroom. Or at least it had been years ago.

"Someone really got murdered here?" Rocky asked Rosa. "Who?"

"I don't know who. But that's what Mr. Brodie said, that there'd been a murder, and he told me to call 911. I didn't see the body for myself though. Please don't make me go in there," the woman quickly added. "I don't want to see a dead body."

Leigh gave her a reassuring pat on the arm. She could easily agree to Rosa's request because if this was indeed a murder, Leigh didn't want the woman anywhere on the scene.

With Rocky at her heels, Leigh made her way down the hall to the *big room*. And yep, it was big all right. The doors to the massive bedroom suite were open, and even though it'd been redecorated in the years since she'd been here, it lived up to the size in her memory.

She didn't see anything remotely resembling a dead body, but there was a live one all right. Leigh immediately spotted Cullen.

And she felt the punch of lust.

There was no other word for it. Pure, hot lust. Of course, Cullen had that effect on plenty of women, what with his rock-star face. Not a used up, has-been rock star, either, but one in his prime who could attract just by breathing. Sizzling blue eyes, midnight-black hair and a face that, well, created those punches of pure, hot lust.

He was seated in a dark red leather chair, a glass of amber liquid in his hand. The top buttons of his rumpled white shirt were undone, and his tie was tossed on the glossy mahogany table in front of him.

His gaze slid over her, settling for a long moment on the badge she had clipped to her belt. "Sheriff," he said, and there wasn't a trace of the smirk or disapproval that some folks doled out when they mentioned her title.

"Mr. Brodie," Leigh greeted in return, and it earned her a raised eyebrow from him. Probably because the only other time she'd been in this room, they'd definitely been on a first-name basis.

Since Leigh didn't want to remember that right now or think about the lust, she got down to business. "You had Rosa call 911 to report a body?"

Cullen nodded, his gesture slow and easy. The same as his movements when he got to his feet. He definitely wasn't dressed like a rancher tonight in his black pants that had no doubt been tailored for that perfect fit.

When he got closer to her, she caught his scent. And she mentally sighed. He smelled expensive.

Leigh followed Cullen to the adjoining bath, but he didn't go in. He stepped to the side to give her a clear view of the stark white room. A view that gave Leigh a gut-jab of reactions and emotions.

Sweet merciful heaven. There was blood. And lots of it. It was spattered on the tub, the walls. Even the mirror.

There was also a body.

The woman was sprawled out on the glossy white marble floor. She was a brunette with her arms and legs flailed out as if she'd tried to break her fall and then crawl away from her attacker. Maybe she'd managed to do that, but if so, she hadn't gotten far, and it hadn't helped save her. Nothing probably could have done that, considering the back of her head had been bashed in.

"Blunt force trauma," Leigh muttered, hoping if she focused on the scene and not the body that her stomach would stop churning.

She didn't normally have this kind of reaction to blood. Or a crime scene. But then, she'd never personally seen one this bad. During her time at the Lubbock Police Academy, she'd stayed on the fringes of murder investigations. An observer there to learn. Well, she wasn't an observer tonight. She was right in the thick of it.

Leigh continued to look around. Continued to study what was right in front of her. There was no weapon that she could see, and there wasn't any blood on the sharp corners of the counters to indicate that's how the woman had been fatally injured.

"Uh, you want me to call Jeb?" Rocky asked, and the shakiness in his voice had gone up some significant notches.

"No." This time Leigh didn't manage to tamp down her glare when she glanced back at him.

Along with the shakiness, Rocky looked ready to boot. She was pretty sure this was his first murder scene, too.

"Go ahead and call the medical examiner and the county CSI team," Leigh instructed. "We also need some deputies to do a room-to-room search and check the grounds. When you're done with that, take Rosa's statement. And the statements of anybody else who's in the house."

"No one else is here," Cullen provided. *Calmly* provided.

If she hadn't looked at Cullen, she might not have noticed the tight muscles in his jaw or the fierce set of his mouth. But she did look. Did notice. And she saw this had given him a gut-punch, too.

"But Jeb oughta be brought in on this," Rocky protested.

This time, Leigh didn't bother with words. She gave her deputy a look that could have frozen El Paso in August, and it was thankfully enough to get Rocky moving.

"I didn't kill her," Cullen said, those jaw muscles stirring again. "I found her when I came to my room after the party."

He didn't have to explain what party he was talking about. Small-town gossips had clued in everyone who'd listen or overhear about that. Cullen had hosted an engagement celebration for his friend Austin Borden and Austin's fiancée, Kali Starling.

According to the bits Leigh had heard, there'd been about a hundred guests, most from Lubbock, about a half hour away. Since Austin lived in Lubbock and it was where Cullen had his main office, that didn't surprise her. It was also no surprise that only a couple of locals had received invitations. Cullen hadn't exactly kept close ties with many in his hometown.

Including her.

Leigh gave Cullen another once-over, and this time she made sure the lust stayed out of it. "You wore those clothes to the party?"

Cullen nodded. "I didn't kill her," he repeated.

She believed him. Whoever had done this would have had blood spatter on him or her, and Leigh didn't see so much as a speck on Cullen. Of course, a smart killer would have changed his clothes before calling in the cops, but Leigh didn't think that was what happened here.

"It's Alexa," Cullen added when Leigh was about to go inside the bathroom.

That sent Leigh whirling back around to face him. "Alexa Daly?" she asked on a rise of breath.

Cullen nodded and had another gulp of his drink while he kept his eyes on the body.

Leigh swallowed hard. This just got a whole lot stickier. Because Alexa was Cullen's ex-girlfriend. There'd been plenty of rumors about that, too. Leigh didn't know how much of what she'd heard about the breakup was actually true, but just about everyone agreed that it'd been a nasty one. There'd been some public arguments and rumors of a restraining order. Later, Leigh would have to suss out how much of that was gossip and how much was fact.

"Did you touch the body?" she continued, stepping inside the room. Leigh was careful to avoid any of the blood while she surveyed the area.

"Yes. I checked for a pulse on her neck. There wasn't one, and her body was already cold so I didn't try CPR. I called out for Rosa to dial 911."

So, there could be trace evidence from Cullen. She wished he hadn't made that a possibility, but it was instinct to make a check like that. Well, instinct for some. Others would have just panicked and run.

She stooped down to get a closer look at the body. Yes, it was Alexa all right, and even death hadn't been able to completely steal her beauty. Someone, however, had definitely stolen her life. Alexa's now blank emerald green eyes stared up at her.

"How many people had access to your bathroom?" Leigh continued her examination of the body and didn't see any self-defense wounds. No blood or tissue under Alexa's perfectly manicured nails, which had been painted bloodred.

"Anyone who came to the party, and that includes any of the catering crew who set things up. Guests don't make a habit of coming back here, but it does happen every now and then."

Leigh looked back at him again to see if that was a little jab at her. After all, she had come to his room fourteen years ago during a party. She hadn't made a habit of doing that, either. In fact, it'd been her first.

Cullen had been her first.

And that was yet something else that she nudged aside.

"I'll need a guest list along with the names of any catering staff," she told him, shifting her focus back to the dead woman. "Include the names of any of your ranch hands or hired help who might have had access."

"I'll have Rosa give it to you. Alexa's name won't be on it," he explained. "She wasn't invited, and I didn't know she was here."

Leigh wasn't surprised that Alexa hadn't been invited, but she was wearing party clothes. A clingy silk dress the color of expensive sapphires. Her wrists, neck and ears glittered with gold and diamonds, which ruled out robbery as a possible motive. Well, unless the would-be thief had panicked after she'd hit the floor.

"Alexa had a key to the place?" Leigh asked.

Cullen shook his head. "I had the locks changed after we broke up, but the house wasn't locked tonight. She could have walked in except…" He paused.

"Except?" she pressed.

"She's not wearing a coat, and I didn't see one in here or in my bedroom. Plus, there's no vehicle unaccounted for in the driveway. I checked out the windows and didn't spot one," he told her. "I also don't see a purse."

"You're observant," Leigh muttered, not at all surprised by that.

The ranch was a huge success, and from all accounts, that was because of Cullen. He might not spend much time at the house, but he still ran it, and observation skills would come in handy for that.

"Did you notice anything unusual about any of your guests?" she went on.

"Do you mean did someone come into the great room

with blood dripping off them?" He cursed, shook his head and seemed to gain control of that quick snap of temper. "No. It was a party. A celebration. And we celebrated."

Cullen turned away from her, groaned. "I don't know who'd do this."

"That's why I'll investigate." She paused, steeled herself up. "But you should know that I have to consider you a possible suspect."

With the same slow movements as he'd had before, Cullen eased back toward her. The breath he dragged in was long and weary. "Leigh," he said.

Just that. Only her name. But he'd made it sound like so much more. There was a plea in his tone, maybe a plea for her to believe he was innocent. And heaven help her, she did. It wasn't just the lack of blood on his clothes.

Or their very brief history together.

It was the whole package, even if that "package" was the assessment she'd been able to make so far. If Alexa and he had argued, if they'd had a fight that'd gotten out of hand, she didn't believe Cullen would have struck the woman from behind. Nor would he have removed the murder weapon only then to leave the body in place. This very well could be a crime of passion, but she didn't feel it in her gut that Cullen was responsible. Of course, she doubted anyone else was going to put much stock in her gut feeling.

Cullen scrubbed his hand over his face. "Will what happened between us get in the way here?"

Since she'd asked herself the same thing, Leigh didn't blister him with a look or insist that nothing would get in the way of her doing her job. She couldn't. Because, yes, their past might get in the way. It wasn't like she could go back and erase memories of her first lover. Or the tangled mess that followed.

Despite her attempts to stop them, some of those memories came now. Not a gentle blur of images but crystal clear ones of Cullen's naked body. He'd been a lot younger when they'd had sex. Just nineteen. But like the rest of him, his body had been memorable even then.

"Our past won't get in the way," she answered, hoping to reassure him, and herself, that it was true. Maybe if she said it enough, both of them would start to believe it.

Stepping around Cullen, Leigh went back into the bedroom and had another look around. No blood or signs of a struggle. It was the same for the sitting area and the adjoining office. Still, the CSIs might be able to find something.

"The bedroom door was open when you came up after the party ended?" she asked.

"Closed." Cullen moved to stand beside her and followed her gaze as it skirted around the room. "Something's missing," he said.

That got Leigh's attention. "What?"

He was already moving to the sitting area, specifically to a corner table next to a leather love seat. "A bronze horse statue. It's a replica of Lobo," he added in a murmur.

The name instantly rang a bell. In the short time that she'd been involved with Cullen, his favorite horse had been named Lobo. He had won plenty of competitions, and Leigh had heard through the grapevine that Cullen had been upset when Lobo died.

"How big was the statue?" she asked.

"About a foot high, and it was heavy." He looked back at her then, and she didn't have to ask what he was thinking. Someone had grabbed it and then used it to murder Alexa.

Leigh turned when she heard the hurried footsteps coming from the hall, and several moments later, an out-of-breath Rocky came rushing into the room. He didn't have much color in his face, and he'd drawn his weapon.

"What's wrong?" Leigh immediately asked.

Rocky's chest was heaving, and it took him a moment to speak. "On one of the side porches," he finally managed to say. "There's been another murder."

Chapter 2

*H*ell.

That was Cullen's first reaction, but he tamped down the string of profanity going through his head and raced up the hall with Leigh. Rocky led the way, threading them through the great room and toward the west side of the house to one of the guest suites.

Cullen saw Rosa huddled in the corner of the room. The woman had obviously followed Rocky, and her breath was gusting out, causing little white wisps of fog in the freezing room. Freezing because the glass doors leading to a patio were wide-open.

"Out there," Rocky said, pointing to the patio. The deputy didn't go closer but instead stepped to the side to make way for Leigh and Cullen. "The doors were open when I came in here so I looked out and saw him."

Leigh went straight outside, her gaze firing around

the side yard before settling on the man who was in a crumpled heap on the mosaic tiles. Like with Alexa's body, there was blood. Unlike Alexa, this guy was wearing a thick coat.

"It's Jamie Wylie," Cullen blurted out the moment he got a good look at the man's face. "He's one of my ranch hands."

Cullen didn't stay put. He hurried out to Jamie even though he figured there was nothing he could do, that the man was already dead.

But Cullen soon learned he was wrong.

Jamie groaned, a weak sound of raw pain, and he moved his head from side to side.

"Call for an ambulance," Leigh shouted, taking the words right out of Cullen's mouth.

Behind them, he heard Rocky make that call, and Cullen dragged the comforter off the bed. With all the blood Jamie had already lost, it was a miracle that he was still alive, but he wouldn't stay that way if he froze.

Leigh caught onto the side of the comforter and helped Cullen cover the man. "I don't want to move him," she explained. Then she threw Rocky a quick glance over her shoulder. "Tell the EMTs to hurry."

Cullen understood the urgency. There was no way to know just how serious Jamie's injuries were, and moving him inside could end up killing him. Of course, a killer could do that, too, and that's why Cullen glanced around to make sure they weren't about to be ambushed.

Beside him, Leigh was doing the same thing.

Unfortunately, this particular part of the yard had a lot of shrubs and trees that stayed thick even in the winter. It'd been landscaped that way to create a little garden oasis for guests. Which meant there were plenty of

places and shadows where someone could hide. There
were no views of the front or back yards, but Cullen
knew there were flagstone stepping-stones that led in
both directions. Alexa's killer could have gone in either direction.

Or neither.

Whoever was responsible for Jamie and Alexa could
still be on the grounds. Definitely not a settling thought.

"Rosa, find one of the portable heaters and bring it
out here," Cullen told the woman.

It would maybe pull her out of the shock along with
helping to keep Jamie warm until the EMTs arrived,
and Cullen knew there were several of the heaters in
the storage room just off the kitchen. They used them
for taking the chill off the patio and porches during
late-night parties.

Cullen went back into the bedroom and grabbed the
spare quilt and pillows from a cedar chest at the foot of
the bed, and he brought those out to Jamie, too.

"It's blunt force trauma," Cullen said, looking down
at the wound. Except this wasn't to the back of the head
like Alexa but rather to the man's left temple. Along
with the blood, there was already a huge, ugly bruise
forming on his face.

Leigh nodded. She didn't touch Jamie but did lean in
so that her face was right over his. "Can you hear me,
Jamie? Can you tell me who did this to you?"

Jamie managed a hoarse moan. Nothing more. His
eyes stayed shut, but Cullen prayed the man would be
able to answer that question soon.

"Are these patio doors usually locked?" Leigh asked,
aiming that question at Cullen.

"Usually, but I had a cleaning crew in the house ear-lier, and they could have left them unlocked."

He'd barely gotten out that answer when Leigh fired off another question. "Any idea what Jamie would have been doing out here?"

Cullen had to shake his head. "He wasn't on duty." But then he paused. "He knew Alexa."

"Knew?" Leigh pressed, and he heard the cop's in-flection of what she meant.

"Nothing sexual as far as I know," Cullen explained. "But Jamie gave her riding lessons here at the ranch."

And Cullen's mind began to play with that connec-tion. Had Jamie brought Alexa here tonight? Cullen could see her being able to talk Jamie into doing some-thing like that.

Maybe.

Jamie wasn't exactly a soft touch, but he was young. Barely twenty-one. And Cullen was pretty sure Jamie had been somewhat dazzled by Cullen's former girl-friend. Then again, Alexa could do lots of dazzling until you got beneath the surface and saw, well, a woman who could be obsessive and vindictive. Still, that didn't explain why Alexa was dead or why Jamie was lying there, clinging to life.

Rocky moved out onto the patio, peering down at his boss and the ranch hand. "Whoever did this musta killed the woman in the bathroom," the deputy con-cluded—which, of course, was stating the obvious. It was also obvious when Rocky turned an accusing gaze on Cullen.

The deputy thought he'd done this.

He doled out one of his hardest glares to Rocky, and Cullen knew for a fact that he was good at it. However, he didn't get a chance to add anything to the expression he knew would intimidate. That's because something caught Cullen's eye.

One of the small shrubs that rimmed the patio had been trampled down. He went closer, and while he didn't see any footprints, it appeared that someone had stepped on it. Maybe the someone who'd attacked Alexa and Jamie.

Leigh stood and moved closer to him, her gaze following what Cullen had spotted. "Rocky, get some photos of this with your phone. Once the EMTs arrive, they'll come rushing back here and might destroy possible evidence. Make sure you don't step on any prints."

The deputy followed her instructions just as Rosa came hurrying to the doorway. She didn't come onto the patio and didn't look at Jamie, but she did plug in the heater that she then set out on the tiles. She also handed Cullen a coat. He certainly hadn't forgotten about how cold it was, but he hadn't wanted to go inside, not with Jamie out here.

Leigh's phone rang, and because Cullen was right there next to her, he saw the name that popped up on the screen. Jeb. And he found it interesting that she hadn't listed him in her contacts as Dad but rather by his first name.

Frowning, she took the call but stepped away from Cullen. However, she continued to volley her attention between Jamie and Rocky, who was already snapping some pictures.

Cullen watched her take the cop attitude up another level and wondered if she even knew she was doing it. Probably not. It might be her go-to response when dealing with her dad. He hadn't had to hear rumors to know there was tension between Jeb and Leigh. Or at least there had been fourteen years ago when Jeb had convinced her to cut Cullen out of her life. It obviously hadn't been that hard for her to do, either, since she'd made the break and hadn't looked back.

But Cullen had.

There were times, like now, when he wondered if he should have pressed Leigh for something more. Even if that *something more* would have put even greater strain on her relationship with her father.

"Rocky shouldn't have called you," Leigh replied in response to whatever her father had just said to her. She smoothed her hand over the top of her dark brown hair that she'd pulled back into a sleek ponytail. The gesture seemed to be a way of steadying herself or maybe giving her fingers something to do other than tighten and clench. "I can handle this."

There was a long pause where Leigh was no doubt listening to Jeb's *advice*. Something that a lot of people did. Many folks still thought of Jeb Mercer as the voice of authority.

The law in Lubbock County.

It didn't matter that Jeb had been the sheriff of Dark River, a small town within the county. His lawman's reputation was legendary throughout this part of Texas.

Cullen just thought of him as a hard-nosed, bitter man who'd never gotten over his toddler son, Joe, being kidnapped twenty-seven years ago. Jeb had devoted a big chunk of his life to finding the boy, who'd now be a grown man if he was still alive. And Cullen wasn't the only one who thought that Jeb's search for his son had come at the expense of his daughter, Leigh, and his estranged son, Cash.

"I'm nowhere near ready to make an arrest," Leigh snapped a moment later, and it was definitely a snap. Judging from the quick glance she gave Cullen, he figured Jeb was already pressuring her to arrest anyone with the surname Brodie.

Hell. Old wounds and bad blood were definitely going to play into this.

"I have to go," Leigh insisted, and she hit the end call button. Cramming her phone in her pocket, she stooped back down beside Jamie and looked up at Cullen. "I'll have to bring you in for a formal interview. And not because Jeb's pressuring to do that, but because it has to be done."

Cullen stared at her, and a dozen things passed between them. Memories. Heat. The past. Yeah. The old wounds were already surfacing.

In the distance, Cullen could hear the wail of the ambulance, but he kept his attention on Leigh. "A formal interview," he repeated, following that through. "Something you'll have to do with anyone who attended the party."

She nodded. "In the meantime be thinking of who'd want Alexa dead."

At least Leigh hadn't said *Other than you, who'd want her dead?* Though Cullen was certain Jeb would be trying to put that bug in her ear. But it wasn't true. Cullen hadn't wanted his ex dead.

"Before tonight, it's been weeks since I've given Alexa a thought," Cullen admitted.

"She didn't make any threats against you?" Leigh pressed. "Or say anything about someone threatening her?"

"No," Cullen could honestly answer. She'd made

threats, yes. But they'd been verbal and none were recent. Of course, that was in part because Cullen no longer took calls from her and had refused to see her.

Leigh probably would have continued to push for info if there hadn't been the sound of hurried footsteps. She immediately rose, laying her hand on her gun. Cullen did the same to the snub-nosed .38 that he always carried in a slide holster at the back waist of his pants. But it wasn't the killer who'd come to finish off Jamie. It was two more of Leigh's deputies. Vance Pickering and Dawn Farley.

Cullen recognized both of them and had even gone to school with Vance. He didn't know Dawn as well, but one of her brothers worked on the Triple R, and he did a good job. Hardly an endorsement for his cop sister's abilities, but at least Cullen hadn't heard anything bad about her.

"We've got a DB in the master bedroom at the back of the house," Leigh explained. "Dawn, I need you to go there and secure the scene until the CSIs and ME arrive."

"Rocky told me it was Alexa Daly?" Dawn said.

Leigh spared her a confirming nod before she shifted back to Rocky. "You will not contact Jeb again about this investigation." She kept her voice low, but Cullen still heard her. He heard her warning tone, too. "Understand?"

"But—" Rocky started.

"You will not contact Jeb," Leigh interrupted. "Now, go to the front porch and direct the EMTs here." Ignoring Rocky's huff, she turned to Vance. "I need you to check the grounds. We're not sure how the DB got here so take down the license plates of any vehicle you see. Jamie lives here at the ranch?" she asked.

It took Cullen a moment to realize that tacked-on question was meant for him, and he nodded. "He lives in the bunkhouse."

Leigh shifted her attention back to Vance as Dawn and Rocky left. "Then check there, too, and see if anyone knows what Jamie was doing on the patio."

Good question. The bunkhouse was a good quarter of a mile away from the main house, and Cullen couldn't think of a good reason why Jamie would be here in this particular spot. But he could think of a bad reason if the ranch hand had indeed helped Alexa. Help that maybe someone had objected to because Cullen doubted that Alexa had bashed Jamie on the head and then sneaked into his bedroom to have her own encounter with a killer. Then again, maybe that was exactly what'd happened.

Vance nodded at Leigh's order and stepped away, but not before giving Cullen the same kind of cop's eye that Rocky had. This time Cullen didn't even bother with a glare because his own phone rang.

Since he didn't recognize the number, Cullen started not to answer, but then he realized it could be one of the ranch hands trying to contact him. Not a hand though because it was Austin.

"It's me," Austin immediately said. "I don't have my phone so the clerk here at the gas station let me borrow his."

Normally, Cullen wouldn't have minded a call from the man he considered a close friend, but it'd been less than an hour since Austin had left the party, and Cullen wasn't in the mood for a chat.

"I figured you'd be home by now," Cullen remarked, hoping to put a quick end to this conversation.

"I was heading that way, but the roads are bad so I was going slow. I nearly ran out of gas, too, so I stopped, and I overheard the clerk talking about his girlfriend getting called out to the Triple R. He said she was a CSI."

Cullen sighed and stepped back into the bedroom to deal with this call. This was the downside to living in a small town. Gossip, especially gossip about bad news, didn't stay hush-hush for long.

"Alexa's dead," Cullen said. "And no, I didn't kill her. I don't have a clue who did."

Austin cursed. "What the hell was she doing there?"

"Don't know that, either. In fact, I don't have answers to much of anything right now." Cullen watched as the EMTs hurried toward the patio to tend to Jamie. "But we might know something soon. Did you see anyone at the party who shouldn't have been there?" Cullen asked.

Austin paused, probably giving that some thought. "No. Are you telling me that someone came into your house and killed Alexa?"

"It looks that way." Cullen dragged in a long breath. "Maybe you could ask Kali if she saw anything? Kali got here early to make sure I didn't need any help so she might have noticed something off."

Austin paused again. "Yeah, I'll call her and ask."

Cullen's forehead bunched up. "She's not with you?"

"No. After she left the party, she went back to her folks' place for the night. I think she and her mom are doing some wedding stuff first thing in the morning. But I can tell you that if Kali had seen anything off, she would have said something to me about it. She was right by my side most of the night."

That was true, but most wasn't *all*. "You stepped outside for a smoke a couple of times," Cullen reminded him. "Did you see anything then?"

"Just one smoke," Austin corrected. "And I didn't see a thing that sent up any red flags."

Cullen pushed a little harder. "Were you anywhere near the guest room patio or the patio off my bedroom?"

"No." Austin's answer was firm and fast. "Is that where you think the killer was?"

"Yeah, along with being in my bedroom. Any chance you were in the hall outside my suite at any time during the night?"

Austin cursed. "This is beginning to sound like an interrogation, but no, I didn't go anywhere near that hall. No reason for it. Ditto for staying outside very long when I went out for that smoke. It was too damn cold."

"Sorry about the interrogation," Cullen said. "But these are questions Leigh will be asking you soon enough."

"Why me?" Austin cursed again. "Does she think I'm a suspect? Because if so, she's crazy. I didn't even see Alexa tonight."

Cullen sighed. "No. You're not a suspect. But right now anyone who was at the party will no doubt be considered a potential witness." Maybe even a person of interest. But Cullen kept that last part to himself. "We just need to find out who came into my house and committed a murder."

Austin stayed quiet a couple of seconds. "And we have to stop this person from coming after anyone else. I got that," Austin said on a heavy breath. "But give me some time to think about who it could be, and I'll get back to you."

"Thanks." Cullen watched as the EMTs loaded Jamie onto a gurney. Leigh was right there, giving them instructions about keeping Jamie secure, assuring them she'd be at the hospital soon.

"That's a lot of noise for just cops," Austin remarked. "That sounds like an ambulance siren to me."

"Because it is. Someone attacked one of my ranch hands. Jamie," Cullen provided.

"Jamie?" Austin questioned. "Hell, is he dead, too?"

"No." Cullen didn't add *not yet, anyway*, because he wanted to hang on to the hope that Jamie would pull through.

"Jamie's alive?" Austin made a sound of relief. "Then, he can tell you who attacked him?"

"To be determined. I have to go. I want to be at the hospital when the doctors examine Jamie." He hoped Leigh wouldn't give him any hassles about that. Even if she did, Cullen would work his way around her.

The anger came now, shoving the shock aside and twisting his muscles into knots. Someone had come into his home and done this. Maybe had murdered and maimed to set him up. Yeah, Cullen would definitely get to the bottom of why this had happened.

"You need me there?" Austin asked, drawing Cullen's attention back to him.

"No. Bad weather's moving in, and I don't want you on the roads. But if you find out anything from Kali, let me know."

"I will," Austin assured him, "and keep me posted about Jamie. Hell, Cullen, he was just a kid."

Cullen didn't want that to eat away at him. But it did.

Mercy, it did. All of this would eat away even when he found out who'd done this.

He ended the call and was about to go back on the patio with Leigh and the EMTs, who were about to move Jamie to the ambulance. But Leigh looked up, her gaze zooming past Cullen's shoulder and landing on someone behind him. Cullen turned and saw someone he definitely didn't want to deal with tonight.

His father, Bowen Brodie.

Bowen had ditched his party clothes and was wearing his usual jeans, including a rodeo buckle that gleamed out from his wide leather belt. Obviously, he'd had time to go to his house about fifteen minutes away and change before making his way back here, but then, Bowen hadn't stayed long at the party. He'd given his congrats to Austin and Kali and had then made an excuse about wanting to leave the shindig to the "young folks."

"I heard about the murder," his father said right off.

"It's the middle of the night," Cullen reminded him, and he didn't bother to take the snarl out of his tone. "Since you don't have ESP, someone must have called you."

Bowen confirmed that with a nod. "One of my assistants is dating the Dark River dispatcher. When he heard there'd been a murder at the Triple R, he called her."

Yeah, and had probably also called anyone and everyone in his contact list. Ditto for the dispatcher. This was big news.

"Normally, I would have cussed out anybody calling me at this hour, but I knew you'd have to deal with Jeb's spawn," Bowen added. "So I came straight over."

Spawn. That was a good way to start off this visit. Cullen was a thousand percent sure that Leigh felt the same way he did about not wanting to deal with his father tonight.

To say that Bowen and Leigh's father had bad blood was like saying the Pacific Ocean had a drop or two of water in it. Cullen knew it went all the way back to the kidnapping and disappearance of Jeb's son. A kidnapping and disappearance that Jeb had always thought Bowen had played a part in.

Heck, maybe he had.

Bowen might be his father, but Cullen could see the man clear enough. Along with making a game of skirting the law, Bowen could be vindictive. And that vindictiveness went back to Jeb arresting Cullen's mother for a DUI. Cullen had been five years old, barely old enough to remember, but Bowen had made an art form of keeping the incident, and what followed, alive by talking about it with anyone who'd listen. That's because Cullen's mother had died in the jail cell. Alcohol poisoning, according to the ME, but Bowen had considered it negligent homicide on Jeb's part.

And so the cycle of bad blood had begun.

A cycle fueled by Jeb's firm belief that Bowen had gotten revenge by kidnapping Jeb's little boy. Apparently, the bad blood was about to continue if his father kept using words like *spawn* and glaring at Leigh.

"You're not going to railroad my son into taking the blame for something he didn't do," Bowen snarled, and he aimed that snarl at Leigh.

Leigh looked at the EMTs, motioned for them to leave. "I'll be at the hospital in a few minutes." With that, she turned to Bowen. "I don't make a habit of rail-roading, and I won't be starting now."

His father made a sound of disgust. "You're a Mercer. Railroading and murder are your specialties."

Cullen groaned and stepped between them, but Leigh obviously wasn't going to have any part of him running interference for her. She moved to Cullen's side and met his father's glare head-on.

"Someone's been murdered," Leigh stated, her voice a whole lot calmer than she probably felt. "I need to do my job."

She started to move past Bowen, but he caught onto her arm. Leigh looked at Bowen's grip, her brown cop's eyes sliding back to his father's equally flat ones.

"You'll want to let go of me," she said. Again, with a calm voice, but there was some fire in her expression.

"I will, when you hear me out. You're not going to pin a murder on my son because Cullen didn't kill any-one." Bowen's hand slid off Leigh's arm. "But I can tell you who did."

Chapter 3

Leigh had intended to walk away from Bowen and his 24-7 bad attitude, but what the man said stopped her in her tracks.

"You know who killed Alexa?" Leigh demanded, her narrowed gaze drilling into Cullen's father.

Bowen huffed, maybe because of her tone, maybe because of her glare. Then again, Bowen never had a positive reaction to her so he was often huffing and glaring around her.

"You need help, Sheriff Mercer?" Rocky asked. The deputy had obviously come back in the house and was eyeing Bowen as if he was a threat. Maybe Rocky thought she'd need some of his "manly" muscle to handle this situation.

She didn't.

"No, thanks," Leigh assured Rocky. "I was just asking Mr. Brodie a few questions."

Rocky gave Bowen a hard stare which didn't surprise Leigh. Rocky was loyal to Jeb, which meant the Brodies were the enemy. Plenty of people in Dark River felt the same way.

"It's freezing," Bowen snarled. "Let's take this inside, and I can tell you all about the kind of woman Alexa was."

Leigh didn't want to go inside. She wanted Bowen to finish with this revelation so she could get to the hospital. Besides, what he had to say might not be a revelation at all but just some ploy to throw suspicion off Cullen. Still, Leigh couldn't totally blow off something that might help with the investigation, so with the tip of her head for Bowen to follow her, she stepped through the patio doors. Rocky didn't leave, but he did step to the side so there'd be room for Bowen and Cullen.

The guest room was quiet, but it wouldn't stay that way. It'd likely be only a matter of minutes before the ME and CSIs arrived. Too bad this second crime scene had already been compromised. Rosa, Cullen and now Bowen had already been in the room. Rosa was no longer there, but, of course, Cullen was right there next to Leigh when she turned to his father.

"Make this quick," Leigh told Bowen. "I'll do a formal interview with you in the morning, but for now I want to hear about who wanted Alexa dead."

"I don't know his name," Bowen explained. "But Alexa met with him."

When he didn't add more, Leigh made a circling motion with her index finger for him to continue. That gesture earned her another huff.

"I hired a PI to follow Alexa," Bowen blurted out, his

gaze shifting to Cullen. "She was threatening you, and I wanted to make sure she didn't do anything stupid."

Leigh volleyed glances at the two men, and she saw the surprise on Cullen's face, the steely resolve on Bowen's. Bowen clearly didn't think he'd done anything wrong by trying to micromanage his son's life.

"I wanted to make sure she didn't do anything stupid," Bowen repeated, the resolve also in his voice. "I didn't want Alexa to try to smear your name. Or worse. Have her try to do something violent. Hell hath no fury like a woman scorned," he added.

Leigh wasn't sure Alexa had actually been scorned, but she wanted to hear more. "I take it this PI found out something about her?"

Bowen nodded, kept his unapologetic eyes on his son. "Yesterday, Alexa had a meeting with a man in a café in Lubbock. The PI said the guy was carrying concealed, that he saw the bulge from a shoulder holster beneath his coat."

"Maybe he had a license to carry concealed," Leigh pointed out when Bowen paused again.

"Maybe," Bowen agreed. "But when the PI took a table near them, he heard Alexa and this man mention Cullen. Specifically, Alexa said she wanted the man to deal with Cullen."

"Deal with?" Leigh and Cullen repeated in unison.

"Yeah, and I don't have specific details of what she meant by that. The PI said that Alexa and this man quit talking when someone else took a table nearby, and they went outside to finish their conversation. The PI wasn't able to hear anything else they said."

Leigh looked at Cullen to see what his take on this was, but he only shook his head. "You believe Alexa was hiring this man to do something to me?" Cullen asked his father.

"Yes, I do. I think that's obvious. She wanted this guy to hurt or kill you."

Well, it wasn't obvious to Leigh. Possible, yes. But not absolute proof of the woman's guilt. Still, Alexa was dead so this could very well be connected.

"I'll want the name of your PI," Leigh insisted.

"Thought you would." Bowen extracted a business card from his coat pocket and handed it to her.

Leigh glanced at the card only to note the PI's name, Tyson Saylor. She'd be calling him very soon.

"This should be enough for you to back off Cullen," Bowen went on. "Alexa probably had her hired goon bring her here tonight. So she could witness him killing or hurting Cullen. Then, I'm guessing something went wrong. Maybe the goon wanted more money, and when Alexa wouldn't pony up, he killed her."

Obviously, Bowen had given this some thought, but it was still just a theory. One that might not have any proof to back it up.

"I'll investigate this—" Leigh assured him.

"And you'll lay off Cullen," Bowen interrupted. "Don't you think about arresting him because of what's gone on between our families."

Leigh heard the weariness in her own sigh. "At the moment I have no plans to arrest Cullen or anyone else for that matter because there's no clear-cut evidence to point to who did this."

Bowen released the breath he appeared to have been holding, and he gave a crisp nod before turning back to Cullen. "Call me if you need anything."

So, she'd apparently appeased Bowen enough for

him to get out of her face. Not Rocky though. Her deputy was aiming a questioning look at her. Probably because he believed there was indeed some *evidence to point to who did this*.

And Rocky no doubt thought the pointing should be at Cullen.

"Check with Dawn and make sure both crime scenes are secure," she instructed Rocky, not only to remind him that she was the sheriff and was therefore in charge but also because it was something that needed to be done. "I'm going to the hospital to get an update on Jamie." With some luck, she might even be able to question the ranch hand.

"I could go with you," Rocky suggested.

"I need you here," she insisted, and Leigh motioned for Cullen to follow her toward the front door. "Depending on how long I'm at the hospital or Jamie's condition, I might be able to get your statement in the next hour or two. I suspect you'll want a lawyer there for that."

Cullen had already opened his mouth, but he seemed to change his mind as to what he'd been about to say. "I'm going to the hospital, too. Jamie works for me," he added in a snap before she could protest.

She saw the weariness on his face. The worry. Not for his own situation but for Jamie. And that's why Leigh didn't tell him to stay put. Even though that would have been the smart thing to do. It'd keep Cullen out of her hair while she gathered evidence. Then again, it would keep him away from the crime scene, too. Cullen would no doubt be able to handle any flak that Rocky tried to dole out to him, but this would hopefully keep Rocky focused on his assigned duties so he wouldn't be able to take jabs at Cullen.

"You can ride in the cruiser with me," she offered, "but you'd have to find your own way back here once we're done at the hospital and my office."

Cullen didn't object to that, so Leigh reached for the knob on the front door. However, before she could open it, Vance called out to her.

"Wait up," the deputy said, hurrying through the great room toward them. "I think I found the murder weapon." He took out his phone, showing her a picture. "I didn't touch it. Figured I'd leave it where it is for the crime scene guys to collect."

It was a bronze horse statue of Lobo.

"Where'd you find that?" Cullen demanded.

Vance waited until he got a nod from Leigh before he answered. "In some bushes on the patio off the master bedroom. I'm guessing the killer went out through the patio doors and tossed it there."

That put a knot in Leigh's stomach. Because anyone wanting to pin this on Cullen would point out that the weapon had been in Cullen's bedroom and that Cullen would be the one to most likely have access to it.

But Cullen wasn't stupid.

Only a stupid killer would have tossed the murder weapon so that it could be easily found. That meant it probably didn't have anything on it that could be linked back to who'd used it to bash in Alexa's head. Then again, maybe the killer had tossed it out of panic. Or because he or she had been in a hurry. Either way, this was going to put some pressure on her to arrest Cullen.

"If the CSIs aren't here before the sleet starts, hold an umbrella over the statue so we don't lose any prints or trace," Leigh told Vance. "Once it's been bagged and tagged, mark it priority and have a courier take it to the lab."

Vance nodded, and as Rocky had done, he gave an uneasy glance at Cullen. "You heading somewhere?"

"Cullen and I are going to the hospital."

Vance's uneasiness seemed to go up a notch. "You okay with that?"

She heard the deputy's underlying concern. That maybe she was about to get in the cruiser with a killer. It didn't sting as much coming from Vance as it had with Rocky. That's because Vance didn't have the fierce loyalty to Jeb that Rocky did. Or the equally fierce hatred of the Brodies.

"I'm okay," she assured Vance. "Call me if you find anything else. I need to know how Alexa got here tonight. And don't forget to question the other ranch hands in the bunkhouse about Jamie. We need to find out how he ended up on the patio. Rocky can help you with that."

Leigh stepped outside and could have sworn the temp had dropped even more. Worse, she heard the first pings of ice start to hit against the porch. She hoped that Vance would get the statue protected in time and considered going back in to make sure that happened. But her best bet at getting to the truth wasn't a statue that had likely been planted to frame Cullen. Her best bet was to question Jamie.

"Before you say anything," Leigh told Cullen as they headed down the steps. "I'm going to Mirandize you."

Cullen didn't curse, but the look he shot her was colder than the sleet needling against her face.

"It's necessary," she explained. "And no, it doesn't mean I've changed my mind about your guilt. It's a way of covering my butt if you happen to say something—

anything—connected to this murder investigation that could seemingly incriminate you."

Cullen still hadn't cursed, but Leigh belted out some mental profanity. Because this was something she should have already done.

"Do you understand your rights?" she asked when she'd finished reciting the Miranda warning.

"I understand" was all he said. Or rather grumbled. And then he got in the passenger's seat of the cruiser.

Cullen was clearly insulted and riled. It was a good thing Leigh hadn't started to weave any fantasies about having a hot night with her former lover.

Except she had.

Mercy, she had. No matter how much she tried to push away this attraction, it just kept coming back.

"Do you have enemies?" she asked, pulling the cruiser out of the driveway. Leigh headed for the road that would take them into town. "Someone who'd want to cause trouble for you?"

"Of course," he readily admitted. "I'm a businessman, and I'm sure more than a few people thought they got the short end of the stick in a deal. But I don't know of anyone who'd set me up by murdering Alexa and bashing in the head of one of my ranch hands."

His voice and expression weren't so cold now. Oh, no. There was heat, and it wasn't from attraction. This was a storm of fury that Cullen was no doubt fighting to rein in. He looked formidable. And dangerous.

"Your father obviously hated Alexa," she pointed out.

"Yes, but Bowen didn't kill her," Cullen snapped before she could add anything else. "My father has bent the law too many times to count, but he wouldn't kill my ex-girlfriend in my bathroom and leave her body for me to find."

On the surface, she had to agree with Cullen about all of that. But maybe Alexa's murder hadn't been planned. Maybe it'd been an impulse kill. Ditto for the attack on Jamie. If so, that changed the rules. People didn't always make good decisions when panicked and trying to cover up a crime.

"Your father was at the party?" she asked. She mentally cursed again. This time when she tried to clear the sleet away with the windshield wipers, it left icy smears on the glass.

"He was." Cullen paused. "He left early. And no, he didn't seem upset or rattled. Maybe distracted," he added in a mumble. "Maybe because he knew he'd have to tell me about the PI he hired."

Maybe. That certainly had to be weighing on Bowen's mind. But it also gave the man a motive for murder. Cullen had no doubt come to the same conclusion.

"My advice," Cullen said a moment later, "have one of your deputies question my father. It'll go easier on both of you if you're not the one to do the interview."

Probably. But Leigh intended to do the questioning herself. When exactly that would happen though, she didn't know. Jamie came first, and then after she'd gotten everything she could from him, she'd need to contact the PI Bowen had hired. PIs often took pictures, and if he had, they might get an ID on the man Alexa had met in the café.

Because she had no choice, she turned on the wipers again and gave the windshield a spray of the cleaner that had a deicer in it. Her tires weren't shimmying on the road yet, but they soon would. Definitely not good because this was a narrow ranch road with deep ditches on each side.

Leigh saw the flash of lights to her left. But only a flash. She barely had time to process it when an SUV came barreling out from a cluster of trees.

And it slammed right into the cruiser.

Chapter 4

The collision happened fast. Too fast for Cullen to do anything to try to lessen the impact.

His shoulder and the side of his head rammed against the side airbag as it deployed. The seat belt snapped and caught, clamping like a vise over his chest and pinning him against the seat.

Probably with some help from the sleet, the cruiser went into a skid, and beside him, Leigh fought with the steering wheel. Trying to keep them on the road. She might have managed it, too, if the driver of the SUV hadn't come at them again. With the headlights on high beams, the SUV rammed them from behind, the front end of it colliding with the rear of the cruiser.

The impact slammed the cruiser headfirst into a tree.

There was the sound of metal tearing into the wood along with the swoosh of the front airbags when they punched into their faces. It knocked the breath out of Cullen for a couple of seconds, and the powder that'd surrounded the airbags flew into his eyes. Still, he forced himself to react, not to give in to the shock. Because he was certain of one thing.

Someone was trying to kill them.

The first impact could have possibly been an accident. Someone losing control as they came out of one of the trails. But the second collision had been intentional and with the purpose of causing them to crash into the tree. Which was exactly what'd happened.

Cullen glanced at Leigh to make sure she was conscious. She was, but she looked a little dazed. Still, she was already fumbling for her gun, which meant that she, too, had figured out that someone was using a vehicle to attack them.

The SUV came at them again.

This time the vehicle didn't just plow into them. Instead, the driver began to inch forward, sandwiching the cruiser between the SUV and the tree. Cullen had no idea if the front end of the SUV could actually crush the cruiser like an accordion, and he wasn't about to wait to find out.

Cullen batted away the airbag so he could take out his gun. It wasn't an easy task since there wasn't much room to move around. He finally managed it and soon saw that Leigh was still struggling to draw her own weapon.

"You need backup. I'm armed and stopping whoever's doing this," Cullen said, giving her a heads-up.

Leigh might have argued with him if she'd actually had her gun out and if this hadn't been a life-and-death situation where there hadn't been time to call for backup. Instead, Leigh just kept frantically shoving the airbag aside and battling to get her damaged door open while Cullen barreled out of the cruiser. He took aim at the windshield of the SUV, right where the driver would be.

Leigh finally got hold of her gun, and she must have given up on getting her door open because she climbed out through the passenger's side. The moment her feet landed on the ground, she lifted her body, and she pointed her gun at the SUV.

"I'm Sheriff Mercer," Leigh called out. "Stop or I'll fire."

Cullen wasn't surprised when the driver stopped. After all, the windshield probably wasn't bulletproof, and he or she had two guns aimed at him. Unfortunately, because of the high beams, the darkness and the heavily tinted windshield, Cullen couldn't see who was behind the wheel.

But it was almost certainly Alexa's killer.

That reminder had Cullen moving several steps closer, and he bracketed his right wrist with his left hand so his aim wouldn't be off.

On the other side of the cruiser, Leigh came forward, too, but she'd barely made it a step when the driver threw the SUV into Reverse and hit the accelerator. The tires fishtailed some, but he managed to keep control.

While he sped away.

Cursing, Cullen ran out onto the road, and he shot at the tires, hoping to disable the vehicle. He needed to see who was inside. Needed to see who was doing this so the snake could be put behind bars.

With her breath gusting and her gun still gripped in her hand, Leigh took aim at the SUV, too, but the driver had already disappeared around a curve. The road led back to the Triple R, but Cullen doubted that's where this clown was going. Not when there were many trails that the driver could use to turn. Trails that would lead back to the main road.

"I need to call this in," Leigh said in between those gusts of breath, and Cullen noticed that she was limping when she went back to the cruiser.

"Are you hurt?" he asked.

"I'm fine." It was the tone of someone who didn't want to be bothered with such questions.

Cullen didn't blame her for the attitude. Not with the adrenaline and anger pumping through them. But maybe she wouldn't put up a protest about being examined by an EMT or doctor.

Behind him, Cullen heard Leigh use the radio in the cruiser to call for backup and put out an all-points bulletin on the SUV. What she couldn't give the dispatcher was the info on the license plates. That's because they were missing, and Cullen figured that was by design. A way of making sure no one ID'd the vehicle or the driver.

Cullen stayed put on the road, and he listened and kept watch just in case the SUV returned for another round. He actually hoped that would happen, and then he could put some bullets through the windshield instead of the tires.

The wind had picked up considerably, and it was whipping the ice pellets through the air. The sleet stung his face, but he stayed put, and a few seconds later, Leigh joined him on his watch.

"Vance will be here in a couple of minutes," Leigh

relayed to him. "He'll look for the SUV along the way. We might get lucky," she added.

Might fell into the slim-to-none category. Unless the driver of the SUV was a complete idiot, that is. Because anyone would have been able to figure out that Leigh would have called for backup, and even if that backup had had to come from town, it wouldn't have taken long for help to arrive.

Leigh looked back at the mangled front end of the cruiser and muttered something under her breath that he didn't catch. Cullen caught the gist of it though.

"Yeah, this is connected to Alexa and Jamie," he said.

Leigh certainly didn't argue with him. "But was I the target, or were you?" she asked.

He looked at her, their gazes connecting, and in that moment it seemed as if all the bad blood between them vanished. Nearly being killed could do that. It could tear down the walls from the past and, well, connect you. Cullen certainly felt very connected to Leigh right now. Protective, too.

And guilty.

Because he could be the reason that she'd nearly just died. Cullen didn't know the specific motive of this killer. Not yet, anyway. But he soon would. He intended to give this plenty of thought and then go after the SOB who was responsible for this hellish night.

"I doubt the SUV will be back this way," Cullen said. The sleet was coming down harder now. "We should probably wait for Vance in the cruiser."

That would not only get them out of the bitter cold, it would also give him a chance to figure out just how badly Leigh was hurt. She was still limping as they

made their way back to the cruiser and slid into the back
seat. Cullen got in beside her to avoid the airbag debris
in the front and so he could examine Leigh. It was too
dark for him to see if there was any blood on her jeans,
but he used the flashlight on his phone.

Yep, there was blood all right.

"You cut your leg," he pointed out.

"More like a scrape," she corrected. "When the SUV
hit my door, it pushed against my knee."

Pushed wasn't the right word. More like *bashed*. But
he couldn't exactly blame her for downplaying her injury. Not when they had much bigger problems to deal
with. Still, he wanted her examined.

Leigh gave the back of the driver's seat a shove, but
Cullen thought the gesture was from frustration rather
than trying to create more legroom. Her frustration
seemed to go up a notch when her phone rang, and she
saw Jeb's name on the screen. She hit the decline button.

"Your father will press you to arrest me," Cullen
threw out there.

She didn't look at him but made a sound of agreement. "But this might convince him that you're not responsible for Alexa's death."

"Maybe. But he might just say I hired someone to
do this so I'd look innocent," Cullen pointed out. "After
all, the collision was mainly on your side of the vehicle.
You stood the greatest chance of being hurt."

Leigh made a quick sound of agreement to that, too,
which meant she'd likely already considered it. Then
she turned her head and stared at him. "You didn't do
this," she said, and then she paused. "Would your father have done it?"

Cullen tried not to be insulted that Leigh had just

asked if his father was a killer. A killer who wouldn't hesitate to murder his own son.

"Not with me in the cruiser. Bowen might be bull-headed and unable to let go of the past, but he wouldn't have put me at risk." Now Cullen was the one who paused. "But perhaps this goes back to the man Alexa met in that café. Maybe he was the one behind the wheel."

Leigh didn't get a chance to give an opinion on that because the approaching headlights grabbed their attention. With their guns ready, they got out of the cruiser, watching and waiting in case this was their attacker returning.

"It's Vance," she said, releasing a breath of what was almost certainly relief.

Cullen didn't relax just yet. He had no intention of standing down until he knew for sure there wasn't another threat. But this wasn't an SUV. It was a silver Ford truck, and it pulled to a stop directly in front of them.

"Are you okay?" the deputy asked the moment he got out. It was Vance all right, and while he'd drawn his gun, he didn't aim it at Leigh or Cullen.

"Fine," Leigh answered. "Any sign of the SUV that hit us?"

"None, and like you said, I made sure to look closely at the trails that lead off the road." Vance studied the cruiser and shook his head. "Man, that looks bad. You sure you're okay?"

"I'll live," she muttered. "No thanks to the driver of the SUV." She looked at Cullen. "You have a vehicle we can use? If not—"

"I have something," Cullen assured her. One that would hopefully handle better on the icy roads than her cruiser. Since there were more than two dozen cars, trucks and four-wheel drive vehicles at the ranch, there wouldn't be any trouble accessing one right away.

Leigh grabbed her purse from the cruiser, and they got in the truck with Vance to head back to the Triple R.

"I got the horse statue secured," Vance told Leigh as he drove. He opened his mouth, probably to continue to update his boss, but then the deputy cast a wary glance at Cullen.

"It's okay," Leigh assured Vance. "Keep going. Tell me what's happening at the ranch."

The deputy gave an uncertain nod but finally continued. "I put crime scene tape around the patio and on the front door of the house and marked the area where the shrub had been trampled. There's an umbrella over the spot in case there's a print we didn't see right off."

"Good. What about Dawn and Rocky?" Leigh asked.

"Dawn's still with the body, but I told Rocky to keep on working to get statements from the ranch hands. Oh, and the CSIs are on the way, but they're having to go slow because of the weather. The roads out of Lubbock are already pretty bad."

That meant it'd be hours, maybe even days, before the CSIs were done processing his house. Cullen could go to his dad's place, but he preferred to be closer in case something broke on the investigation. He'd use either the bunkhouse or else get a room at the inn in town.

"Once you're back at the ranch, call Rocky and have him ask the hands about the SUV," Leigh instructed. "It's dark blue, has heavily tinted windows and will have some front end damage. The license plates have been removed. I don't want the driver lying in wait at the Triple R."

Cullen sure as hell didn't want that, either, and he whipped out his phone to send a text to his top hand, Mack Cuevas. He told Mack to be on the lookout for the SUV and to assist Rocky and the other deputies with whatever needed to be done.

"I'll also need the CSIs to take a look at my cruiser," Leigh continued as they approached the ranch. "There'll be paint transfer from the SUV."

Yeah, there would be, which meant the driver would likely ditch the vehicle as soon as possible. Of course, there was always the possibility that the driver would leave traces of himself inside the SUV. Traces that the lab could use to ID him.

"Rosa mentioned that a lot of the guests were taking pictures at the party," Vance went on, pulling to a stop in the driveway in front of the house. "She thought they were posting them on social media. Might be worth having a look at them and any other pictures on the guests' phones. If you want, I'll do that first chance I get."

"Yes, do that," Leigh agreed.

Cullen went back over the night, something he was certain he'd be doing until Alexa's killer was caught, and he did indeed remember lots of picture-taking going on. However, he was pretty sure he would have remembered if anything wasn't as it should be.

"This way to the garage," Cullen told Leigh when they stepped from Vance's truck.

They started in that direction but had only made it a few steps when Leigh's phone rang again. Judging from the huff she made, she expected it to be her father again. But it wasn't.

"It's the hospital," Leigh muttered, hurrying to answer it. She didn't put the call on speaker, but Cullen had no trouble hearing what the caller said.

"Sheriff, this is Dr. Denton. I figured you'd want to know that Jamie Wylie has regained consciousness."

Leigh released another of those hard breaths. "Is he okay?"

The doctor didn't jump to answer that. "I haven't finished the exam, but I should know something soon. In the meantime, Jamie's insisting that he talk to Cullen and you right away. He says he needs to tell both of you about what went on with Alexa tonight."

Chapter 5

Leigh tried to ignore the adrenaline crash that was coursing through every inch of her body. Especially her head. She'd known it would happen, but she didn't have time to come down right now. She also didn't have time to process that someone had just tried to murder Cullen and her. She had to focus on talking to Jamie.

Because he might be able to ID a killer.

First though, Cullen and she had to get to the hospital, and that wasn't an easy task. As predicted, the roads were an icy mess and were giving even Cullen's huge truck some trouble. She felt the tires shimmy more than a couple of times, but Leigh consoled herself with the reminder that the road conditions might prevent the driver of that SUV from trying to come after them again. Or going after Jamie.

Leigh had beefed up security as best she could by arranging to have the hospital's lone security guard posted with Jamie. That wouldn't necessarily stop someone from coming in with guns blazing, but so far this particular killer hadn't used a gun. The bronze horse statue had been a weapon of opportunity. Maybe the SUV had, too, if the driver had stolen it. But if this guy got desperate to cover his tracks by eliminating Jamie, then there was no telling what he'd do. The security guard was armed, but she didn't know how he'd react in an actual crisis. There weren't many crisis tests at the Dark River Hospital.

There were other pieces of the investigation that she needed to put together, too. She had to get into Alexa's house and her workplace to see if the woman had left any clues as to who'd killed her. That meant Leigh would likely need warrants since she would have to access emails, phone records and such.

"Thinking?" Cullen asked, his question jarring her from her thoughts. "Or trying not to think?"

She considered that a moment. "Both, I guess. I need to go over the details of the investigation, but I'd rather not relive the SUV crashing into us." Leigh looked out the window, hoping that Cullen wouldn't see her shudder when she got a flash image of that crash.

"First time anyone's tried to kill you?" he asked.

"Yes." Leigh glanced at him. "You?"

"Second. A guy in a bar once drew a gun on me. He pulled the trigger, too, but it jammed."

He'd said it almost flippantly, as if it weren't a big deal, but the muscle that tightened in his jaw told her that it had indeed been big. Of course, she doubted anyone could ever get accustomed to having someone try to kill them.

Leigh motioned to the back waist of his pants. "Is that why you always carry a gun, even to a party? At least I'm guessing you had it at the party. Or maybe you holstered it afterward?"

The tightened jaw muscle relaxed into a quick smile. Not one of humor, either. "Always trying to get details that might or might not apply to the case. You're a cop to the bone, Leigh," he remarked.

"So many people would argue with that," she disagreed, and she wanted to kick herself for opening this particular can of worms.

"So many people would be wrong." Cullen smiled when she tossed him a scowl, and this time there was some humor in it. "No, I'm not saying that to get on your good side so you won't arrest me." He paused. "And yes, I always carry a weapon. Or two."

That last remark had a dangerous edge to it. Like the man himself. Leigh was attracted to that danger. To that edge. To the part of him that she thought might never fall into the "tame" category.

And that made her an idiot.

She needed an untamed, dangerous man about as much as she needed more criticism about her having the badge or living up to the lofty standards Jeb had set. Still, her body wasn't giving her a break when it came to Cullen. Hopefully though, once the adrenaline crash was done, her head would stay steady, and she would remember that he could complicate her life in the worst kind of way. There were people who were looking for a chance to oust her as sheriff, and those people would use Cullen as ammunition to get rid of her.

Leigh checked the hospital parking lot when Cullen pulled into it. He did the same, and she knew they were both looking for that SUV. Or any signs they were about to be attacked again. But the parking lot was practically empty. She considered that to be a small blessing but continued to keep watch as he parked right by the ER doors.

Another small blessing was the police department was just up the street. Less than two blocks away. Three of her eight deputies were already tied up at the Triple R, but that left one, Kerry Yancy, on duty to man the police station and back up the security guard on Jamie. Still, Kerry could respond in just a couple of minutes if she needed help, and if things went from bad to worse, Leigh could call in the day-shift deputies. Most of them lived just a few miles from town.

Ducking their heads against the sleet and cold, Cullen and she hurried into the hospital, heading straight to the room where she saw the security guard. "Jamie's in there," the guard said.

Leigh knew him, of course. He was Harry Harbin, and when he'd been in his prime, he'd been one of her father's deputies. That explained the cool look he aimed at Cullen. And the dismissive one he gave her. She made a mental note to have Vance schedule a reserve deputy to do security detail. Guarding Jamie was critical, and Leigh didn't want any misplaced righteousness playing into this.

She knocked once on the door but didn't wait for a response before she entered, and she immediately spotted Jamie in the bed. He was indeed conscious, with his gaze zooming straight to Cullen and her.

"Thank you for coming," Jamie muttered, his voice hoarse and weak. He was hooked up to some machines and an IV.

Dr. Denton nodded a greeting to them. So did the nurse, Amber Murdock. Amber's silent greeting, however, warmed up considerably when her attention shifted to Cullen. Leigh didn't know if Amber had been one of Cullen's bedmates or if Amber was just hoping to become one. Women in Dark River generally fell into one of those two categories.

Sadly, Leigh was both.

Well, a confirmed former lover, whose body wanted the *former* label to switch to *current*. She was going to do everything in her power to disappoint her body about that.

"Is it true?" Jamie asked right off. "Is Alexa really dead?"

Leigh glanced at the doctor and the nurse, and it only took her one look to figure out the news of Alexa's death had come from Amber.

"It's true," Leigh verified. No need to hold back on the news since it was obviously already the talk of the town, and the hospital.

Tears filled Jamie's eyes. "Dead," he repeated. "She's really dead."

Leigh gauged his reaction. His grief and shock seemed genuine enough, but for all she knew Jamie had been the one to kill Alexa. Of course, that didn't explain how Jamie had then gotten hurt, and that's why she had plenty of questions lined up for him. Apparently though, Jamie had some for her as well.

"Who killed Alexa?" Jamie demanded. "How did she die?"

"I don't know who killed her," Leigh admitted. "I'm hoping you can help with that."

Jamie started to answer, but then he shifted his attention to the doctor. "Jamie insists on talking to the two of you alone," Dr. Denton explained, and clearly the doctor wasn't happy about that. "We have more tests that need to be done, and I don't want him getting agitated or upset."

Leigh didn't fault the doctor for wanting to do what was best for his patient. But she had a job to do as well. "I think Jamie will be less agitated and upset if I'm able to arrest the person who hurt him and killed Alexa. This chat is important," she added, purposely using *chat* instead of *interview*.

On a heavy breath and with a ton of obvious reluctance, Dr. Denton nodded, and with the tip of his head, he motioned for Amber to follow him. "Keep the visit short," the doctor insisted as he left with Amber.

Leigh shut the door and went closer to the bed. She didn't bother with greetings or niceties since Jamie did indeed look exhausted, and she figured she wouldn't have much time with him. "Who attacked you?"

"I don't know," Jamie muttered. Groaning softly, he took a moment to gather his breath. "I heard footsteps, but before I could see who it was, someone bashed me on the side of the head."

Leigh wanted to curse. Cullen probably did, too. It would have put a quick end to the investigation if Jamie had been able to give them a name. And he still might be able to do that. Sometimes witnesses and victims remembered plenty of details once they were questioned, and questioning him was exactly what Leigh planned to do.

"How did Alexa die?" Jamie pressed.

"Blunt force trauma," Leigh explained. "I think once the ME has had a chance to examine her that he'll say she had a wound similar to yours. Hers was just a lot worse."

Jamie's tears returned. "I brought Alexa to the Triple R," he blurted out and looked at Cullen. "I'm so sorry. I shouldn't have done it."

"Why did you?" Cullen asked. His voice was steady, not a trace of judgment in it, but Leigh figured he wasn't pleased about one of his hands bringing his ex to a party at the ranch.

Jamie groaned, squeezed his eyes shut a moment, and he eased his head back onto the pillow. Tears continued to slide down his cheeks. "She called me right about the time the party was starting, around seven, I guess, and said she was in town and that she wanted to know if I'd give her a ride out to the ranch. She said her car was acting up and that she didn't want to risk driving it on the country road."

"You came and got her?" Leigh pressed when Jamie didn't continue.

He groaned again, nodded. "She talked me into it. I swear, I didn't know she was gonna be killed."

Cullen came closer and sat on the edge of the bed. "How'd Alexa talk you into driving her?"

Jamie's eyes met Cullen's, and a look passed between them. Leigh supposed it was a guys' understanding thing, but she figured she got it, too.

"Alexa sweet-talked you," Leigh concluded, and it had likely involved some flirting. Maybe even the hint that she'd be interested in being with Jamie in a romantic or sexual kind of way.

"At first I told her no," Jamie went on, "that I didn't think it was a good idea for her to crash the party, but she said she wouldn't be crashing. She said she just needed a quick word with you, that she wanted you to know that she was ready to move on with her life and that she wouldn't be bothering you anymore. She insisted she wouldn't make a big scene or anything and that her chat with Cullen would be private."

"And you didn't think the party would be a bad place for her to do that?" Leigh questioned.

"Yeah, I did," Jamie readily agreed. "That's why I tried to convince her to wait, to try to see Cullen another time, but she…well, she convinced me to go get her and drive her there."

Leigh reminded herself that Jamie was very young. And if Alexa was anything like her reputation, Jamie would have been putty in her hands.

"So, you picked her up and drove her to the Triple R," Leigh summed up. "What happened next?"

His forehead bunched up. "I guess it must have been about eight o'clock by then. Some guests were still arriving so she had me drop her off at the side of the house because she said she was going to slip in and have someone on the kitchen staff go and get Cullen for her. That way, she wouldn't have to go in where the party was going on." Jamie shook his head, obviously disgusted with himself. "I know all of this sounds stupid, and I shouldn't have let Alexa talk me into taking her there."

Agreed. But Leigh had to wonder if the woman had told Jamie the truth. Had she truly just wanted to talk to Cullen? Or was there a lot more to it than that? Leigh was betting it was the latter.

"You dropped Alexa off at the side of the house where you were attacked?" Cullen asked.

Jamie nodded. "The driveway is only a couple of yards behind the trees and shrubs around the patio."

It was, and Alexa would no doubt have known the particular layout. Heck, she'd maybe even stayed in that very guest room at one time or another. At least she could have stayed there when she wasn't sharing Cullen's bed, but Leigh had heard that Alexa had started visiting the Triple R before Cullen and she had gotten involved. That was definitely something Leigh needed to question Cullen about, but according to the rumor mill, Austin's fiancée, Kali, and Alexa were close friends, and Kali had brought Alexa there often.

When Jamie reached and then fumbled for the cup of water on the table next to the bed, Cullen helped him with it. Jamie took a small sip and swallowed hard before he continued.

"After I dropped off Alexa, she told me to wait for her, that she'd only be in the house about ten minutes or so and then I could drive her back into town. She was going to get a room at the inn until she could have someone take a look at her car. She said she wouldn't be driving back to her place tonight because of the bad weather moving in."

So, Alexa hadn't planned on staying at the ranch that night. Ten minutes. Not much time for a talk to try to reassure Cullen that she wasn't going to give him any more trouble.

"Were the patio doors locked?" Leigh asked Jamie.

"No." But then Jamie stopped and shook his head. "Maybe. I didn't watch when Alexa was opening the doors so she might have had a key."

Or she could have picked the lock since Cullen had already told her that he'd changed the locks after he'd ended things with Alexa. But there was a third possibility. Someone had left the doors unlocked for Alexa.

Maybe the killer. Maybe someone else she'd sweet-talked on the catering crew or the household staff. The place was so big that there was no telling how long that door had been unsecured.

"Alexa went inside the house, but she didn't come out after ten minutes," Jamie went on. "I waited, but then I started to get worried about her." His mouth trembled, more tears came, and he kept his attention pinned to Cullen. "I thought she might be getting in a row with you. I thought you two might be arguing." His voice cracked. "But now I know she was dead."

Leigh didn't have to guess that Jamie was feeling plenty guilty about that, and he began to sob. It didn't look as if it was going to be a short cry, either. Still, she had to press him on another point.

"How long did you wait outside before you were hit over the head?" Leigh asked.

"I don't know," he answered through the sob. "Maybe twenty minutes or a half hour."

Not much time for someone to kill Alexa and then go outside to attack Jamie. And that led Leigh to another problem. How had the killer known that Jamie was on the patio waiting for Alexa?

"And you're sure you didn't see who hit you?" Cullen pushed.

Jamie shook his head again. "No. I heard the footsteps, like I said, but that was it."

"Heavy or light footsteps?" Cullen continued. "Fast or slow?"

Since Leigh had been about to ask Jamie variations of those questions, she didn't object.

Jamie's forehead bunched up again. "Fast and heavy. Like someone was running at me."

So, the killer was in a hurry to take care of Jamie. Probably because he or she hadn't wanted to be seen. That made sense. After all, Jamie was young and fit and could have probably fended off a physical attack had he gotten the chance.

But why kill Jamie at all?

Leigh figured that went back to Alexa, too. It was possible the killer thought she'd told Jamie the real reason she'd come to the house. And Leigh didn't believe that real reason was to see Cullen. Not solely, anyway. This might indeed go back to the man she'd met with in the café. Maybe she hadn't trusted him to do the job if she'd actually hired him to hurt Cullen? Or maybe she'd gone there to pay him.

"My head hurts real bad now," Jamie said. "You think you could ask the doctor to give me some meds?"

"Sure," Leigh readily agreed. "I'll be back later today to check on you." And to see if he remembered anything else. "In the meantime, there'll be a guard on your door so you'll be safe."

Jamie gave an almost absent nod to that along with wincing from the pain. She gave his hand a gentle squeeze and headed for the door.

"If you need anything, just let me know," Cullen assured Jamie, and he walked out with Leigh.

"No one other than medical staff gets near Jamie," Leigh reminded the guard.

When she only got a grunt of acknowledgment from Harry, she repeated it and stared at him until he verbally answered. "Yes, I got that."

"I can bring out a couple of my other ranch hands to do security," Cullen suggested. Clearly, he wasn't pleased with Harry's attitude, either.

"I'll ask Vance to arrange for a reserve deputy," she said, taking out her phone.

While Leigh fired off the text, she glanced around the ER to locate the doctor. There was no sign of him, but Amber was obviously waiting for them because she moved away from the reception desk and made a bee-line toward them.

"Jamie says he's in pain and needs meds," Leigh immediately relayed.

Amber nodded. "Dr. Denton will be right back and I can let him know." She shifted her attention to Cullen. "We just got a call from the Department of Transportation. The roads in and out of town are closed."

At the exact moment Amber was relaying that info, Leigh got a text giving her the same alert. She hadn't figured she'd actually make it home for hours anyway, but with the sleet projected to continue until midmorning, there was no telling when the roads would be clear enough to drive.

"I knew you'd be stuck," Amber went on, still talking to Cullen, "so I just called the inn, and they don't have any rooms."

Leigh wasn't actually surprised by that. The inn only had four guest rooms, and anyone who'd gotten stuck because of the weather would have already snapped those up.

"I could probably find you someplace to stay here in the hospital," Amber added to Cullen.

Leigh didn't smirk, but it was obvious that Amber's *interest* in him had gotten him that particular offer. An offer that Cullen apparently wasn't going to accept.

"Thanks," he said, "but Leigh and I are going to the police station."

She was indeed heading there as planned. Not only could she get started on work, but if she had to crash for a couple of hours, there was a cot and a sofa in the break room. Though Leigh hadn't counted on sharing such cramped quarters with Cullen. But she rethought that. Neither of them would likely get any sleep anyway, and this way she could go ahead and take his official statement.

"I need to bag the clothes you're wearing," Leigh said to him as they walked away from Amber.

Cullen's mouth quivered a little. "I'm guessing it's to cover all bases and not because you want me to strip down."

She frowned. Or rather tried to do that. Leigh knew she didn't quite pull it off. "Yes, to cover the bases. I can find something at the police station for you to wear."

"I've got a change of clothes in my truck. I keep a duffel bag behind the seat."

Now she did frown. "For sleepovers with admirers like Amber," Leigh muttered, cursing herself the moment the words were out of her mouth. She so didn't need to be bringing up Cullen's sexual conquests.

"Well, actually, it has more to do with horses than admirers." That sounded very tongue-in-cheek, and he let it linger a couple of moments before he added, "I've learned the hard way to have extra clothes because I often go out to other ranches to look at horses I'm considering buying. I can get pretty sweaty, and I don't like driving back when I smell worse than the livestock."

That explanation made her silently curse herself even more. Because it gave her a giddy little punch of relief to know that he didn't make a habit of sleepovers. Then again, he could, and probably did, simply have his lovers come to his place.

Once they were outside, Leigh considered just walking to the office, but the arctic blast of air had her climbing inside Cullen's truck when he opened the door for her. He started the engine and took the time for it to warm up, which thankfully wasn't long. He pulled out of the very slippery parking lot just as Leigh's phone rang.

"It's Vance," she relayed to Cullen, and she took the call, putting it on speaker. "Guess you got the alert about the roads being closed?" she asked Vance.

"I did, and Rosa was going to call Cullen to ask if it was okay if we all stayed the night here."

"Tell Rosa that's fine," Cullen spoke up.

"Thanks, I'll tell her," Vance replied. Then, he paused. "Uh, I questioned some of the ranch hands, and I might have something."

Leigh understood the subtext in Vance's tone. She might not want Cullen to hear the *something*. But Leigh figured anything that came out of the investigation would soon make it back to Cullen's ears anyway.

"What do you have?" Leigh asked Vance.

She heard Vance take a deep breath before he answered. "Wilmer Smalley is one of the ranch hands here, and he seems reliable enough."

"He is," Cullen assured them. "Did Wilmer see someone?"

"He did," Vance verified. "He said that he spotted two people outside the house when the party was going on. One was at the back of the house, right about where Cullen's bedroom is."

"No one should have been out there," Cullen provided before Leigh could ask him. "The catering staff would have come in through the kitchen entrance."

"Yeah, that's what Rosa said, too," Vance verified. "But he saw a man there. At least he's pretty sure it was a man, wearing a coat. He didn't get a good look at him."

"Height? Weight?" Leigh pushed.

"Wilmer couldn't say. He got just a glimpse of him before the person ducked out of sight. He said he didn't think anything of it at the time, that he figured Cullen had maybe stepped out for some reason. But he's obviously giving it plenty of thought right now."

Yes, he would be. But it helped that Wilmer hadn't immediately thought it was Cullen outside the bedroom. Even with just a glimpse, the hand should have known if it was the big boss.

"So far no one on the kitchen staff is owning up to being near Cullen's room," Vance went on. "And the kitchen entrance isn't near Cullen's room or the patio where Jamie was attacked." He paused again. "But Wilmer did see someone there."

Leigh jumped right on that. "Someone on the patio?"

"Yeah," Vance repeated. "And this time, Wilmer got a decent look at the guy's face. He says it was Cullen's good friend Austin."

"Austin?" Cullen said, the shock in his voice and on his face.

"Wilmer said he was positive that's who it was," Vance added.

Leigh immediately looked at Cullen. "Any idea

what Austin would be doing out there on that particular patio?"

"None." Cullen pulled the truck to a stop in front of the police department and took out his phone. "But I'm about to find out."

Chapter 6

Cullen figured there wasn't enough caffeine in the entire state of Texas to get rid of the fog in his head. Or the headache that'd been throbbing at his temples for the past six hours. Still, he tried, and downed his umpteenth cup of coffee.

Leigh was drinking a Coke, her beverage of choice to keep her alert, but at the moment she didn't seem to be faring any better than he was. He saw her eyes droop more than once while she sat at her desk and typed away on her computer or sent texts to her deputies.

Apparently, the catnap she'd taken around 7:00 a.m. had been enough to at least keep her going, and she appeared to actually be getting work done. That included taking his official statement.

Cullen had managed some, too, in the chair next to her desk and while using a laptop that Leigh had lent him, but work was similar to coffee and his own catnap. No amount of either was going to block the images of Alexa's dead body.

Or the fact that Austin still hadn't returned his call.

Cullen had attempted the first call right after learning that Austin had been on the patio the night of the party. Something that Austin definitely hadn't mentioned in their earlier conversation. Cullen had tried three more times to get in touch with Austin, but each had gone straight to voice mail. He left another voice mail on Austin's phone at work.

It was possible the winter storm had caused some outages. Equally possible that Austin had just turned off his phone for the night and was now sleeping in. But Cullen needed to talk to his friend. So did Leigh. She'd made her own attempts to contact him, and Cullen knew those attempts would continue until she could have a conversation with him.

An official one.

Cullen didn't believe that Austin was a person of interest in Leigh's investigation, but he could tell from the terse voice mail messages she left for Austin that she suspected the man was guilty of something. Maybe the something was simply going out for a smoke. However, if Austin had used the patio for that, why hadn't he just said so? Cullen didn't know, but he just couldn't see how this connected to what had happened to Alexa and Jamie. Austin could be reckless and cocky, but he wasn't a killer.

And Cullen hoped he continued to feel that way after he heard Austin's explanation.

He doubted Leigh's deputies would give Austin the benefit of the doubt when it came to innocence or guilt.

Neither would plenty of others in Dark River. Folks would want someone arrested for Alexa's murder if for no other reason than so they could feel safe in their own homes. Austin wasn't local, and worse, he had the disadvantage of being Cullen's friend. The pressure to drag Austin in and hammer away at him would grow. Well, it would once the deputies and anybody else actually managed to get into Leigh's office.

Right now, Leigh and he had the entire building to themselves since she'd sent the night deputy, Kerry Yancy, home several hours earlier. Kerry lived in an apartment just up the street so he hadn't had to drive to get there. Good thing, too, because the street glistened with ice in the morning sun, and it was too dangerous to be out driving. It would no doubt keep away any visitors—including Austin. But judging from the messages Leigh had left for Austin, she wanted him to do a phone interview and then another one with him in person as soon as the roads were clear enough for that to happen.

Leigh stood, stretched and motioned toward the break room, a location that Cullen had gotten very familiar with since it was where the coffee maker was located. "I'm going to grab a shower."

Cullen had already made use of the shower in the break room's bathroom when he'd changed into his jeans and work shirt. Thankfully, he'd had some toiletries in the bag, too, and had even managed to brush his teeth.

"There's stuff in the fridge if you want to nuke something for breakfast," Leigh added, yawning.

Her eyes met his, something that she'd been careful not to do throughout the hours they'd spent in her office. It was as if *out of sight, out of mind* was the way to go.

It wasn't. And she no doubt got a full jolting reminder of that when her gaze collided with his.

She groaned, then sighed and shook her head. "I can't get involved with you," she muttered. But it sounded to Cullen as if she was trying to convince herself.

"So you've said." He let that hang in the air, and it kept hanging until Leigh mumbled something he didn't catch and walked away.

He followed her to the break room to get another refill on the coffee, and he settled down on the sofa to try to get in touch with Austin again. When he had no luck reaching him, Cullen checked the time. It was barely ten in the morning, but he was tired of waiting for Austin to return his calls so he tried Kali and cursed when she didn't answer, either.

Cullen remembered Austin saying that Kali was spending the night with her folks, but he didn't have their number so he moved on to the next call he had to make. To Mack, his ranch hand. The ever-reliable Mack answered on the first ring.

"How are things there?" Cullen asked.

"Tense," Mack said after a short pause. "The hands are nervous because the deputies have questioned them."

Cullen wished he could tell them that wouldn't continue, but it would. Each and every one of them would have to make a statement. Especially Wilmer. "Did any of the others see Austin outside during the party?"

"No. And nobody saw the other man Wilmer described, the one in the coat who he got a glimpse of by your bedroom. I'm guessing it was someone at the party who stepped out?"

"Maybe. But there were a lot of vehicles coming and

going, and he could have parked somewhere and walked to that spot." He decided to go ahead and lay it out for Mack. "The guy in the coat could have been the one who killed Alexa."

"Yeah," Mack said after some thought. The word *tense* applied to him, too. Cullen could hear it in his voice.

"How's Jamie?" Mack asked.

"He's doing all right." Mostly, anyway. "He texted me after they finished running tests on him. He's got a concussion but the doctor says the signs are good that he'll make a full recovery." Dr. Denton had confirmed that when he'd called Leigh earlier.

"He's lucky," Mack concluded, and Cullen had to agree.

It'd taken nearly two dozen stitches to sew up the wound, but it could have been so much worse. If Rocky hadn't found him on the patio, Jamie might have frozen to death.

"I don't know how long it'll be before I can get back to the ranch," Cullen continued. "But keep an eye on things. And if you hear anything about the investigation, let me know."

"I can let you know that Rocky believes you're guilty," Mack readily admitted.

That came as no surprise whatsoever to Cullen. And Rocky wouldn't be the only one who thought he'd killed his ex-girlfriend. That was why it was important to Cullen that the snake who'd killed Alexa be caught. He didn't give a rat what people thought of him, but this could spill back on Leigh if enough gossips thought she wasn't doing her job by not arresting him.

Cullen ended the call with Mack and sent a text to

Rosa to check and see how she was doing. He also made a mental note to give her a huge bonus for everything she was having to deal with right now. When he got a quick answer that she was okay, Cullen frowned and wished he had another text or call so he wouldn't keep thinking about Leigh.

Specifically, about a naked Leigh in the shower.

Well, at least the thought of her managed to clear out some of the cobwebs from his head. The thoughts of joining her, naked, cleared out a whole bunch more. Over the years he'd never forgotten her, but being around her like this had a way of reminding him that forgetting her was impossible.

He finally heard her turn off the water in the shower, and Cullen hoped that would quell any notion of him going in there. It didn't. Because he started to think about her dressing. Leigh had had an amazing body as a teenager, but he was betting she'd gotten even more amazing over the years.

Cullen was certain he looked guilty, and aroused, by the time Leigh came out of the bathroom. But she didn't notice, thank goodness, because she had her attention pinned to her phone.

"I got the search warrant for Alexa's home and office," she said, still focusing on the phone screen. "I'll be going through her emails, phone records, et cetera. Is there anything you'd like to tell me before I look at them?"

Cullen didn't answer right away, and he did that on purpose. He waited for Leigh to lift her gaze and look at him. "I hadn't been in touch with Alexa in months, but it's possible she kept some old emails or texts from me," he explained. "If so, there won't be any threats."

"Nothing that can be construed as a threat?" she pressed.

He gave a weary smile and went to her. "No. I don't make a habit of pouring out my heart—or my temper—in emails or texts."

She met him eye to eye. "Did you pour them out verbally?"

"Not threats. Promises," he clarified, causing her to frown.

"Promises," she repeated. "Spoken like a true bad boy."

"I'm not a boy," Cullen stated. It was stupid, but he wanted to prove that to her. Prove it in an equally stupid way. And he did that by leaning in and brushing his mouth over hers.

It was too light of a touch to qualify as a kiss, but it sure as hell packed a wallop. He could have sworn that he felt it in every inch of his body.

He pulled back, gauging her reaction, and didn't think he was wrong in that she'd felt it, too. There was plenty of heat in her eyes, and it wasn't just anger that he'd done such a stupid thing.

She smelled good. Damn good. And her scent didn't have anything to do with the soap. No. This was her own underlying scent that added an extra kick to the effects of the kiss that hadn't been a real kiss.

"Leigh?" someone called out from the front of the building.

She backed away from Cullen as if he'd scalded her, and she groaned. Because it was her father's voice.

"Leigh?" Jeb called out again, and Cullen heard the man's footsteps heading their way.

Cullen didn't move, but Leigh sure as heck did. She

put several feet of space between them and turned to face her father head-on when Jeb stepped through the open door. Cullen faced him, too, and he saw the instant sweep of Jeb's gaze. From Leigh to Cullen. Unless Jeb was an idiot, then he was no doubt picking up on the heated vibes in the room.

Cullen didn't see Jeb often, which he was sure both of them considered a good thing, and it'd been several years since he'd laid eyes on him. It seemed to Cullen that Jeb had aged considerably during that time. He looked older than his sixtysomething years, and being out in the cold hadn't helped his appearance. His face was chapped and red. His lips, brittle and cracked.

"The roads are closed. You shouldn't have come," Leigh insisted.

Cullen had to hand it to her. Her voice was solid, and she never once dodged her father's intense gaze.

"The county crews salted the roads about an hour ago so they should be opening back up soon. I used my big truck so I could come and check on you." Jeb paused. "I talked to Rocky, and he told me that Cullen and you had spent the night here."

Leigh nodded. "We were at the hospital when the roads were closed so we came here."

Jeb nodded, too, but it was obvious he was processing that. Along with likely trying to decide if his daughter had had sex with a man he considered a suspect.

"How's Jamie?" Jeb asked, walking past them and going to the coffeepot. He poured himself a cup and sipped while continuing to watch them.

"He's better," Leigh said just as Cullen answered, "Fine." It was Leigh who added, "But he wasn't able to ID the person who attacked him."

With just a flick of his gaze to Cullen, Jeb let her know that he was looking at the person he thought had done it. "Rocky said you'd had all the Triple R hands questioned, and—"

"I'm running the investigation by the book," Leigh interrupted. "It's all under control." Which was no doubt her way of saying her father should butt out.

Jeb didn't.

"If you were by the book," Jeb stated, his jaw tight and set, "we wouldn't be having this conversation in front of the man who should be on your suspect list."

"I didn't start this conversation," Leigh snapped. "You did when you came in here and started slinging around accusations and giving me *advice* that I don't need or want."

There was some serious temper in her tone, but it didn't last. Cullen could see that she reined herself right in. Probably because she'd had a lot of experience doing that over the years.

"Everything's under control," she repeated, much calmer this time.

She had a staring match with Jeb that lasted several long moments before Jeb huffed. "I'm worried about you," Jeb finally said, and he'd reined in most of his own temper as well. *Most*. "Someone tried to kill you."

"Someone tried to kill *us*," Leigh corrected, and she hiked her thumb toward Cullen. "We don't know which of us was the target."

Jeb opened his mouth but then closed it. He nodded, conceding that she had a point, and he downed a good bit of his coffee like medicine.

"I'm going across the street to the diner to see if Minnie needs anything," Jeb said.

Minnie Orr was the owner of the diner and someone that most folks classified as Jeb's *friend*. They were
probably lovers and likely had been for years.

"Give Minnie my best," Leigh said, and she walked
out of the break room, heading back in the direction
of her office.

Jeb didn't follow her. Neither did Cullen, and he suspected that her father had a whole lot left to say to him.
And he was right.

"You need to keep away from her," Jeb warned him,
his voice a growling whisper. "Leigh doesn't need your
kind of *help*."

"She apparently doesn't need yours, either," Cullen
threw back at him, and he didn't whisper. No way was
he going to cover up for Jeb Mercer taking a dig at him.

Jeb flinched, finished off his coffee and slapped the
cup on the table. "If you killed Alexa, I'll make sure
you end up behind bars."

Cullen looked him straight in the eyes. He wasn't a
cop, never had been, but he knew how to stare someone down. "Same goes for you."

Now Jeb did more than flinch. His eyes widened.
"What the hell are you talking about?"

"You were a smart cop so follow the dots," Cullen
spat out. "Someone killed my ex in my home. Someone
who might have wanted to cause trouble for me. When
I come up with possibilities of who'd want to cause that
kind of trouble for me or my family, your name's always
at the top of the list."

Oh, Jeb's temper returned. He aimed his index finger
at Cullen, and the man's hand was shaking. "You—"

But that was all Jeb managed to say before his face
went pasty white, and he staggered back a step. Since

Jeb looked ready to pass out, Cullen hurried to him and caught onto his arm.

"I'm all right," Jeb insisted, and he tried to bat Cullen's hand away, but he held on. Jeb dragged in several short breaths, wincing with each one. "You don't say a word about this to Leigh, understand?"

Cullen ignored that and went with a question of his own. "Are you sick?"

"No. I'm just a little light-headed. I need to get something to eat at the diner." Jeb finally managed to get out of Cullen's grip, and he stepped back, making eye contact with him. "Not a word about this to Leigh," he repeated.

Cullen had no intention of agreeing to that, but if Jeb was truly sick, and Cullen thought he was, then Leigh would figure it out soon enough. An illness would explain though why Jeb had decided to retire while his approval ratings had still been sky-high. Of course, Jeb hadn't hinted at any health problems, only that he was ready to turn in his badge and take some time off to pursue the search for his missing son.

"I'm not going to hurt Leigh," Cullen told him while he had the man's attention. "I care for her. I've always cared for her, and I believe we would have ended up together had it not been for Bowen and you. And for me," Cullen added. "I was young and stupid and didn't stand up to the two of you back then. But I sure as hell will stand up now."

Jeb continued to stare at him for what felt like an eternity, but the man finally nodded, turned and walked out. Cullen stood there, watching him go, and wondering what the hell was going on.

Cullen took his time going to Leigh's office just in

case she wanted to have a private word with her dad. Apparently though, she hadn't, because Jeb had already left and Leigh was on the phone.

"Rocky, I don't want you leaking any more info about the investigation," she snapped. She glanced up at Cullen, who stopped in the doorway, but she continued her conversation. Or rather the dressing-down of her deputy. "Yes, leaking details to my father or anyone else. Any info that needs to be doled out will come through me. Got that?"

Cullen couldn't hear how the deputy responded, but he doubted Rocky would like having Leigh go at him like that. But Rocky deserved it. It showed disrespect, going behind her back by talking to Jeb.

Leigh stabbed the end call button and shoved her phone back in her pocket. She groaned softly, pushed some wisps of hair from her face.

"How much grief did Jeb give you after I left?" she asked.

"I gave him grief right back," Cullen settled for saying. He went closer and tapped her badge. "Do you wear that because of Jeb or in spite of him?"

Leigh shook her head, and he thought she might be annoyed with the shift in conversation. Or maybe she was just annoyed. Period. She certainly had a right to be.

"I've wanted to be a cop for as long as I can remember. Not a cop like my dad," she emphasized. "I always disapproved of punishing enemies or playing favorites when it came to justice." Leigh stopped, gave a hollow laugh. "Which is exactly what Jeb thinks I'm doing now."

Cullen studied her a moment. "No, you're not doing

that. If the evidence had pointed to me killing Alexa, I'd be in a holding cell right now."

She studied him, too. Then nodded. "You would be. The badge means something to me, and if I'd been Jeb's son instead of his daughter, he would have given me his blessing about becoming sheriff. And he'd put a stop to Rocky undermining me every chance he gets." Leigh paused. "But I'm not Jeb's son."

She didn't sound bitter about that. Just resigned. And in that moment Cullen despised Jeb even more than he already had. Damn the man and his backward way of thinking. Damn him, too, for hiding whatever health problems he had from Leigh and trying to make Cullen part of that secret.

"You were elected sheriff," Cullen reminded her.

"Barely," she muttered and then quickly waved that off.

Cullen didn't wave it off though. He took hold of her chin, lifting it so their gazes met. "You were elected sheriff," he repeated. "And what you said to Jeb wasn't lip service. You *are* handling this investigation."

She turned away from him. "If I fail at this, if I don't get reelected, I'll have to move. Dark River's my home, but I'll have to move so I can get another job in law enforcement. I couldn't just go back to being a deputy. Plus, whoever beats me in the next election wouldn't want to keep me around anyway."

Cullen understood the "home" roots. He had them. Ironic, since his life was often calmer and easier when he wasn't in Dark River. It would probably be the same for Leigh, but she was as grounded here as he was.

"We have more in common than you think," he reminded her. "That's why we became lovers in the first place."

She looked back at him, the corner of her mouth lifting into a smile. "That was hormones along with the thrill of being star-crossed lovers." Leigh made air quotes for "thrill."

No way could he pretend that the heat hadn't played into her being in his bed that night. But there was more, and Cullen was certain he wasn't the only one who'd felt it. He would have reminded her of that *more*, too, but the phone on her desk rang, and the moment was lost.

Leigh hit the answer button. The speaker function, too. "Sheriff Mercer," she said.

"Sheriff Mercer," the man repeated. "I'm Tyson Saylor."

It took Cullen a couple of seconds to remember that Saylor was the PI his father had hired to follow Alexa.

"Thank you for getting back to me," Leigh told him. "I have some questions for you."

"Well, let's hope I have the right answers," Saylor replied. "In fact, I believe I have something that's going to help with your investigation."

Chapter 7

Leigh didn't let her hopes soar, but she truly hoped that Saylor was right and that he could help. Because heaven knew, she needed some help right now.

"As Bowen told you, he hired me to keep an eye on Alexa," Saylor continued a moment later. "He thought she might be planning on doing something to cause his son some trouble."

"And was she?" Leigh asked when she saw that was the question on Cullen's face.

"That'd be my guess, but, of course, it's all circumstantial."

Leigh sighed. "I need more than just guesses."

"I understand, and I've got a lot more than that," Saylor assured her.

She tried to manage her expectations but, mercy, that was hard, especially since none of the other evidence was falling in place just yet.

"Bowen told you that Alexa met with a man in a diner, a man who was carrying a weapon," the PI continued. "Well, it turns out that the guy is indeed a thug. I was able to ID him by asking around at the diner, and his name is James McNash."

Leigh hurried to type that into the search engine on her laptop.

"A waitress at the diner says he goes by Jimbo," Saylor explained while she typed and skimmed what popped up. "He's big, mean, and he's got a sheet for multiple assaults. He spent two years in jail on one conviction and six months on another. He's got a rep for being hired muscle."

So, a criminal with violent tendencies. That didn't mean he'd killed Alexa, but it was worth looking into. Also worth looking into why Alexa was meeting with such a man.

"What's the connection between Alexa and this Jimbo?" Leigh pressed. "How'd they know each other?"

"Don't know that, but after I did some pushing, and a little bribing, one of the waitresses finally admitted to me that Alexa and Jimbo had met more than once and that she'd overheard Alexa mention Cullen's name. The waitress also heard Alexa talk about paying Jimbo for the job. Not *a* job," he emphasized. "*The* job."

"And you think the job might have been Cullen," Leigh concluded.

She looked at Cullen, but his expression had gone icy cold. She was betting beneath all that ice, there was the heat of temper.

"I think it's a strong possibility," Saylor agreed.

So did she. But it bothered her that the waitress had offered up so much info. Yes, there'd been payment involved, but it was a lot to tell a PI. What didn't surprise Leigh was that the waitress would remember Cullen being mentioned. It wasn't a common name, and because of his wealth and power—and yes, his looks—Cullen was somewhat of a celebrity.

"I can't get into Alexa's financials, but you might be able to trace a payment to Jimbo," Saylor suggested. "And, of course, you'll want to have a talk with him for yourself. He lives on what used to be his grandfather's farm, about ten miles from Dark River."

Leigh hoped the roads were clear enough soon because she wanted to have a chat with the man today. The sooner, the better.

"I want to go with you to see him," Cullen insisted, his voice low enough that Saylor likely hadn't heard him.

Leigh sighed because she'd known that would be his reaction. She wanted to say no, but if she did, she had no doubts, none, that Cullen would just go visit Jimbo on his own. If Alexa had indeed hired a thug to hurt or kill him, then Cullen wasn't going to back off.

"We'll discuss it later," she muttered to him, holding her hand over the receiver of the phone. Then, she could try to make Cullen see that it would hurt her investigation if he was with her when she interviewed a possible suspect.

"There's more," Saylor added, getting Leigh's attention. "Over the past month, Alexa met with two other men. I don't know the identity of one of them, and she only met with him once while I had her under surveillance. I didn't get any help from any of the waitstaff on IDing the guy. Not even when I offered money. But

I'm running the photo through facial recognition, and we might get lucky."

Leigh thought about that a moment. "Did Bowen see the picture? If so, he might recognize him."

Saylor made a sound of agreement. "I sent him the pictures as an attachment to emails, but Bowen's not good at opening that sort of thing. I'll call him and tell him to have a look, that it's important."

Yes, it was. "Any chance you could send me the photos so I can show Cullen?" she asked. "He might also know who he is."

"I can do that. I don't have the pictures on my phone, and my internet's down right now, but as soon as it's up and running, I'll fire them off to you." Saylor paused. "But Cullen won't need a picture for the third man who met with Alexa. I got an ID on him from some of the background data I collected on Cullen and Alexa. It's Cullen's friend Austin Borden."

Leigh's mind did a mental stutter, and the iciness vanished from Cullen's face. "Austin?" he repeated, and this time it was plenty loud enough for Saylor to hear.

"Cullen's here with me," Leigh quickly explained to the PI. "You're sure it was Austin Borden?" she pressed.

"Positive. I'm guessing he didn't mention any of those meetings to you?"

"No," Cullen said, the surprise and confusion in his voice. *"Meetings?"* he repeated. "How many of them were there?"

"Four over the past month. They met in a café once, and the other times I trailed her going into his office."

Leigh tried to figure out why Austin would have done that, and she only came up with one possibility. Well, one possibility that didn't involve anything illegal or shady. "Maybe Alexa had business with him?" Leigh suggested.

She looked at Cullen to see if that was a possibility even though she knew it'd be a slim one. Austin was a cattle broker, and Alexa didn't seem the type to need such services. Still—

Cullen shook his head in response to her silent question, and making a frustrated groan, he scrubbed his hand over his face. He also whipped out his phone, no doubt to try to call Austin again, but Leigh lifted her hand to have him hold off on that. If Austin finally answered, she wanted the first crack at him.

"I'll get those pictures to you first chance I get," the PI added a moment later. "Good luck with your investigation, Sheriff."

The moment Leigh ended the call, she turned to Cullen. He wasn't going to like her having a go at him like this, but it had to be done. "Tell me why you think Alexa would have visited Austin," she insisted. "Were they friends?"

"Friendly," Cullen answered after a long pause. He cursed. "Hell, they were all friends. Austin, Kali and Alexa. Austin and Kali are the ones who introduced me to Alexa."

Leigh tried to jump on the "no way was Austin guilty" bandwagon, but this wasn't looking good. Especially since Austin had been spotted on the patio while the party had been going on. Added to that, the man wasn't answering his phone, and the cop in her wondered if that was because he had something to hide.

"Maybe the meetings have something to do with Austin and Kali's engagement," Cullen said several moments later. He was obviously trying to make sense of this, too. "It's possible Alexa helped him pick out the ring." He paused. "It's equally possible that Alexa was working Austin so she could figure out the best way to send a thug after me."

Of those possibilities, Leigh was choosing the last option Cullen had come up with. If it'd been something as simple as ring selection, Austin probably wouldn't have kept it from Cullen. Then again, maybe Austin felt it was best not to bring up anything to Cullen about his ex. The relationship lines became a little blurred when there was a breakup of a couple in a group of friends. Austin might not have wanted it to get around that he was staying in touch with Cullen's ex.

"All right," Leigh said, "go ahead and try to call Austin again. I've already left a message insisting he contact me immediately for questioning and then to come into the station the moment the roads are clear. If you're able to reach him, let him know I want that interview to happen ASAP."

Cullen nodded, made the call and then cursed when it went to voice mail again. She hoped Austin wasn't just trying to avoid them, but if so, she'd just pay him a personal visit after she talked with Jimbo. If he continued to dodge her, she'd be forced to get a warrant to compel him to come in for questioning.

"I'll try to call Kali again," Cullen insisted. "I can leave her another voice mail, too."

However, before he could do that, Leigh's own phone rang. She answered it and immediately heard a familiar voice.

"It's me, Jamie," the ranch hand blurted out. "Someone just threatened to kill me."

Cullen must have noticed the change in her body

language and expression because he hurried to her. "Jamie," she said so that Cullen would know who was on the phone. And she put the call on speaker. "Who threatened to kill you?"

"I don't know." Jamie's voice was shaky, and she figured that shakiness applied to the rest of him, too. "I got a call from a man. It popped up on my screen as unknown, but I answered it anyway because I thought it might be somebody from the Triple R. The man's voice was muffled, but he told me if I kept talking to the cops that I'd end up like Alexa."

Sweet heaven. Leigh reined in what would have been a brusque cop tone because she knew Jamie had to be terrified. "You're still in the hospital?" she asked.

"I am, but I asked the security guard to come in the room with me. Don't tell anybody I called you. At least not until I'm out of the hospital and can fend for myself."

"I have no intention of letting you fend for yourself. The guard will stay with you and make sure you're safe. Now, tell me about this call you got." She started with an easy question. "You're sure it was a man?"

"It sure sounded like one," he answered after a pause long enough to let her know he was giving it some thought, "but like I said, his voice was muffled. You know, like someone with a bad sore throat."

The person had obviously tried to disguise his voice. Maybe because the caller had believed Jamie would recognize him.

"He threatened to kill me," Jamie repeated, and his fear had gone up another notch.

"I know. And I'm sorry. Cullen and I are just up the street. We'll be there in a few minutes and will stay with you until a deputy arrives." Leigh started putting on her coat. "I'll also need to take a look at your phone to see if we can trace the call."

"You have to trace it," Jamie insisted. "You have to stop him from killing me."

Leigh would do her best on both counts, but the trace was a long shot since the person had likely used a burner cell.

"Jamie, did Alexa ever mention someone named Jimbo McNash?" Leigh asked.

He repeated the name several times. "No. Why? Is he the man who just threatened me?"

"I don't know. But I'll find out," she promised him. "Cullen and I will be there in a couple of minutes, and we'll talk more then."

Cullen grabbed his coat, too, putting it on as they headed to the door. Leigh hated locking up, but if anyone called in with an emergency, it would go through dispatch, who would in turn notify her. She was hoping though that there wouldn't be anything else that required her attention because she already had a full plate.

"I'm texting Kerry Yancy, the night deputy, and asking him to come in," she told Cullen, and she took care of that before they went outside.

They hurried to Cullen's truck and found the windshield scabbed with ice. Since it would take precious moments to defrost it, they headed to the hospital on foot.

And they both kept watch.

Apparently, there was no need to mention to Cullen that this could be a lure to get them out into the open so that the driver of that SUV could try to kill them again. But it was a risk she had to take. Leigh wouldn't have felt right being holed up in the office while a killer went after Jamie.

"Whoever made that call could be desperate," Leigh concluded. She lowered her head against the howling wind and tried not to think of the ache that the cold air put in her lungs. "Desperate enough to try to silence Jamie, or scare him into being silenced, anyway. I need to get out the word that he didn't see anything and can't ID his attacker. In this case, the truth might keep him safe."

"I can arrange for some of the ranch hands to stand guard in the parking lot and keep an eye on who comes and goes," Cullen suggested.

Something like that would certainly cause gossip. The wrong kind of gossip, that Cullen had his nose deep in this investigation. Still, it might prevent Jamie from being hurt again.

"You trust all your ranch hands and don't believe any one of them could have had a part in Alexa's murder?"

"I trust them," Cullen said without hesitation. "If I didn't, they wouldn't be working for me."

She considered what he said for the last block they had to walk and nodded. "Have them come out when the roads are open, but I want them to stay in the parking lot. I'll make sure security is posted inside."

And maybe none of these measures would even be necessary. It was entirely possible that the caller who'd threatened Jamie had done that as a ploy to keep the young man quiet. Thankfully, Jamie had trusted her enough to let her know about it, and Leigh wanted to make sure his trust wasn't misplaced.

They hurried into the ER, and Amber was there, waiting for them. "We've moved Jamie to another room.

He was very upset so the doctor had me give him a sedative. Follow me, and I'll take you to him."

Jamie must have told Amber about the threatening call as well because the nurse was clearly shaken.

As it had been before, the hospital was still practically empty, but Leigh kept her eyes open, looking for any signs of trouble. They made their way down a hall to a room in the center of what was the patients' ward, and Cullen and she were about to go in when his phone rang.

"It's Kali," he relayed when he saw the screen. He looked at Amber when she stayed put. "I need to take this call." Cullen didn't add "in private," but Amber got the message because she strolled away, heading back to the ER.

"Kali," Cullen greeted, putting the call on speaker for Leigh. "I've been trying to get in touch with you."

"Yes." That was all Kali said for several long moments. "I got your messages, but I...well, I needed some time before I talked to you."

Oh, mercy. There was definitely something wrong, and it sounded as if the woman had been crying.

"I have to speak to Austin," Cullen continued, obviously zooming right in on what needed to be done. "Where is he?"

The next sound that Leigh heard from Kali was a sob. One that put Leigh's stomach in knots.

"What's wrong?" Cullen pressed. "What happened?"

Kali didn't answer right away. Probably because of all the crying. "I thought Austin would be with you. That's why I'm driving to Dark River now."

Cullen cursed under his breath. "Kali, it's not safe for you to be out on the roads."

"I have to see him, and he's not home. I figured he'd go to your house."

"No. If he had, someone would have called me. I'm at the hospital right now. One of my ranch hands was injured, but if Austin had shown up at the ranch, Rosa would have told me."

"Then where is he?" Kali demanded.

Apparently, Leigh wasn't the only one who wanted to know the answer to that. "I'll try to find out," Cullen tried to reassure her.

Kali didn't sound the least bit reassured though. "Did you know?" she blurted out. "Did you know about Austin?"

Because her arm was against Cullen's, Leigh felt his muscles turn to iron. "Know what?" Cullen demanded.

"That Austin was having an affair." The words rushed out, followed by another sob.

Oh, mercy. This was a new wrinkle, and Leigh already had a bad feeling about it.

"No, I didn't know about any affair. You're sure he was cheating?" Cullen pressed.

"I'm sure. I found out last night. I accidently took his phone with me."

Well, that explained why they hadn't been able to reach Austin.

"Austin's always forgetting his password so when it rang, I answered it," Kali went on. "It was just his dad wanting to make sure he got home all right after the party, but that's when I saw the texts."

"What texts?" Cullen demanded.

"God, Cullen," Kali said on a hoarse sob, "Austin's been having an affair with Alexa."

Chapter 8

Cullen felt Kali's words land like an actual punch to his gut. Words that he had to mentally repeat a couple of times just so they'd sink in. Obviously though, Leigh wasn't having any trouble processing what Kali had said.

"Austin had an affair with Alexa?" Leigh asked.

"Who is that?" Kali demanded. "Who's listening?"

"Sheriff Leigh Mercer," she said.

Cullen could have told Leigh it was a mistake to volunteer who she was, and Kali's gasp proved it. He wasn't the least bit surprised when Kali hung up on him. On a heavy sigh, Cullen tried to call the woman back, but Kali didn't answer.

"For legal reasons, I had to identify myself," Leigh muttered. "And I didn't want her to say anything incriminating that I couldn't use because her lawyer wouldn't allow it into evidence."

Yeah, Cullen understood that, but he wished he'd been able to ask Kali if she was certain about Austin having an affair with Alexa. Then again, Leigh would almost certainly ask her when she had Kali in for questioning.

Which Leigh would do.

No way could Leigh dismiss a bombshell like that. No way could Kali dodge questioning, either, because this was a murder investigation. An investigation where Kali had just revealed a possible motive for Austin murdering Alexa. Because affairs didn't often end well. Hell, Alexa wouldn't have let it end well unless she'd been the one to call it quits.

"Let me make sure Jamie is okay," Leigh said, peering into the room. "And then we can discuss what I'm going to have to do about this situation with Austin and Alexa."

What she was going to have to do would likely include warrants. Maybe even an arrest. Yeah, this was like a punch to the gut all right.

Cullen looked in Jamie's room, too, and saw that his eyes were closed. So whatever meds Amber had given him had already taken effect. The guard, Harry Harbin, was there as well, and he actually appeared to be interested in doing his job. He was standing at the foot of the bed and had his hand on the butt of his gun.

"You need me to wake him up?" Harry asked her.

Leigh shook her head. "No. Not yet. Stay in here with him. I'll be right outside in the hall for a couple more minutes."

Harry nodded, and the moment Leigh shut the door, she turned back to Cullen. "Is Austin the type to have an affair?" she whispered. "An affair with your ex," she tacked on to her question.

"I didn't think so." Or rather Cullen didn't *want* to think so. "But obviously Kali saw something on Austin's phone to make her believe it was true. Plus, the PI said that he'd seen Alexa meet with Austin."

And there it was—the proof in a nutshell.

When he added that Austin had been spotted on the patio and that he'd kept his relationship with Alexa a secret, Cullen knew that Austin had just become Leigh's prime suspect. But Cullen could see this from one more angle.

"Even if Austin had the affair, it doesn't mean he murdered Alexa," Cullen said, thinking out loud. "But if someone found out what he was doing, they might have wanted to kill Alexa at the party to make him look guilty. That, in turn, would sling some mud on me because some would think I'd cover for him."

Cullen was thankful when Leigh didn't ask if he would have indeed covered for his friend. He wouldn't have.

"I'm guessing Austin didn't tell you about the affair," Leigh continued a moment later, "because he…what? Would have thought you'd tell Kali?"

"I wouldn't have," Cullen insisted. "But this would have put a wedge between Austin and me. Not because he was having sex with my ex but because he was cheating on Kali. I would have tried to talk him into either ending the affair or breaking things off with Kali."

Leigh groaned softly and leaned back against the wall while she studied him. "You know this gives both Kali and Austin motive for murder. Yes, Kali said she didn't learn about the affair until she saw Austin's phone, but she could have found out sooner."

Cullen tried to imagine Kali bashing in Alexa's head, and he could see it happening if she was in a rage. But what was hard for him to fathom was that Kali would clean herself up and then come back into the party as if nothing had happened. Plus, there was the problem of Jamie. Cullen hadn't kept track of Kali's whereabouts all evening, but he just couldn't see her sneaking up on his ranch hand and trying to kill him.

Then again, people did all sorts of things to cover themselves.

And Kali might have felt the need to get rid of Jamie if she'd thought he could link her back to Alexa. Maybe Alexa had even claimed to have told Jamie that she was meeting with Kali and that if anything happened to her, Jamie would know. Again, that felt like a huge stretch.

"I need to call Mack," Cullen said, shifting his thoughts. "I want to have some extra ranch hands stand guard in the parking lot."

Leigh nodded and studied him as if she was trying to figure out just how much this latest development was eating away at him. It hurt all right, but Cullen didn't hide it from her. Wasn't sure he could.

On a sigh, she touched his arm, rubbed lightly. "I'll go in and get Jamie's phone so I can get started on the possible trace."

"Thanks for that," he said, tipping his head to the arm she'd just rubbed.

Her next sigh was louder, and despite their situation, it made him smile. This attraction was really messing with both of them.

Cullen waited until she'd gone in with Jamie before

he called Mack, and as expected, the ranch hand answered right away.

"I was about to call you," Mack said. He heard the man drag in a deep breath. "I took one of the horses over to the east trail. Just to have a look around. I wasn't far from the house when I found an SUV. There's damage to the front end so I bet it's the one used to ram into the sheriff's cruiser."

Yeah, that was a safe bet. "I'm guessing no one was inside it?"

"No one," Mack verified. "I didn't touch it, because I knew the CSIs would want to process it so I just let them know. They'll probably be calling the sheriff about it."

Again, that was a safe bet.

"It's one of the Triple R's vehicles," Mack added a moment later.

Hell. Of course it was. If the killer wanted to add another twist to muddy the waters even more than they already were, then it made sense to use one of Cullen's own SUVs. There were several on the ranch, along with a large number of trucks, and the vehicles were parked all around. There probably wouldn't have been keys in the ignition, but someone capable of killing could likely know how to hot-wire a car.

"Boss, if you're thinking one of the hands could have done this," Mack said, "you're wrong."

"I wasn't thinking along those lines. But it could have been someone who had been at the party. Someone who maybe stayed back when I thought they had left."

That would be something a killer would do—stay around to tie up any loose ends. Hell, for that matter the killer could have hidden in one of the rooms in the house. No one had done a head count to make sure all the guests had been accounted for.

And that led Cullen back to Austin.

Kali, too, since she and Austin hadn't left the party together. Plus, either one of them would have known where the SUVs were kept.

"If Austin or Kali show up at the ranch, let me know and then bring them straight in for questioning," Cullen instructed Mack. "Also, I need two more hands out to the hospital parking lot to stand guard. Jamie got a threatening phone call that shook him up."

"Will do." There was concern and some alarm in Mack's voice. "Look, I can get into town if you want me there with him."

"No, I'd rather you stay at the ranch and put out any fires that might pop up." Because after all, it was possible the killer was still nearby.

It was an unsettling thought that grew even stronger when Cullen saw Austin coming up the hall toward him.

"I have to go," Cullen told Mack, and he ended the call so he could give Austin the once-over.

His friend looked like hell. Dark shadows under his eyes. Scruff that went well past a fashion statement, and it looked as if he'd grabbed the jeans and T-shirt he was wearing off the floor of his room. His coat was unbuttoned and flapped against his sides with his hurried strides.

"I still haven't been able to find my phone so I accessed my office messages and found all these calls from Leigh and you," Austin said right off. "What the heck's going on?"

Cullen wasn't sure where to start, and it turned out that he didn't have to make a decision about that. Leigh must have heard Austin's voice, because she came out of Jamie's room.

"What the heck's going on?" Austin repeated to Leigh.

She glanced around and motioned for him to follow her. Leigh led Austin to a small visitors' room just a few doors down from Jamie's room. Cullen went with them since he had every intention of hearing what Austin had to say. However, he waited in the doorway so he could see if someone tried to get into Jamie's room. Leigh and Austin took seats at the small metal table.

"I'm going to read you your rights," Leigh said to Austin, and she proceeded to do just that.

Austin sat in what appeared to be stunned silence before he turned his accusing gaze on Cullen. "You believe I killed Alexa?" Austin came out and demanded.

"I have questions, and I have to make sure all the legal bases are covered," Leigh insisted before Cullen could speak. "You want to call a lawyer?"

"Do I need a lawyer?" Austin fired back, but he immediately waved that off. "Let's just clear all of this up. And I can clear it up," he insisted.

The angry fire in Austin's eyes was just as much for Cullen as it was for Leigh. Cullen didn't mind. There'd be fire in his own eyes if it turned out that Austin had indeed had any part in this.

"Let's start with your whereabouts during the party," Leigh started, and she took out her phone and put on the recorder. "Were you on the patio of the guest room at the Triple R?"

Austin opened his mouth, but it seemed to Cullen that he changed his mind as to what he'd been about to say. "Yes. I was there."

"You said you smoked on the front porch," Cullen pointed out.

"Well, I misspoke." Austin stood and poured himself a cup of what looked more like sludge than coffee. It probably tasted like sludge, too, because Austin grimaced when he took a sip. "It was on the patio. It was cold, and I left the doors open so I wouldn't freeze while I was out there."

"What time was this?" Leigh said, asking the very question that Cullen knew she would.

They didn't have a time of death on Alexa, but according to Jamie, he'd dropped her off around eight. A half hour or so later, Jamie had been attacked. So, Alexa had likely died between eight and eight thirty.

"I'm not sure." Austin's forehead bunched up. "Maybe seven thirty or a little later. It was still early, but I needed a smoke before all the toasts got started so I popped outside. It was so cold that I decided to take just a few drags off the cigarette and then get a hit with the nicotine gum I carry so I wouldn't have to stay outside."

If Austin was telling the truth, then his timing for that smoke would clear him. But Leigh probably had plenty of doubts about that "if."

"Did you see anyone else on or around the patio when you were out there?" Leigh asked, and there was some skepticism not only in her voice but also in her flat cop's eyes.

"No." Austin stopped for a moment. "Well, other than a few of the ranch hands. I saw a couple of them going to and from the barn."

"Only the ranch hands?" Leigh pressed. "No one else?" When Austin shook his head, she moved on to the next question. "Did you leave the patio doors un-locked when you came back into the house?"

Again, Austin's forehead bunched up. "Maybe. Sorry, I can't remember." He huffed. "Look, I didn't kill Alexa or hurt Jamie so all of this is unnecessary."

"This is a murder investigation," Leigh argued. "All the details are necessary. Did you see Alexa during the party?" she tacked on without even pausing.

"No." However, Austin certainly did some pausing. "But she did text me. She wanted me to meet her, and I told her no."

Leigh jumped right on that. "Meet her where and why?"

Austin lifted his shoulder. "She didn't say."

"So, she could have wanted you to meet her in the house? In Cullen's bedroom?" Leigh continued.

"She didn't say," Austin repeated, and this time he snapped it. "And from the sound of these questions, I think I should call my lawyer after all."

"Go ahead." Leigh stood. "As soon as I get one of my deputies here for guard duty, I'll meet your lawyer and you at the police station. Deputy Yancy's already there and can show you to an interview room. He texted me when I was with Jamie," she let Cullen know.

Austin stood as well, and was no doubt about to ver-bally blast Leigh for treating him like the suspect that he was, but he didn't get the chance. Looking as harried as Austin had when he'd arrived, Kali came rushing in.

"The nurse said she saw the three of you come in here," Kali explained, her voice shaky and her glare already on Austin.

"Kali." Austin went to her and tried to pull her into his arms, but Kali batted him away and turned to Cullen. "You've told Austin that I know about his affair with Alexa?"

The color drained from Austin's face.

"No, I didn't tell him," Cullen admitted.

"Kali," Austin repeated, and again he reached for her. This time, Kali slapped him. Not a gentle hit, either. The sound of it cracked through the room.

Cullen stepped in, putting himself between the two while Leigh took hold of Austin and pulled him back.

"Don't you dare try to deny it," Kali spat out, aiming her venomous gaze on Austin. She held up what was almost certainly Austin's phone. "I found your texts to her."

It was hard for Cullen to believe this was the couple who'd been so happy just the night before. Or rather, they'd *appeared* happy. Obviously, appearances weren't accurate.

"I was going to break things off with Alexa," Austin pled. "I swear. I made a huge mistake by being with her, and I told her it was over, that I wanted to be with you. I want us to get married, Kali. I want a life with you."

The sound Kali made was a low, rumbling growl. "You'll never have a life with me."

She started cursing him, calling him vile names, but the fit of temper soon gave way to tears. Judging from her red eyes, these tears weren't the first of the day.

The sobs seemed to weaken her, and Kali sagged against Cullen. He helped her to the table and had her sit.

"I'm sorry," Austin said, but Leigh blocked him from going closer to Kali. "So sorry. You have to believe me when I tell you it was over with Alexa."

"I don't have to believe anything you say." Kali spoke

through the wet sobs, and Cullen located a box of tissues for her.

"Please," Austin tried again. "Let me make this up to you."

But Kali didn't answer. She buried her face in her folded arms on the table and continued to cry.

"When did you break up with Alexa?" Cullen asked Austin, knowing that it was something Leigh also needed to know.

Austin cursed, groaned and squeezed his fists on the sides of his head. "Right before the party. She called me and said she wanted to have sex with me in your bed."

Cullen wanted to curse, too. Hell. That was something Alexa definitely would have done.

"She sent Austin a naked picture of herself," Kali provided, thrusting out the phone to Cullen.

That caused Austin to groan again, but he sure as heck didn't deny it. And Cullen could see how this had played out. Alexa had probably thought this was the way to get back at him.

Cullen took the phone from Kali and passed it to Leigh. "Did you see Alexa at any time during the party?" Leigh asked, scrolling past the naked photo to get to the texts.

"No, I swear," Austin insisted. "After she texted me, I told her I had no intentions of having sex with her in Cullen's bed or anywhere else for that matter, and I let her know that it was over. Then, I blocked her because I didn't want to have her texting or trying to call me during the party."

Leigh continued to scroll through Austin's phone. "You had this text conversation with her about the same time you said you were on the patio having a smoke," Leigh pointed out.

Austin was scowling when he whipped toward her. "I was having a smoke and texting her. You can see—I ended things with her. I ended things with her," he repeated, this time to Kali.

"I don't care," Kali snapped. "I never want to see you again."

"Unfortunately, you'll have to," Leigh said to Kali. "I'll need to interview both Austin and you. And take this into evidence," she added, holding up the phone. She looked at Austin. "Do I need a search warrant to examine the clothes you wore to the party last night, or will you give me permission to have them sent to the lab?"

Austin stared at her a long time. "You'll need a search warrant," he snarled. "Since I find myself without a phone, text Doug for me," he added to Cullen. "Tell him I'll meet him at the Dark River PD. I won't be saying anything else to Sheriff Mercer until he arrives, and I damn sure won't be giving her my clothes unless he says different."

Doug Franklin was a lawyer friend of theirs and had been at the party the night before. On a heavy sigh, Cullen sent him a text as Austin stormed out.

"I don't want to go to the police station right now," Kali muttered. "Let me just sit here for a little while and try to steady myself." She pulled off her engagement ring and practically shoved it into Cullen's hand. "Give that to him and tell him I hope he chokes on it."

"That should be fun," Cullen mumbled, slipping it into his pocket, and he stepped out into the hall with Leigh.

"I doubt they're flight risks," Leigh whispered to him, "but I want to go ahead and take Kali in after I get a deputy here to keep tabs on Jamie." She sent a text to arrange for a deputy to come to the hospital.

Cullen couldn't blame Leigh for wanting to get Kali in for questioning. The sooner they got answers, the better. Well, Cullen thought it would be better, anyway, and he hoped the woman he'd kissed less than an hour ago didn't have to arrest his friend for murder.

Leigh was no doubt trying to contain it, but the stress was starting to show, and Cullen gave her one of those arm rubs she'd given him earlier.

"That shouldn't feel good," she said, her voice still a whisper. "It can't feel good," she amended with her eyes lifting to meet his. She groaned. "This is really turning into a nasty mess."

Cullen figured he was part of that mess. A complication added to the fact that Leigh now had two suspects. Or rather three since she hadn't had a chance to talk to Jimbo McNash yet. Cullen was hoping the thug would just confess to the murder and the attacks just so the investigation wouldn't be looming over them. Then, Leigh and he could...

Well, he didn't know where they'd go from there, but one thing was for certain. He needed to figure out a way to keep her in his life. Along with getting her in his bed.

Her phone rang, and she slid Austin's cell in her jeans pocket so she could answer it and put it on speaker. "This is Saylor again," the PI greeted.

"What can I do for you?" Leigh asked.

"I got your number from Deputy Yancy when I called your office. Thought you'd want to know that Bowen had a look at the rest of the surveillance photos of Alexa, and he was able to ID the other man she met with."

Cullen leaned in so that he wouldn't miss this.

"My internet's working so I just sent the photos to you," Saylor added. "But you'll recognize the man, too."

"Oh?" Leigh asked.

"Yeah," Saylor verified. "Because it's your deputy Rocky Callaway."

Chapter 9

The sudden shock hit Leigh to the core. "Rocky?" she managed to say to the PI. "You're sure?"

"Bowen said he's positive." Saylor paused. "He also wants to talk to you about this."

Of course he did. He'd demand to know if Rocky had conspired with Alexa to cause trouble for Cullen. Maybe for her, too. And right now, Leigh didn't have the answer to that, but she soon would.

"I photographed only one meeting that Alexa had with your deputy," Saylor continued. "But it's possible there were more."

Yes, and that was something else she would ask her deputy.

"When did this meeting with Rocky take place?" Leigh asked.

"Three days ago."

So, two days before the party. Rocky definitely should

have mentioned speaking to Alexa that close to the date of her murder. Especially since Leigh hadn't heard a peep about Rocky being friends or even friendly with the woman.

"Thanks for the info," Leigh told him, and she ended the call so she could access her email on her phone.

"I'm guessing Rocky didn't tell you about these meetings?" Cullen asked.

Leigh shook her head, pulled up the file with the photos, and the moment the first one loaded, she wanted to curse. It was Rocky all right, and she turned her phone so that he could see. Rocky and Alexa weren't exactly cozy-looking, the way lovers might be, but they were clearly having an intimate conversation.

"How bad does Rocky want to see you fail as sheriff?" Cullen asked.

Leigh suspected the answer to that was *very bad.* But she didn't voice that opinion because she spotted Cecile Taggart, a reserve deputy, heading her way. Cecile was in her early fifties and had plenty of experience. Better yet, she was someone Leigh trusted.

"I was already heading into town when I got your text," Cecile greeted. "Which one is Jamie's room?"

Leigh pointed to it. "The security guard's with him now, but I'd rather you be in there. The guard can stay on the door."

Cecile's eyebrow winged up. "Are you expecting big trouble?"

"Trying to avoid it," Leigh explained. "Jamie's sedated right now, but he's scared. Stay with him at all times."

"Will do. I've got my laptop with me," she added, patting the bag she had hooked over her shoulder. "If you need any help with the murder investigation, just let me know. I'll probably have some downtime while I'm with Jamie."

True, especially since Jamie was asleep and might be that way for a while. "There's a search warrant to go through Alexa's files and phone records. Get started on making that happen. I need you to earmark any communication Alexa had with Austin Borden, Kali Starling and James McNash, aka Jimbo. Also with Cullen and Bowen Brodie."

Cecile's eyebrow came up again, and she glanced at Cullen, probably to see how he felt about that. Cullen merely shrugged.

"I'm covering the bases," Leigh muttered to Cullen. But, of course, she hadn't. Because she'd left Rocky's name off that list. No doubt because Leigh didn't want Rocky to know he was under investigation. And that was probably why she also added to Cecile, "Flag anything that's connected to anyone involved in this investigation. *Anyone*," Leigh emphasized.

"Will do," Cecile repeated. "You headed home to get some shut-eye?"

Leigh shook her head. "I'll be in my office."

She waited until Cecile was in with Jamie before turning back to the visitors' room. Kali was still sitting there, but she'd stopped crying. She was staring blankly at the table.

"Would you like to walk with us to my office?" Leigh asked.

Kali shook her head. "I need a few more minutes. I'll be there soon." Now she turned and looked at Leigh. "Just make sure Austin's in a room somewhere when

I get there. I meant it when I said I didn't want to see him."

Leigh gave a confirming nod, and with Cullen right beside her, they started for the exit. As she walked, she pressed Rocky's number, and he answered after several rings.

"Yo," he grumbled, sounding as if she'd woken him.

"I want you at the office right now," Leigh told him.

"But the roads—"

"Are obviously clear enough since I've got two people already waiting in Interview," Leigh interrupted.

Rocky yawned. "You want me to do the interviews?"

"I want you in the office," she repeated, a snap in her voice, and ended the call.

"Are you okay?" Cullen asked her.

No, she wasn't, and Leigh made a sound that could have meant anything so that she didn't have to verify that she was far from okay. It was possible that Rocky had withheld evidence pertinent to a murder investigation. If he had, then that would be obstruction of justice.

And possibly more.

"I'm not okay," Leigh grumbled as Cullen and she walked.

"I got that. It was a tough night, followed by a tough morning."

Yes, it had been. "Thanks for not giving me any flak about having Cecile look for correspondence between Alexa and you."

"I figured you've already got enough flak. Plus, it'll be interesting to see what she kept. Like I told you, I didn't pour out my heart in emails."

She believed him. Leigh mentally groaned because it was more than just believing him. For reasons she didn't especially want to explore, she trusted Cullen, and right now, she very much needed someone who wasn't going to stab her in the back.

Deputy Yancy was at his desk when they went into the police department, and he stood, giving a nodded greeting to Cullen.

"Austin Borden's in the interview room," Yancy volunteered. "But he said he's not saying anything else until his lawyer gets here."

"I can talk to him," Cullen suggested.

But Leigh shook her head. If Austin told Cullen he was indeed a killer, she didn't want the lawyer throwing out the confession or trying to have it suppressed. Austin's lawyer could even claim that Cullen had coerced him to admit to murdering Alexa.

"When the lawyer gets here, I want you to be the one to take Austin's statement," Leigh instructed Yancy. "He's already riled at me, and you might be able to get more out of him."

Yancy was laid-back and had more of a friendly-officer style when it came to interviews. Austin might respond better to that. Heck, he might respond better to anyone other than her. Because right now, Cullen and she were the enemy.

"Dawn and Vance finished interviewing the Triple R ranch hands and the catering staff," Yancy explained. "Nothing new so far."

Leigh figured that would be the case. Still, it was a box that had to be checked.

"You know about the blue SUV being found at the ranch, right?" Yancy asked.

She nodded. "I got a text about it. Let me know when the CSIs have it processed."

"Will do. You've also got a bunch of emails and had some phone calls," Yancy added, handing her a sheet listing the calls.

"I'll get to them," Leigh said, heading into her office. "In the meantime, I need you to start securing a warrant to search Austin's home. I specifically want to get the clothes he wore to the party last night."

Yancy's eyes went a little wide. "You think there might be blood on them?"

Leigh shrugged. "We'll see when we have the clothes. Vance and Dawn might have photos from some of the guests. They were going to try to collect them. If they've managed to do that already, we'll know what clothes to include in the warrant. Unless..." She turned to Cullen. "Do you remember?"

Cullen closed his eyes a moment as if trying to call up the image. "A black suit with a blue tie. Kali was wearing a blue dress." He opened his eyes, looked at her. "I figured you'd want to know that in case you got a warrant for her clothes, too."

"I do," Leigh confirmed, giving Yancy instructions to get the warrant for that as well. She added a search of Kali's parents' house since the woman had spent the night there. "Try to stretch the warrant to include her computer, emails and phone records." She turned back to Cullen. "And I'll have your clothes couriered to the lab this morning."

In fact, she'd already done the paperwork to get that started, and the courier would no doubt soon be on the way now that the roads were clearing. She was certain there'd be no blood on Cullen's clothes, and that might stave off those who thought he was guilty. Ironically, her own deputy Rocky was one of the ones fanning those particular "Cullen's guilty" flames, and now Leigh wanted to know if that was because Rocky had something to hide.

Because she desperately needed a caffeine hit, she went into her office to make a fresh pot. Cullen followed her, of course, and he shut the door.

"Are you going to test Rocky's clothes, too?" Cullen asked.

"If I have probable cause."

Leigh was about to continue with some legal babble to explain how she would do her job, but she cursed and gave the leg of her desk a good kick. It hurt, the pain vibrating through her boot to her toes, but she hadn't been able to hold back the frustration. No, it was more than frustration. It was a gut-punch of anger.

"Rocky will fight me every step of the way," she said on a heavy sigh. "And while he's fighting me, it'll also be a distraction from the investigation. *You're* a distraction," she added when Cullen reached for her. "You and your clothes," she grumbled.

He looked, well, amused by that, and as if she would put up no protest whatsoever—which she didn't—he pulled her into his arms and brushed a kiss on the top of her head. "My party suit or the clothes I'm wearing now?"

"The latter." She squeezed her eyes shut, and just for a moment, she let her body sag against him. "Hot cowboy clothes."

Leigh couldn't see his face, but she suspected he was smiling. After all, she'd just confessed that his well-worn jeans, faded blue work shirt and scuffed boots appealed to her more than his suit had. Then again,

Cullen looked good in anything. And nothing. Especially nothing.

That, of course, only proved to her that he was a distraction.

She forced herself away from him so she could get some coffee and do some work while they waited for Rocky, Kali and Austin's lawyer. That was the plan, anyway, but the plan took a little detour when Cullen leaned in and kissed her. This was no peck like the one earlier in the break room. No. This was the full deal.

Cullen certainly hadn't lost any skills in the kissing department. He was still darn good at moving his mouth over hers. Still good at making a kiss feel as if it was full-blown foreplay. And his taste. Mercy. It was foreplay, too.

He dropped his hands to her waist, nudging her closer while also nudging her lips apart with his tongue. She remembered this. Another kick of heat. The urgency he created when he deepened the kiss.

Leigh sank into him, all the while the sane part of her yelling that she should knock this off. She listened to the sane part, knew that it was right, but she lingered a little longer, letting the kiss and Cullen's touch slide through her.

It took some willpower, but Leigh finally untangled herself from Cullen and stepped back. She didn't dodge his gaze because she needed him to see that this had to stop. Maybe she got that point across, maybe not, but either way, he didn't reach for her.

They stood there, their breaths heavy, and with the heat searing around them. She might have been tempted to go back for another round, but she was saved by the bell when her phone rang.

"It's Cash," she muttered after glancing at the name on the screen.

There was no need for her to explain that Cash was her brother, because Cullen and Cash had gone to school together. Had both been star football players. They hadn't stayed close, but then, like Cullen, Cash hadn't stayed particularly close with anyone in Dark River.

Including her.

It'd been at least six months since she'd gotten a call from him, and Leigh doubted it was a coincidence that Cash was getting in touch with her now while she was neck-deep in a murder investigation.

"Leigh," her brother greeted the moment she answered. "I just got a call from one of your deputies, Yancy. He gave me a heads-up that you'll be initiating a search warrant for Kali Starling's and her parents' residences."

Yancy worked fast, and it took Leigh several moments to realize why Cash was telling her this. Cash was the sheriff of Clay Ridge, a town about twenty miles from Dark River, and Kali and her parents lived in Clay Ridge.

"Yes," Leigh verified. "Kali was on scene at a party last night where a woman was killed."

"I heard. The dead woman was Cullen's ex. I also heard you haven't arrested Cullen." Cash paused. "How much grief is Jeb giving you over this?"

"Enough," Leigh answered honestly, knowing it was going to cause Cash to curse.

It did.

"Damn it, Leigh, you shouldn't let him run roughshod over you like that," Cash snarled.

And there was their sibling conflict in a nutshell.

After doing almost daily battle with Jeb, Cash had left home and hadn't come back. Not even for her when Leigh had insisted on staying. Cash saw that as a weakness on her part, claiming that she was Jeb's doormat. But Leigh saw it as putting up with Jeb so she could be where she wanted to be and have the job she'd always wanted.

"Jeb's never going to accept you as sheriff," Cash went on. "Not really. I mean, he might say he's okay with it, but I promise you he wanted one of his sons to take over the job."

"That's probably true," she agreed. "That's why I'm focusing on the badge. You understand that," Leigh reminded him.

Cash paused for a very long time. "Yeah. I understand." She heard him drag in a long breath. "I'll help grease the way for the warrant and will have one of my deputies execute it. What exactly do you need from Kali's place?"

"Any and all blue dresses. She wore a blue dress to the party," Leigh explained when Cash made a "huh" sound. "Also, if the warrant includes it, I want a look at her computer. Specifically, her emails. Her car is here in Dark River so one of my deputies will handle that search in case the dress is in there."

"I'll see what I can do," Cash assured her just as there was a knock on her door.

The visitor didn't wait for her to invite him in. Rocky threw open the door, his narrowed gaze spearing into Leigh.

"Thanks for everything," she told her brother. "I'll call you back later."

And she turned to Rocky.

"Cullen," she said, "could you step out while I speak with my deputy?"

Cullen moved toward the door, but Rocky stepped in front of him. "What the hell have you been telling her?" He jabbed his index finger at Leigh.

"Nothing," Leigh assured him. "But I know you've met with Alexa."

The shock widened Rocky's eyes but only for a second. Then, the anger returned with a vengeance. "Nothing," Rocky repeated, and it was coated with venom. Venom that he aimed at Cullen. "You're bad-mouthing me to Leigh because you know it should be your butt that's in jail right now."

Oh, that was not the right thing to say, and it caused Cullen to send Rocky a steely, dangerous glare. "I don't have to bad-mouth you, you idiot. You did this to yourself by meeting with Alexa."

Since Cullen was apparently going to be part of this conversation, Leigh stepped around the men and shut the door. Yancy probably wouldn't repeat anything he heard, but Leigh didn't want to air this particular dirty laundry to anyone who happened to come into the police department.

"Sit down," she ordered Rocky, and yes, she made sure it sounded like an order.

Rocky tossed out some glares of his own, both to Cullen and her, but he dropped down in the seat across from her desk.

"Before you deny meeting with Alexa," Leigh continued, "you should know that Alexa was under surveillance by a PI. He took photographs. I've personally seen the photos, and I know it's you."

Part of her hadn't wanted to give Rocky a cushion

like that. A part of her had wanted him to go ahead and lie so she could reprimand him. But getting to the truth was more important than any discipline she doled out. Plus, she could dole out discipline later.

"I'm going to read you your rights," Leigh told Rocky, and she proceeded to do just that. Of course, it didn't improve his mood, and he grew angrier with each word she recited.

"You're arresting me?" Rocky spat out when she'd finished. "Good luck making any bogus charges stick."

"If I arrest you, the charges won't be bogus," she assured him. "Now, tell me why you met with Alexa, and then you can explain why you withheld this information during a murder investigation. You've been a cop long enough to know that could be considered obstruction of justice."

Rocky didn't jump to answer that, and Leigh half expected him to yell for a lawyer. But he didn't. Leigh watched as Rocky seemed to make an effort to steady himself. Maybe because he remembered that how he handled this could determine if he kept his badge. Despite his attitude, Leigh knew that wearing the badge was important to Rocky.

"Alexa called me a couple of days ago and asked if I'd see her," Rocky said. "We aren't exactly friends, but I've met her a couple of times when she's been in town with Kali. Alexa told me that she had some questions about you."

It took Leigh a moment to realize the "you" was her and not Cullen.

"I had some business in Lubbock so I agreed to hook up with her at a diner," Rocky went on. "Alexa had heard some rumors and wanted to know if Cullen and you had started seeing each other again. I told her you weren't stupid so you wouldn't get involved with Cullen. Guess I was wrong about that," he added in a barely audible mutter.

Leigh didn't bother to blister him with a scathing look. She just motioned for him to continue.

"That was it," Rocky insisted. "Alexa just wanted to know if you two were sleeping together. When she figured out I didn't have any gossip to dish up to her, she paid for my lunch and left. And as for obstruction of justice, that's bull. I didn't obstruct squat because the meeting wasn't important. Hell, I'd forgotten all about it."

Leigh figured that last part was a huge lie. When he'd seen Alexa's dead body, it would have been logical for him to say something about the meeting he'd had with her just days earlier. Then again, maybe Rocky thought that might add him to the suspect list.

And it would have.

"Did you know that Alexa was going to the party at the Triple R?" Leigh pressed.

Rocky paused, shrugged. "She asked me about the party, wondered if me or any of the other deputies were doing security. You know, like Vance and Yancy sometimes do."

She did indeed know about that. Vance and Yancy had done some off-duty work like that when there'd been big events at the Triple R, but none of her deputies had been tapped for the engagement party.

"In hindsight, I guess Alexa asked me about that because maybe she thought I could get her into the party, but I didn't think of that until later. I didn't think of a lot of things." Rocky looked at Cullen. "I got the feeling that Alexa would do anything to get back at you."

"Well, she didn't kill herself," Leigh pointed out.

"No," Rocky quietly agreed. "But I think she was trying to stir up some kind of trouble."

"Something specific?" Cullen asked when Rocky paused.

"I'm not sure, but I figure she planned on doing something at the party. I mean, why else would she want to make sure she got in?"

If Austin was telling the truth, then Alexa had indeed planned on doing *something*, and that was getting into Cullen's bed with Austin. But Leigh figured Alexa intended to do more than just that. Maybe the woman had intended for Cullen to walk in on Austin and her.

"Why didn't you tell me about this sooner?" Leigh pressed.

"Because like I said, I'd forgotten all about it. See?" Rocky added, and some of his usual cockiness was back in his voice. "No obstruction of justice. No withholding evidence. I simply had lunch with a woman who might or might not have tried to manipulate me. Either way, I didn't have anything to do with Alexa getting into the party or being murdered, and you don't have any evidence to say otherwise."

She didn't. Leigh would give him a written reprimand for not volunteering the meeting with Alexa, but Rocky would no doubt believe it was petty. That the reprimand was because he was Jeb's ally and that he actually hadn't broken the law.

"Can I go now, *Sheriff*?" Rocky snarled, getting to his feet before she could nix that or agree. Of course, he used a mocking tone on her title. "I'm way past my normal shift hours and need some shut-eye."

Leigh nodded and watched as Rocky breezed out

of her office. She battled with her temper, tamping it
down—and trying not to kick the trash can again.

Rocky walked out to the dispatch desk, where Yancy
was sitting, and struck up a conversation with his fellow deputy. All the while keeping an eye on Leigh. Of
course, she was keeping an eye on him as well.

"Rocky could have been the one who came after us
in the SUV," Cullen pointed out.

She nodded again. Heck, Rocky could have killed
Alexa, hurt Jamie and then tried to kill Cullen and
her—and all because he hated her and wanted her job.
Then again, it was indeed possible that Rocky had done
nothing wrong other than forgetting a meeting with a
dead woman.

Her phone rang, and with her attention still on Rocky,
Leigh pressed Answer. However, her attention wasn't on
Rocky for long because the deputy gave Yancy a pat on
the back and then headed out the front door.

"This is Jimbo McNash," the caller greeted Leigh.
His voice was like gravel. "You left me a couple of messages, said it was real important that I call you back."

That got her attention firmly focused on the "thug"
who Alexa had met at the diner. "Yes, it is important,"
she verified. "I have some questions for you."

"Cops," he grumbled in the same tone as Rocky had
said *sheriff*. "Got a call from Cullen Brodie, too. Now,
he's somebody I'd be interested in having another chat
with."

Leigh didn't know that Cullen had tried to get in
touch with the man, and she hit the speaker function on
her phone so he could hear the rest of the conversation.

"You said Cullen Brodie called you?" she pressed.

"Yep. This morning."

Cullen shook his head. *I didn't call him*, he mouthed.

"What exactly did Cullen say to you?" Leigh asked McNash.

"He said he'd heard I'd been meeting with his woman. His ex-woman," McNash emphasized. "And he said he'd be willing to pay me to hear anything his ex told me."

"And you agreed to that?" Leigh continued.

"Sure did. So, when you come out to see me, make sure you bring Cullen and his money with you," McNash snapped right before he ended the call.

Chapter 10

"I didn't call McNash," Cullen repeated as Leigh put her phone back in her pocket.

She nodded. "I believe you. And that means someone wanted either McNash or me to believe you'd called him."

Yeah, and Cullen had a good idea of who'd done that. "The killer or someone the killer hired."

Which, of course, didn't rule out Kali. Both Austin and she had had ample opportunity to contact McNash. Rocky had, too. But that led Cullen to another question.

"How would the killer have known about Alexa's meetings with McNash?" Cullen threw out there, but the moment the question was out of his mouth, he came up with possible answers. "Alexa told the killer. Or else McNash was the one who killed her." He paused, huffed. "Am I going to have to convince you to take me along on this visit to McNash's place?"

"No." She didn't hesitate, either. "If money's his motive, I'm counting on him telling you exactly what Alexa and he discussed. Then, if he presses you for payment, I'll arrest him for extortion." Leigh took a deep breath. "For now though, I need to find out why Kali hasn't gotten here yet."

However, Leigh didn't get a chance to do that because her phone dinged with a text.

"It's from Vance," she relayed. "The ME's finally taken Alexa's body to the morgue. We should have a verified time of death soon."

Cullen figured the TOD wasn't going to vary much from the 8:00 to 8:30 p.m. range that Jamie's timeline had already given them. Still, it was something Leigh needed to know. It was possible she'd be able to use the timeline and the photos from the guests to determine who was in the great room and who wasn't when Alexa had been murdered.

"You have Kali's number?" she asked, firing off a response to Vance's text.

Cullen took out his phone, pulled up Kali's contact, and Leigh called the woman. She put the call on speaker just as Kali answered.

"This is Sheriff Mercer. You're on your way to the police station." Leigh definitely didn't make that a question.

"No." And Cullen heard Kali sobbing again. "I'm on my way home. I need to try to settle my nerves. I'm not running away or anything," Kali quickly added. "I just have to get myself together before you start asking me a bunch of questions."

Leigh huffed. "You should have come here."

"I know." Kali continued to sob. "But I didn't want

to risk having Austin see me like this. I don't want him to know that he's crushed me. I'll be there in a couple of hours, I swear, and I'll tell you whatever I can. Promise."

Leigh's scowl deepened, and she checked the time. It was almost noon. "All right. I should be back from another interview in about three hours, and you can come in then." She paused a heartbeat. "Kali, just so you know. This interview isn't optional. If you don't show, I'll have to send a couple of my deputies over to escort you here."

"That's not necessary. I'll be there."

Leigh ended the call and glanced down at the torn knee of her jeans. And at the dried blood. It was a reminder that she hadn't gotten any medical attention. Maybe she didn't need it, but Cullen made a mental note to give her a push in that direction the next time they visited Jamie.

"I'll need to stop by my house and change my clothes," she muttered, reaching for her coat. She was still putting it on when Yancy came to the door.

"There's a problem with Austin Borden's lawyer," Yancy said. "The roads still aren't clear between here and his office in Ransom Ridge, and he can't come until later this afternoon."

"Great," Leigh muttered, and Cullen understood her frustration. Not only did she want answers from Austin, she probably also didn't want Kali and Austin squaring off when they were in the building together. "You confirmed that it's true about the roads not being clear?"

"I did," Yancy verified. "The work crews are just now salting the roads so there's still plenty of ice."

Leigh nodded. "All right. Cut Austin loose for a while. Tell him to be back here by four o'clock. Since you haven't gotten much sleep, Vance or Dawn can interview Austin and Kali. They should be back here once they're able to get away from the Triple R."

"I'm okay," Yancy assured. "I can do at least one of the interviews."

She seemed to consider that a moment and then nodded again. "All right. Make sure you do it by the book. I'm going to visit Jimbo McNash."

"I just saw that name on a preliminary report from Cecile," Yancy explained. "She sent it to you and all the deputies."

"Did Cecile see Jimbo's name in any of Alexa's emails?" Leigh quickly asked.

"Not that she said. I don't think she's had time to go through them yet. This was just a quick report to say that she'd be looking for that particular connection." Yancy paused. "You think this guy had something to do with Alexa's murder?"

"That's what I intend to find out. I intend to question him after I've made a quick stop at my house for a change of clothes."

"Then you should probably take backup," Yancy said, the concern in his voice.

Leigh slid a glance to Cullen, maybe deciding that he could play backup if necessary. Maybe also calculating how long it would delay this visit if she had to wait for one of the other deputies to arrive.

"I have a license to carry," Cullen simply reminded her. "And you know I'm carrying." Though the reminder wasn't necessary since she'd seen him fire at the SUV that had attacked them.

"All right, I can legally deputize you," Leigh said after

a short pause. "Temporarily deputize you," she emphasized.

Cullen didn't smile. Or curse. But he wasn't sure how he felt about being a cop. Even a temporary one. Still, this was about protecting Leigh and getting answers, so he'd handle the deputy label for the next couple of hours.

Leigh started toward the door but then stopped and looked at Yancy. "If possible, arrange the interviews so that Kali and Austin aren't in here at the same time."

Yancy assured her that he would, and Cullen and she headed out, only to have Leigh stop again when she glanced around the parking lot. "My cruiser's wrecked," she muttered.

"We can take my truck," Cullen offered.

She didn't turn him down, though Cullen suspected she would have preferred to use an official vehicle for this visit with a suspect. Especially since she might have to arrest the man. But if that happened, Cullen's truck did have a narrow back seat they could use to transport him back to the police station.

Cullen deiced the windshield, noting that there were more people out and about now. People who noticed Leigh in the truck with him, and he wondered how much gossip and grief that was going to cause her.

"I'm muddying your reputation," Cullen joked, hoping to get a smile out of her.

No such luck. She looked at him with a slew of emotions crossing her face. Two of those emotions might have been frustration and regret, but there was also the heat.

"I would kiss you here and now just because I'm riled enough at the people who love picking my every move apart." Leigh took in a deep breath. "But that'd be using you."

Now he smiled. "If you kissed me, I'm positive that I'd feel plenty of things, but *used* isn't one of them."

She smiled, too, while shaking her head. Much to his disappointment though, she didn't kiss him.

Cullen drove to her place on the edge of town. Her one-story white limestone house sat in the center of four acres surrounded by white fence. A small red barn was behind the house, and he spotted a couple of bay mares inside. He'd known that Leigh was a horse lover, which wasn't a surprise since she'd been raised on a ranch.

He pulled up in front of her house, and both of them glanced around, looking for any signs of trouble, before she used her phone to disengage her security system. As they got out, Cullen pushed open the side of his jacket in case he had to go for his gun, but when Leigh unlocked the door and they went in, nothing seemed to be out of place.

"I won't be long," she said, leaving him in the foyer. But she only made it a couple of steps before she turned back, caught onto him.

And she kissed him.

Cullen didn't even care that she'd chosen to do this behind closed doors. What he cared about was the instant slam of heat and need. The feel of her mouth. The pressure of her body against his. She didn't linger long, just enough to assure him that this attraction wasn't going away anytime soon.

Mumbling something he didn't catch, she pushed away from him and headed for the hall. "Help yourself to whatever you find in the fridge."

He wasn't the least bit interested in her fridge and

considered going after her and seeing how far he could take things. Of course, he already knew that would just lead them to bed, and they couldn't take the time for that now. The sooner they got to Jimbo, the sooner they might have the answers they needed.

Forcing himself to go anywhere but to her bedroom, Cullen strolled into the living room. No fuss and frills here. There was a comfortable leather sofa the color of caramel, and from the looks of the way things were arranged, Leigh spent time in here reading, watching TV and working on a laptop that was open on a rustic coffee table.

He went to the fireplace to have a closer look at the single framed photograph on the mantel. A family shot of Cash, Leigh, their mother and their missing brother, Joe. It'd been taken when Leigh had been about five. That would have meant Cash was about seven and Joe three and a half. They were all smiling, and Cash was holding up a fish that he'd likely just caught.

It was a happy photo of a happy family, taken on a sunny summer day. There probably hadn't been many happy days after that because by Cullen's estimation, Joe had gone missing shortly afterward. A year later, Helen Mercer had died in a car accident that many had considered suicide. Losing her mother when she'd been so young was something they had in common.

"It used to hurt when I'd see that picture," Leigh said from behind him.

Cullen looked back at her, at the clean pair of jeans she was wearing. She'd also freed her hair from the ponytail, and it fell loose just below her shoulders.

"But now it gives me, well, comfort," she added. "Jeb took the picture. That's why he's not in it."

She probably didn't know that there was a tinge of bitterness in her tone when she said her father's name, and Cullen doubted that photo would be there for a daily reminder had Jeb actually been a visual part of the "happy" scene.

"You remember your mom?" he asked.

"Some. I have good memories, then the memories of her crying after Joe was taken." Leigh motioned for him to go with her to the door. "What about you? Do you remember your mother?"

"Some," he said, echoing her answer. And like Leigh, there were some good memories, but there'd been plenty of times when his mother had had way too much to drink. Something she'd done the night she died. As a child he couldn't see it. Now he knew she'd been an alcoholic. A mostly out-of-control one who'd made a habit of drinking and driving.

"You blame Bowen for her death?" Leigh asked.

"No." That was the truth. "But I love my father. Most of the time, anyway. So it's not something I talk about with him. Mostly though, I just blame my mother for not getting the help she obviously needed. Then again, I should put some of that blame on my dad, too, because he had to have known that the drinking had gotten way out of hand."

Leigh made a sound of agreement and added a genuine sounding "I'm sorry" as they went to his truck, and she reset the security system with her phone. She then gave him Jimbo's address so he could put it in the GPS.

"How much grief would your father give you…" But Leigh stopped and waved that off.

"How much grief would he give me if I started seeing you again?" Cullen finished for her. "Plenty," he readily admitted, "but that won't stop me. At this point, I doubt there's much of anything that'd stop us."

She didn't disagree with that, but the long breath she took let him know that she'd be getting plenty of grief as well.

"Your father approved of Alexa?" she asked.

Cullen nearly laughed when he recalled the many arguments Bowen and Alexa had had. "No. Not one little bit. He thought she had too much flash, too much temper."

Which was true, but Cullen had been attracted to her. That attraction was a drop in the bucket though compared to what he felt for Leigh. And he knew it was best to keep that to himself. He could coax Leigh into having an affair with him, but she wouldn't want to know how deep his feelings for her ran.

Cullen wasn't sure *he* wanted to know.

It had crushed him all the way to the bone, or rather the heart, the last time Leigh walked out of his life and he didn't want another round of that. Still, he was going to have to take the risk.

The roads were mostly clear and there was almost no traffic, but Cullen kept watch as they made their way out of Dark River and to the farm road that led to Jimbo's place. With each passing mile, Cullen's concerns grew, and he forced his mind off Leigh and back on the danger hanging over them.

"If Jimbo killed Alexa and was the one driving that SUV, he might try to finish us off," Cullen reminded her.

"Yes." She said it so fast that it'd obviously been on her mind. "I think the best way for us to do this is for me to call Jimbo when we get to his house. I'll insist that he come out so I can check him for weapons."

That was a good start, but Cullen wanted to go one step further. "You could question him while we're in the truck. That way, you're not out in the open in case he has a partner in crime."

She stayed quiet a moment. "Jimbo might not go for standing out in the cold while I talk to him."

"He might if he thinks this could lead to a payoff," Cullen quickly fired back.

Cullen gave her some time to work that around in her mind. Leigh finally nodded and took out her phone. She didn't press Jimbo's number though until Cullen took the final turn toward the farm.

And that's when Cullen saw the smoke.

There were dark coils of it rising into the sky, but the winter wind was whipping away at it, scattering it almost as soon as it rose. Since it was way too much smoke for an ordinary fireplace, Cullen got a very bad feeling in his gut.

"Jimbo's not answering," Leigh said, her attention focused on the smoke.

It was less than thirty seconds before they reached the house. Or rather what was left of it. The structure was engulfed in flames.

The sight of those flames sent Leigh's stomach to her knees. In that instant, she knew the chances were very high that this wasn't an accidental fire.

And that Jimbo might be dead.

Because she doubted the man had set this fire. Then again, maybe he had if he'd thought he was about to be arrested for murder. There was a problem with that theory because of the truck parked in front of the house, and she was betting the truck belonged to Jimbo. Still, she wanted to hold out hope that he'd caught a ride with someone and torched his house to conceal any evidence inside.

Even though she didn't like the idea of a prime suspect being in the wind, it was better than the alternative of the man being dead. Dead men couldn't give her answers about those meetings with Alexa.

Since Leigh already had her phone in her hand, she called 911 to get the fire department out to Jimbo's house. But she could already see that they wouldn't get there in time to save the place.

She glanced around the yard, at the rusted-out farm equipment, overgrown trees and piles of junk. No Jimbo. In fact, no sign of anyone, but if he'd been attacked, then maybe he'd managed to make it outside before he would have been overcome by the smoke and fire.

"I'm keeping watch," Cullen assured her.

Leigh was already doing the same thing. Because even if Jimbo had been the one to set the fire, it was possible he'd stayed around to try to ambush them. That possibility, however, bit the dust when she saw Jimbo stagger out the front door.

The man's head and chest were bleeding, and he was clearly dazed. Added to that, his shirt was on fire.

Cullen and she threw open their doors at the same time. They also drew their guns as one. Cullen sprinted across the yard toward Jimbo, catching onto him to take his weight and slapping out the fire with the sleeve of his coat. Leigh went to help, but she also looked all around the yard to make sure there was no other threat.

Jimbo mumbled something she couldn't understand and collapsed. If Cullen hadn't had hold of him, he would have fallen face-first to the ground. Cullen grabbed the man's arms, dragging him away from the house.

In the nick of time.

Because a chunk of the roof came crashing down and sent out a cloud of smoke, ash and cinders. When some of those cinders landed on Cullen, she had to use her own sleeve to stop them from igniting into full flames.

From the corner of her eye, she caught some movement to the right, but the wind shifted, sending the thick smoke right at them. She couldn't see her hand in front of her face much less someone who could be yards away. But the good news about that was the person might not be able to see them, either.

Leigh heard the sharp cracking sound, and for a split second she thought the rest of the house was collapsing. But then she knew what it was.

Gunfire.

Someone had just taken a shot at them, and the bullet tore into the ground just a few feet from where they were dragging Jimbo.

Cullen cursed, and he tried to shove Leigh behind him. "Get down," he snapped.

No way would Leigh do that. Not with someone shooting at them. She moved to take Jimbo's other arm to help Cullen drag him to the side of the truck so they'd have cover.

"Did you see the shooter?" Leigh asked Cullen. "I think he was running up from the right."

"I didn't see anyone," he said. His words rushed together with his heavy breath, and he peered over the front end of his truck. The shot came right away, skimming across the metal hood and slamming into a tree behind him. Cursing him, Leigh grabbed Cullen and forced him back down.

What he'd just done was way past being dangerous, but it'd helped pinpoint the direction of the shooter. He was in or near that area with the old farm equipment. Equipment that was plenty large enough to conceal whomever it was she'd glimpsed from the corner of her eye.

It had to be the killer.

But why hadn't he been in place to shoot them when they'd arrived? It would have been the perfect time since their attention was mostly focused on the burning house. Later, she'd give that some thought, but for now she needed to work on how to get them out of this.

They couldn't stay put. They were too close to the house, and it would collapse. No doubts about that. And when it went, some of those fiery chunks of wood could land on them. Plus, Jimbo was bleeding and needed medical attention ASAP. Leigh sent a quick text for an ambulance and backup.

More shots came, all of them slamming into the truck, but some of the bullets seemed to have come from different angles. The gunman could be on the move, maybe making his way to them so he could shoot them the moment he rounded the truck.

"Watch the front. I'll keep an eye on the rear," Leigh told Cullen.

Cullen dropped down on the ground next to Jimbo so he could look out underneath the truck. "He's coming this way," he snarled, and he shifted his gun to take aim.

Cullen fired.

The pain shot through Leigh's ears. It'd been necessary though. With the angle of his shot, Cullen would have likely only managed to wound the gunman in the leg, but that might be enough to stop him.

Cullen cursed again. "Smoke," he snapped.

That was the only warning Leigh got before another cloud of smoke came at them. It was thick and smothering, and it must have gotten to the gunman as well because she heard someone cough. And then she heard something else. More of the house collapsed, and the blazing debris landed between them and the shooter.

"I'm dying," Jimbo muttered, drawing her attention back to him. Unlike Cullen and her, he wasn't coughing, and the man seemed to be on his last breath.

Leigh needed him alive, and the only chance they had was to get him to a hospital fast. She reached up, fumbling for the door, and opened it as wide as she could manage.

"Get in and stay down," Cullen told her through his coughs.

"You do the same," she insisted.

She took hold of Jimbo's arm, and while Cullen and she both tried to keep watch, they hauled the man into the center of the seat. Cullen quickly followed, getting behind the wheel. He threw the truck into Reverse and gunned the engine.

Leigh braced herself for the hail of gunfire.

But it didn't come.

Still, she kept her gun ready while Cullen sped out of the driveway. Once they were out of the cloud of smoke, she looked around, trying to pick through the yard to spot the person who'd just tried to kill them.

Nothing.

The shooter was nowhere in sight.

Chapter 11

Cullen could feel the exhaustion all the way to his bones, and he figured it was the same for Leigh. They were both dragging when they walked into her house, nearly ten hours after they'd left to do the interview with Jimbo. What was supposed to have been a short trip had turned into a grueling ordeal. One that could have ended with Leigh and him dead.

Like Jimbo.

Despite their efforts to save him, Jimbo had died shortly after they'd arrived at the hospital. He hadn't been able to tell anyone who'd put the two bullets in his chest that'd killed him. And with his house a total loss, his killer hadn't left any evidence behind. In fact, he'd left nothing behind. The local cops hadn't been able to find him or a vehicle he'd used to get to Jimbo's. It was as if the guy had vanished like the smoke from the fire.

At least during the ten hours, Leigh's deputies had done the interviews with Austin and Kali. According to the updates Leigh had gotten, neither had given any new info, but the interviews ticked off some necessary legal boxes. So had the searches of both Kali's and her parents' houses. Some blue dresses had been collected at both and had been sent to the lab.

"The bathroom's there," Leigh said, motioning toward the hall. "The guest room's right next to it." She glanced at his jeans and shirt that were stained with Jimbo's blood. "I'll see if I can find you something to wear while you wash those. The laundry room's just off the kitchen."

Cullen wasn't sure if he wanted to think about why she'd have men's clothes in her house, and he sure as heck wasn't going to press on getting something from the Triple R. According to Mack, the ranch was still being processed as a crime scene, and the CSIs didn't want anything removed until they were finished.

Leigh glanced down at her own clothes, at the blood there, and she groaned softly. It didn't matter that Jimbo had been a thug with a long criminal history. A man was dead, and he'd almost certainly died because Alexa's killer had wanted to tie up any loose ends.

But how had the killer known to go after Jimbo?

That was a question that'd been circling in Cullen's mind. No doubt circling in Leigh's, too.

"Help yourself to anything in the kitchen," she added. "Once you're done with your shower, let me know, and I'll take one."

Neither of them moved, and exhaustion was only part of the reason why. Cullen could practically feel the guilt coming off her.

"You couldn't have saved Jimbo," Cullen insisted.

"I could have if I'd realized the killer would go after him." She muttered some profanity and then groaned. "I should have realized it. I should have asked the locals to provide him protection until I could get out to his place."

He could have reminded her that she'd been embroiled in a murder investigation and that she was functioning on very little sleep. But she'd see that as part of the job so he saved his breath. Instead, he went to her and pulled her into his arms. Maybe it was the exhaustion playing into this again, but she didn't resist. She went body to body with him and dropped her head on his shoulder.

Cullen knew she was allowing this because she needed some comfort, and there weren't exactly a lot of people in Dark River who could offer her that. Heck, he needed what she was giving as well. It'd been a damn long day, and it felt good to stand there with her like this.

"Don't kiss me," she said. "I don't have the willpower to do anything about it."

Cullen managed to laugh. "That's probably not something you should tell me."

"Yes, it is," Leigh argued. "Because underneath all that bad boy, you're a decent guy."

Well, hell. How could he kiss her after she'd said that? And yes, he had indeed been thinking about a kiss or two. Nothing more though. When they ended up having sex again, he wanted them to have enough energy to enjoy it. Still, Cullen settled for brushing a kiss on her forehead because there was indeed some bad boy beneath the decency.

The kiss caused her to chuckle a little, and she stepped

back to meet his gaze. Mercy, she was beautiful even now with those tired eyes.

"You're not thinking about sex, are you?" he asked, hoping that she'd managed to get a second wind.

"No." The corner of her mouth lifted in a smile. A smile that quickly faded. "I was thinking about how the killer knew to go after Jimbo."

So, her mind had indeed been toying with that.

"Let me change my clothes," she added a moment later, "and then I'd like to hear your theories on how that could have happened." She went into her bedroom but didn't close the door all the way. "I'm thinking Alexa could have told her killer about Jimbo. Maybe she did that in passing, and then the killer might have decided that Alexa could have told Jimbo about him or her."

Cullen could see that happening with Austin or Kali. Austin because he was having an affair with Alexa, and Kali because Alexa was her friend. He'd heard Leigh talking on the phone with Yancy, and the deputy had taken both Austin's and Kali's statements, and it'd be interesting to see if there was any connection to Jimbo.

When the killer was finally identified and locked up, Cullen knew he was also going to have to deal with the impact of his best friend having a relationship with his ex. Even though Cullen had no longer loved Alexa, the affair still felt like a betrayal. One that he'd need to process. Process and then hopefully put aside since he had a lot of things to deal with. That included his feelings for Leigh.

"Or maybe Jimbo had a partner," Leigh added a moment later, "and the partner killed him rather than risk Jimbo tying him or her to a murder."

Despite the seriousness of the conversation, it took

Cullen a moment to focus on something other than remembering Leigh and her beautiful, tired eyes from moments ago. "Either of those are possible," he said, leaning against the wall outside her door. "But Rocky would have gotten the preliminary report that your other deputy sent out. He knew you'd be earmarking any emails or texts between Alexa and Jimbo."

He had no trouble hearing her quick sound of agreement which meant that had already occurred to her.

"This rules out your father," Leigh went on. "He knew about Jimbo before Alexa's murder, and if he was a killer, he probably wouldn't have waited hours to eliminate someone who could have incriminated him."

"Bowen will be pleased to hear that." And yeah, he added a little tongue and cheek to that comment.

"Jeb won't be pleased." Leigh had a tongue-in-cheek tone, too.

At the mention of her father's name, Cullen recalled what'd happened in the break room when Jeb had had the dizzy spell. Or whatever the heck it'd been. He nearly brought it up now, but Leigh continued before he could say anything.

"But I'd prefer to arrest the person responsible rather than the person I want it to be," she said, and he heard her sigh.

"You want it to be Rocky," he concluded. "He's withheld evidence and backbites you any chance he gets."

"And that's why I'm being very careful about how I'm dealing with him. I don't want to project something on him that might not be there. He might not be more than just a backbiter."

She opened the door, and he saw that she was wearing a white terry cloth bathrobe. It wasn't clinging, low-cut or anything else provocative, but it still got his attention.

Before he could give in to the temptation of sliding his hand inside that robe, she thrust out a pair of black pj bottoms.

"Sorry," she said. "It's the best I can do. Cash stayed here about six years ago when his house was being painted, and he left them behind. Just the bottoms," Leigh clarified. "So, you'll have to do the bare-chest thing while your clothes are being washed."

He was about to joke and ask her if she'd be watching for that, but her doorbell rang. Leigh whirled around, scooping up her holster. At the same time, Cullen also drew his gun.

"I doubt the killer would ring the doorbell," he said, trying to steady her nerves. But Cullen didn't plan on putting his gun away until he was sure who was at the door.

Cullen went to one of the side windows. Leigh went to the other. And they both groaned when they spotted Austin on her porch.

"I have to talk to you," Austin called out, ringing the bell again.

"I'll get rid of him," Cullen offered, and he didn't wait for Leigh to object.

He held on to his gun as he opened the door and faced his friend. That would be *former* friend since one look at Austin and Cullen knew Austin was still riled. Heck, Cullen was, too.

"Where's Leigh?" Austin demanded.

With just those two words, Cullen got a whiff of Austin's breath. He'd clearly been drinking.

"What do you want?" Leigh asked, moving in front of Cullen to face Austin head-on.

"Kali thinks I murdered Alexa," Austin blurted out, pointing his index finger at Leigh. "You made her believe that."

Hell. This was not what Leigh needed to be dealing with after the day they'd already had. "Leigh was doing her job," Cullen quickly pointed out. "And you didn't exactly volunteer information about your affair with Alexa."

Austin's rage-filled eyes slashed to Cullen. "Because it was my personal business. My mistake. There was no reason for me to tell a cop."

"No," Leigh disagreed. "There's no such thing as personal business in a murder investigation."

"Have you tried to ruin Cullen the way you're ruining me?" Austin fired back. Then, he smirked. "No, you haven't because you're sleeping with him again." He gave a hollow laugh. "Alexa was right about that."

Cullen stared at Austin. "What do you mean by that?"

Austin continued the smirk. "Alexa saw you looking at an old picture of the two of you. The one taken at a party when Leigh was still in high school."

The party where Leigh had lost her virginity to him. Cullen did indeed have a picture, but he didn't remember looking at it while Alexa was around.

"Alexa was so jealous of you," Austin continued, his comment aimed at Leigh. "And she had a vindictive streak and wouldn't have wanted Cullen and you to be together. I could have sent her after you like that." He snapped his fingers. "Too bad I didn't. If I had, you wouldn't have ruined my life."

Enough was enough. Cullen stepped in front of Leigh again. "You ruined your own life," Cullen snarled. "By not keeping your jeans zipped when you were around your fiancée's best friend. If you want to put the blame on someone, just look in the mirror."

Austin clearly didn't care much for that, and he reached out as if he might try to clamp onto Leigh's arm. Cullen didn't let that happen. The punch he landed on Austin's jaw was hard and fast. Austin staggered back, the blood already oozing from his mouth, and he glared at Cullen.

"You two deserve each other," Austin snarled, and weaving, he started off the porch and toward his truck in the driveway.

Leigh sighed, took out her phone. "You've been drinking," she called out to Austin, "and you're not getting behind the wheel. We have a couple of people in town doing Uber, and I'll get you a ride."

"I don't want a ride," he insisted, although he didn't get in his truck. He started walking back toward town. Cullen was about to go after him, but he saw the truck approaching the house.

"Great," Leigh muttered. "It's Jeb."

Cullen hadn't thought this day could get any worse, but he'd apparently been wrong. Jeb stopped his truck next to Austin and lowered the window. Cullen couldn't hear what they said, but they had a very short conversation before Austin got in the passenger's seat.

Jeb drove to the house, got out and was sporting a serious scowl as he walked to the porch. "I'll see that Austin gets to the inn. There should be rooms open by now."

"Thanks," Cullen said, and he was glad Jeb was seeing to this. Austin was in no shape to drive or walk in the cold.

Jeb didn't acknowledge Cullen's thanks. In fact, he didn't acknowledge Cullen at all. He stared at his daughter.

"I came to give you a heads-up," Jeb said. "Rocky's asked the town council to have a meeting tomorrow. You'll need to be there."

"And why would I need to do that?" Leigh asked.

Jeb swore under his breath and scrubbed his hand over his face. "Because Rocky's going to present what he says is evidence to have you removed as sheriff."

Leigh read through the CSI and ME reports and tried to stay focused. Hard to do because she'd had yet another night with little sleep.

Cullen probably hadn't fared much better in the sleep department, and he looked as tired as she was as he worked on a laptop in her living room. She wanted to tell him to take a break, especially since she'd have to be heading into her office soon, but he was going through the photos that the deputies had collected from the party guests. Those photos might end up holding some clues as to what had happened that night.

She desperately needed answers. Desperately needed the attacks to stop before anyone else died. She could still feel Jimbo's blood on her hands. Could still hear the sound of gunfire.

She pushed back what would have been a shudder, drank her coffee and kept reading. Basically, there was no news in either report that she could use to make an arrest, but the ME had concluded that Alexa had recently had sex. That didn't necessarily mean that sex

had been with Austin, but Leigh would need to take another look at Cullen's friend. Before she did that though,
she wanted the lab results on the clothes that'd been
taken from Austin's house. There was no telling when
those would be processed, but she'd give the lab a call
and try to hurry them.

If she had a job, that is.

She tried not to think that she could lose her badge
today. It could happen though. She doubted that Rocky
had any actual evidence to present to the town council,
but he could use her connection with Cullen. That was a
darn good reason for her to put some distance between
Cullen and her. But if she did that, it would be for all the
wrong reasons—because she'd been pressured into it.

There were right reasons for distancing herself. A
possible broken heart and butting heads with Bowen.
However, one look at Cullen, and Leigh knew she didn't
exactly have a choice about her feelings for him.

"Problem?" Cullen asked, and that was when Leigh
realized he'd caught her staring at him.

She waved that off just as her phone rang. "Jeb," she
muttered and hit the decline button. Leigh wasn't in the
mood for a lecture or advice.

Cullen stood, facing her, and he crammed his hands
in the pockets of his jeans. It seemed to her that he was
having a debate about what he wanted to say. "Is your
father okay?" he asked.

Of all the things Leigh had thought Cullen might
say, that wasn't one of them. And his tone only added
to her surprise. He seemed concerned, and that didn't
mesh with his usual feelings about Jeb.

"Why do you ask?" she countered, and she hoped

this wasn't about to turn into a discussion of whether or not Jeb could have killed Alexa and Jimbo.

Again, Cullen hesitated. He shook his head, then huffed. "Jeb wanted me to swear not to tell you, but he had a dizzy spell yesterday in the break room. It happened shortly after you left for your office."

Everything inside Leigh went still while she tried to wrap her mind around that. "A dizzy spell?"

Cullen nodded. "He went pale and staggered back before I caught him. If he hadn't told me to keep it from you, I might have dismissed it as nothing. But it feels like something," he added.

Yes, it did, and Leigh tried to wrap her mind around that, too. Was Jeb sick? Or was it worse than that? Either way, she could see him wanting to keep it from her. Maybe because he didn't want her thinking he was weak. Or perhaps because it was just something he wanted to keep to himself. Neither of those excuses would work on her. Jeb and she might not be close, but she wanted to know if he was having health problems.

Leigh pressed Jeb's number, and since he'd just tried to call her, she expected him to answer. He didn't. In fact, it went to voice mail, but before she could leave him a message, she got an incoming call from the reserve deputy Cecile Taggart.

"Is everything okay with Jamie?" Leigh immediately asked.

"He's fine. In fact, the doctor might let him go home late today or tomorrow."

Leigh released the breath she was holding. That was good news. No one had tried to kill Jamie again, but his release would pose a few new problems. She'd need to get with Cullen on that and see how they could protect him while he was on the Triple R.

"I was calling about those emails and phone records you wanted me to check," Cecile continued a moment later. "Alexa's emails and phone records," she explained. "I've been going through them, and I think I found something."

"I'm listening," Leigh assured her, and she was. So was Cullen, who'd moved closer to her. Leigh put the call on speaker so he'd be able to hear.

"Well, it might be nothing, but there's a text from Alexa to Kali Starling where Alexa confesses that she's having an affair with Kali's fiancé."

Leigh was reasonably sure this wasn't *nothing*. "When did Alexa send that?"

"About four hours before the start of the party," Cecile quickly answered. "It appears Alexa deleted some other texts from her sent folder but not this one."

"Did Kali respond to the text?"

"Not with a text, but there's a record of an incoming call from Kali shortly after she would have gotten the text."

Leigh groaned. It would have been better to have that particular conversation in writing, but maybe Kali could fill in the blanks. "I want you to forward me that text," Leigh instructed.

"Will do, but there's more. Vance and Dawn have been going through the pictures of the guests at the party. I don't think it's my imagination that Kali looks pretty upset in several of them. In one, she looks sort of disheveled. Windblown, I guess you'd say. Her hair is a little messy, and she looks as if she's been crying."

Interesting, and Leigh very much wanted to know

what Kali had to say about that. She ended the call with Cecile and immediately contacted Kali. Leigh almost expected the woman to dodge her, but she answered.

"Kali, one of my deputies just went through Alexa's texts," Leigh said, going right to the heart of the matter. "Anything you want to tell me that you left out of your interview?"

"W-what?" Kali answered, slurring the word.

"Alexa's texts," Leigh repeated.

Kali moaned softly. "Uh, I can't think right now." That was slurred, too.

"Kali, are you all right?" Leigh demanded.

There were more moans. "Sleeping now. I took something to help me sleep." And with that, the woman ended the call.

Leigh cursed and immediately contacted dispatch. "I need someone to go to Kali Starling's residence and do a welfare check. Make it fast," she told the dispatcher. "It's possible the woman has overdosed on sleeping pills."

If she had, hopefully help wouldn't be late in getting there.

"Would Kali try to kill herself?" Leigh asked Cullen.

He lifted his shoulder. "I don't know. But if you think it'll be a while before someone can get to her place, I'll go."

Leigh considered it, then shook her head. "If Kali's the killer, this could be a trap." And that was something Leigh relayed to the dispatcher when she called him back.

She'd just put her phone away when there was a knock at her door. Heck, what now? Frustrated, she went to the side window, looked out and spotted Jeb. He must have known she would peer out like that because his gaze zoomed right to hers.

"I need to see you," he said.

Leigh looked at him, studying his face to see if there were any signs of the paleness and staggering that Cullen had described. Nothing out of the ordinary except his eyes were tired. Then again, her eyes were probably tired, too.

She went to the door and opened it. "I'm not up to a long visit," she said, "but I do have questions for you."

With his mouth tightening, Jeb shifted his attention to Cullen. "If something's wrong with you, Leigh should know," Cullen told him.

"No time for that," Jeb insisted, turning back to Leigh. "The mayor just called, and he's assembled the town council. You're about to get a call from him, and he'll tell you that they want you there right now."

Chapter 12

Cullen thought the mood in the town hall felt like a witch hunt. And he was pretty sure that at least some of the council considered Leigh to be the witch. But Cullen hoped that Rocky hadn't been able to turn all of them against the woman the majority of residents had elected sheriff.

"If the town council votes to start the process to oust you," Jeb explained as they paused outside the door of the meeting room, "it wouldn't be immediate."

Leigh nodded. "They'd have to initiate a recall." Her jaw was tight. Eyes, narrowed. "The voters would have to decide if I should stay or go."

Cullen couldn't blame her for being riled to the core. He knew how much the badge meant to her, and how devastated she'd be if it was taken away.

Leigh stepped ahead of them and opened the door. She didn't hesitate but instead walked into the room and went straight to the front. The mayor, Noble Henning, was there at the center of the rectangular table, and part of his mayoral duties was to head the council. He was flanked by the five other members who made up the town council. Those other members were business owners or prominent citizens—which explained why Jeb was on it. He took his seat at the far end of the table.

Noble was a huge man with an equally huge belly. Since he was a rancher, Cullen had done business with him and had found him fair enough. Right now though, nothing felt fair, and Cullen cursed Noble, Rocky and everyone at the council table for putting Leigh through this.

Rocky was there in the front row, and he made a point of staring at Leigh as she stood in front of the people who could decide her fate. Word of the meeting apparently hadn't gotten out because other than the mayor and the members of the council, Rocky was the only other person there.

Cullen stayed at the back of the room, but Leigh went all the way to the table to face the council along with giving Rocky a cold, hard glance that was effective enough to cause him to look away.

Noble cleared his throat and also had some trouble looking Leigh in the eye. Instead, he read from his notes. "Sheriff Mercer, there have been complaints and concerns about you being negligent in carrying out your duties in the murders you're currently investigating. Deputy Rocky Callaway claims you've shown preferential treatment to a suspect and have failed to arrest that suspect because you're having a sexual relationship with him."

That got Cullen moving forward, but Leigh spoke before he could say anything.

"I'm assuming that my deputy is referring to Cullen Brodie." Leigh's voice was calm, but Cullen suspected there was no calmness beneath the surface.

Noble nodded just as Rocky blurted out, "You should have arrested Cullen instead of sleeping with him."

"There was no evidence to make that arrest," Leigh countered, turning her attention back to the mayor. "Cullen's clothes were taken to the lab and there was no blood on them. The CSIs used a UV light on other clothes in his closet and didn't detect any blood. According to the assessment of the crime scene, the killer would have gotten some blood spatter on themselves."

"Cullen was alone with the body—" Rocky started, but the mayor motioned for him to hush.

"The lab is still testing the clothing of others who attended the party," Leigh continued without missing a beat, "and once I have those results I might be able to make an arrest if the evidence warrants that. There are several people who have means, motive and opportunity, and some, including Deputy Callaway, weren't forthcoming with information about the victim."

Rocky practically jumped to his feet. "I wasn't forthcoming because it wasn't relevant."

"I decide what's relevant in a murder investigation." Leigh tapped her badge. "And you failed to tell me about a meeting you had with the victim."

Noble made another motion for Rocky to sit back down. The deputy did after several snail-crawling moments. Then, Noble's gaze shifted to Cullen.

"I'm guessing you've got something you want to say to the council?" Noble asked.

Cullen was certain his body language conveyed that, yes, he did have something to say. He wanted to tell them all to go to hell and take the backstabbing Rocky with them. But that venom wouldn't help Leigh.

"I'm not especially happy that any one of you would think I'd need to sleep with the sheriff in order to keep myself out of jail," Cullen snarled. "It especially pisses me off that you'd think Leigh would sleep with someone she believes could bash in a woman's head."

"Are you saying you haven't shared the sheriff's bed?" Noble asked.

"I'm saying it's none of your business," he snapped at the same time Leigh said, "Cullen's not a suspect so you don't have cause to ask that question."

Rocky smirked, obviously pleased because he probably thought Leigh was digging herself into a huge hole.

The door practically flew open, and Vance, Dawn and Yancy all came rushing in. They glanced around the room as if assessing the situation and then went to the front to stand by Leigh.

"Sorry," Vance said, "but we just got the word that the sheriff was having some trouble here. We didn't want her facing that trouble alone."

Leigh made eye contact with all three of them and nodded her appreciation. "Thank you," she said plenty loud enough for everyone in the room to hear.

"The *trouble* is," Noble spoke up, emphasizing the word, "the sheriff doesn't seem to be close to arresting anybody for murder."

"She's had less than two days," Cullen argued and got sounds and mumbles of agreement from the three deputies standing with her. "You want her to arrest the wrong person just so you'll have someone behind bars? I don't think you want that kind of justice doled out here."

"No, I don't want the wrong person arrested," Noble countered, "but I want the threat gone. I want people to know they're safe in their own homes."

"This might help," Vance said, and he handed Leigh a piece of paper.

She read through what was written on it, and while she didn't smile, Cullen thought he saw some relief. "The SUV that rammed into my cruiser was sent to the lab for processing," Leigh relayed to the council. "The steering wheel had been wiped, but they found a partial print. The lab's going to try to match it."

Noble blew out what Cullen thought might be a breath of relief. "Good," he said. "Then, we'll postpone this meeting until you've had a chance to get the match."

It didn't seem nearly enough. More postponing the witch hunt rather than giving Leigh the credit she was due.

Jeb stood as if he might say something for, or against, his daughter, but Leigh's attention wasn't on her father. Or anyone else on the council. It was on her phone as it rang.

"It's Austin," she relayed in a whisper to Cullen and her three standing deputies. While Noble officially ended the meeting, Leigh stepped to the side of the room to take the call. Cullen went with her.

"Something's happened to Kali," he heard Austin blurt out.

Cullen thought of the part of the phone conversation he'd heard when Leigh had been talking to Kali. Leigh had been concerned enough to send someone out to check on the woman.

"What's wrong?" Leigh demanded.

"I came to her house to check on her, but she's not here." Austin groaned. "And there's blood on her back porch. Leigh, you need to come right away."

Leigh had plenty on her mind as Cullen and she hurried out of the town hall toward his truck. She still had plenty of anger about the town council meeting that Rocky had been able to wrangle. Plenty of anger directed at Rocky, too. But right now, her focus was on Kali.

She certainly hadn't forgotten about her brief conversation with Kali, and Leigh had suspected then that the woman was in some kind of trouble. Not the kind of trouble that would cause blood to be on her porch though. No. However, Leigh knew this could have turned out to be an overdose, either accidental or intentional.

"Where are you now?" Leigh asked Austin.

"I'm trying to figure out a way inside Kali's house. She must have changed the locks because my key doesn't work, and all the windows are locked up."

It didn't surprise her that Kali would change the locks. The woman had been very upset over Austin's cheating. But that led Leigh to another question. "Why call me and not the locals?"

"Uh, I don't know the locals," Austin answered. "I know you."

Yes, and it was a huge understatement to say he didn't much care for her. Still, it was possible this wasn't a trap and had nothing to do with his feelings about her. Maybe Austin was truly panicked about Kali, and he would have had her phone number right there in his contacts.

"Call an ambulance," Leigh instructed Austin, "but don't go in." Because if this wasn't an overdose, it could be another murder. The killer could still be inside. "There should be someone from Clay Ridge PD arriving soon. Tell him or her what you just told me."

She ended the call and instructed her own deputies—Vance, Yancy and Dawn—to go back to whatever needed to be done, that she would handle things with Kali. Then, Leigh called her brother, and she was thankful when Cash answered right away.

"One of my deputies, Karen Wheatly, should be at Kali's house soon," Cash said without any kind of greeting. "I'm guessing that's why you're calling?"

"I am," Leigh confirmed. The moment they'd buckled up, Cullen took off, heading out of town. "Her former fiancé is there now, and he says there's blood on the porch."

Cash cursed. "The dispatcher didn't say there were any signs of foul play or danger so I didn't send any backup with Karen."

"I just now found out about the blood, and Cullen and I are on the way there now," Leigh assured him. "Call your deputy and tell her to approach with caution. The same person who killed Jimbo could have gone after Kali."

Cash belted out some more profanity. "I'm in Lubbock right now and won't be able to get there for at least thirty minutes. You'll be backing up my deputy?"

"I will. I'll keep you posted," she added and ended the call. Leigh immediately started glancing around, no doubt to make sure they weren't about to be attacked.

"Are you okay?" Cullen asked, but he, too, kept watch.

It took Leigh a couple of seconds to shift gears from

her conversation with Cash, but she knew what Cullen was really asking. He wanted to know how she was handling what had just happened in the town hall.

"If I don't make an arrest soon, the mayor could press for a recall and have me ousted from office," she said. "Rocky might have been the one to set everything in motion, but Noble will get pressure, and he just might cave."

Still, Noble wouldn't be able to start the recall process to get rid of her by himself. It would take a majority vote from the council. Leigh had no idea just how many, or how few, votes would swing her way. Heck, she couldn't even count on getting Jeb's support. But that wouldn't stop her from doing her job for as long as she held the badge.

"I know you won't want it, but Bowen could put some pressure on Noble," Cullen offered.

She gave him a thin smile. "You're right. I don't want it." She paused. "But thanks. Right now, you and the three deputies who showed up are my biggest supporters."

The sound of agreement that Cullen made let her know that he was more than that. Yes, he was. Even though they weren't lovers, Leigh knew that would soon change. She'd land in bed with him, but she needed to keep her heart and the heat in check until after she'd finished this murder investigation.

Thankfully, the temps had warmed up enough that most of the ice was gone so the trip to Clay Ridge didn't take that long. Good thing, too, because Kali didn't live in town as Leigh had expected. According to the background data Leigh pulled up on her phone, Kali's house was situated on ten acres where she had horses. And it wasn't a sprawling, expensive place, either. The white frame house looked simple and cozy.

When Cullen pulled into the driveway, she spotted the cruiser and the lanky female deputy who was in the front yard with Austin. Leigh immediately looked to see if he was armed. He didn't have a gun in his hand, but that didn't mean he wasn't carrying one beneath his bulky coat.

"The blood's back here," Austin said the moment Leigh and Cullen were out of his truck. He motioned for them to follow him. But Leigh took a moment to introduce herself and Cullen to Deputy Karen Wheatly.

"I haven't been here long," Karen explained, "but Mr. Borden's right about the blood. There are some drops on the back porch."

"Drops," Leigh repeated. That was better than a huge amount, but it was still troublesome. "You haven't been inside?"

"I was about to do that now. I've knocked on the door, and Kali hasn't responded so that and the blood gives me probable cause to break the lock."

It did indeed, but before Leigh could ask if the deputy had a crowbar with her, Cullen pulled out a utility knife from his pocket. "I can get us in."

He didn't wait for permission, either. With Austin right on his heels and telling him to hurry, Cullen went to the front door. He had the lock open within a matter of seconds.

"Nick," Cullen said as an explanation.

Since his brother, Nick, was an ATF agent, Leigh figured that he'd taught Cullen how to get through locks. She was glad Noble or Rocky hadn't been around to see him use those skills or they probably would have considered it more reason for her to arrest him.

They stepped into the house, and Leigh noted that no security alarm went off. Maybe Kali had disengaged it. It wasn't a large place, but all the furniture appeared to be high-end. There also didn't seem to be anything out of place. Definitely no signs of a struggle.

"Kali?" Austin called out, and he would have bolted toward the hall had Cullen not took hold of him.

"It might not be safe," Cullen warned him.

"But Kali could be hurt," Austin insisted.

He slung off Cullen's grip. However, he waited, going with Karen, Leigh and Cullen as they went through the place room by room. Like the other parts of the house, there was nothing to indicate there'd been a problem.

Until they reached the kitchen.

There were what appeared to be drops of blood on the floor. Again, it wasn't a large amount and there was no spatter on the walls or counters to indicate blunt force trauma.

"The back door's locked," Karen pointed out.

Yes, and that was puzzling. The blood clearly led toward the door so if Kali had been attacked or hurt, why would she or her attacker take the time to lock up behind them?

Karen unlocked the door, and stepping around the blood, they went onto the back porch. More drops here, and these would have been the ones that Austin and Karen had already spotted. Leigh hoped that Austin hadn't compromised the scene by touching anything. As it was, he was going to be a suspect if anything had happened to Kali, and it'd be worse for him if he'd left traces of himself behind.

Leigh went down the steps, spotting a few more blood drops on the brown winter grass. She continued a few more feet, but when Leigh didn't see any more blood, she stopped and glanced around.

Kali's place was a lot like Leigh's. There was a small barn, what appeared to be a storage shed and plenty of fenced pastures. There was a heavily treed area to the right and a creek on the left. Leigh felt her stomach tighten because she didn't want Kali to have ended up in the icy water. Austin must have had that same thought because he started to run in that direction.

"I'll go with him," Karen insisted. "Why don't you two have a look around the barn?"

Leigh nodded, but before she moved, she spoke to Karen in a whisper. "I'm not sure I can trust Austin so watch your back."

Karen's eyes widened a little when she glanced at Austin. "Thanks." She slid her hand over the butt of her weapon and went after him.

Leigh continued to keep an eye on Austin until Cullen and she made it to the barn. Both drew their guns and stepped inside. She went still, listening, but didn't hear anything. She also didn't see any signs of blood.

"This doesn't make sense," Leigh muttered. She was hoping if she spoke her thoughts aloud that Cullen could help her understand what'd gone on here. "If Kali was taken, why would her kidnapper have brought her out through the back door? Why wouldn't he have just put her in his vehicle?"

They stepped out of the barn, and Cullen tipped his head to the woods. "There are probably trails out there where the kidnapper could have left his vehicle." He stopped and shook his head. "But it's a long way to take an injured woman. Especially since none of her neighbors are close enough to see if he'd taken her out through the front."

True, and that left Leigh with an unsettling theory. "If Kali tried to kill herself, she could have maybe staggered out of the house and collapsed somewhere." In this bitter cold, she wouldn't last long.

"The shed." Cullen motioned toward it, and that's when Leigh noticed the door was slightly ajar.

Mercy. Was Kali in there? Hurt and maybe hiding?

"Kali?" Leigh called out. "It's Sheriff Mercer. Cullen's with me. Do you need help?"

When Leigh got no answer, Cullen and she started in that direction. But they didn't get far. Only a couple of steps. Before they heard the scream. Not coming from the shed but rather from the woods.

"Kali," Leigh said on a rise of breath, and they began running toward the scream.

The shot rang out before they even made it past the shed.

Leigh was already moving to take cover, but Cullen hurried that along. He took hold of her, dragging her back behind the shed. Just as another shot blasted through the air.

Her adrenaline kicked in. So did the memories of the shooting just the day before. A shooting where Cullen and she had come close to dying. Hard to not let that play into this now, but Leigh battled the fear and forced herself to focus.

"The shot came from the woods," she said.

"Yeah, and it sounded like a rifle," Cullen agreed. "I'm pretty sure it came from the same area as the scream."

Leigh believed that, too, and it could mean that Kali had just been shot. Or worse. Killed. Her instincts were to go after Kali, to try to save her. But that would be suicide, and it could get Cullen killed, too, because there was no way he'd let her go out there alone.

"Kali?" Leigh called out again.

Her voice would give away their position, but the shooter probably already knew their exact location. She got confirmation of that when more shots came, and all of them smacked into the storage shed.

Cullen cursed and dragged Leigh to the ground, until they were practically on their bellies. Leigh only hoped that Karen and Austin were also taking cover.

"Kali?" Leigh tried again, not expecting the woman to answer.

And that's why it surprised Leigh when she did.

"I'm here!" Kali shouted. She was definitely in the woods. "Someone's trying to kill me."

Welcome to the club. Since the shots all seemed to be coming right at the shed, maybe that meant the gunman wasn't actually firing at Kali. Then again, if the shooter had injured her and taken her into the woods, it was possible Kali was the target and the guy was just missing.

But Leigh didn't believe that.

No. The bullets were coming too close for them not to be in the crosshairs of this snake.

"Help me!" Kali shouted.

"Get down!" Leigh yelled back. "Take cover."

"I'll create a diversion," Cullen said. "I'll get the shooter to focus on me."

Leigh didn't even get the chance to say no to that because Cullen got up and hurried to the back end of the shed. He kept low, but Leigh knew it wouldn't be nearly low enough for the bullets that were still coming their way.

"Don't do this," Leigh snapped.

He didn't listen. Cullen peeled off his jacket, and he thrust it out from cover. It drew immediate gunfire and sent Leigh's heart into a tailspin. Mercy. He was making himself a target, and if the shots went just a little to the left, they'd hit Cullen.

Hurrying, she crawled to him, took hold of his leg and jerked him back down. Cullen didn't go easily. He was obviously still hell-bent on saving Kali because he tossed out his jacket, probably with the idea of drawing gunfire while Kali managed to take cover.

But the shots stopped.

Suddenly, it was quiet, and the only sounds were their ragged breaths and her pulse throbbing in her ears.

"He's getting away again," Leigh murmured.

She groaned and punched the shed with the side of her fist. The frustration and anger washed over her. Catching the shooter was the only way to stop these attacks. The only way to stop him from killing again. But part of her was relieved, too. If the shots stopped, then Cullen wouldn't be gunned down.

"Don't ever do anything like that again," she snapped. At least she'd intended to snap, but her voice was too breathy and her words too broken.

Cullen looked at her. But he didn't nod or make any sounds of agreement. Instead, he kissed her. It was hard, fast and like another punch of adrenaline.

"Sheriff Mercer?" Karen called out. "Are you both okay?"

"Yes." Leigh had to steady herself to add more. "What about Austin and you?"

"I'm fine. Not sure about Austin. He got away from me before I could even get to the creek. I don't know where he went."

Cullen's gaze met hers, and in his eyes, Leigh could see the same emotions that were no doubt in hers. Damn. This wasn't good. Leigh hated to think the worst about the man, but it was possible Austin had planted a rifle before Cullen, the deputy or she arrived, and he could have been the one to fire the shots.

"Any signs of the shooter?" Leigh asked the deputy.

"No. And none of the shots came my way."

"Good. Stay put until we're sure it's clear."

But the words had barely left her mouth when Leigh heard Austin. "I found her," he shouted. "I found Kali."

Chapter 13

Cullen steeled himself, preparing for the worst when he saw Kali. But she was nowhere in the "worst" category.

He saw that right away when Kali came running out of the woods.

Leigh, Karen and he all started toward her. Kali's hair was disheveled, and there were smudges of dirt on her face, but he couldn't see any injuries that would have left those blood drops.

"Kali, wait!" Austin called out to her.

But Kali kept running, and she practically collapsed into Cullen's arms when he caught her. "I don't want Austin here."

In the grand scheme of things, that seemed small compared to everything else that had just happened. And to everything that could still happen. The shooter could still be out there, ready to fire off more shots, and that's why Cullen led Kali to the side of the shed so they'd have some cover.

"Are you hurt?" Leigh asked her.

With her breath gusting, Kali nodded. Then shook her head. She lifted her hand, to show them the gash on her palm. "I cut myself in the kitchen." It was deep enough that she'd need stitches, but it wasn't life-threatening. Unlike those shots.

"What happened?" Leigh pressed, still glancing around and no doubt keeping an eye out for the gunman. "Why were you in the woods?"

Kali sobbed, throwing herself against Cullen again. Her face landed against his shoulder. "Someone was breaking in through the front door so I ran out the back."

"But the back door was locked when we got here," Cullen pointed out.

"It locks automatically unless you adjust the thumb turn. And I didn't. I just ran and kept running so I could hide in the trees, but I didn't have my phone with me so I couldn't call anybody."

"Kali, are you all right?" Austin tried again.

"Make him leave," Kali snapped.

Cullen gave Austin a hard stare, hoping that he wouldn't give them any trouble about this.

"She needs to go to the hospital," Austin insisted, but he turned and headed toward the house.

"I'll have to question you later," Karen called out to him. "And question you, too," she added to Kali. "But Austin's right about you needing to go to the hospital. You should have someone take a look at that cut."

Kali turned not to Karen but to Leigh. "But what if the killer comes back?"

Leigh met her eye to eye. "You saw the killer?"

"No, but he shot at me." Kali paused, then shook her head again. "At least I think he was shooting at me. I didn't see him though."

Hell. Cullen had hoped Kali had at least gotten a glimpse of him. That could have put an end to the danger if they'd gotten an ID. But maybe the CSIs would be able to find something.

Karen stepped to the side to call in the shooting. It didn't take long, and when she was finished, she looked at Leigh. "Two other deputies are on the way here now so they can search the woods." Glancing up at the sun that would be setting in the next hour or so, she added, "A thorough search might have to wait until morning though."

That meant valuable trace could be lost, and it would sure as heck give the shooter plenty of time to get away.

"I'll go ahead and take Kali into the ER and get her statement," Karen continued a moment later. "I'll send you a copy. Cash will also need statements from Cullen and you."

"I'll make sure he gets them," Leigh told her. "I'd also like to see reports on any evidence the CSIs collect."

"Will do," Karen assured her, and she led Kali away while she kept watch around them.

Cullen and Leigh kept watch as well, but they didn't speak until they were in his truck. "Austin could have been the one to fire those shots," Leigh said.

Since Cullen had already considered the same thing, he nodded. "Or Kali could have."

Leigh's sound of agreement was fast and firm, causing Cullen to curse. Not because he was upset with her but because Kali and Austin had been his friends, and now he wasn't sure if one of them was a killer.

"Rocky could have gotten out here, too. I didn't see anyone following us, but it's possible he overheard us at the town hall."

Definitely possible, and he could have arrived after them and slipped into the woods. He would have had plenty of time to set up a shooting while Leigh and he had been searching inside Kali's house.

But Rocky couldn't have been responsible for the blood drops on the porch.

No. Not enough time for that so maybe Rocky had an accomplice.

Leigh took out her phone, probably to start the calls and texts that a sheriff needed to make when she'd just been under attack, but she stared at the screen a moment and put it away. That's when Cullen noticed that her hands were trembling a little.

"I don't want to go back to the office," she murmured. "I don't want my deputies to see me like this."

It didn't surprise him that she'd held things together while she'd been talking to Kali. That was the job for Leigh. But with the pressure she had coming at her from all sides, she wouldn't want anyone to think she was weak. And Leigh would definitely see trembling hands as weak.

Since his own house still hadn't been cleared by the CSIs, Cullen drove her home, and he hoped like the devil that they wouldn't have any visitors. Leigh didn't need another round with Austin, Rocky or Jeb tonight. Didn't need to tangle with him, either, and that's why he'd give her some space so that maybe she'd be able to get some sleep.

Leigh kept her eyes open, still watching for the gunman, but she lay her head back against the seat. Not relaxing. No. She'd balled her trembling hands into fists, and she was no doubt reliving each and every one of the bullets that'd come at them.

"Rocky's not that good of a shot," she said, getting his attention. "He barely qualifies at the shooting range when he has to take his annual test. What about Austin? Is he into guns?"

Cullen sighed, wishing that she'd been able to turn off her mind at least for this short drive but apparently not. Besides, it was a darn good question.

"Austin collects guns," Cullen explained. "I've never seen him fire one, but people who collect usually know how to use them. That doesn't mean that he's a good shot though."

She made a sound of agreement. "And Kali? I didn't see any guns in her house."

"Don't have a clue if she can shoot or not. But her father is a rancher so she's probably been around firearms." He paused. "Will your brother have Kali and Austin tested for gunshot residue?"

"Probably, but GSR doesn't always show up. And these shots likely came from a rifle so there might not be any GSR on their clothes."

So, it could be another dead end, but at this point any and all evidence could fall into that category.

Cullen pulled to a stop in front of Leigh's house, and he was pleased when exterior security lights flared on. It made it much easier for them to see that her yard was empty. Still, Cullen didn't take any chances.

When they went inside, they both shed their coats and checked to make sure no one had gotten in. The place was just as they'd left it to go to the meeting at the town hall.

Leigh used her phone to reset the security system, and then she just stood there in the hall. She did the same when her phone rang. She stared at the screen as if debating if she should answer it. Groaning softly, she finally hit the answer button and put the call on speaker.

"Jeb," she said. "What do you want?"

"I want to make sure you're okay and that you're not alone."

She took a couple of moments before she responded. "Cullen's here. He's staying the night again."

Cullen figured that would earn her a lecture from Jeb, but it didn't. "Good," Jeb said. "Because it's not a good idea for you not to have some backup."

"Backup," she repeated. There was both weariness and a little surprise in her tone. "So, you no longer believe I should be arresting him?"

"No." Jeb paused, sighed. "I heard about the shooting. Heard, too, that Cullen was with you again. If he was behind these attacks, he wouldn't keep putting himself in the line of fire like that."

Leigh sighed as well. "He's not behind the attacks nor the murders. You might have put him in the same tainted light as Bowen, but Cullen's not—"

"I did do that," Jeb admitted. "And I'm sorry."

Leigh pulled back her shoulders. Cullen had a similar reaction because Jeb was not the sort of man to admit a mistake. Worse, this conversation was starting to sound like a last-ditch effort to mend the rift between Leigh and him.

"What's wrong?" Leigh demanded. "Are you sick?"

Jeb's laugh was quick and dry. "I don't have to be

sick to tell you that you were right about Cullen. Right about the way you've handled the investigation. Right about a lot of things," he added in a mutter.

"Am I right about you being sick?" she asked.

Jeb's silence confirmed that she was. "I'm waiting on test results, but the docs think it's my heart. Might need bypass. Might need something more. I won't know for a couple more days, and I hadn't planned on telling you until I knew for sure."

Leigh drew in a long, slow breath. "Does Cash know?"

"No. He doesn't take my calls. And before you say anything, I know he's got reasons for that. So do you. But thanks for hearing me out. If you want, I'll tell you the test results when I have them."

"I want that," she assured him.

It seemed to Cullen that Jeb blew out a sigh of relief. "Good night, Leigh," he added and ended the call.

Once again, Leigh just stood there, but she looked even more exhausted than she had been before Jeb's call.

"I'm sorry," Cullen told her.

She nodded, put her phone away and then turned to him. Their eyes met. Held.

"Don't sleep in the guest room tonight," she whispered, taking hold of his hand. "Come to bed with me."

Leigh figured she should just tell Cullen this was a mistake. Maybe then he'd do the right thing and back away from her.

She knew for a fact that she wouldn't be doing the backing away.

This was despite the lecture she'd given herself about waiting until after the investigation to get involved with him. She should wait. But the fear and emotions were crushing her like an avalanche, and Cullen was the one person who could make that stop. For a little while, anyway.

"The timing for this isn't good," Cullen said. "You want to talk about Jeb?"

Leigh didn't have to take time to consider her answer. "No. I don't want to talk about anything at all. It doesn't have to be sex tonight…" She groaned, pushed her hair from her face and kept her gaze nailed to his. "Yes, it does."

The corner of his mouth lifted, and she got a flash of that hot smile that had no doubt lured many women to his bed. But tonight she was doing the luring. Leigh rethought that though when Cullen pulled her to him and kissed her.

His kiss was exactly what she needed. She sank into it. Sank into his arms, too. Because, mercy, she needed this.

She needed him.

The years they'd been apart vanished, and it felt as if they'd always been together like this. Always *should* be together. But now wasn't the time for Cullen to hear that or for her to realize it.

Cullen picked up on her need for him by her deepening the kiss, and he didn't waste any time backing her into her bedroom. They moved together without breaking the kiss or the arms she'd locked around him.

"I should give you a chance to reconsider," he said, getting off her boots before easing her back on the bed. He looked down at her. "Don't reconsider."

Now it was her turn to smile, and Leigh pulled him down on top of her. All in all, it was a great place for him to be. The weight of his body on hers only fueled this ache she had for him. The kisses did as well when Cullen took his mouth to her neck.

She remembered this part. The foreplay and fire. The urgent heat that started to build inside her. Cullen was very good at the building. At making her need him more than her next breath.

He did something about her breath. He made it vanish when he lowered the kisses to her stomach. He shoved up her top, his mouth teasing her bare skin and kicking up the urgency even more.

Leigh reached for his shirt, but he pinned her hands to the bed and kept on kissing her. Going lower until he reached the zipper of her jeans. With his own hands locked with hers, he simply used his mouth. And his breath. Cullen kissed her through the denim and kept kissing her until Leigh could take no more.

She rolled with him, reversing their positions so she could go after his shirt. She wanted her mouth on his chest. Wanted to touch him. And she did both. She took a moment to admire the view—the man was built—but she couldn't stave off Cullen.

Once she had his shirt off, he did another flip, straddling her so he could rid her of her shirt. He flicked open her front-hook bra and gave her a quick reminder that breast kisses were hot spots for her. He fanned the heat even higher, managing to kiss one breast, then the other, before he moved lower to shimmy her out of her jeans and panties. He kicked off his own boots as well.

Then, he kept kissing her.

Leigh had no choice but to hang on and enjoy the ride. She fisted her hands on the quilt, anchoring herself, but she knew that if he kept up those clever flicks of his tongue that she'd climax too fast.

"We do this together," she insisted.

She maneuvered away from him so that she could tackle his jeans. And finally his boxers. Yes, the man was built, and the past decade had only improved everything about him.

"Condom," he ground out when she ran her hand the long length of him. "In my wallet."

Since she wanted that long length inside her, Leigh rummaged through his jeans, located the wallet, then the condom.

Cullen did some more maneuvering, flipping their positions again so that he was on top of her. Thankfully, it didn't take him long to get the condom on, and with their gazes locked, he slipped inside her.

The pleasure speared through her, and the sound she made was a long, slow moan. It felt as if she'd been waiting for this for way too long.

Cullen made his own sound of pleasure, and he began to move inside her. Building the fire with each maddening stroke. Making everything pinpoint to the need to finish this. And that's what he did.

He finished it.

Leigh held on to Cullen and let him finish her.

Chapter 14

Cullen sipped his coffee while he stared out Leigh's kitchen window. It was a good view of the frost-covered pastures, the barn and the horses.

Leigh had set up automatic feed dispensers, probably because of the long hours she often worked, and he'd heard talk that she had part-time help for the chores that came with running a small horse ranch. But for this morning, they had the place to themselves.

That's why he'd found it damn hard to leave her bed.

However, Cullen had forced himself away from her and into the shower. Then, into the kitchen so he could give her some thinking time. He fully expected when she came to her senses that she'd tell him they'd made a huge mistake by having sex. And maybe they had. But at the moment it felt like something he wanted to continue doing beyond just this time together. First though, they had to find a killer and stop him or her from coming after them again.

He continued to sip coffee, and then saw Leigh. Not in the house but headed toward the pasture. Since she hadn't come through the kitchen, she'd likely gone out through the patio doors off her bedroom.

Wearing a bulky buckskin work coat, she stopped at the pasture fence, and a bay mare immediately came to her. Leigh ran her hand over the horse and murmured something. Even though Cullen couldn't hear what she said, he smiled. Obviously, they had common ground when it came to their love of horses.

His smile faded though when he remembered that it wasn't a good idea for her to be out in the open like that. Not with a killer on the loose. A killer who favored taking shots at them. Cullen grabbed his coat and went to join her.

The sun was out, making everything look as if it'd been doused with diamond dust, but the cold air still had a sting to it. His boots crunched on the ice-crusted grass, and it was that sound that likely alerted her, because with her hand still stroking the mare, Leigh turned to look at him.

"I know," she said before he could speak. "I shouldn't be out here. But being around the horses helps me clear my mind."

He smiled again. Yeah, they had common ground all right.

"This is Buttercup," Leigh said, introducing him to the mare. "And that's Smoky and Honey." She tipped her head to two other horses, who were also heading their way. "If they'd caught a stranger's scent, they would let me know about it. Like now." All three horses were snorting and whinnying.

Well, they weren't as good as guard dogs in sending up an alarm, but it was better than nothing.

Because he wanted the taste of her, Cullen moved closer and brushed his mouth over hers. That also got him some attention from the mare, who gave his arm a nudge. He gave her a quick rub, then lingered a moment longer on the kiss with Leigh.

Leigh eased back, her eyes partly closed and a dreamy look on her face. Obviously, the kiss had been just as potent for her as it was for him. But potency aside, being out here was too dangerous. Cullen hooked his arm around Leigh to lead her back to the house. He considered trying to coax her to bed, but they'd barely made it inside the kitchen when her phone rang.

"It's Vance," she said, answering and putting the call on speaker.

Since this almost certainly had something to do with the investigation, Cullen was very interested in what the deputy had to say.

"Just got off the phone with the crime lab," Vance explained. "It's not good news. The fingerprint on the SUV is too smudged for them to get a match."

Leigh didn't groan, probably because she'd already considered that might be the outcome. She shucked off her coat and put it on the peg by the door. Cullen did the same.

"I want you to put out the word that the print isn't smudged and that the crime lab believes they'll be able to get a match from the database," she told Vance after a short pause. "Tell everyone you know because I want word to get back to the killer. But also alert the lab so they've got full security in place in case the killer tries to eliminate the evidence."

"Will do," Vance assured her.

Cullen could help with that, too, and he fired off a quick text to Austin. He told Austin that it was good news, that the killer might soon be ID'd. If Austin was guilty and did indeed try to destroy evidence against him, then he'd be caught. That still felt like a heavyweight's punch, but it was better than having Austin come after Leigh.

"I'll be in the office soon," Leigh added to Vance a moment later. She ended the call, but before she could put her phone away, it rang again.

"Cash," she said, glancing at the screen. The muscles stirred in her jaw. "I'm not going to tell him about Jeb. Not over the phone. I'll pay him a visit to give him the news."

That made sense, and her tone let Cullen know that her father's illness was weighing on her. Despite the rift between them, she almost certainly still loved him.

As she'd done with Vance, Leigh put the call on speaker while she helped herself to a cup of coffee. "Please tell me you found the shooter," Leigh greeted her brother.

"No," Cash answered after a huff. "And I'm about to add another complication to your murder investigation."

"What happened?" Leigh demanded.

"I'd better start with what didn't happen," Cash explained. "Kali didn't have a break-in, and she didn't run into the woods because she was afraid. During the interview, she broke down and admitted that it was all staged. She claimed she knew Austin was coming over because he'd texted her and said he was. So, she told me that she set up her injury to leave the blood drops, and then she ran and hid so it'd make him sick with worry."

Leigh groaned and set her coffee aside so she could scrub her hands over her face. "And what about the shooter?"

"Kali insists she doesn't have a clue about that. Says she didn't see anyone in the woods before or after the shots started."

"You believe her?" Leigh pressed.

This time Cash wasn't so fast to answer. "Not sure. Plenty of people are good liars, and I don't know if she's one of them. But if she fired those shots, then the rifle is probably still somewhere in the woods, and the CSIs are out looking for it now."

Leigh gathered her breath before she spoke again. "Did Kali agree to let you test for GSR?"

"She did. Nada. Then again, the EMTs had their hands all over her clothes when they examined her. She had a panic attack in the ambulance, and they had to restrain her."

Cullen didn't even bother to curse. Leigh had already known that the GSR would be a long shot.

"Unless I can prove Kali's the shooter," Cash went on, "I can't charge her with anything other than a misdemeanor for wasting law enforcement resources. She didn't make a false 911 call, and she admitted the ruse once I got her in interview. I can't arrest her for wanting to worry her ex-boyfriend."

No, but it did show how desperate and hurt Kali was. So desperate and so hurt that she might have killed Alexa. Especially if Alexa had taunted Kali about her affair with Austin.

Leigh finished her call with her brother, gulped down

some more coffee and gave her shoulder harness an adjustment. "You should be able to go back to the Triple R sometime this morning," she said, her gaze lifting to meet his. "But you're welcome to stay here."

That was an invitation Cullen had no intention of turning down. Not just because he wanted to be with Leigh but also because he wasn't about to leave her alone as long as the killer was still gunning for them. Cullen would have told her that, too, but they got another call. This time, it was his phone.

"It's Jamie," he said, answering right away. He also put it on speaker. "Are you okay?" Cullen immediately asked him.

Jamie, however, didn't give him an immediate answer. "I'm getting out of the hospital. Deputy Cecile Taggart is still here, and she's going to drive me to the bunkhouse."

Cullen was thankful Jamie would still have police protection, but something was wrong. He didn't think he was mistaken about the worry he'd heard in Jamie's voice.

"Did something happen?" Cullen came out and asked.

"Yeah. And that's why I need to talk to the sheriff and you." Again, Jamie hesitated, and he lowered his voice to a whisper. "The killer called me again."

Leigh resisted snatching the phone right out of Cullen's hand, but she did hurry to get closer so that Jamie would have no trouble hearing her. "What did the killer say to you?" she demanded.

"I don't want to get into it here over the phone," Jamie said, still hesitating, still whispering. "Deputy

Taggart and I will be at your house soon. I need to talk to you about going into protective custody or something. I can't go on like this."

Jamie hung up before she could demand again that he tell her about the phone call he'd gotten from the killer.

"I should go to the hospital," Leigh grumbled.

"You could end up passing him and Cecile on the road," Cullen quickly pointed out.

His voice was calm and reasonable. Too bad she wasn't feeling either at the moment. She wanted to know about the killer, and Jamie might have key information. Information that could possibly stop another attack.

"Witness protection," she repeated like profanity. "I'm guessing that means the killer threatened him again." And that reminder sent some fresh alarm through her. "I should send Cecile backup."

She whipped out her phone and called the deputy, and Cecile must have been expecting her call, because she answered on the first ring.

"Jamie's fine," Cecile said right off. "He's just scared. We're heading out of the hospital right now, and then I'll drive him straight to your place."

"Why is he scared? What did the killer tell him?" Leigh pressed.

"I don't know. I didn't hear any of the actual call, but he's insisting on talking to you about it. I called your office and they said you were still home so I figured that's where I'd bring him. I had Dawn come here to the hospital, too, so she'll ride along with us."

Some of the tightness eased in Leigh's chest. She had good cops working for her, and this was proof of it. Cecile had arranged for backup on her own. Maybe it wouldn't be necessary, but taking precautions was the right call.

"Come straight here," Leigh instructed. "If we end up doing protective custody, I've got contacts with the marshals that I can bring in. That way, they could meet with Jamie here so he doesn't have to go back out again."

"Will do," Cecile assured her. "We're getting in the cruiser right now and will be there in just a couple of minutes," she added before she ended the call.

"I can arrange for security at the ranch, too, if Jamie wants to go back to the bunkhouse," Cullen offered. "Or if he wants to go to his folks' place, I can send men there with him."

Leigh gave his arm a gentle squeeze. "Thank you." She took a deep breath. "I just wish I knew if Jamie was in actual danger or if the killer is just trying to intimidate him. Either way, he needs protection," she added in a mumble.

"Nick might be able to help," Cullen suggested.

It'd been a while since she'd seen his brother, but since Nick was an ATF agent, it was highly likely that he had other contacts in law enforcement. Nick might be able to streamline the process for Jamie.

When she heard the sound of an engine approaching the house, Cullen and she hurried to the front window. But it wasn't a police cruiser. It was a big silver four-by-four truck that maneuvered over the dirt and gravel like a bulldozer, and it pulled to a stop behind Cullen's truck.

Cullen groaned. "It's Bowen."

Leigh wanted to groan as well. She didn't have time for a visit from a man who was likely there to give her grief.

She disarmed the security system so Cullen could open the front door, and Leigh went onto the porch with him when he faced down his father. Bowen stepped from his truck, leaving the engine running and door open as he started toward them. He sighed in obvious disapproval when he saw them.

"It's true, then," Bowen said to Cullen. He stopped at the bottom porch step and stared up at them. A stare from narrowed eyes. "You're staying here with Leigh."

Yep, she'd been right about the grief-giving, and apparently Bowen was going to dole some of it out to Cullen as well as her.

"Last I heard I didn't have to check with you about my sleeping arrangements," Cullen fired back.

"Well, you should because you know Jeb will use this to try to lock you up." Bowen flung his index finger at Leigh. "And she might not be able to save you. They're trying to kick her out of office."

"Yes," Cullen agreed, "and they're trying that because she won't give in to the gossip that I killed Alexa." He put his hands on his hips, shook his head. "You and Jeb are a lot alike, you know. He was at the station and had the same complaint."

"Of course he did," Bowen snarled. "He'd rather see you dead than with his daughter."

That might be true, but Leigh didn't believe Jeb would do anything to cause Cullen's demise. However, Jeb might indeed want to rid her of her badge so she couldn't tarnish the reputation he had in the county.

"I'm pretty sure I'm in love with Leigh," Cullen said, stunning his father.

However, Bowen's reaction was a drop in the bucket compared to Leigh's. "What?" she managed to say.

Cullen had likely tossed that out in anger. Something to get his father off his back. But one look at him, and Leigh thought it might be true.

Well, heck.

This wasn't good. Not now, anyway. She didn't have the focus or time to sort out how she felt about that announcement. Or how she felt about Cullen for that matter. Yes, she had feelings for him. Deep ones. Always had. But love?

It was something she had to push to the back of her mind though because the cruiser pulled into the driveway. Dawn was behind the wheel, and she pulled up in front of Bowen's truck.

"This conversation isn't over," Bowen said like a warning. "I'll come back after you've dealt with business."

"Just stay put a couple more seconds," Leigh instructed, keeping her attention on the cruiser. "You can leave after Jamie's inside the house."

"Jamie?" Bowen asked, and there seemed to be genuine concern in his voice. "What's he doing here?'"

"Business," Leigh said, using Bowen's own choice of words.

The young ranch hand got out from the back seat of the cruiser. There was a white bandage on his head, and he looked more than a little pale and wobbly. The unsteadiness was probably why Cecile rushed around the cruiser to take hold of Jamie's arm. Leigh went into the yard, too, with Cullen right behind her. Something Leigh appreciated. If Jamie was about to collapse, they might need Cullen's muscle to get him into the house.

Leigh intended to call the doctor as soon as Jamie was safe. No way did he look ready to have been released from the hospital. Then again, maybe Jamie had pushed for his release because he'd been afraid the killer would get to him.

With Cullen on one side of Jamie and Cecile on the other, they started toward the house.

"Is the boy all right?" Bowen asked.

Leigh was asking herself the same thing. But she didn't get a chance to answer Bowen.

Before someone fired a shot.

Cullen moved fast when he heard the gunshot. He hooked his arm around Leigh's waist and pulled her to the ground next to some shrubs and landscape boulders. Cecile did the same with Jamie. But the deputy wasn't fast enough.

The bullet slammed into her shoulder.

"Cecile," Leigh said on a gasp, and she pulled away from Cullen so she could go to her deputy.

Apparently, Dawn was trying to do the same thing. Cullen heard the cruiser door open. Heard the shot that followed. And because he was on the ground, he could see Dawn fall on the other side of the cruiser.

Hell.

There were two deputies down.

Cecile was alive. Cullen could see that. But he could also see the blood that was already spreading across the front of her coat. Cecile was also writhing in pain. Pain that would get a whole lot worse if the shooter managed to put another bullet in her.

Cullen couldn't see Dawn well enough to know if she was alive, but she wasn't moving. Definitely not a good sign.

"Oh, God," Jamie muttered, and he kept repeating it.

Another shot came, this one slamming into the ground between them and Bowen.

"Get down!" Cullen yelled to his father, and he drew his gun.

But there really wasn't any cover where he was. Ditto for Leigh, Jamie, Cecile and him. They were all literally out in the open in the yard with two injured cops and a ranch hand who looked on the verge of a full-out panic attack.

While Leigh applied pressure to Cecile's wound, Cullen made a quick call to the police station to get them some backup. It wouldn't take long for the other deputies to arrive, but a gunman could take them all out in just a matter of seconds.

Cullen had to do something about that. He couldn't just let Dawn and Cecile bleed out. He glanced around, looking for a way to get everyone to safety. The cruiser was a good fifteen feet away. It was the same for Bowen's truck. They'd be easy targets if they tried to get to them.

Another bullet cracked through the air, and because he'd been waiting for it, Cullen used the sound to pinpoint the location. The shooter was to the right of Leigh's yard, probably in the thick cluster of oak and pecan trees.

"Get flat on the ground next to those bushes and try to crawl to the left side of the house," he told Bowen, but his father was already scrambling to do that.

More shots came, and none seemed to be aimed at Bowen. They all came toward Leigh. Even though Cullen knew she wasn't going to like it, he climbed over her, took aim in the direction of the shooter, and he fired. It didn't faze the shooter one bit because he sent more bullets their way.

Making a sound of outrage, Leigh levered herself up, and she, too, fired at the gunman. Cullen figured the chances of either of them hitting the guy were slim to none, but they needed a lull in the gunfire so they could get to the side of the house where Bowen was.

"I'll get to Bowen's truck," Cullen told Leigh, and he made sure it sounded like a plan of action and not a suggestion. "I'll bring it here so we can get Jamie and Cecile inside."

Leigh was already shaking her head before he finished. "He'll shoot you before you can get to it."

Maybe. *Probably*, Cullen silently amended. "You can try to take him out when his attention's focused on me."

She was still shaking her head when they heard the sound of more gunfire. But this hadn't come from the direction of the shooter. No. This was coming from the far right, behind Leigh's house. And it wasn't aimed at Leigh and him but rather at the shooter.

"Bowen," Leigh said, glancing in the direction where Cullen had last seen his father. Bowen was no longer there. Since his father always carried a gun, he'd probably gone around the back of the house so he could try to stop the gunman.

And it worked.

Well, it worked in distracting the gunman, anyway, because the shots began to go in Bowen's direction. Cullen knew Bowen was taking a huge risk. One that Cullen hoped didn't cost him his life. But maybe it would be enough of a diversion for him to get Leigh, Jamie and Cecile behind cover.

"Jamie, you need to stay down and move," Cullen

told him, and he hoisted Cecile over his shoulder in a fireman's carry. The deputy moaned in pain, but she was still conscious.

Leigh's eyes met Cullen's. It was just a split-second glance, but a lot of things passed between them. The fear. And the hope. This was their chance, and they had to take it.

"We need to get to the left side of the house," Leigh added.

Cullen was right there with her, and once he was sure Jamie was in a crouching position, Cullen got them moving. Leigh turned, covering their backs as they hurried across the stretch of yard.

It didn't take long for the bullets to come their way.

They smacked into the ground, tearing up the grass and dirt. But Bowen didn't let up. He continued to fire shots at the gunman, and Cullen figured that slowed the guy down at least a little.

Each inch across the yard seemed to take an eternity, and with each step, Cullen's heart pounded even harder. His fears skyrocketed. Not for himself. But for Leigh. She was putting herself between them and the shooter. Not only that, she was almost certainly the primary target.

The moment Cullen reached the left side of the house, he caught onto Jamie, dragging him to the ground and handing him Cecile. Thankfully, Jamie took the injured deputy and that freed up Cullen to lean out and give Leigh and Bowen some help. He fired at the gunman until Leigh was able to scramble next to him.

"I need to get some help for Dawn," Leigh immediately said, taking out her phone.

She called dispatch to request medical assistance, but Cullen tuned her out when he heard the hurried footsteps coming from the back of the house. He pivoted in that direction, bringing up his gun, but it wasn't the threat his body had braced for.

It was Bowen.

His father wasn't hurt, which was somewhat of a miracle, and with his gun still drawn, he hurried toward them.

"Who's trying to kill us?" Bowen snarled.

Cullen shook his head and turned back to the front yard so he could keep watch. He didn't see the gunman, but he saw something else. Dawn. The deputy was crawling to the front of the cruiser. Like Cecile, she was bleeding, but at least she was alive. She might not be that way for long though if they couldn't get an ambulance out here.

"I can try to make a run for my truck," Bowen said, causing Cullen to glance back at him.

There were times his father's stubbornness could irritate the heck out of him, but Bowen was no coward. He would indeed go out there just as he'd drawn fire so that the rest of them could get to cover.

"There's an ATV in the barn," Leigh said when she finished her call. "One of us could use it to get Cecile to the trail at the back of my property. The trail leads out to the road. She needs to get to the hospital ASAP," she added, looking directly at Cullen.

Cullen had no doubts that Leigh meant for him to be getting Cecile out of there. He wouldn't have minded doing just that if it didn't mean leaving Leigh behind.

Where he knew for a fact that she would take huge risks to try to get to Dawn.

"And what about Dawn?" Cullen asked her.

"I can go through the back door into my house. One of the windows on that side should make it easier to take out the shooter."

It would. And Leigh would have the added advantage of having some cover.

"You'll take Cecile to the ATV in the barn?" Cullen asked his father.

Bowen hesitated, but that was probably because he, too, was thinking of the danger to those who stayed behind. His father finally nodded and hoisted Cecile as Cullen had done. "But, damn it, don't do anything stupid."

Cullen didn't make him any promises. Couldn't. Because he'd definitely do something stupid if it meant keeping Leigh safe. Unfortunately, she probably had the same thing in mind when it came to him.

"I'll be in the house with Leigh," Cullen explained, still keeping watch of the front and back yards. He didn't want the shooter sneaking up on them from behind.

"I can help Mr. Brodie with Cecile," Jamie volunteered. "Then, I can wait in the barn until it's okay to come out."

Leigh nodded. "Let's go."

As she'd done in the yard, Leigh took the back position, and Cullen jogged ahead so he could make sure the gunman wasn't lying in wait for them. He didn't see anyone so he gave Bowen and Jamie the go-ahead to get to the barn. They were only about halfway there when Cullen heard something he definitely hadn't wanted to hear.

Not a gunshot.

But an engine.

It was Bowen's massive truck, and when the driver hit the accelerator, the truck barreled right toward them.

Chapter 15

Leigh got a quick flash of images from when the SUV had rammed into her cruiser. Those had been some terrifying moments, but at least she and Cullen had been in the vehicle. There'd been some protection.

Not now though.

They were out in the open, where they could be mowed down and killed.

"Run!" she shouted.

That order wasn't just to Cullen but to Bowen and Jamie. They weren't in the barn yet, and they were out in the open, too, where they'd be easy targets. Especially since Bowen was carrying Cecile and Jamie obviously wasn't in any shape to outrun a truck with a driver hell-bent on killing them.

Leigh didn't dare take the time to look back to see how close the truck was to them. Every second counted now, and the moment she reached the back porch, she cursed the railing. It was too high to vault over, and if she tried to climb it, she could be sideswiped. That meant going around and up the steps.

But she didn't get a chance to do that.

From the corner of her eye, she saw Jamie fall, but it was just a blur of motion because she was moving. Or rather Cullen was moving her. He caught onto her arm, jerking her away from the porch.

And it wasn't a second too soon.

Because the truck rammed into the exact spot where she'd just been.

Neither Cullen nor she had had time to fire at the driver, but Cullen's momentum got them away from the impact. They fell, but immediately scrambled to get up. However, Jamie wasn't doing the same. He was still down, and Bowen must not have even noticed because he was still barreling toward the barn with Cecile in tow.

The railing on the porch gave way. So did part of the porch. However, the truck didn't seem damaged at all. The driver spun it around, taking aim at Cullen and her again.

Leigh had to make a quick decision. If Cullen and she ran toward Jamie, they might not be able to get him up in time to stop him from being run over. Obviously, Cullen had the same concern because he took hold of her arm and started running toward the front of the house.

Where the cruiser was.

And Dawn.

The truck would almost certainly follow them, but if they could get the deputy into the cruiser, then they stood a chance of protecting her. Then, they could drive back around to the barn to help Jamie and Bowen.

Leigh braced herself in case someone fired shots at them. After all, the driver could be working with a partner. But the only threat came from the truck itself. The driver managed to get it turned around and came at Cullen and her again when they reached the front yard. Because the windshield was so heavily tinted, they couldn't see who was trying to kill them.

Once again, Cullen and she had to dive out of the way of the speeding truck. It whipped right past them, so close that Leigh could feel the heat of the engine. They fell again. Hard. Leigh rammed into some rocks, causing the pain to shoot through her. The impact also knocked the breath out of her, and she lost critical moments of time fighting for air. No way could she stand when she couldn't breathe.

Cullen helped with that though. He got to his feet, hauling her up and practically dragging her out of the way. Good thing, too. Because the driver threw the truck into Reverse and came at them again.

Leigh was thankful that Cullen still had hold of her because he got them out of the way again, this time diving behind some landscape boulders. Still, they'd just come close to dying, and it was obvious the driver wasn't finished. He did a doughnut in the yard, the tires slinging up dirt and rocks. Obviously, taking aim at them again.

But he didn't hit the accelerator.

He just sat there, revving the engine. Waiting. But for what? Maybe he thought it would shred the tires if he hit the boulders. And it might. But the two-foot-high rocks wouldn't give them enough protection if he started shooting. That's why Leigh had to try to stop him from doing that. She still had hold of her gun so she pointed it at the windshield.

And she fired.

Just as the driver sped forward. Her bullet tore through the safety glass, and she cursed when she realized her shot had been off. Not directly at the driver but a little to the left. She might have injured him, but it likely hadn't been a headshot. Right now, she figured killing him was the only way for the rest of them to survive. If this killer managed to take out Cullen and her, he'd take out the rest. No way would he want to leave witnesses behind.

Cullen pulled her to her feet again, and they darted to the left. But not far. The driver would have to at least clip the boulders to get to them. That would certainly slow him down.

However, he didn't come at them again.

The driver spun around, speeding not toward them but rather in the direction of the barn. Leigh's stomach went to her knees because she was pretty sure she knew what he was doing. He was going after Jamie, Bowen and Cecile.

"No!" Leigh shouted, hoping to draw the driver's attention.

But she didn't. The truck kept going, past the house and into the backyard. Straight to Jamie. He was still on the ground, but he was conscious, because he was struggling to get up and out of the way.

With the howl of police and ambulance sirens just up the road, Cullen and she started running. Hoping to stop the driver from killing the ranch hand. However, there was a lot of distance between Jamie and them.

The driver slammed on the brakes, but Leigh couldn't tell if he'd hit Jamie or not. She couldn't tell if Jamie was still alive. Worse, she couldn't see the driver. But she heard what she thought was the passenger's-side door opening.

"He's grabbing Jamie," Cullen said, pulling up so he could take aim.

Leigh immediately understood why he'd do that. The killer had to know backup was on the way, and he could use Jamie to escape. But there was a possibility that was much worse. Maybe he was about to kill Jamie so he could eliminate him as a loose end.

"I can't risk shooting," Cullen snarled like profanity.

No, he couldn't. Because he might hit Jamie instead. The windshield wouldn't help with that, either. There was a gaping hole from her own shot, but the rest of the glass had cracked and webbed. It was as effective as putting a mask on the killer.

She heard the door slam, and the driver quickly turned the truck around. So that it was facing Cullen and her again. It came at them. Slowly this time. Like a predator stalking its prey. Since that slow pace could mean the driver was preparing to fire at them, Cullen and she moved back behind the boulders. Even if they were belly-down, it wouldn't stop them from being shot, but it was better than standing out in the open with a killer bearing down on them.

"Be ready to jump out of the way," Leigh warned Cullen.

The driver held the snail-crawling pace until he stopped just a few yards away from them. Leigh saw some movement behind the damaged glass, and a moment later, Jamie peered through the fist-sized hole in the windshield. She could only see part of his face, but it was enough for her to know he was terrified.

"Me for you," Jamie said, his voice trembling with fear. He aimed those fear-filled eyes at Leigh. "That's the deal I'm supposed to tell you. If you don't trade places with me, I'll die."

Hell. That was the one word that kept going through Cullen's mind.

It was bad enough that Leigh and he had to face down a killer, but now Jamie was in the middle of it.

Cullen seriously doubted that Jamie was in any shape to fight off the killer, especially since he was almost certainly being held at gunpoint. Being told what to say, too. The killer had no doubt told Jamie word for word what he was supposed to say to Leigh and him.

He made a quick glance at the road and spotted a cruiser and an ambulance. They'd turned off their sirens, but their lights were still flaring. Leigh obviously saw them, too, and she fired off a text. "I told Vance to try to get Dawn out of here and take her to the EMTs," she relayed to Cullen. "I don't want him or the ambulance coming any closer."

That was a wise decision. If the cruiser came speeding in, it might help Leigh and him by giving them some cover, but it could be a deadly move for Jamie. If the killer didn't shoot him on the spot, he might try to flee with him. Then, the snake could just murder Jamie once he was in the clear.

But Cullen wanted to make sure this SOB didn't get away.

"Me for you," Jamie repeated.

"And how do I know you won't gun all three of us

down if we make this trade?" Leigh called out to the driver.

There was a short silence, probably for Jamie to get his instructions, and he finally said, "You don't know. It's a risk you'll have to take if you want to keep me alive." Jamie's voice trembled. Then, it broke. "Don't take the risk," he blurted out. "Don't trade yourselves for me."

Cullen could see enough of Jamie to spot the barrel of a gun as it jammed into the ranch hand's temple.

"All of this is to cover up you murdering Alexa," Leigh called out. "And it's stupid. Backup's already arrived, and you won't be able to get out of here. Just toss down your weapon, let Jamie go, and I'll see what kind of deal I can work out."

Jamie winced when the gun dug even harder into his head, but he didn't say anything for several seconds. "You're lying. There'll be no deal," he said, obviously repeating what the killer had told him.

The killer was right about that. No way would he get a reduced sentence when he'd murdered at least two people and attempted to murder others, including cops. Still, maybe there was a way to bargain with him.

Or her.

Cullen couldn't rule out that it was Kali behind the wheel. It wouldn't have taken much muscle to force Jamie into the truck at gunpoint.

"If your plan is to get away, you'll need money," Cullen called out to the killer. "You could consider it a ransom. I'll pay you to release Jamie."

"Money won't fix this," Jamie said, repeating his instructions. "But Leigh and you will. This is your last chance," Jamie added. "Me for you."

"Any chance you have a shot?" Leigh asked him.

Cullen studied the distorted images behind the heavily tinted glass. "Maybe. I figure the killer is still behind the wheel. Maybe keeping low. But I could keep the shot to the side so that it won't hit Jamie."

Well, maybe it wouldn't. Cullen doubted the driver had Jamie fully in front of him like a human shield—there wouldn't be enough room for that—but any shot would be a risk. If Cullen didn't kill the driver, then he or she could turn the gun on Jamie. Of course, the odds of that happening were already sky-high.

That's why they had to go for it.

"I'll take the shot," Cullen told her.

She nodded, her breath mixing with the cold air and creating a wispy fog between them. "On the count of three, you fire, and I'll run to the side of the house. That might buy Jamie some time."

Yeah, it would. Because the killer would turn the gun on Leigh.

"No." Cullen couldn't say that fast enough. "You're not running out there."

Leigh looked him straight in the eyes. "Neither one of us can crouch here and let Jamie die. It's what has to be done."

Cullen cursed, ready to argue with her, but then he spotted something he definitely hadn't wanted to see.

Bowen.

Crouched down, his father had come out of the barn, and it was obvious he was trying to sneak up on the driver of the truck. Not directly behind it. But rather to the side. It'd be a damn good way for Bowen to get himself killed.

"What the heck is he doing?" Leigh snarled. "Text him. Tell him to get down right now."

Even if Bowen read the text, he wouldn't just get down. His father's stubborn streak wasn't reserved just for Jeb and members of his family. However, Cullen had to try, and he motioned for Bowen to drop.

He didn't.

Bowen took aim at the back tires of the truck, and he started firing. Not one shot but a barrage of them that would almost certainly flatten the tires and prevent a quick escape. But it wasn't escape that Cullen was immediately worried about. It was Bowen and Jamie.

The driver's-side door flew open, and Cullen saw Jamie being dragged out of the vehicle. Now he was a human shield, and that position prevented Cullen from seeing who was holding him, especially since his captor was hunkering down.

"Keep that up, and I die," Jamie yelled.

Again, it was the words the killer wanted him to say, and Cullen was thankful he could actually say them. Because it meant he was still alive. The killer hadn't panicked and just taken him out.

Not yet, anyway.

However, the fact that Jamie was being forced to do all the talking meant the killer didn't want Cullen or Leigh to hear his or her voice because they would recognize who it was.

Bowen did stop firing, and he had the sense to drop down on the ground. That, and the fact that he was on the other side of the truck from the killer, might prevent him from being shot.

Leigh levered herself up a little and took aim. Cullen had to resist the need to push her back down. To give her that small margin of cover. But she was a cop, and no way would she put her safety over Jamie's.

"Bring the cruiser around to the back," Jamie said.

So, the killer wasn't panicking or giving up. He could use the cruiser to escape, and if he managed that, then Leigh wouldn't be safe. This snake would just keep coming after her.

"I'm going to take that shot now," Cullen whispered to Leigh. "I'll aim for their legs. If I miss and shoot Jamie, he'll drop down. That'll give you a clearer shot at the killer."

She pulled her gaze from the truck for just a second, and in that quick flash of time, he could see her trying to work out whether or not that was the right thing to do. It might or might not be. Cullen knew that. And so did she. But they had to do something before this escalated even more.

"The cruiser now," Jamie shouted. "You've got one minute."

Leigh nodded. "Take the shot," she told Cullen.

She got into a crouch, and he knew what she had in mind. She was going to make that run to the side of her house to create a distraction. And to get herself in a better position to take a kill shot. Again, he had to do battle with his instincts to try to keep her safe. Instead, he brushed a quick kiss on her mouth and took aim.

"Now," Cullen said.

And Leigh took off running.

Cullen kept the shot low, going for the edge of the boot that he saw behind Jamie's, and he pulled the trigger. The shot blasted through the air. So did the howl of pain.

A man's howl.

Bowen lifted his head and his gun, trying to take aim. The killer shifted, staggering a little. Enough to let Cullen know that he'd hit his target. But the killer quickly recovered. At the exact moment Leigh reached the side of her house, the killer pivoted, hooking his arm around Jamie's neck and dragging his human shield back in front of him.

"Big mistake," the killer yelled. "Now Jamie dies."

The words were like fists, but Cullen now knew exactly who they were dealing with because he had no trouble recognizing the voice.

Rocky was the killer.

Leigh had known that it could be Rocky behind the wheel of the truck. But it still brought on an avalanche of emotions. Anger, betrayal, shock. He'd worked side by side with her, and until the last twenty-four hours, she hadn't seen any signs that he was a killer.

But she was seeing them now.

Rocky had a gun to Jamie's head, and Leigh knew with absolute certainty that he'd kill Jamie. In fact, the only reason Rocky hadn't already pulled the trigger was because he needed a shield, and the terrified Jamie was it. However, it wasn't Jamie Rocky wanted.

No.

He wanted her. Probably Cullen, too, but Leigh wasn't sure she knew the reason for that.

"Have you always wanted me dead?" Leigh called out to him. "Or were you worried I'd prove that you're the one who murdered Alexa and McNash?"

"You don't deserve the badge," Rocky spat out.

His response surprised her. Not because of his obvious venom, but because he'd answered her at all.

Leigh had figured he'd just spout out his demand for the cruiser so he could make his escape.

Something she wanted to make sure didn't happen.

That's why Leigh glanced around to try to figure out how to stop him. Rocky was going to pay for the murders—which he hadn't denied. Pay for the attacks against Cullen and her, too. And he was especially going to pay for the hell he was putting Jamie through.

From the angle she had now, she could no longer see Bowen, but it was possible he'd try to sneak up on Rocky. Which wouldn't be a good thing. It could cause Rocky to have a knee-jerk reaction and pull the trigger. Especially since Rocky was already hurt. There was blood on his leg just above his boot.

Cullen was still on the ground, using the boulders for cover, but he also had his gun aimed and ready. If he got a shot, she could count on him to take it—and not miss.

She didn't know where Vance was but suspected the text she'd just gotten was from him. Probably asking for instructions on what he should do. Without taking her attention, or her aim, off Rocky, Leigh motioned toward the last spot where she'd seen Dawn. If Vance hadn't gotten to her already, then maybe he'd do that now.

The one person Leigh didn't want to look at was Jamie. She could practically feel the fear coming off him in hot, slick waves, and she couldn't let her worry for him get in the way. He could help best by diffusing this mess.

"So, you wanted me dead because I'm the sheriff," Leigh called out to Rocky.

"You're sleeping with Cullen Brodie," Rocky snapped. "Now, quit yapping and get me that cruiser." He peppered that *request* with a lot of crude profanity.

Again, she wasn't surprised that Rocky was enraged about her relationship with Cullen. With a Brodie. Jeb's anger toward Bowen might not have erupted into violence, but it had spilled over to Rocky. Still, she wasn't putting a drop of the blame on Jeb. This was Rocky's deal, and she was betting at the core that it had less to do with his feelings about Cullen than it did with him trying to cover up Alexa's murder.

And she'd try to use that.

"You killed Alexa in the heat of the moment," Leigh said, trying to keep her voice calm. "That's second-degree murder. Maybe even manslaughter."

Rocky gave a hollow laugh. "You expect me to believe you'd offer me a deal! Don't insult me. I'm a cop. A better cop than you'll ever be."

She could have pointed out that he was a killer and had also committed numerous other felonies, but that wouldn't help diffuse this. Maybe nothing would help, but she had to try for Jamie's sake.

"Maybe you are a better cop," she said. "Because I can't figure out why you'd kill Alexa."

"No more yapping," he yelled. "Get me that cruiser now."

"It'll take a couple of minutes. Vance used it to get Dawn to the ambulance. She's hurt, Rocky, and she needs the EMTs so she won't bleed out."

Rocky cursed. "She got in the way. She got herself shot. Like Alexa."

Wincing, Rocky staggered back a step. Obviously, the gunshot wound was giving him some pain, and pain didn't go well with logical thought.

"The cruiser," Rocky shouted. "Get it now, or I'll start putting bullets in Jamie. While I'm at it, I'll send some shots at Cullen and you. I might get real lucky and finish you both off."

Even with Rocky's stagger, Cullen still didn't have a shot so Leigh sent a quick text to Vance to have him bring the cruiser around. She had no intention of letting Rocky get in with Jamie, but with all the maneuvering around that would take, it would increase their chances of one of them getting that clean shot.

She heard the movement behind her and thought it was Vance. Still, she pivoted in case Rocky was working with a partner. So did Cullen. And they saw Jeb walking toward them.

"Get back," Leigh warned him.

But Jeb kept on walking, and he wasn't using anything for cover. He was out in the open, and he had his hands lifted, maybe in surrender, maybe to show Rocky he wasn't armed.

"You don't want to do this, Rocky," Jeb said, his voice as calm as a lake. "You're scaring the boy. Let Jamie go, and we can talk this out."

"I got no choice," Rocky argued. "You understand that." There was nothing calm about his voice. Every word had a sharp, raw edge to it.

Leigh wanted to curse her father for doing this. For putting himself in the direct line of fire. But if she went into the yard to drag him back, it could get them both killed.

"I understand. But you've got choices," Jeb argued back. "You can drop your gun and let Jamie go."

"No!" Rocky shouted, and he volleyed wild-eyed glances from Jeb to her to Cullen. "I can't go to jail." He tapped the badge he still had clipped to the waist of his jeans. "You know what they do to cops in jail."

Jeb nodded. "I know, but you could be placed in solitary confinement—"

"I don't want to talk to you," Rocky interrupted, and this time the edges were even sharper. The man was losing it. "Leigh's the one who messed this up. She shouldn't be the sheriff. I should be."

But he stopped, and he didn't say anything else. She wondered if what he'd said had just sunk in. He was a killer, and there was no way he should be sheriff. He'd broken the very laws he'd sworn to uphold. Yes, the first—Alexa's murder—had no doubt been committed in the heat of the moment, but everything else since had been calculated.

So was what Leigh was about to do.

It was a risk, but she didn't want Rocky killing Jeb because he didn't want to hear what her father had to say. Leigh stepped out, took aim at Rocky.

"You have no right to wear that badge," she said, staring him right in the eyes.

With his gun trained on Rocky, Cullen stood, too, moving to Jeb's other side. Leigh wanted to yell at him for doing that. Especially since she figured that Rocky would indeed try to kill Cullen. But she knew he was feeling the same thing she was. Neither of them wanted the other to die. She could include Jeb in that, too.

"Don't you dare take a bullet for me," she snapped, aiming that at both Jeb and Cullen.

She might as well have been talking to the air though because she knew both of them would. Because they loved her.

Leigh stared at Rocky. "Put down your gun now."

Again, Rocky staggered back just a little, and Jamie made a strangled sound. Maybe because he thought this was all about to come to a head and that he'd die. And he might. Leigh couldn't make any guarantees that any of them would make it out of this alive.

"Do the right thing, Rocky," Jeb said.

Just as all hell broke loose.

The gunshot tore through the air. And also tore right into Rocky's leg. It took Leigh a moment to figure out where the shot had come from, but then she spotted Bowen. He was belly-down on the ground behind the truck, and he'd been the one to put another bullet in Rocky.

Rocky howled in pain, cursed and shoved Jamie forward. In the same motion, he brought up his gun.

Taking aim at Leigh.

Chapter 16

Cullen didn't think. He just pulled the trigger, double-tapping it and sending two shots into Rocky's chest.

The moment seemed to freeze with the sound of the bullets echoing through the icy air. Rocky just stood there, his face masked with shock, and the blood already spreading across the front of his coat. Finally, he crumpled, dropping first to his knees before collapsing to the ground.

With Leigh right beside him, Cullen ran toward him. And behind them, he heard Jeb shout for the EMTs to come to the backyard. Rocky still had hold of his gun, and Cullen didn't want him having a chance to try to kill Leigh. They reached Rocky at the same time, and Leigh ripped the gun from his hand. She also frisked him for other weapons and found a backup gun and a knife in his boot holsters.

"Where's Cecile?" Leigh asked, aiming her question at Bowen.

"I used the ATV to take her to the ambulance. I left her with the EMTs while I came back to try to help."

Leigh released the breath she seemed to have been holding. "Thank you. You did help. Thank you for that, too."

Cullen doubted this would be the end of the bad blood between their families, but it was a good start. It was too bad that it'd nearly taken them all being killed before it happened.

Jamie pushed himself away from the truck and staggered toward Bowen, who caught him in his arms. "You okay?" Bowen asked him.

Jamie nodded, but Cullen thought the ranch hand was far from okay. He'd likely have to be admitted to the hospital again. But at least this time, there wouldn't be the threat of danger.

Well, maybe.

Rocky probably didn't have much time left. He was bleeding out fast, and even the EMTs likely wouldn't be able to keep him alive. That's why Cullen had to press him for answers now. If not, Leigh and Jamie might never have peace of mind.

Cullen got right in Rocky's face. "You said Alexa got herself killed? How?"

Clamming up, Rocky laid his head back on the frozen ground and looked up at the sky. Leigh didn't stay quiet though. She read Rocky his rights. That was the smart thing to do in case Rocky survived.

"You really want to take all of this to the grave?" Cullen shrugged and shifted as if to get up. "Suit yourself. You'll be remembered for being an idiot and a coward."

"I'm neither of those things," Rocky snapped. He coughed, grimaced and then gathered his breath again. "Alexa got herself killed because she hated your guts. That's why. And she wanted me to help her set you up because she knew I could. She knew I was just that good." He was actually bragging now, puffing up his bloody chest. "Alexa was going to bruise up her face some and get me to say I'd witnessed you assaulting her."

Cullen felt his jaw tighten. Hell. If Alexa and Rocky had done that, it would have definitely caused him some trouble. Leigh might have had to arrest him after all. Especially with Alexa and Rocky pushing her to do just that.

"You were going to help Alexa frame Cullen?" Leigh demanded.

Rocky narrowed his eyes and gave her a defiant glare. "Yeah. But when I met her in Cullen's bathroom the night of the party, she said she'd changed her mind, that she was giving up on Cullen and wanted Austin instead."

Cullen gave that a moment to sink in. Yeah, he could see Alexa moving on to her next mark, and she might have enjoyed trying to twist up Austin and Kali.

"I told Alexa no, that I wasn't going to let you off the hook," Rocky snarled, and he aimed all that anger at Cullen. "I told her that if she didn't go through with it, then I'd go to Leigh and rat her out."

"I'm guessing Alexa didn't care much for that?" Leigh prompted.

"She didn't," Rocky verified in a snarl. "That's when

Alexa called me, well, a lot of names. She shoved me, told me to get lost. Nobody talks to me that way. *Nobody.* I got the horse statue and bashed her on her idiot head."

Cullen could see all of that playing out. See it playing out with Jamie, too. He was betting that Alexa had mentioned Jamie bringing her to the Triple R. Rocky had probably wanted to make sure Alexa hadn't told Jamie that she was there to meet him. It would have been something similar with McNash. Rocky couldn't risk that Alexa had told the thug about her hiring Rocky.

And that left Kali and Austin.

With everything Rocky had just spelled out for them, Cullen doubted Austin and Kali had had any part in the attacks. Austin had lied and cheated, and Kali had set up the ruse to get back at Austin, but if Rocky could have put some of this blame on them, he would have.

The EMTs came closer, but Rocky waved them off. "Nobody touches me. You think I want to live behind bars for the rest of my life? I don't," he said, answering his own question. He shifted his gaze to Leigh, who was staring down at him. "I want to say my piece. I want both of you to know how much I hate your guts."

The hatred was obvious, but it didn't enrage Cullen nearly as much as Rocky using that hatred to try to kill Leigh. He darn near succeeded, too. Any one of those fired shots could have left her dead.

"You're the one who called me," Jamie said. "Threatened me. You told me you'd kill me if I went to the cops."

Cullen glanced at his ranch hand, who was now being treated by the EMTs. Jamie was still plenty shaky. With good reason. He'd just come close to dying again.

But there was some steel in Jamie's eyes, too. Ditto for Bowen's. His father moved away from Jamie to come closer to Rocky and them.

"So what if I threatened you?" Rocky snapped, dismissing Jamie with a split-second glance. "I didn't want you remembering that I was the one who nearly bashed in your brains. I figured the calls would make you shut up."

"I didn't know it was you," Jamie fired back. "Not for sure, anyway. But I'd got to thinking that it could be you and that's why I wanted to talk to Leigh and Cullen after I got out of the hospital. I wouldn't have had any proof it was you if you hadn't kidnapped me."

"Oh, boo-hoo," Rocky taunted. "You whiner. Go home to your mommy."

"Oops," Bowen said, his voice dripping with sarcasm. He stepped on Rocky's leg. Right in the spot where Bowen had shot him minutes earlier.

Rocky gave a feral howl of pain. But nobody felt sorry for him. And nobody did anything to stop Bowen from adding even more pressure before he finally stepped back.

Leigh stooped down, and she waited until Rocky tore his narrowed gaze from Bowen and moved it back to her. "Who helped you with McNash's murder and the attacks against Cullen and me?" Leigh demanded. She didn't sound hateful or filled with anger. She sounded like a cop.

"Nobody," Rocky spat out. "I didn't need any help. I'm the one who fired those shots in the woods by Kali's house." He paused, winced and dragged in a ragged breath.

"Austin and Kali didn't work with you?" Leigh pressed.

Despite the obvious pain, Rocky managed a dry, nearly soundless laugh. "No, I didn't need them. Both of them are stupid. Austin was cheating with Alexa, and Kali was too blind to see what was right in front of her face. Alexa was a viper, ready to ruin anyone who got in her path." He looked at Cullen. "You were stupid, too, to ever get involved with her."

"It wasn't my finest moment," Cullen admitted. "But you've had some damn un-fine moments yourself. You wanted to kill Leigh because she beat you in the election. Because the majority of people in Dark River wanted her and not you for their sheriff. Considering what you've done, that was a seriously good decision on their part."

The light might have been dwindling from Rocky's eyes, but there was still plenty of bitterness and hatred in them. He looked past them at Jeb. "She shouldn't have the badge, Jeb. You shouldn't have the right to call her your daughter. She betrayed you with Cullen."

"*You* betrayed me," Jeb said, his voice hard and mean. "I'll be damned if you'll die wearing this." He reached down, tore off Rocky's badge and handed it to Leigh. "Now, go to hell, where you belong."

Jeb stepped back, letting the EMTs move in to start treating Rocky. Leigh stepped away, too, heading to Vance, who was making his way to them.

"How are Dawn and Cecile?" she immediately asked.

"They'll be okay. I had another ambulance come, and they're both on the way to the hospital."

Cullen knew Leigh would be checking on her deputies as soon as she could wrap up everything with

Rocky. Leigh would also have to deal with some guilt for their injuries, and it wouldn't matter that it wasn't her fault. She'd still feel responsible that she hadn't been able to stop Rocky before he did so much damage.

"We also found a truck near Leigh's house," Vance added. "It's probably the vehicle Rocky used to get here." He glanced at Rocky. "He tried to kill you?"

Leigh nodded. "And he succeeded in killing Alexa and McNash. He just confessed."

Vance shook his head, muttered some profanity. "I'm sorry, Leigh," he said. "So sorry."

Cullen figured there was some guilt playing into that apology as well. Vance was a good cop, and he'd be kicking himself for not seeing that he'd been working with a dirty one.

"Is Rocky going to live?" Vance asked a moment later.

But the moment the question was out of his mouth, one of the EMTs stood and checked his watch. "Time of death is 9:35. You want me to go ahead and call the ME?"

She gave a weary nod, sighed and closed her eyes for a moment. Steadying herself. Cullen tried to help with that. He went to her, and despite the fact that they had an audience, he pulled her into his arms. Judging from the way she leaned into him, she needed the hug as much as he did.

While Vance dealt with the EMTs and the body, Cullen led Leigh up the back porch steps and into her kitchen. He left the door open though so they could still keep watch of what was going on.

"I'm not going to ask you if you're okay," Cullen whispered.

"Good. I won't ask you, either." But she did look up at him as if trying to see just how much this had shaken him.

He was shaken all right and could still hear the roar of the truck engine bearing down on them. But flashbacks and bad memories weren't going to overshadow the good feelings he had about Leigh. That was why he brushed a quick kiss over her mouth. It packed a punch despite being barely more than a peck.

"Should I have seen that Rocky was dirty?" she asked.

Cullen didn't even have to think about this. "No. Rocky hid the depth of his hatred. Well, until the end when he knew he was caught."

She stared at him, obviously considering that, and nodded. That nod was a victory and the start of her accepting that what Rocky had done was beyond her control.

Leigh moved out of the hug when Jeb came to the doorway, but she stayed close. Arm to arm with Cullen. And because they were still touching, he felt Leigh tense up a little. Probably because she didn't know what she was about to face with her father. Jeb obviously hadn't condoned Rocky's actions, but then, he might not condone her kissing Cullen, either.

"The town council won't have a leg to stand on if they try to dismiss you," Jeb said. His voice, like the rest of him, was coated in weariness. A man who'd seen way too much. Maybe there was some guilt, too, because he hadn't seen the dirty cop who'd worshiped him. "You held your ground and didn't arrest an innocent man."

"But I didn't arrest the guilty one before he could kill again," she muttered.

Jeb lifted his shoulder. "The town council, including me, gave Rocky the green light to go after you. We'll be eating that particular dish of crow for a while." He met her eye to eye. "Nobody's going to challenge you… Sheriff."

Leigh's arm tightened again when Jeb stuck out his hand for her to shake. It was hardly a tender family gesture, but coming from Jeb, it was practically a blessing of his support. Maybe his love, too.

Leigh shook his hand. Then relaxed. "Thank you. You taught me well."

Again, not especially tender, but Jeb blinked hard as if trying to keep his eyes dry. "What will you two do now?" he asked.

The timing was lousy, but Cullen decided to go ahead and declare his intentions. All of them. "I'm going to ask Leigh on a date. If she says yes, then I'll ask her on a second date. Then, a third. Then, a—"

"Yes," Leigh interrupted. And even though the timing was just as lousy for her, she smiled a little. "That's yes to the first, second and third."

"What about a fourth?" Cullen pressed.

She looked up at him. "Yes to that, too."

Cullen smiled as well, and he would have kissed her long and hard if Jeb hadn't cleared his throat.

"I'll be going," Jeb muttered. He turned to leave, then stopped, his gaze going to Leigh's. "You probably don't want my opinion, but I think yes is the right answer. You should go on those dates with Cullen."

"She should," Bowen said.

Cullen hadn't realized his father was close enough to have heard their conversation, but obviously he had been.

"My son's in love with your daughter," Bowen added, sparing Jeb the briefest of glances.

Jeb nodded. "And she's in love with him." He lifted his hand in farewell and walked away.

Leigh stood there. Her eyes wide. Her body still.

"You look stunned," Cullen said.

"I am," she admitted.

"Because you didn't know you were in love with me?" Cullen clarified, sliding his arm back around her.

"No, because our fathers didn't take swipes at each other." She looked up at him. "I'd already figured out I was in love with you."

Now Cullen did kiss her, and he didn't give a rat that his father and everybody else was watching.

"I know you're about to get busy with reports and such, but I'll want to hear more about how you figured out you were in love with me," he said with his mouth against hers.

"We can get into that on our fifth date," Leigh whispered, and she kissed him right back.

* * * * *